Black Velvet Out of the Ashes

Maggie Parker

http://www.facebook.com/maggieparkerauthor

Black Velvet: Out of the Ashes

Maggie Parker

Paperback Edition First Published in the United Kingdom
in 2016 by aSys Publishing

eBook Edition First Published in the United Kingdom
in 2016 by aSys Publishing

Disclaimer

This is a work of fiction. Names, characters, businesses, places,
events and incidents are either the products of the author's
imagination or used in a fictitious manner. Any resemblance
to actual persons, living or dead, or actual events
is purely coincidental.

Cover Artwork: Christine Moody

ISBN: 978-1-910757-78-9

aSys Publishing
http://www.asys-publishing.co.uk

For Kevin, still the one.

CHAPTER
ONE

(Story so Far)

The rock group Black Velvet, comprising of childhood friends; vocalist Vickie D'Angelo, bass guitarist Jamie Connolly, drummer Andy Cowan, lead guitarist Johnny Vincent and his brother rhythm guitarist Christopher. The group met at school in a small Scottish west coast town. Their rise to fame, under the Svengali-like Tony Gorman, was meteoric.

A tragic plane crash took the lives of Vickie's husband Billy, his mother Gillian, Johnny's pregnant wife Ali, her sister Caroline, Andy's mother Hannah, brother Jake, and Jamie's only relative, his younger sister Lyndsey. In the aftermath of the crash Tony allows Vickie to be drugged by a doctor, and she and Johnny sleep together.

Supporting each other through the shock and horror of the accident and grieving, the band members move into Vickie's home where they live as a family, looked after by Annie, Vickie's former nanny, who is also Johnny and Chris's maternal aunt.

At the time of the crash Vickie and Billy were trying to conceive a child, having already got two young sons. When Vickie discovers she is pregnant it gives her the will to carry on. She is shocked to find out from her paediatrician father, Clinton Malone, that the twin daughters she has given birth to have not been fathered by Billy but are the children of Johnny. Johnny and Vickie enter a relationship, and their friends accept them as a couple.

The male band members concerned about Tony's management of them, and rumours around his sexual preferences, want to sack him and change management. Vickie, however, feels she and the others owe a lot to Tony. She wants to wait until his contract expires. When Tony, however, is suspected by the band of being responsible for the drugging and rape of Vickie's prodigy, teenage singer Dania Phillips, Vickie struggles to accept Tony is capable of this kind of assault.

The band's accountant discovers Tony, who is already taking 50% of everything they make, has been syphoning money from their earnings. When Tony calls Vickie and threatens her, the band sack him and begin working with Simon Forsyth as their manager.

CHAPTER

TWO

February 19th 2012
Greenwich Park London

Vickie looked up from her iPhone as Tony Gorman walked over and stood beside her. He smiled sadly, "Vickie you look great, thanks for meeting me. I know this is a difficult time for you with the anniversary of the accident. Why did you choose here?"

"Greenwich Park?" Vickie looked him in the eye. "Public place, Tony!" She put the phone in her pocket.

Tony looked hurt but continued to talk. "Do you want a coffee? We can go down by the river to talk; you have nothing to fear from me Vickie, I swear."

Vickie sighed and nodded. Tony walked over to the coffee stall and he returned holding two cardboard cups. They found a picnic table in a secluded spot away from the path, out of earshot but still in sight of the public. Vickie sat with her back to the park, pushed back her furry parka hood then took off her black knitted gloves.

Tony took a sip of his coffee and made a face. "Vickie, you

can't possibly believe I had anything to do with Dania being attacked? I wish I hadn't taken her home now!"

"Why did you? She says she wasn't drunk!"

"Vickie, she was drunk, really wasted. She was with Pixie Fields and her crowd. They just went off and left her, she was almost legless. I took her home and left her there. I swear I never touched her; I didn't even take her jacket off. I just put her on the couch with a bucket, locked up, put the keys through the letterbox and left." His eyes filled up with tears, "I admit I quite like younger women, but it's consensual; I'd never force myself on anyone. I think of you and her as my daughters, Vickie, you know I've never done anything to make you think otherwise."

"Why younger women Tony?" Vickie asked, her eyes narrowing. "You can't possibly think they are with you for anything other than publicity or your money?"

"Vickie, I don't live in a house without mirrors! When I was your age, I didn't have anything going for me. Short, fat and shy, that was me, the butt of everyone's jokes! I was bullied within an inch of my life. It was like that years ago. No one cared, you were just told to get on with it. I was a virgin till I was 23 and even then, I paid for it." Tony looked sadly at her. "Hookers don't care if you're ugly."

Vickie glanced at him, "I'm sorry you experienced that Tony."

Tony shrugged, "grandad died, left me some money. I started the company, never looked back. I had the gift of the gab, when it came to promotions people listened to me. I also loved music, and all those nights alone in my bedroom with my stereo meant I knew a lot about it. I didn't really need the money when I took you on Vickie. I had enough to be comfortably off. I heard you sing, I knew you were something special." He laughed bitterly, "I knew you would be a star, you just had that quality, your voice, your stage presence. Even without the boys, you could have made it; you're the star not them. I know you were the one who didn't want to part company with me Vickie. You trusted me, knew I had all your best interests at heart. I know you Vickie," Tony said, looking her in the eye. "If you thought for one minute I had hurt Dania, you wouldn't have agreed to meet me."

Vickie finished her coffee, stood up, put the cup in the bin across from them and then looked at Tony. "So, what happened Tony? Who did it? I might not think it was you, but someone drugged and raped her. You had keys to that flat."

"Vickie, she was really drunk, incoherent, that's why I took her home. I have gone over and over it in my mind. I told you, I locked the door and put the key back through the letterbox. My keys were in the office Vickie. After the boys and Lynne moved out, it lay empty until I put Dania in it." He shrugged, "I never changed the locks. You know what those four were like? They partied constantly, anyone could have had keys. Jamie loses his keys almost on a weekly basis, you know he does. You said, on the phone, she had been attacked in the house. What do the police say?"

"She hasn't gone to them, she doesn't remember anything. Tony, what about the men you were with?"

"We went to a strip club after we dropped her at the flat, then to a massage place in Mayfair. They're business men, they fancied her yes, but they were with me. I dropped Dania about eleven, went home about three am. I left them at their hotel."

Tony took Vickie's hand in his, he studied it. "I know you're with Johnny now. I'm pleased for you, I really am. After losing Billy and Ali you both deserve happiness. He's the best of the bunch, will treat you like a princess. Please, don't let him and Chris influence how you see me. I realise it's over, in terms of me managing you, and I'm going to just let it go, but I need you in my life. You're the daughter I never had. I love you . . . not in a sexual way. I feel the same about Dania."

Vickie sighed. She looked into his eyes, "someone hurt her Tony, she was raped. She's terrified and doesn't know who did it."

"I tried to speak to her Vickie, but her father threatened me. The boys have turned everyone against me." He looked at Vickie and wiped away a tear, "your brother came to my office and told me he would kill me. I could have gone to the police, got him charged but he's young, it could have ended his career."

"Thanks Tony," Vickie said, patting his hand. "Patrick was really upset. Him and Dania, well, they were close."

"Vickie, you know I'd never do anything to hurt you or Dania! You know I'd never see her or you as sexual objects."

"Tony, I believe you, but it's so hard, The boys believe you were responsible!"

Tony shook his head. "You know the boys wanted to end my contract, they think they're too big for me now. They're influencing you."

"What about the money Tony? The accountants say you've been moving money around for years. They found a lot of financial irregularities!"

"The money the accountants are talking about was in a separate account Vickie. It was rainy day money, nothing more. Look darling!" he said, putting his hand over hers, "can we please stay friends? I . . . I don't think I can ever forgive the others for what they've done to me and my reputation. I know you're not into that, I know you believe me." Tony smiled sadly then patted her hand before letting it go. "Knowing you trust me is enough."

Vickie nodded, saying nothing. She felt there was nothing left to say.

"Vickie, I'm going to take off now, I have a meeting over at Canary Warf. Could I give you a call from time to time? Maybe take you out for dinner occasionally? You've been in my life so long now; I'd really like to keep in touch."

"I don't know Tony? Johnny wouldn't like it, he really does believe you were either responsible or knew about the attack on Dania." Vickie sighed. She frowned, remembering, "he saw her the night I found out. He was with me when I went around to the flat."

Tony stood up and looked at her, "you know I didn't have anything to do with it. Look, call me sometime darling." Vickie stood up. She nodded, hugged him feeling awkward, and then sat down, watching as he walked away.

Vickie bought another coffee then sat for a long time thinking about the situation. She realised Tony had offered a plausible explanation as to the attack on Dania. Vickie knew during the time Chris, Jamie, Andy and Lynne shared the flat, there had been many parties. A lot of people could have keys to it. Vickie also knew the boys had been only too happy to believe Tony's guilt in relation to the attack on Dania and the allegedly embezzled finances. She didn't know who or what to believe. However, in her heart, she knew she trusted Johnny and the others more than Tony. Billy, Vickie's late husband, had quite early in the relationship with Tony, before the band's global success, mistrusted him. Vickie knew Billy's perception and insight was usually correct. Johnny was sure Tony had either attacked Dania, or set it up for someone else.

Vickie's mind wandered as she sat there. Thinking of Johnny made her smile. The only thing they disagreed on was Tony Gorman. She knew she wouldn't call Tony; she didn't want him in her life. She would always feel grateful to him for what he had done, but she didn't want to go against the man she loved.

Vickie still missed Billy, but he was always there in her heart. She and Johnny allowed each other to love their dead partners. The bond between the two young couples had been so close, there was no resentment. Vickie thought she knew both Billy and Ali well enough to know they would want this. She knew the love she felt for Johnny wasn't more than she'd had for her husband, it was just different.

Vickie began thinking about the connection she felt to the others. She and Chris had always been friends. Close, but neither of them had ever seriously wanted to be anything more. Andy and Jamie, Vickie loved in a brotherly way. They were like brothers to her, protective but teasing her a lot of the time.

All of them mistrusted Tony. Billy had hated Tony, often telling Vickie to be careful of him. Billy had refused to come on tour with the band in the last year of his life, so great was his dislike of the band's manager. Vickie did not feel uncomfortable around

Tony, never had. When she had discovered Dania, she had automatically spoken to Tony about the talented young singer, knowing he could guide her career.

Vickie continued to speak to Dania every day, supporting her from afar. The young woman was undergoing counselling in respect of the attack on her almost two months previously. Dania was unsure as to whether she wanted to resume her career.

Dania had also not made an official complaint to the police in relation to the attack on her. Although she had undergone a medical, and there was, as a result, forensic evidence stored. The young girl, however, had been too traumatised and afraid to pursue this. She could not remember anything after being in a club with Tony, having a drink with him and two other men. Dania had told Vickie she had not had a lot to drink. Tony had just told her Dania was heavily under the influence of alcohol when he met her the night she was attacked.

CHAPTER
THREE

February 21st

Los Angeles, California.

"Christ, you look beautiful babe; you're going to wow them in that." Vickie twirled around, her white trouser suit showed her figure to perfection without displaying any real flesh. She was, however, showing cleavage, the single button of the jacket sewed together to avoid any wardrobe malfunction. Johnny, wearing a kilt and dress shirt, pulled her into his arms, kissing her.

"Hey put her down Jovi!" Nicky, their stylist gasped. "That suit is pure silk; don't want your sweaty handprints all over her before she's photographed." She looked at his groin, "at least we won't be able to see your erection when you put your sporran on."

"I don't have an erection Nicky!" Johnny cried, looking down at the front of his kilt and blushing.

"Jovi, you must have a really big willie then, because I can see it."

"See what?" Chris Vincent asked, coming into the room also in highland dress, his bow tie and sporran in his hand.

"Jovi has a hardon!" Nicky laughed.

Chris squinted at his brother's groin, then at Vickie. "Hmm, no wonder, you look sensational babe, that suit really works. Turn around. Yeah it clings in all the right places. You should lose the knickers though, you have a VPL. I'm going to have wet dreams tonight, just thinking about it."

"Is nothing sacred with you lot?" Vickie laughed. "What do you think Nicky? Knickers or no knickers?"

"No knickers," Nicky said smiling, "the trousers are lined. Even if they weren't, I gave her a Hollywood wax yesterday. Imagine that Chris, when you're having wet dreams."

"Wow, I'll be having wet dreams too!" Vickie looked up as her best friend Lynne entered the room.

"Lynne, you made it!" Vickie moved over to hug her. Lynne laughed, shook her head and air-kissed Vickie without touching her,

"That suit is silk babe. It'll stain if you touch it, white silk does. You won't be able to sit for long either. Wait until you've been photographed going in, been up for awards, then take it off, put on the other one. It looks the same but it's a cotton mix. Then we can get pissed. Roberto, won't care, he'll be over the moon you're wearing it. He's pissed off at me because I'm wearing Stella. Hey, she asked me first, she's my friend too."

Chris leaned over. He kissed Vickie's cheek, keeping his hands raised in the air. "You look great Lynne. The dress is superb, much better than Roberto's stuff! Sorry Vickie, that's sexy because it's on you, not because of anything he did."

Lynne grinned at Vickie and nudged Chris, "touch of the green-eyed monster, Vincent? Not like you to bother."

"How many times must I say, Lynne, Roberto is a wanker; it's not about him and you!" He grinned at her, pulled her close kissing her on the mouth, "for tonight though, it's just you and me. Got any Charlie babe? It's going to be a long evening and an even longer night. If you're taking off for Florida in the morning, well, we should party. What about you Nic, want some?"

10

Nicky looked at Chris, "I'll join your party if you don't mind?"

Lynne grinned at Nicky, "oh babe, you joining our party is his favourite fantasy just now, so don't encourage him." She nudged Chris and smiled, "funny how you're getting snippy about me being with other men but encouraging me to do women."

Vickie watched them go. She looked at Johnny, "do you ever miss it?"

"What, other women? I was never into that Vic."

"No, the party drugs! You used to do drugs. Billy used to slip in and out of it. It always worried me I made him give up something he enjoyed." She smiled and sighed, "I did acid a couple of times with him; I suppose I needed to know what it was like. With me it was, okay, I've done that now, so what's next? I know the others used to do it a lot when they talked about sex on it being phenomenal. It was good, but I prefer it natural." Vickie looked at Johnny and sighed, "we dropped an 'e' one night too. To be honest, I thought it was quite boring. Yet look what happened after the crash, the reaction we both had?"

"You know that was the mix of drugs Vickie, it was an unusual reaction," Johnny replied. "You don't need it babe, you and I, our connection is amazing."

"I was the same with coke; I can take blow or leave it. You changed when you stopped using Johnny! I just thought you might miss that life style?"

Johnny smiled and looked at her, "not really. I was never as into it as the others, it was only ever recreational with me. Now, I get a big enough rush from being with you. Ali and I, we stopped when we started talking about her getting pregnant. I missed it at first; I could always think better when I was doing coke. I thought I was more creative I suppose. That's when I started running. We went on a health kick, one addiction for another likely, though. I just couldn't kick the fags, though I'm down to one or two a day now and the occasional toke."

"What about other women? Do you ever think you're missing out?"

"No, why are you asking? Do you think you missed out Vickie?"

"No never, but I sometimes think that I'm a bit odd. I like that you and I have not had loads of experience. I've never really been into other people; why would I when it's so good with you?"

Johnny smiled, "so much for the rock and roll lifestyle eh?" He pulled Vickie closer, sliding his hands under the silk jacket.

"Do you think those three have gone to have sex Johnny?"

"Not unless they are doing it at lightning speed, they're getting amped. The sex might happen later. They've done threesomes with Nicky before."

"I don't get it Johnny, they've been together on and off for years yet they don't get jealous."

"You don't either Vickie . . . get jealous."

"Only because I know you're faithful. I'd go mad if you went with someone else, and I certainly wouldn't want to watch."

Johnny smiled. He pulled Vickie close again and nibbled on her ear, "I'll never want anyone else and know what? I don't think those two really do either. I see a difference in Topher. He is getting annoyed at her being with other men. Have you noticed he never brings anyone home now?"

Vickie looked thoughtful, "they made a pact years ago, if they got to 30 and were still single, they'd be exclusive. I think you might be right babe. Lynne sees Roberto, and she goes around with that Saudi Prince, but she drops them as soon as Chris is around again."

"Uh huh!"

"So why don't they just give in?"

Johnny shrugged. "Who knows, probably neither wants to be the one to suggest it. I do know she's provoking him, trying to make him jealous just now, and he's biting. Probably best just to leave them to it. Let's get wasted tonight Vickie, stop being sensible, party, not necessarily a lot of drugs. We're going straight back to London in the morning."

"I'm breast feeding, so unless you want your daughters to

be pissed too, I can't. I'm going to try to do it for another few months. I have nine months in my head; they should be starting to take solids then. Dad reckons that's the time to wean them. There's a part of me doesn't want to stop. We're not going to have more kids," Vickie sighed and looked away, "so when I stop feeding the twins then that's it." She looked back and grinned. "When I do, we can have a party for your birthday in August, and I'll indulge. I do miss being able to have a drink without planning it. I haven't even had an occasional smoke since I found out I was pregnant."

"What about the Brits? Can't you express enough milk for a day or so, and have a drink?"

"Hmm, we'll see how it goes, but I suppose I could if I start the day before. I'll speak to Laura or my dad about it."

* * *

As the plane crossed the Atlantic en route for London, Vickie smiled, looking down at Chiara, who lay content, asleep at her breast. She glanced over at Johnny who was holding Chiara's twin Billie. "It was good, wasn't it? I'm so glad we went now; they were so nice to us. Five awards for a British Act! Quite something. I forgot how much I enjoyed the buzz of awards shows. I'm glad Simon refused the invitation for us to sing live, I liked just getting ready and going to the show without having to worry."

"Sexiest female, woo hoo." Johnny grinned at her. "Although I could have told them that, they didn't need to vote! I can't wait to get you home. I keep seeing you with that white tuxedo on, it made me really horny. Pity I was too drunk to do anything." He laughed. "All those other women in their evening dresses, showing off their bodies, and there you were, covered from head to foot apart from a spectacular cleavage, and you still made the front pages. You were sexier than them all, and you have the trophy to prove it." Johnny lay back and looked around the little compartment. "These seats are definitely worth the money Vickie; we'll be rested and able to go the full nine yards."

13

Vickie nodded and smiled. "This is as good as a chartered jet; so much room." She fluttered her eyelashes, "want to join the mile-high club babe? The toilet is just ours. We could do it, no one need know."

Johnny grinned and looked over at her. "Oh yes, I think that would be most acceptable Mrs D'Angelo, a first for me in fact. Billy told me about you and him on that flight to Barbados, Vickie. Ali would never try it."

"Well, I've got no knickers on under my skirt Johnny, just right for a quickie. I can't believe Billy told you about that!" she grinned, remembering, "it was pretty spectacular though."

"He told me a lot of stuff Vickie," Johnny looked sadly at her. "I confided in him, we trusted each other with secrets. It's what mates do, isn't it?"

Vickie sat up and wiped Chiara's mouth, smiling as the sleeping baby continued to make sucking movements. She stood up, laid Chiara down in her sky cot and tightened the seat belt around it. "Now you're looking at my arse, trying to decide if I'm lying!" Vickie said without looking back.

"No, I'm wondering if we could just put a blanket over us and do it here, cut out the can, too little room."

"That's part of the attraction Johnny boy, the lack of space; you must decide who straddles who, or do it from the back," Vickie grinned, "you had no problem with doggy-style the other night . . ."

Vickie stopped talking as Marnie and the three other members of their band came through and perched on the seats. Johnny looked up then pulled his blanket over the lower half of his body. Vickie smiled. She knew he was annoyed because he had an erection. "Oh, good you're all here," Johnny said quickly, "can we talk about rehearsals for the Brits? We need to get started!" Vickie realised he was, by suggesting they work, giving them an excuse to leave. This normally had the desired effect.

"What, right now?" Andy sighed. "Give us a break Jovi, fuck sake!"

Johnny frowned. "We're really going to struggle; we haven't played live for over a year."

Chris shook his head. "We've been in the studio."

"It's not the same Toph and you fucking know it," Johnny retorted. He glanced at Vickie, who raised an eyebrow but said nothing. "We really do need to rehearse; it's quite an honour to be asked to open."

Jamie shrugged and tossed back his red curls. "We've been playing together for years Jovi, we'll be fine; it's only two numbers."

Vickie smiled. "I get to choose the second one?"

"We're not doing the Frozen song Vickie," Johnny said grinning, "just because Denis likes it so much! You do sound good singing it though, but it's not exactly us is it?"

Jamie shook his head. "We need to teach Denis to be a bit more macho. All these Disney Princesses Jovi, it's not good for a boy."

"Oh, so you think you would be a good role model, when he fucking thinks you are one, Merida?" Johnny cried, nudging Jamie.

"We need to toughen him up, get him a tattoo or something," Jamie retorted, smiling at Vickie who was frowning at him. She looked up as Denis, wearing pyjamas and slippers, toddled through from the cabin next door. They all knew her views on gender identity of children. Vickie and Billy had allowed their children to be relaxed about toys, games and identity.

Denis climbed up on to Jamie's knee, his thumb in his mouth. Jamie kissed the top of his head. Denis snuggled in and put his fingers into Jamie's hair.

Chris looked at Jamie and snorted. "Tattoos never toughened you up; you still look like a fucking girl. Look at you, big sap, you love him playing with your hair."

"Chris! Language!" Vickie sighed, nodding over at Denis.

Johnny sat up and looked at his friends. He frowned. "We really need to rehearse though guys and Vickie, just choose a fucking song please?"

15

"You too Johnny, please mind your language!"

Laura, their senior nanny, appeared from behind the curtain. "There you are you little rascal. Denis, back through to the other cabin please, the film you chose is starting, and we have popcorn." Laura smiled as she untangled the little boy's hand from Jamie's curls and lifted him into her arms.

Vickie reached up and kissed Denis as Laura held him over her. She watched as he was carried out of the cabin. "Oh, lighten up Johnny, you worry too much. I think we would be good at that duet Anna and the prince sing. Marnie and I are taking them to a Frozen sing-along tomorrow, you should come."

"I'll be sorry to miss that, a theatre full of screaming weans. Have fun." Johnny looked around him. "Okay we have four days; we'll start rehearsal tomorrow, late morning."

Everyone groaned. Chris nudged his brother. "I thought now you were getting regular nooky, you would loosen up a bit bro."

Vickie smiled. "It's hormones. We were planning to explore the possibility of the mile-high club when you lot came through."

Jamie looked over at her, "Fuck sake! Haven't you had enough?"

"You two must be breaking some kind of records these days. Fuck me, your cock must be about to drop off bro," Chris laughed, nudging Johnny.

"Oh, ha ha!" Johnny said, his face breaking into a smile. "Suddenly we're all comedians. We're working our way through the Kamasutra. Now fuck off back to your own seats please? I've got position thirty to try then I want to sleep."

"He's not joking folks," Vickie laughed, "he's downloaded an app to his phone, different position every day."

"Thirty is no use on a plane like this, try thirty-two," Andy said grinning, "that's my default for air travel. Thirty used to work in the back of the van, what's it called again? Splitting bamboo."

"Fuck you're a late starter Jovi, I'd done the Kamasutra by the time I was 20, Jamie said, his face serious, "it's all about rehearsal, sexual position! I always find that you need to work to how you're feeling, how much energy you've got. I like the frog, myself!" he said, glancing at Marnie, who blushed and looked away. "This is making me horny," Jamie looked at his watch, "still four hours to go; fuck, I need to get off this plane!"

"You'd better remember about band rehearsal; don't disappear when we get to London," Johnny said, pushing Jamie who was sitting on the edge of his seat.

"We will rehearse," Andy groaned, "but can we just do it in our studio? At least give me time to get over this jetlag."

"Andy, you don't have jetlag, you have a fucking hangover! Those shots were a big mistake on top of everything else we had. I'm fucked too" Chris groaned, pushing Vickie over and getting on the seat beside her.

"Chris, get off; go to your own seat."

"No this one's better; it's quieter through here. You move over and lie with your man Vickie, give me the bed. Try the slide, not sure I know what number it is. Always works for me when I need to be discreet, I'll pretend I've not noticed. I need to fucking sleep the drink off somewhere quiet."

"It's quiet because your seat isn't here; Chris I'm warning you, if you don't sleep, I'll fucking choke you." Vickie slid onto Johnny's reclined seat with him.

"Vickie, language dear!" Johnny laughed, wrapping his arms around her.

The others disappeared back through the curtain. Eventually Chris stood up. "It's too fucking quiet in here, I can't sleep." Johnny watched him go then pulled the blanket covering him over Vickie. Hidden, his hands slid under her t-shirt and onto her breast.

"No bra either!" he whispered in her ear. She felt him slide his free hand under her skirt, his fingers moving, rubbing her intimately. After a few minutes Vickie rolled over and got up. Pulling Johnny to his feet she led him, on tiptoe, across the small compartment to the toilet.

Inside the cubicle Vickie pulled Johnny's jeans over his hips. She gasped. "You're commando too!"

Johnny grinned and sat down on the toilet. "Yeah and you're on top but facing me, I need to see you babe!" Vickie, now fully aroused, began to kiss his mouth and neck, before pulling her skirt up and straddling him. Johnny pushed Vickie's t-shirt up, exposing her breasts, rubbing them as she moved against him. "Fuck! I'm close Vickie, you better let go before I do. God sweetheart, I love you, you're fucking amazing." Johnny moved his hands to her waist and held her, his groin pushed up against hers. He cried out, holding her tighter.

"Fuck Johnny!" Vickie gasped. "Just a second, please, hold back, just . . . oh God, keep doing that. I love you." Vickie felt her orgasm begin. She looked at Johnny, noting he was climaxing along with her. She gasped as the tidal wave overtook her. Vickie's body shook as she let go. She watched Johnny's eyes roll upwards and his face contort. She leaned forward, he held her, kissing her neck and shoulders.

"Fuck you're amazing Vickie; each time I think it can't get any better, you go and surprise me. We're definitely doing that again!"

Back in their seat, Vickie lay comfortably wrapped in her lover's arms, her head on his chest. She drifted off to sleep. Johnny lay awake holding her. Looking down at the face of the woman he loved, he felt blessed. He thought back with sadness, to the crash, the loss of Ali and their unborn daughter. At that time Johnny couldn't believe he would ever feel happy again. Yet here he was, just a year later, in love and fulfilled, by a girl he had known all his life. He smiled, kissed Vickie, closed his eyes and slept.

* * *

It was after midnight when they arrived home; everyone except the children suffering from jet lag and awake. Vickie was always glad to be home. Brickstead manor was her safe place, her sanctuary. Creeping into the nursery Vickie fed the twins, and with help from Catriona put them in their cots whilst Laura and

Johnny got the boys, already dressed in their pj's, into their beds. Denis and James had fallen asleep in the car.

Downstairs, the others sat out on the courtyard patio. It was 1am and they were passing a joint between them. Keeping quiet was not their strong point. They were giggling and sharing stories about the after-show party they had attended.

A window above them opened, Douglas Cowan leaned out. "Hope that's a Marlboro you're holding son!"

"Dad! I didn't think you were coming in until Tuesday. Sorry I wasn't here."

"Dougie, come down and join us. Have a smoke, it'll help you to sleep," Jamie laughed, looking up at his friend's father. "Hope you haven't been pestering Annie for a date again, she'll kick your head in mate. *Ouch!*" he cried, as Annie, having crept up behind him in her long velour dressing gown, slapped him on the back of the head. "Didn't see you there Annie, did we waken you?"

"I would think that you wakened people in Kingston High Street Jamie, you have a voice like a foghorn! Andy, I really don't want to know who you scored with in the toilet. Didn't he go with Janelle Taerquy last year?" Annie asked, looking at Jamie," she's the Jailbreak actress, isn't she?" "You've not been sharing women again have you?"

"No, when we share, we generally do it together Annie," Jamie said, shaking his head. "I had a brief thing with Janny, but she actually prefers women. She must be seen with a few men so no one finds out. Bit daft, actually. Her publicist reckons that if people find out she's gay, her sex appeal will be affected. Stupid really, it opens a whole new market, I think."

Andy nudged Annie and smiled. "I was actually in the can with Margot Henry, got a bit crowded. Margot, she's married, so Janelle took the wrap. She did give me a blow job, wasted talent."

"You really are sexual deviants, you three! Johnny and I went to bed early Annie," Vickie, perched on Johnny's knee, laughed and looked up at him.

19

Annie turned in the doorway, "who wants hot chocolate or Horlicks? I'm going to make some. Sexual deviancy is not a subject I want to hear about. It's bad enough reading about your exploits in the newspapers, without witnessing the post mortem. You really have no shame, you young people."

"You should be like us!" Johnny laughed, nudging his brother and taking the spliff from behind his back as Annie disappeared.

"Yeah, cos there's no sexual deviancy with you two is there?" Chris said looking at them. "My fucking bedroom is below yours! Remember that fact when you leave the window open! I hear it all, especially when you're in the hot tub folks."

"You being a sensitive little perv, it must upset you to be hearing someone getting laid when you're not involved. Why are you listening anyway?" Jamie gasped, "that would just make me horny."

"Enough! You lot, stop it, or you can all move rooms to the ground floor. I won't be able to do anything without wondering if you're below me," Vickie cried.

Johnny grinned, "that dear was an unfortunate phrase to utter." He threw the end of the spliff over the wall as Doug, a steaming mug of cocoa in his hand, came out onto the patio. He sat down beside Vickie who put her arms around him and kissed his cheek.

"Oh, so you can discuss sex in front of me and Annie, but you can't do blow!" Doug said, laughing and nudging Andy.

"Do you want some Dad?" Andy asked, offering his father an unlit spliff.

"No thanks son. Not in front of Annie anyway," he said, winking at Vickie.

"How long can you stay Doug?" Vickie asked looking at the handsome man, so like Andy, just older and greyer. Doug smiled then looked at Andy.

"Oh a few weeks, if it's okay folks? I'm here for some interviews. I want to come back to the UK; Dubai is getting a bit I don't know ... lonely! He put his hand on Andy's arm, "I think losing Jake and your mum has made me think more about you and I, Andy."

"Oh, he could do with the guiding hand Doug!" Annie laughed, sitting down beside Andy's father on the wooden bench. "They all could, reprobates the five of them."

"Hey Annie! That's uncalled for!" Johnny gasped. "Don't tar Vickie and me with the same brush as them."

Annie looked at him and snorted, "well, close your bedroom windows then son!"

* * *

Vickie walked into the kitchen; she looked at the big clock, it read 10.30. "Nothing quite like that first night back in your own bed after travelling!" she said, kissing Annie, who was cooking breakfast at the stove, talking to Doug.

Sitting at the table, a mug of coffee in his hand, Doug winked at her. "Especially if it's on Annie's clean sheets," he laughed.

Vickie could hear the washing machine whirring in the utility room, and when she looked out on to the drying green, two rows of washing was already blowing about. "Tell me you're not doing their washing again Annie?" Vickie looked at the utility room floor where piles of clothes lay waiting to go in the machine. "Annie, enough is enough, it's too much, you doing everything! I'm going to hire someone to help you, no argument. I'll get Marnie to put an advert in the local paper, you can interview, but it's happening."

"You saying I can't cope?" Annie asked, her eyes narrowing.

"Annie, you were looking after me, Billy, and the kids; two adults and two children and a four-bedroom flat." Vickie looked at Annie as she spoke and realised she was listening. "We now have ten adults permanently here, four children, a cat and who-ever else they bring home. It's far too much. I'm going to look for a few people, even just part time, laundry and housework, helping with meals. That lot are just taking the piss now! They could do their own washing, I do mine and the kids."

21

"She's right Annie. In fact, I think you should have a night off! Let me take you out to dinner, you've looked after me many times." Doug smiled at Vickie and winked, knowing what Annie's response would be. It always was the same.

"I don't have time to swan off to dinner, Doug Cowan," Annie said pushing him, "I have work to do. As she says, I have fourteen people and you to cook for. If you really want to help, you can come back later and peel the potatoes for me." She glanced over at Vickie, "okay hire some help then, but I have final say on who it is." She grimaced, "I don't want anyone under the age of forty five, cos I've enough to do without worrying about those three sleeping with the help. Whilst you're at it, advertise for a gardener come handyman; old Jake is retiring next month. Someone who looks like George Clooney would be good."

"What about someone who looks like Douglas Cowan?" Doug said laughing. "I could do the gardening!"

Realising she had just scored a major victory with Annie, Vickie went in search of Marnie and made sure there would be an advert in the local paper.

* * *

When Vickie walked into the studio in the basement of the house, only Sam their sound engineer, Jamie and Andy were there. Johnny had, they told her, gone out running, and Chris was still in bed. Together they ran through the lyrics of their new single. When Johnny arrived, he asked where Chris was, then shaking his head in annoyance went off up the back stairs, to find his brother.

Chris appeared with a tray of bacon sandwiches a few minutes later from the main stairs. Vickie had to agree, the aroma made her want to eat.

"Where the fuck've you been?" Chris asked, grinning, when his brother eventually came back through the door.

Johnny looked around him. "Where's mine? I could smell bacon right through the house."

"It was getting cold Jovi," Jamie said, laughing. "Andy ate it. If you're not fast you're last in this house mate."

"Annie's making more; she'll bring them down when they're ready babe. She was doing a fry up for Doug when I passed through." Vickie said smiling, "I saved you a bite of mine. You looked like the Bisto Kid, there!"

"That's love mate, when your woman gives you her last bite!" Andy laughed, swallowing the last of his own sandwich. "I think the third one tasted better because I knew it was yours."

Johnny, ignoring Andy, looked around. "Okay let's run through the new single. Vickie, have you decided on a second song?"

Vickie smiled, "I want to do Black Velvet again. I haven't sung it for years, and it's my favourite. We've not done it since we were doing the pub circuit."

"Ooh can we stand it? Makes me horny that song!" Jamie laughed.

"Jamie, everything makes you horny! Trains, buses, planes, drunk, sober, you name it you've got excited, and you fucking tell us," Andy cried. "You said that as though it was only Vickie singing."

Jamie grinned and nudged Chris, "honestly, the moment I hear the intro, I'm in those pubs. Out back shagging against a wall because you two had the van. I always pulled last."

"Ah the old van, I learned all there was to know about sex in that, perfected the art of seduction. We should have kept it. I bet it would be worth money these days," Andy said smiling, remembering, "I did two in one night in that old tin can then got a blow job on the way back."

Vickie punched him on the arm. "You are a sexist git, you never fail to lower the tone do you Andy? She grinned, "actually, the van's still in the garage at Gillian's! I've got some pretty steamy memories of it too. Billy wouldn't get rid of it. It's still taxed, we pay it every year, couldn't bear to SORN it. There's a painting Billy did of us with it, in the attic here, if you want it Andy?"

"Okay enough reminiscing!" Sam cried, "let's get some work

done please folks. Come on Jamie let's hear that intro, see if you've all still got it."

"What, hardons?" Jamie laughed tossing back his red curls, he picked up his guitar.

* * *

Vickie sat watching the others playing, they always took far longer than she did to record anything. Chris, for all his laid-back, lazy personality, was a perfectionist when it came to his music. He also played more instruments than anyone else, so he did a lot of the backing for their tracks. Vickie looked around the studio; for the first time in a year she felt blessed. Great friends, wonderful lover, four healthy, happy children and a beautiful home. The pain of losing Billy, was still there, still acute at times, she saw him in her boys all the time, sometimes it made her happy, other times desperately sad. Living here with her friends helped.

She realised, when she thought about it, she and the others were family; they did all the things families did. Vickie looked over at Johnny. He winked at her and poked his tongue out. Her heart filled with love. *'Life does not get much better than this!'* she wrote on the chalk board on the studio wall.

Andy came over and sat down beside her. Vickie looked up, "Andy I didn't want to say anything without speaking to you but can I ask your dad if he wants to live here? If he's coming back to the UK, he'll need somewhere. He might not want to, but we've got loads of room and it might be good for you and him."

"Suppose so, we actually get on okay these days, he wasn't around much when I was growing up. You know him and mum split when I was ten, but he was always a good provider. As he says, the accident has made us all think about what's important. Leave it for now Vick, I'll talk to him. I'd actually like him to stop working, take it easy. He's hitting sixty and should be able to retire."

"Andy he's fifty five, same age as Annie, that's not old."

As if on cue, Annie put her head around the studio door,

24

"Vickie there's a call for you darling. I tried to transfer it down here but it won't go." Vickie followed her out, up the stairs to the kitchen. "It's Dania, Vickie, she sounds upset. I'll put it through to your room so you can talk in private. Tell the wee soul I'm thinking about her!"

* * *

"Hi babe, how're you today?"

"Vickie, hi, I'm okay I guess, just a bit emotional. I'm sorry I missed your call yesterday." There was a short pause before Dania spoke again, "I was out all day, then it was too late, you would have been in mid-flight."

"You're bound to be emotional Dania; you've been through a lot sweetheart. It's going to take time, but I'm glad you're going out. That's a start."

Vickie heard Dania take a deep breath. "I was with Paddy; he came down for a few days to help me with something. We went out for dinner before he went back last night." There was a long pause, and Vickie realised Dania was struggling to speak, "I've done it Vickie, I've given a statement to the police, the day you went to America."

"I'm glad you've done it babe, but why didn't you tell me Dania?"

"Oh, the police asked me not to say anything to anyone; I wanted to tell you but had to wait till you came back from America. It was hard, but they were great. They brought two female detectives from London to do it, and it was okay. Paddy got some leave, and he sat through it with me as a support. I couldn't say some things in front of my mum. He's great Vickie; I've explained to him about me asking you to keep it from him, and he gets it. I think he's a bit embarrassed now at the scene he caused. I really hate that I came between you two. He talked me into going to the police. I'm scared but glad I did. I have to know who it was Vickie; I keep wondering if it was Tony. Paddy's sure it was him, he says the boys all think he did it. Maybe this way we'll find out."

25

"So, what happens now Dania?"

"They're going to look at CCTV footage from the club and from the streets in Fulham. They're also going to track down the cabbie who took us to my house, to see where Tony and his friends went afterwards. It'll take a few weeks they think, to do it all, but it's better to wait and get it right. The DNA from me and the bed is to be put into the system first, just in case there's a match. If not, they'll ask Tony to provide a sample for comparison."

"They're going to speak to him then Dania?"

"Yes, and ask him for the names of the two men he was with. They're also going to interview all past tenants of the flat, to see who has keys. Chris gave me the set he still had months ago, so there may be others. Lynne said they used to party a lot, so there could have been people with keys. Part of me wants it not to be Tony, Vickie. Do you know what I mean?"

"Are you still going to go with Steven Forsyth as your manager then? Even if it wasn't Tony?"

"Yeah, if I decide to carry on, which I think I really want to! Now you're away from him it wouldn't make sense for me to stay with Tony. The contract runs out in July anyway, I took Johnny's advice, only signed year to year. I'm thinking about coming back down south. Is the offer of a room with you still there Vickie?" She hesitated. When she spoke again Vickie could hear the emotion in her voice, "I don't think I would want to live alone now."

"Of course it is babe!" Vickie said quietly, "what about the help you've been getting in Manchester though?"

"The counsellor I've been seeing says I can continue to speak to her by Skype if I need to. I don't remember anything clearly, other than being in the club, and that's still affecting me, but they don't think I'll ever remember. Your dad was great to talk to Vickie; it's the one thing that helped. He said it was like getting an anaesthetic. I was unconscious and will only remember before I was drugged. I was really scared it would be like you and Johnny, and I would start to remember. He explained what

26

different drugs do, how they work. How with you and Johnny, it was the combination of different drugs."

"You know there's a room for you here Dania, just say the word! We'd all feel better if you accepted, don't need to think twice about it."

"There are a lot of things I'll think twice about now that I never considered before." Vickie could hear the sadness in Dania's voice. "I'll certainly never take a drink I don't see being made. I'll hire security to look after me. I told you I got all the test results back now. I'm not pregnant and don't have any STD's, so that's lucky I guess."

"Can I tell the others Dania?"

"Vickie, the police, they've asked that I don't talk about their investigation. Would you mind not telling anyone yet? Even Johnny? Obviously, Paddy and my parents know I did it. You and Johnny were so good to me that night. I'll always be grateful to you. I trust you both, but the fewer people who know just now, the better."

"Johnny and I don't see eye to eye on it, Dania. So, I'm quite happy to just leave it for you to tell him you've spoken to the police. I know it happened babe, but I'm really confused about Tony being involved. I just can't accept he was. Johnny goes ape-shit at me for not believing Tony is capable of it! We don't disagree on much, but this has become such an issue, it's better to not say anything." Vickie sighed and whispered, "hopefully we'll know one way or another soon Dania. What about the awards? There's still two days to go, are you going to come down for it? There's a place at our table if you want to come; you would be with us the whole time. I could get Nicky to find you a dress, send Arfur for you tomorrow, if you want. I'd love to see you."

"I have a dress, but I don't think I'm ready for being out in public yet. Someone knows they raped me Vickie, does that make sense? Until I know who it is, I don't think I'd be good in company. I would like to come and see you and the kids. The twins are growing up and changing, the photos are great, but

I'd love a cuddle. Maybe Friday, hopefully everyone will be over their hangovers."

"That will be fine babe, can't wait to see you and the boys will be the same. Do you want someone to come get you?"

"No, Paddy brought me my car. He's away for a month on exercise, by the way. He's going to email you. Vickie, I'll be watching on TV. So, give me a wave and a sign babe! Oh, and if I win anything, can you accept it for me, say I've got flu? Love you Vickie, give the kids a kiss for me and say hi to the boys will you?"

CHAPTER

FOUR

Vickie smoothed down the glittering black dress and spun around. "Wow!" Nicky gasped, "it's even better than we thought. You look sensational Vic; you'll have their tongues hanging out." The dress was a floor length, long sleeved, wrap around style, open at the side, showing Vickie's legs.

"Like a fucking princess!" Chris Vincent said, putting his head around the door. "You'll definitely add sexiest British woman award to our haul." He whistled. "Come on! Everyone's already downstairs, waiting for you. Marnie wants to get some pictures before we leave. She's not coming tonight; the papers have picked up on her and Jamie."

Vickie giggled, "she's still playing hard to get! He's openly chasing her now, which is amazing. Well it's really not her thing, being in the limelight, is it?"

Nicky smiled. "Best leave them to it I suppose, but it won't take long for him to fuck up will it?"

"Oh, I don't know!" Chris said, shrugging, "he's been different since we came back from holiday. Who knows with Jamie? He's a fucking maniac when he gets an idea in his head. Did you see the roses? It must have cost several thousand pounds for that number of flowers. Anyway, you might be right Nic, best leave him to it. Okay, you ready Vickie? Come on, let's wow them."

"You suit a kilt Chris, almost as much as your brother," Vickie said smiling, as they walked down stairs. "He kind of has the edge on you all."

"What he does with what he has under the kilt, is not relevant Vickie." Chris laughed and put his arm around her shoulder.

"Oh, you look amazing!" Marnie cried, as Vickie entered the living room. "Quick, line up, I need to get a photo of this. Guys sit on the sofa, Vickie lie across their knees, film star pose. Chris, come on. Sit beside Andy and hold her feet!" Marnie said, holding up the camera.

Chris was leaning over the back of the sofa behind his brother, who had Vickie's head resting on his chest. Chris grinned then leaned forward. Pretending to leer, he rubbed his hands together. "The view's better from here, I can see right down her cleavage and it's a feat of modern science, her underwear. Must have a scaffold to hold them up."

Vickie looked up at Johnny, "are you going to slap him, defend my honour, or something?"

"He can only look babe; I get to see and touch them. So, let him ogle, it's the charitable thing to do. They're still curious about how they feel Vickie. I just smile when they ask and roll my eyes. I've no idea what fake ones feel like. It's hard to tell whilst you're still breastfeeding. They're really firm, but maybe when there's no milk they'll feel different."

"Well you might not find out mate!" Vickie snapped, glaring at Johnny. "You are as bad as them with the sexist stuff!"

"Hey hold it, that's a great picture!" Marnie cried, "you looking up at him like that."

Nicky and Marnie looked at the still and began to laugh. "Every one of you is looking at her tits," Nicky gasped.

"You lot seriously need to grow up, juveniles! Bet you used to look at the bras in the mail-order catalogues," Vickie gasped, sitting up and slapping Johnny.

"They're only doing it because it winds you up Vickie, ignore them." Marnie laughed, "they'd have heart attacks if you got them out, so don't let them fool you. They only go on about it because there is no chance of you letting them, and they like noising you up. Now move away; I want one of the guys in their kilts. One! Two!" Vickie moved over to stand beside Marnie. Andy winked at Johnny as she clicked on three; the four of them lifted the front of their kilts.

"Argh, gross, we are mentally scarred for life," Vickie cried. "Not a bit of underwear amongst you. Chris, have you got a ribbon on your willie?"

"It's gift wrapped! Want to unwrap it Vickie? Marnie? Nicky?"

"Fuck off, never. You don't know where it's been!" Marnie said, nudging Vickie.

"Real Scotsmen!" Johnny laughed, pulling Vickie towards him, kissing her on the mouth.

"How original, just make sure you keep your legs crossed on stage. Especially you Johnny, I don't want other women looking at your bits and Chris, try to keep it hidden for a change."

"Oh, I will, but there won't be many women there who haven't seen my dick anyway. Do you think we've won anything Johnny? They were talking about us on the radio this morning. Apparently, it's a new record, the amount of nominations we've got. It's a lot for one act," Chris said, looking at his brother.

"Hmm we must be in with a shout? We've done so much in the studio this year though; we've put out an original album and a greatest hits CD. We'll go straight up with the new song, after we do it tonight, it's out in the morning."

"I still don't know whether I'm happy with it," Andy sighed.

"It's good Andy, best we've done so far. Just wait and see."

"You always say that!"

"I'm usually right. Getting to do it live on prime-time TV is a marketing gift. You always get negative when there's a new one out. Vickie, you think it's good don't you?"

"Fuck, Johnny, I have baby brain." Vickie slapped the side of her head. "Do you know what I've done?"

31

Johnny put his hand to her head. "Not unless I'm a mind reader dear!"

"I've left your car in the O2 car park! Marnie had mine because Jamie blocked her in and went off with the keys. So, I took yours to take the boys to school and I came straight to meet you. Then, I came home with you and Jamie, I forgot I had it. I'll stick the keys in my bag. If anyone is sober enough they can bring it back, it won't be me." She nudged Johnny, "I've expressed enough milk for tonight and tomorrow; I'm going to have a good time"

"Security can do it, take it to the flat, we're staying there tonight!" Johnny said, smiling and putting his arm around her. "Okay folks the limo is here, and the red carpet awaits. Vickie, you look sensational, really elegant but wow, wow, wow!" He leaned forward and whispered in her ear, "I wish we weren't going in the same car as them. I so want to make love to you right now babe I've got a boner; I'm having to think of my mum naked to try to get rid of it!"

Vickie shook her head and gasped. "You're as bad as them. You all need to grow up. Chris, where's Lynne? I thought she was doing that shoot in New York and flying back yesterday?"

"We fell out in Los Angeles. She got in a strop, told me to go fuck myself. She's with that fucking Saudi Prince, likely! I think it may be over this time actually; she was really angry."

"What have you done now?"

"How do you know it was something he done?" Jamie asked, smiling.

"Because it always is!"

"You could be wrong!"

"Am I Chris?"

"Nah, I fucked up!"

Vicky caught a look between Chris and Nicky, and she realised that there was a story. She moved over towards Chris, who immediately turned his back and poured champagne into a glass.

"Oh, she'll be back when she's punished you enough!" Andy said, laughing, "she always is!"

"Maybe, but this was serious mate," Chris took a gulp from the glass, "I really fucked up!"

"I'm intrigued Topher, what could possibly cause a permanent rift between you two?" Johnny said, shaking his head.

"Look, could we just leave it for now folks? I really don't want to think about it; I need to party. I'll deal with it some other time." He smiled and nudged Vickie, "and before you start Mrs D'Angelo, I don't want to talk about it, well at least not just now!" Vickie looked at him. She saw a look in his eye which told her he was upset.

Marnie began to laugh, "the UK's four most eligible bachelors; only Johnny has a date, and he can't tell anyone." She looked straight at Jamie who blew her a kiss.

* * *

Outside, Simon sat in the limo. He smiled, and whistled as Vickie got in, "You look sensational Vickie!" Simon's partner Rodney gasped, smiling at her, "not that you don't normally but that dress, your figure is amazing in it."

Simon nodded and looked at Johnny, "defo sexiest female award. You're up against Dania and a few others, but I reckon you'll take it."

"Is Dania coming?" Chris asked, "she said no, but I was kind of hoping Steven would talk her into it."

"No, not a good idea," Simon sighed, "we're trying to get her out of her contract with Tony. Steven saw her yesterday. She's still pretty traumatised and not sure if she wants to come back. What a fucking waste of talent! Tony's not going to let her go without a fight. She needs to officially report the attack, but she still won't go to the police."

Vickie opened her mouth to speak then, seeing the dark look from Johnny, she closed it and said nothing. She had been about to tell them about her discussion with Dania then remembered Dania asking her not to tell anyone. Vickie generally avoided speaking to Johnny about Dania these days, it was a taboo subject. Johnny was adamant Vickie was wrong about Tony, they had argued a lot about it over the last few weeks.

Vickie had spoken to Dania again earlier in the day when she'd called to say she'd be coming down to visit. She told Vickie that Tony had been contacted by the police and asked to attend his local police station to provide a statement. After they had studied CCTV coverage of both the club, and of one of their neighbours, the police said they had a suspect. They would not say who this was, but Dania had been asked to come to London and look at photographs. For Vickie, this indicated that it couldn't have been Tony as Dania could identify him.

Vickie was aware her trust in people was sometimes undeserved. Tony may have tricked them financially, but she still felt they owed him their success. She was sure he had not attacked Dania; she felt she knew him well enough to know.

* * *

Arriving at the venue to crowds and camera flashes, Vickie decided speaking to Johnny about Dania could wait another day. She took Jamie's hand as they walked towards the red carpet. The others walked behind, shaking hands, signing autographs and posing for selfies with fans in the crowd.

Backstage, the boys took off their jackets, left on the waistcoats, removed their bow ties and rolled up their shirt sleeves. "We are going to fucking burn out there," Jamie said. He looked thoughtful. Then took his shirt off, tossed it over a chair and put his waistcoat back on.

"You too can have a body like mine but why starve," Johnny said, laughing and high fiving Andy.

Chris looked at Jamie, then at the others. "I can never get used to an Englishman in a kilt, there's something just so wrong about it!"

"For the last time, I'm fucking Irish. The English accent is because of where I grew up!" Jamie cried, looking around.

Johnny shook his head, "don't wind him up Toph, that's racist bro. Nothing wrong with being English, Jamie!"

34

"Fuck off the lot of you!" Jamie said through gritted teeth.

"Okay are you ready for this?" Nicky said, putting her head around the door. She held it open and Vickie entered the room.

"Fuck! Where's the rest of it?" Jamie asked, looking at her dress.

Nicky laughed. "It is a wonderful idea; the coat part comes off, leaving a strapless, very sexy dress, but you can't tell when it's on that it's two dresses. You're all so used to seeing her in jeans and t-shirts, you've forgotten how sexy she can look!"

Nicky tousled Vickie's hair and placed a small sparkling tiara on the up do. Thigh length, spikey heeled, black leather boots finished the look.

Johnny moved over to stand beside her. "Love the boots. Please take them home with you?" he whispered, putting his hands on her bottom. *"Have you got underwear on?"* he gasped.

"No dear, I'm commando too; does that make me a real Scotswoman?"

"That dress is quite short Vickie; don't get too close to the edge of the stage," Jamie laughed. "Blokes hold up cameras just for that reason."

Vickie put her mouth to Johnny's ear. "It's all good, Hollywood wax redone yesterday," she whispered.

Johnny smiled. Putting his arms around her, he whispered back, "you're a fucking tease Vickie, just wait till I get you and those boots home tonight; you won't be able to walk when I'm finished with you." Johnny kissed her on the mouth then nuzzled her neck. "God, you are so beautiful darling, I almost want to just forget about the show, go straight home."

"Hey Jovi, put her down before we need to go and get a bucket of water." Jamie grinned, "you're giving off so many pheromones, I want to fuck you mate."

Sam, their sound engineer, came into the green room, a headset on. "Vickie! You look ... wow, sexy, fuck me! I don't think I've ever seen you look like that." Still looking at Vickie, he called, "guys you are on in five, get yourselves into position please. Phew mate!" Sam said, nudging Johnny, "fuck sake, she's going to knock them dead! Okay four minutes folks. Come on now, you can look at her later."

"No time for you to put knickers on then?" Johnny whispered. He looked at her chest. "Or a bra? You'd better hope you don't start leaking milk on stage."

"Nipple pads, great invention. Nicky taped them on with industrial toupee tape. It needs to be taken off carefully." She giggled. "So, no ripping off my clothes later to ravish me."

"You do look amazing though babe," Johnny conceded, pinching her bare bum as he passed her. The boys picked up their instruments and followed Sam through the corridor to the stage.

Andy lifted his drumsticks and put his free arm around Vickie's shoulder. "Your tits look huge in that dress Vickie."

"You shouldn't be looking!" Vickie said, pretending to be angry. "You really do have a thing about breasts Andy. Freud would say that you have an oral complex, weren't breast fed long enough or something."

Andy considered this and grinned, "I think it was the opposite. I was on the tit until I went to primary school Vickie. Honestly, apparently I used to lift my mum's top and suck. Then she got pregnant with Jake and stopped. I was about four, so you're probably right."

"You are such a liar Andy! Hannah told me, when Denis was a baby, she didn't feed either of you. Stop looking at my tits or I'll fucking bite you."

Andy nudged her and laughed. "Hard not to notice when they're almost touching your chin. You'd need to move them out of the way to bite anything." Still laughing, the revolving set brought them around to face the audience. They performed their new song as their first number. The crowd erupted into loud cheers and whistles as Vickie sang the last note.

Vickie smiled. Taking the microphone from the stand, she addressed the crowd and the cameras. "Thank you all so much, you have no idea what that means to us to see so many of our peers here tonight, including some of our own musical heroes, cheering us on. Thank you for asking us to do this; it's a great honour to open this event. Last year was not our best year as you all know." Vickie smiled sadly into the camera. "We would like to take you back to our roots and dedicate this next number to everyone who died on flight 17-2C. This song is where we got our name; it's the first song I sang when I joined the band nearly six years ago. It's one of my all-time favourites, used to be my karaoke number. I haven't sung it for about 5 years, so here goes."

As the boys began to play, she sang the opening line of Black Velvet. The crowd remained hushed throughout the number. Vickie sank to her knees, leaning over Andy, as she sang the final line. He continued to play his drums, pretending to ignore her. As the music died, the crowd went wild. "Andy!" Vickie hissed, "I can't get up, it's the fucking boots." Andy burst out laughing, scooped Vickie up, carrying her in his arms to the front of the stage to join the others; both unable to breathe for laughter. She threw his drumsticks into the crowd for him.

Johnny held his hand up and lifted the microphone. "Thank you, thank you. Most of you here have just heard Vickie sing this song for the first time. I first heard her sing it in a little Scottish pub, nearly six years ago. I looked at this skinny little girl, with the great boobs, my mate had just married."

The audience cheered and whistled.

"What, the boobs?" Johnny laughed. "Come on, like no one noticed. Anyway, her singing! She sang that song. I had known Vickie most of my life; I'd no idea she could sing. Her voice made the hair on the back of my neck stand up. I got shivers down my spine then, and it still does it for me now. The rest, as they say, is history. As Vickie said though, we need to thank you all for being there for us this year. None of us will ever forget the support we've had. Now, we need to go work on getting drunk. It's good to be back, thank you all."

"That went well!" Jamie said, as they walked backstage.

"Vickie, are you going to put the rest of your dress back on?" Andy said grinning, putting his arm around her waist. "Fuck me those boots! I really want to fight Jovi for you when you're dressed like that. Especially when I know you're not wearing knickers." He nudged her. "I could see your bare arse when you got stuck."

"Yeah, I feel good Andy, but I think I'm more comfortable showing a bit less skin. The boots are the most uncomfortable footwear I've ever worn. I must have looked like something from the zombie apocalypse trying to dance in them. I could barely walk." She nudged him, "thanks for being a gentleman."

Re-dressed, they walked back to their table. The presenter stopped talking to allow yet another round of applause. "Ladies and gentlemen, please put your hands together once again for the legend that is the pride of Scotland! Black Velvet!"

The boys turned around, lifted their kilts and mooned the cameras. The crowd went wild. Vickie shook her head and buried her face in her hands. "You're mad. You do know this is tomorrow's front pages?"

"Oh, I think we can be forgiven a bit of fun Vickie," Andy laughed. "You should have joined in, seeing as you're going commando too."

"It's great to be able to relax," Johnny said, sliding into the seat beside her. Vickie leaned in closer to him. Johnny put his arm around her shoulder and kissed the top of her head. "We literally brought the house down. We should release Black Velvet as a single; you're superb."

"You never wanted to do it!" Vickie gasped, choking and spitting out her drink. ***You said no covers."*** Johnny handed her a napkin and grinned. "That's because you singing it didn't just make the hair on the back of my neck stand up . . . it made my cock stand up too. Yes Vickie, even then, it terrified me what I wanted to do to you." He grinned, "it was purely fantasy stuff I thought but fuck, Vickie, our sex life just gets better and better."

"Was it a shock, with me?"

"Truth? Yes. Although he never elaborated, Billy used to say you were adventurous. I kind of thought that was just him trying to make excuses for being faithful. I'll never forget that first night with you, 1ˢᵗ of January 2012, 12.37!"

"You know the exact time?"

Johnny grinned. "As I had that first orgasm, I looked up, I was trying to hold back, to let you come! My eyes were drawn to the clock above the tub." He giggled, "I get a rager every time I see that fucking clock now."

Vickie slid her hand under the long table cloth and into the front of his kilt, his penis instantly responding. He grinned at her. "I dare you! You just wait till I get you back to the flat, you're going to be begging me to let you sleep. I'm going to make love to you all night, just you, me and those boots. I told Nicky to put them in your bag. Arfur has taken said bag to the flat."

"Do you know what?" Vickie whispered in Johnny's ear. "I reckon I could get under the table and give you head without anyone else noticing! The table covers go to the floor Johnny. I could be in and out in a heartbeat, you're so hard." Vickie giggled and nudged him, "you actually had that first orgasm, at 12.29 though. That clock is eight minutes fast!"

Chris leaned over. "You'd better take your hand off his knob, Vickie. Or we could be up on that stage with his sporran hanging at a very odd angle, cos we're likely to win something." He slapped his brother on the back of his head, "still does it to you, doesn't it?"

"Oh yes."

"The song? Why?" Vickie asked. "Billy was the same when I sang it."

Johnny smiled. "It's not just the song Vickie, it's your voice, the way your sing it. Andy and I are always trying to write a song that makes us feel that way."

"Shoosh," Andy hissed. "They're about to announce the album award. We've probably got it for Sober When Operating."

The presenter began to speak; he read out the nominations for Best Album then announced that Black Velvet had indeed won for their last album. As the cameras focused on their table, hitching up her dress, Vickie jumped up and wrapped her arms around Johnny. He kissed her on the mouth. Vickie then walked through the audience with Chris, his arm slung casually over her shoulder.

The audience, on their feet, cheered as Vickie and the boys crowded onto the stage. Flashes of white light lit up the room; she took the award then handed it to Andy. Andy stepped up to the microphone, he smiled. "As Vickie and Johnny said earlier, tonight is bittersweet for us but this award, like the others, we dedicate to those who we loved and lost. Many of the tracks on the album capture our feelings. The title, which we're often asked about, was something Vickie's dad, who's a doctor, said to me one Christmas. I was trying to get him to have a drink when he was on call. He said, *'If one of the kids has an accident tonight, you'll be thankful I'm sober when operating.'* It stuck in my mind. All five of us are thankful for a lot of things. We're thankful for having each other and for the support we've had." He held up the statue. "This means the world to us. Cheers folks."

Four more times Black Velvet were called up and given an award; they were over the moon. The images of them celebrating were flashed all over the world. Vickie also accepted the Best Newcomer award on behalf of Dania. She waved into the camera, holding up the award. "Get well soon, babe!"

Finally, the presenter called for quiet**.** *"A special award,"* he announced. He turned to the crowd. "We need now to recognise the achievement of one act, in terms of the way they've dealt with adversity and tragedy they've come back stronger than ever." Everyone turned to look at the Black Velvet table. "Last year this ceremony was marred by our pain at their huge tragic loss. It had only been a few days, and we were all in shock. The track they released in memory of those who died became the highest selling single of the last year, and all proceeds went to the charity the band set up. They raised an obscene amount of money which has gone to open twelve '2/17' centres for young musicians, across the country."

"Vickie!" Johnny said, nudging her. "They're really wasted, look!" he said, nodding in the direction of Chris, "need to keep them from talking on stage, especially Jamie and Chris. Fuck knows what they'll say."

The presenter continued speaking. "They're a credit to us all, the way they have come through with dignity." He looked over at the Black Velvet table and saluted. "We want to recognise and respect the strength it has taken for them to get back up and carry on. It must have been so difficult. In the last few months they've released some of their best work. Ladies and gentlemen, please stand for Black Velvet."

On stage, and overwhelmed, Vickie stood in front of the microphone. "Thank you for this, but we didn't do anything special. If we're honest, we'd rather not be standing here. At first, in those mind numbingly, grief stricken days, we just could not believe we could carry on. In fact, until tonight, we'd not sung live since the crash! Probably as therapy, and avoidance, we got back into the studio and recorded some of our best material. The writing Johnny and Andy have done this last year was inspired by their feelings, their way of dealing with emotions." Vickie paused trying to not cry, emotion obvious in her voice. Johnny nudged Andy, who stepped forward and put his arm around her waist. Vickie gulped back tears but continued to speak. "We lost some of our most loved people that night. We survived, came back because of the support of the public here and abroad, the love and support of each other and the team around us. We lead a very unorthodox life and are often in the gossip columns, some of it is true, some just nonsense. What I will say is, we have always been more than just friends. We'll still be more than friends, long after Black Velvet is reduced to a dusty CD cover at a car boot sale." She began to cry.

Jamie took the microphone from her and continued, his own voice hoarse with emotion. "However, for now, we are under new management and ready to go again. The best is yet to come."

Vickie nodded, "I'm sorry about the boys lack of clothing;

what can I say?" she smiled, dabbing her eyes with a tissue, "but there's worse things to look at I suppose. They do have nice asses don't they?" The audience relaxed, and laughter could be heard. Vickie looked around her before continuing. She smiled and nudged Jamie, "I've four children to feed, we obviously can't afford that and underwear."

Chris took the mike and grinned. "We also have a very hungry ex-manager to feed." He looked at Vickie pretended to leer at her, *"she's commando too, by the way*!" I mean, could you see a VPL in that dress?" Chris shouted, pulling Vickie towards him. Vickie giggled and shook her head.

Tony Gorman threw a glass at his television screen. He stood up**. "They'll be fucking paying before this night is out,"** he growled, rummaging in his dinner suit jacket pocket. He pulled out a handful of tablets, swallowing some and returning the rest to his pocket. "Just you fucking wait, Vincent, we'll see who laughs last!" Picking up the telephone, he pressed a button, "hello, remember that favour you owe me? Well it's payback time; here's what I want you to do." As he put the phone down his front doorbell rang, he looked at the security monitor above the door. Shaking his head, he moved towards the back door and out into the alley beyond.

* * *

"Oh well, what after show parties should we go to?" Vickie smiled, as Johnny put his hand on her back, leading her out of the venue towards the waiting press. "Fuck Vickie, I must be getting old, I just want to go to the flat and take you to bed, to sleep! The drink really fucks me now!" he added.

"Come on, we need to go to at least one of the parties," Vickie said, moving closer to him, "then I believe I'm on a promise."

Their security team came around to meet them at the door.

"Colin, my new Range Rover is parked out in the car park," Johnny said, looking around at the big bodyguard. "Nicky has the key. Can you get it and take us to . . . ? Where, Chris?"

Chris looked thoughtful. "The record company offices. We'd better go there first cos I'm putting money on you two boring bastards disappearing; it's just around the corner from the flat."

Johnny smiled and winked at Vickie. "Arfur, you and Zac go in the limo with the others, we'll take mine."

"Where you going first?" a reporter called out as they got into the car. "Record company offices in Hammersmith Road," Chris said. Jimmy Murphy from the Mirror, a good friend of the band's, raised his thumb.

"Chris! What did you tell them for? They will be there waiting now. I just saw Ratfink run off, he'll be jumping on his bike as we speak." Andy gasped, "come on Zac, Jamie, let's go try to get in before they get there. See you there folks."

CHAPTER

FIVE

Colin stopped the car in front of the venue. "Fuck, what's he doing here? What do you want me to do Jovi?"

"Absolutely nothing!" Vickie said firmly.

Johnny scowled at Vickie as they watched Tony go in. "He'd better stay away from you Vickie!"

"He manages other bands Johnny; he'll still be invited." She looked sternly at him then pushed Chris. "Just try to be civilised both of you. If you can't, then just stay out of his way; it's in the hands of the legal team now. He was drunk when he spoke to me honey, he doesn't even remember."

"You can't possibly believe what he said in that letter?" Johnny hissed, his voice angry, his eyes narrowing.

"He apologised for that Johnny, it's over, let it go."

"What about Dania, Vickie? Have you forgotten the state she was in?"

"No of course not, but I keep saying, we don't actually know if he was involved Johnny. He has an addiction that caused some of his behaviour in the last year. He said it was the trauma of the crash and our grief. If he had been taking drugs and drinking like he said and he's getting help now . . . ?"

"Vickie, there's no excuse for that kind of sexual violence babe. There've been other allegations about him, from girls in the office. Marnie told Jamie about a couple. Billy always said he was a sexual predator, I heard him tell you that loads of times." Chris looked around as he spoke. "Vickie, I've used every drug known to man and a few that aren't. I've drunk myself unconscious, but I've never raped or beaten anyone. Even if he did have a problem, which I think he probably did, it does not excuse what happened to Dania.

"But Chris . . . " Vickie cut in.

"No, Vickie, let me finish," Chris held up his hand to silence her. "Okay you don't believe he did it, we've no evidence but Vickie we've also no evidence he didn't!"

"I'm not condoning it Chris," Vickie whispered, "I just think we actually don't know what happened and neither does Dania! Can I remind you, in this country, you're innocent until proven guilty?"

Johnny stared at her then shook his head. "No fucking way Vickie, you can't possibly believe that it's okay? You fucking saw what he did."

"Johnny, he might not have done anything. We knew him for nearly five years and I never ever felt uncomfortable in his company. I just can't see it, but if he was taking combinations of drugs . . . "

"Vickie, for Christ sake babe, listen to yourself!" "You can't possibly think that what he did can be excused by saying he was out his face?"

Vickie sighed, "Johnny look at what happened with us after the crash, we didn't know we had sex, I still don't have any memory of it."

Johnny looked at her, his eyes narrowed, "Dania was drugged, brutally raped by several men; you saw the fucking bruises Vickie! Whatever happened between us, it wasn't deliberate and you know it!"

"That's not what I'm saying Johnny, I'm not condoning what was done to Dania! I'm saying I don't believe he did it!"

"Vickie I'm seriously disturbed by what you've just said. I

can't believe that you can find any way to condone that dirty bastard. More disturbing, you're condoning rape!"

Vickie sighed, "I'm not Johnny. She doesn't remember what happened. I don't think I could be that wrong about him, Johnny." Vickie looked at Johnny and sighed again. "I don't know, maybe the alternative, for me, is too awful to contemplate so I have to excuse it in my mind. I just can't believe I was so wrong about him. He was good to me Johnny, looked after me. Please can we just drop it. I love you, I hate arguing with you."

Johnny sighed, put his arm around her and kissed the top of her head, his other hand moved to her breast. He kissed her on the mouth. "Darling, you'd find something good to say about Old Nick himself. It's one of the things I love about you, your compassion and naivety! Look babe, I hate fighting with you too. Let's just leave this conversation for another time. He's out of our hair now anyway, so can we just avoid being near him tonight?"

Chris turned around and looked at his brother. "You'd better take your hand off Vickie's tit bro, before someone takes a picture."

"Fuck, I do that without thinking now." He looked down, "but they do look huge in that dress," Johnny said as he lifted Vickie down from the car.

"Look, there's Lynne!" Vickie waved at her friend who detached herself from a small group, stopped to pose for Jimmy Murphy, kissed him and then walked towards Vickie.

"Like I said earlier, she's really pissed off with me!" Chris whispered. "I don't want a scene here, Jimmy's a mate but he fancies her, so I'd better make myself scarce."

Lynne moved away from the reporter and sidled over to them. She looked beautiful, every inch the supermodel she was. Her blonde hair was hanging down her back; she wore a red silk mini dress and red knee length boots accentuating her long legs. *"Fucking shit-bag,"* she hissed, as Chris moved swiftly inside the door. Blowing Lynne a kiss, he disappeared into the crowd.

"Excuse me?" Johnny laughed. "I may just join my brother at

the bar. Vickie, stay with Lynne!" he whispered in her ear.

Lynne looked furious. Vickie shook her head and hugged her friend, "what's he done this time?"

"Oh, I'll tell you the long version later, it's not that important actually. I bared my fucking soul to him in LA, said I wanted to settle down with him, be an exclusive couple . . . he fucking laughed Vickie."

"Laughed! He should have been hysterical?" Vickie gasped, her eyes wide, her mouth open. "You can't really blame him Lynne, it would be funny. You were even more adamant than him, it was always going to be casual."

Lynne sighed and looked away, her face showing how hurt she was. Vickie, watching her, realised Lynne was close to tears. "Even more reason for him to realise I was serious. I have been doing it with him since I was 15 and he fucking laughed." Vickie watched, astounded, as Lynne quickly wiped away a tear from her eye. "He really hurt me Vickie, but I'll live." She smiled sadly, "I love him Vic, always have. I thought I wanted excitement and to be free but I don't anymore. I want him."

"What happened?" Vickie gasped, "what changed your mind? I'm struggling to take this in, and I believe in fairy tales."

Lynne sighed, "It was the night of the Grammy's, we had a session with Nicky, and well, I suddenly felt jealous." She smiled through tears. "It was a bolt from the blue. I want what you and Jovi have. Oh, it's not over, I'll end up with him again, no one else comes close. He doesn't need to know that, I need to let him squirm. I've been seeing Arahan, the Saudi Prince again. If Chris doesn't want me, others will." Lynne sighed and rummaged in her evening bag, "I need to go powder my nose; I'll be back in a moment."

"Lynne, go easy on the Columbian marching powder. That's what causes a lot of your problems with Chris, the cocktails of drink and drugs!"

"Oh, I know. I only have a little coke on me, but I'm thinking I'll need it tonight." She sighed. "I need the stimulation. Arahan, well, he's not as good in bed as Chris, but he is more fucking reliable."

Vickie laughed and hugged her friend. "Lynne, our cat is more reliable than Chris." Vickie looked up and smiled as Colin moved over to stand beside her.

Colin handed Vickie Johnny's car keys. "Jovi said to give it to you to put in your bag. He's forgotten the flat key, there's one on that ring. His car's parked out front Vickie; we're within walking distance of Hammersmith View so you can just leave it here. It should be safe enough, there are cameras on this building and it's alarmed. Do you mind if I go and get something to eat? I'm starving."

Vickie laughed, Colin was always hungry. "No, we'll be here for a while, I'm just waiting for Lynne then I'll go and find Johnny." Vickie smiled. She stood on tip toes and kissed his cheek. "You go and get food Colin."

"Okay boss, just promise me you'll stay inside until I get back. Don't speak to fucking Gorman either. Johnny's right about him Vickie, and there's some real weirdo's out there too."

Vickie looked around her, "there are probably more nutters inside here Colin."

As she walked towards the cloakroom Vickie heard her phone ring. She took it out, Catriona's name came up. She couldn't hear so she stepped out into the street to listen. "Catriona is everything alright?"

"No Vickie!" Catriona cried. Vickie could hear the panic in the young woman's voice. "It's Chiara, she's really not well. I tried to call your dad, but he's not answering. I need you to come home . . . **oh my God Vickie, she's stopped breathing.** I don't know what to do. Vickie, I'm so scared."

"Call an ambulance Catriona. Where's Laura? I'll be straight home." The line went dead.

Fingers shaking, Vickie dialled Johnny's number then Chris's; both went straight on to answering service. She threw her phone into her bag and looked around, she couldn't see anyone. She ran back towards the venue hoping to catch Arfur. The foyer was busy with people, shoulder to shoulder, trying to get through into the bar area. Suddenly she remembered the car keys in her bag.

"What's wrong Vickie?" She looked up. Tony was standing in the street beside her. "Vickie, are you alright darling? I saw you on the phone and you looked upset!"

"Tony, it's Chiara, she's ill, I have to get home. I can't find anyone; Catriona has just called and Chiara was not breathing. I have Johnny's keys but Colin has gone to get something to eat. I can't drive, I've been drinking." Everything was coming out in a rush. Vickie knew she was panicking, but she couldn't see Johnny. Frantically she dialled his mobile again then Chris's but they both just rang out then went to recorded message.

"I can take you!" Tony said. "Vickie I'm not an ogre, you know I'm not. Come on, let's go, you can phone the others whilst I drive. I haven't drunk much, I just got here, but my car is quite a bit away, and we would have problems getting a taxi. Give me the key?" Vickie handed him the keys. She got in the passenger seat beside him. "Nice car!" Tony sighed. "It's new!"

"Johnny got it . . . I don't know, about three weeks ago. Tony, please, just get me home; we can do it in an hour."

"Won't they take the baby to hospital? Vickie you'd better call Catriona back, ask her. Try not to worry babe, these things happen with babies. Look, it will probably be the nearest A&E in Kingston they take her to. We'll head there; you keep trying to reach her."

Vickie tried again, there was no answer. Her heart was beating loudly, pounding in her chest. She could hardly speak; her mouth was dry. "Please God!" she prayed. "Don't let anything happen to her." Vickie heard the central locking click as Tony started the car.

"Better to be safe love, carjackers, this is a prestige motor." Tony didn't say much as he drove, appearing to concentrate on the road. It began to snow. Tony slowed down and put on the windscreen wipers; they scraped against the dry windscreen.

Vickie was too scared to care. When he turned off the main road, onto a side one, Vickie looked at him.

"Tony, is this the quickest way?"

"Yes, it's a short cut, don't worry. Try the nanny again. Ask where they're taking Chiara."

With shaking fingers Vickie dialled the number, but there was no reply. Frantic, she dialled the internal house number, Laura answered. "Vickie I've been watching on TV, well done."

"What the fuck?" Vickie cried. "Where's my baby . . . where's Catriona?"

"What are you talking about? Catriona's in bed!"

"She called. She was hysterical, saying Chiara was really ill." There was an echo, Vickie could hear her own voice after every word. Vickie became aware of Laura's confusion. She looked at Tony who appeared to be watching the road, oblivious to what Vickie was saying.

"Catriona? What did you say? Catriona called you? Vickie I can't hear what you're saying, the lines really echoic, like you are under water. Catriona didn't call you; she went to bed with a migraine over an hour ago, after the last feed. The babies are fine. I have just been up and checked. The monitor is in front of me, they're both asleep."

"What?"

Suddenly the phone was taken from her.

"Tony, you bastard, what are you up to? You must have known this was a hoax? Why are you doing this to me? Let me out of this fucking car." She began to try to open the door, it but it was locked. She tried to hit him, but he lifted his hand and slapped her face.

"Don't make me hurt you Vickie!" he said through gritted teeth. "Just don't. I only want to talk to you. You said we could be friends then you ignored me!" He looked at her and laughed, "Catriona was working for me all along, little spy in the camp Vickie; you thought you were safe but she told me everything. I knew about you and Johnny being together because she told me."

He began to laugh harder. "I told you lots of lies Vickie; you're going to have to try to work out what I actually lied about."

Vickie pulled off her seat belt and tried to open the door. Tony grabbed her, pulling her roughly towards him and then pushed her against the side window. Realising she was trapped Vickie began to scratch and kick him. The car swayed over the road.

"You fucking little wildcat, I'm going to teach you a lesson you'll never forget. You think you can get away from me just like that? I warned that fucking prick you are shagging. I told them all, there would be consequences if they fired me!" Tony pulled Vickie's face towards him, *"We have payback time. If it hurts when I fuck you, blame your friends Vickie."* Tony opened the driver window; he threw her phone out onto the road. Stopping the car, he pushed Vickie back, straddled her. Pulling a pair of handcuffs from his pocket, he quickly over-powered her, handcuffing her hands behind her head and through the headrest. He pulled the seat belt back around Vickie, put his hand on her face and squeezed her cheek. Vickie cried out as pain shot through her face and head.

"Oh, that will just be the start if you don't sit there and shut up. I'm in the shit now Vickie, I've just kidnapped you. So babe, I have nothing to lose, remember that!" He moved towards her, grabbed her chin and kissed her hard on the mouth. "I'll sample the goods later." He looked at her. Vickie realised she just didn't know this person hissing at her. "Did you know she was going to the police when you met me for coffee? Did you fucking know I was going to be questioned? Did you know they had DNA Vickie?"

"Fuck off!" She tried to bring her foot up to kick him. He slapped her hard; Vickie felt as though her eye had come out of its socket. He grabbed her hair and pulled her closer, she could smell whisky, she knew she was trapped, she spat in his face. He reacted quickly, punching her hard in the face; the force sent her into the side window once more. Dazed, she slid down the seat, her eye hurt, she couldn't see.

51

"Don't Vickie, don't be brave; you just sit there, take it babe." He pulled at her long skirt and it opened as the front came away from the clips holding it in place. "Ah the slutty dress, I thought it was underneath." He put his hand up her skirt. "Ah, aha, Chris wasn't joking, no panties either. Same as the boys, true Scotswoman; is that what it is Vickie? Hollywood wax too, I do like a smooth ride. Were you ready for Vincent's knob? Know what Vickie? Mine's bigger and you are going to have it in every orifice before this is over."

"You wouldn't dare Tony! They'll lock you up," she hissed, her body shaking. She knew her voice reflected her fear but she continued. "When they find out what you've done, they'll throw away the key."

Tony laughed. "It'll be your word against mine babe. Besides, when they find out that you have been putting it around your band for years, will anyone believe that you weren't having an affair with me too? Fuck, you and Johnny were shagging before Billy and Ali were even cold. I know it all Vickie; Catriona heard it all. It should have been me, I got you all drugged up to do you that night. The night they died, but fucking Johnny wouldn't leave you. Then you fucked him instead of me."

"I made you Vickie, I own you." He pushed two fingers into her vagina; she cried out in pain as his nails scratched her. He pulled the fingers out and put them in his mouth then took a photograph of his fingers. Vickie braced herself. Noting this, Tony stopped and laughed. "It's like a honey pot in there, isn't it? No wonder they're all after you."

Vickie screamed. She pulled away from him, the handcuffs bit into her wrists.

"Oh, not here, I want to see you in all your glory Vickie. I want what that sap Billy got, what Johnny is getting now. You're a classy bird, Vickie; the car isn't the place to ride someone like you."

"Tony, stop this now. Let me go! " Vickie was terrified,

she had never experienced anything like this, had no idea what to do. "I promise I won't tell anyone, it's not too late, please Tony?"

He grabbed her face again and squeezed, laughing when she cried out at the pain. "Oh, I like it when you beg. You'll be begging me in a little while Vickie, begging me to keep riding you. Begging me to take my great big cock out of your tight little arse. Nearly six years I've been thinking about this; I wanted you but I wanted the money you made me more."

"You're fucking mad Tony; this can't be happening."

"Oh, it's real babe, very real!" He looked at her and laughed; Vickie watched, fear growing in her stomach, as he popped some pills into his mouth. "Viagra Vickie, just so I can keep going. I'd hate to disappoint you. You're all mine Vickie, not like little Dania, I got 500K for her virginity, and I got to watch. She really was a virgin, there was blood and everything. I have a film of her being fucked for the first time. Don't know what excited me more, watching her getting it or when I counted the half a million later. I did her too but it was like necrophilia, she was totally out of it."

"You bastard, you dirty bastard, you made me believe you didn't know about it." Vickie looked at him. Despite the pain she was in she shook her head. "I trusted you Tony, I defended you. Why?"

"I couldn't believe it when I was offered half a million for her, I couldn't turn it down could I? Half a fucking million? It was planned Vickie; it wasn't just by chance I met her that night. Never used rohypnol before, not my thing, but fuck it worked quickly. If I had managed to get you as well, I could have got more. You're not a virgin but there's a market for you, with those huge tits and a Hollywood wax. I might share you later. I could phone a friend, make some money from you. But you are going to feel every bit of it Mrs D'Angelo, every fucking thrust."

Vickie, now terrified beyond her worst nightmares, knew he meant it. She also knew it was possible no one would realise in the crowded party that she was missing. She remembered the state Dania was in, the bruising, the report of vaginal and pelvic trauma. Her mind was racing, could she just lie back and let him, she didn't know. Everything she knew about sexual assault told her not to fight him, just let him do it.

Meanwhile, Johnny was looking for Vickie. When she had not joined him at the bar he had tried to call her. Noticing the missed calls, he had called her phone which went straight on to voicemail. He called Laura who had also rung him. She told him about the call from Vickie. "Johnny, she was with Tony." Laura sobbed, "he was hurting her, I heard him. I think he was hitting her Johnny. He told her he was going to rape her; I heard it all, there was an echo it must have been coming through the Bluetooth in the car. Johnny, I'm so scared. Then I heard traffic, then nothing."

"Hi boss, everything okay?" Colin appeared beside Johnny.

"Where's Vickie Colin?" Johnny cried. *"She was with you; you were supposed to stay with her!"*

"I went to get some food. I left her in the foyer waiting for Lynne."

Johnny ran through the crowded party, pushing people out of the way. He spotted Lynne standing at the bar with a man of Arab appearance. "Come with me." He grabbed her arm and dragged her through the crowd. Jamie and Andy looked up as he passed them and followed.

Colin pushed his way through the crowd towards them. "Jovi, it's getting worse mate. Your car has gone; I gave Vickie the keys." He pointed out the glass wall, to an empty space in the road.

"Lynne, did you see her with anyone?" Johnny cried. *"Fucking think Lynne, did you see Tony near her?"*

"Hm, I went to the toilet, did some coke. When I came back out I could see her through the glass, on the phone. I went to get us a drink, when I came back she was gone. I just thought she was in the party. She won't be far away Jovi. She's probably talking to someone inside; some wee Ned likely stole the car."

Johnny's phone buzzed and Tony's name flashed up, with a photograph of two fingers. The text above it read, 'These fingers have just been in your woman's fanny. I'm about to make her cum all over your cream leather seats.'

"Colin, call the police, get them here! That bastard has taken her."

"What bastard?" Chris asked, appearing beside him.

"Gorman, I think he's kidnapped Vickie."

"Fuck Johnny, you're havering now. After what happened to Dania Vickie wouldn't be stupid enough to go anywhere with Tony! If he'd kidnapped her from here, someone would have stopped him."

"Well let's just find her Chris then you can say I told you so."

Chris's phone buzzed. He took it out of his pocket. A photograph flashed up clearly showing a woman naked from the waist down, the black sparkling dress hitched up around her waist, the distinctive Celtic band tattoo, Vickie's tattoo. 'This is what you are missing Christopher,' the text underneath said.

"Oh, fuck Johnny!" Chris gasped, handing the phone to his brother, a look of horror on his face. "Fuck sake, she wouldn't do that willingly."

"Jovi, if they're in your car you can use the tracker!" Colin cried.

"Fuck, of course; I can link in through my phone."

In the car, Vickie was trying hard to be brave, not show Tony how scared she was. She was, however, terrified. "Tony, please? Can you at least think about what you're doing? It's not gone too far for you to stop this! They'll be looking for me now. Have you taken leave of your senses?"

He turned and looked at her; for a second Vickie thought that he might be considering her request. However, he lifted his hand and hit her hard across the face. Her lip split, she banged her head on the side window again. She could taste blood. "Shut the fuck up, Vickie. You need to be taught a lesson, I'm going to teach you. Like I said, I've nothing left to lose. I may just finish you off, bury you, because they would need to prove it wouldn't they? You'd better pray I do finish you off properly. I've got a grave all ready for you. I'd hate to bury you alive!"

Vickie tried not to cry, but tears welled up in her eyes. She began to shake violently, her teeth chattered. She would never see her children or Johnny again."

"You scared?" he asked calmly.

Vickie nodded, unable to speak because of the fear and shaking; she realised she had wet herself.

"Good, you fucking should be. Now if you are good to me, I'll finish you off quickly; I won't let you suffer. Then you and sweet William can be together again. Tell me Vickie, how do you think he would feel about you fucking his best friend?"

"Tony, why?" Vickie stammered, "why are you doing this to me? We were friends!"

"Shut up Vickie, I told you, you and those fucking posers need to be taught who is boss. You undermined my authority; they ruined my reputation. They've been telling everyone I'm a rapist, now Dania has gone to the police. They came for me tonight Vickie, but I left by the back door and came to find you. Helmut told me where you were, so I got little Catriona to call you. No more Vickie, I'm finished now. Besides I want to fuck you, I always have, I know you like it rough! I'm going to have you before they lock me up. Better to get hung for a sheep, than a lamb."

Johnny followed the tracker system across the busy traffic of London. He was in the back of a police car with Chris and Lynne; the others were behind in the staff car driven by Colin.

"Where's he going?" Johnny gasped. "It looks as though he's heading for Windsor."

"Of course he is, he has a cottage there; it's quite isolated, he used to rent it out as a holiday home. Andy and I stayed there once, years ago. It's in the middle of a wood, nothing for miles, except the river," Chris cried. He took out his mobile phone. "Andy, what was the name of Tony's cottage, the one near Windsor; remember the place he lent us when we were with those two sisters? Yeah, the one in the woods, near the racecourse, yes. Can you take Colin there, you're good with directions." Chris nudged the policeman in the passenger seat, "Frogmore cottage!"

"Fuck this for a game of soldiers!" the policeman driving said, switching on the siren and blue light. He called in with the information on Tony. He asked that local police in Windsor be alerted.

CHAPTER

SIX

"Get out Vickie! Come on, I won't hurt you, I was only joking about killing you. I just want to touch you, let's have a little fun. If you behave and give me some of that body then I'll take you home afterwards. You know I'm not a killer." Tony unclipped the handcuffs and pulled Vickie roughly towards him. He dragged her, screaming, into the house. "Scream all you want babe! There's no one for miles. Nobody will hear you." He pushed her into the hallway. Vickie caught sight of herself in the large hall mirror. He noticed. "You don't look too pretty Vickie! Sorry about messing up your face, you just got me so angry. Your body is alright, no blemishes there yet." He opened a door, Vickie looked around her. She could see it was a bedroom, dimly lit and decorated in black and purple, a large Victorian iron bed sat in the middle of the room.

Tony pushed Vickie roughly onto the bed, threaded the single handcuff through a chain attached to the headboard and fastened it to her other wrist. He began to laugh. "Ha-ha, look at you! Not so smart now Mrs D'Angelo, not so snooty. Fuck I'm going to enjoy this; I've imagined fucking you for years. First you are going to suck me off, just for an appetiser. I saw you do it before baby, many, many times. I had cameras all over that house in Glasgow I put you in. Fuck, you and Billy had some fun. Same

58

with the Fulham house; I watched them, fucking unbelievable what they got up to. Then there was Dania, she was getting close to doing it with that fucking brother of yours. Another week, she wouldn't have been as saleable."

Vickie watched him, terror growing in her heart. She silently prayed.

Tony stood up and threw his dinner jacket on to the floor. He undid the fly of his trousers, letting them fall to the ground he stepped out of them. His manhood sprang out; he came towards her rubbing it. "Look at me, that's what thinking about fucking you does to me Vickie. I still have a wank to those films sometimes, there's loads of material. You were like a fucking bunny, the amount of shagging you did and you're a fucking contortionist too. Johnny and Ali were so boring in comparison; he must think all his birthdays have come at once doing you now."

He pushed Vickie's head back, she cried out at the pain in her face and head. Her head crashed against the headboard and she felt the metal cut into her. Her mouth ached. He pulled her around and made her sit on the edge of the bed. Holding her hair he wound it around his hand and held her as he forced his penis into her mouth. He began to thrust, she gagged. "Oh, am I fucking choking you?" He grabbed her head and pushed her again. Vickie felt her teeth scrape and he cried out and hit her hard on the head. *"Be fucking careful."*

Suddenly he gripped her head and his breathing became heavier as he ejaculated. Tony withdrew. He grabbed her face, closing her mouth. "Fucking swallow bitch. You did with Billy I watched you swallow." Vickie tried, but she began to gag and vomited. He disappeared, reappeared with a sponge and a towel, cleaned her up roughly then pushed her back onto the bed.

He picked up his jacket from the floor, rummaged around in the pocket, brought out a small bag and a straw. Vickie watched him lay out and cut white powder with a credit card then snort it. He repeated the action and cut another line of what she supposed was cocaine then walked towards her. He grabbed her dress and in one swift movement, ripped it down the front.

Vickie screamed in agony, as the tape Nicky had carefully applied tore her skin. She tried to move away but he pulled her towards him. His white dress shirt was splattered with what she realised was her blood. "Oh, baby what a body!" Grabbing her breast, he lowered his head and bit her. He laughed as she screamed.

He put his lips to her nipple and she felt his teeth bite in to her again. He spat a mouthful of breast milk at her then hit her hard across the face with the back of his hand. Moving away, he licked his finger and ran it along the line of coke on the bedside table then he pushed the finger up in to her vagina. "You are going to love this Vickie, it's amazing. You'll feel every thrust."

"I want you on your knees now!" He pushed her around, grabbing her hair, pulling her head back. She felt the handcuffs bite into her wrist and then immense pain shooting up her arm as her left wrist snapped. He tried to enter her from behind and Vickie cried out, sickening pain ripped through her body as he pushed against her. "Fucking dry as a stick!" he shouted. "Fucking bitch, I can't get in." He thrust again, she screamed in agony.

"Please Tony, you're hurting me!" she cried, willing her body to respond, to stop the pain.

He fell heavily on top of her. She hit her face hard on the headboard, the weight of his body pushing her face into the metal. Her front teeth burst through her lip, blood filled her mouth. He pulled away then left the room and returned a few seconds later with a small cold cream tub in his hand. He held her by her hair and made her watch as he smeared the cream around his penis with his free hand. Getting behind her again, he forced his penis into her anus, pulling her backwards towards him by her hair.

She cried out as pain engulfed her. Her head spun and Vickie knew she was going to faint before she did pass out. After a few thrusts, realising her body had gone limp, he pulled out of her, letting her fall like a discarded piece of trash. "I prefer the fanny

Vickie, don't you?" he hissed in her ear. He turned her around to face him. Vickie was only half conscious by this time, fighting hard to stay awake; she knew that if she passed out again she might not wake up.

Feeling something cold around her vagina she cried out in agony, the pain waking her as whatever he had used smarted and burned. She tried to close her legs. He pushed them apart and forced his way inside her. Vickie screamed in terror and pain. As his face contorted, he forced his mouth on hers. She retched, swallowing blood and vomit; she felt herself suffocating. For Vickie, it seemed to go on for an eternity. She fought to stay awake, her head spun. He began to grunt and groaned, "oh fuck, you are just like a tight little honey pot! Come on Vickie don't just lie there, you need to enjoy it. How about I make it better?" He put his hand on her throat and began to squeeze.

Vickie couldn't breathe, her head banged against the hard-cold iron headboard. Panic overtook thoughts in her head, "*I'm going to die now.*" Mentally saying goodbye to her children, picturing their faces, she felt calmness descend. She gave in to the blackness; the pain stopped. She heard voices, people calling her name. She saw Johnny's face.

CHAPTER

SEVEN

Tony climaxed, his body shook; he felt an amazing surge. He pushed on her throat and watched her lips turn blue, her eyes lost their panic and fear, glazed over; her body became limp. "*Now no one has you!*" he whispered. Suddenly he was flying, being kicked and punched, he became aware of voices.

Chris's face was contorted with fury. "You fucking bastard, what have you done to her?" He threw himself on top of Tony, smashing his fist into Tony's mouth. Chris began to pummel Tony's face with his fists. Two uniformed police officers appeared beside him and pulled Chris away.

Tony began to laugh, he cackled. "You fucking loser Vincent, hungry manager, stupid fucker!" he spat. "You never had her and I did. Fuck you Chris! Who's hungry now?"

Chris lifted his right leg and kicked out, his foot connected with Tony's jaw. As Tony cried out, Chris fell to the floor, weeping.

Tony struggled with the police officers as they handcuffed him. Looking over to the bed he saw Lynne bending over the body of Vickie, so tall she looked huge next to the tiny half naked figure. Johnny was thumping on Vickie's chest. "Where's the key to the handcuffs?" The police officer punched Tony on the side of the head and held him. "Where's the fucking key?" Tony began to laugh. Blood ran from his mouth and sprayed out.

Lynne jumped up and grabbed the jacket from the floor. Tony saw her go through the pockets then run back towards the bed.

The door flew opened. Andy ran into the room, closely followed by Jamie and Colin, all three surveying the scene. "You dirty, fucking, bastard!" Andy screamed, launching himself at Tony, who was still being held by the two police officers. "What have you done to her?" He grabbed Tony, head-butting him. Colin put his arms around Andy's waist, separating him from Tony and the policemen. Bright red blood ran down Tony's face.

Still holding Andy back, Colin lifted his foot and kicked Tony in the groin. The force of the big man's foot caused the two policemen to fall backwards. Tony screamed, doubled up then slumped. Jamie stood rooted to the spot in the middle of the room, his mouth open, shock on his face. His red curls standing up as he ran his hand through them. A paramedic rushed into the room, followed by another police officer in full motorcycle gear. The policeman was shouting into his radio.

"Everyone out of here! Give me some space," the paramedic cried.

Johnny shook his head. *"No chance, I'm not leaving her. She's breathing again but her lips are still blue. Please help her?"* Johnny pulled a throw from the bottom of the bed and covered Vickie up. "She's so cold!" he sobbed, the horror and reality of the situation suddenly hitting him. "She doesn't like being cold." They heard an ambulance siren, and seconds later another paramedic appeared beside them.

Lynne put her arm around Johnny, gently pulling him back from the bed. "Jovi, you need to let them work with her, she's badly hurt babe." She grabbed his face with her two hands, "Johnny, listen to me please? Listen, she's breathing, we got her to breathe! As long as she is alive we can deal with anything."

Chris sat in the corner crying, his head in his blood-covered hands. Andy tried to pull him to his feet, but he slapped him away.

A third paramedic knelt beside Chris. "Are you okay pal?" he said, his accent unmistakably Scottish.

"Where are you from?" Andy asked.

"Glasgow originally, but I've been down here for 20 years. Now can I just check you over, your hand, it's bleeding. Chris, isn't it?"

Chris looked at his hand, blood dripped onto the floor. "I don't know how I done that."

"You took out that fucker's teeth by the look of it, there's one stuck in your hand." The medic pulled the tooth out and put it in a small clear bag one of the policemen held out.

Chris began to shake. "Has he killed her? Is Vickie dead?" The man looked over his shoulder at his colleagues working with Vickie on the bed.

"No, but she's badly hurt, we'll do everything we can for her pal."

Lynne and Johnny, holding on to each other, watched the paramedics, their faces showing their terror as Vickie was put on to a board. The paramedic gently placed an oxygen mask on her face. "Can I go with her?" Johnny asked, his voice barely audible.

"Sure, it may help if she comes around and sees a familiar face." The paramedic looked around him. "Okay she's stable, let's go folks."

"Where are you taking her?" Andy asked.

"The nearest A&E, she'll need to be assessed. Once they know what her injuries are, they can make decisions."

"You do know who she is, don't you?" Andy asked.

"Oh yes!" The paramedic put his hand on his arm. "Andy, they'll take good care of her. There's another ambulance coming for Chris; he needs an x-ray and stitches in that hand. He also needs some specialist treatment. A human bite is worse than a dog bite. You and Jamie could do with some treatment for shock. You're running on adrenaline mate, he's been standing there without moving since I got here. Come in the ambulance with Chris. Your minder is outside, vomiting all over the garden, best bring him too." The paramedic put his hand on Andy's shoulder. "Everything can be dealt with later, for now you need to help get your pals into the ambulance."

"Will she live?" Johnny asked the paramedic who was tending to Vickie. He watched the man gently adjusting the mask on her face and smoothing back her hair.

"I think so; she's fairly stable now. We don't know how long she was starved of oxygen though, so we need to wait for her to wake up. We're pumping it in now. We'll need to get her to hospital and assessed, before there's a prognosis."

At the hospital, Vickie, still unconscious, was taken away. Johnny was shown into a private relative's room. He was joined by Jamie, Colin and Andy a few minutes later, all of them clearly upset and shocked. "I phoned Arfur to go get Clinton," Colin told him quietly. "I just told him there'd been an accident. How the fuck do we tell anyone this?" The big black man sat down and buried his face in his hands sobbing. "I should have stayed with her, I'm her fucking security. You told me to look after her and I let this happen."

"Colin the only person to blame here is Gorman, fucking sick bastard," Jamie said, putting his hand on the big man's arm.

Johnny stood up and began pacing the floor. "I fucking left her too Colin, I fucking knew Gorman was dangerous. I knew Vickie didn't believe he was, and I fucking left her. I knew he was around."

Andy, his face pale and tear stained, the shock of the events finally hitting him, looked around the room. "What was she doing with him Jovi? Why would she go with him? If he had kidnapped her, someone would have noticed."

"I don't know Andy; she thought the way he spoke to her was because of drugs. He had said in that letter he was getting help. Vickie didn't really believe he had anything to do with Dania. Fuck, Dania didn't think it was him either."

Johnny looked around at his friends. "Laura said when Vickie called her she was saying something about Catriona telling her that Chiara was ill. Laura said Catriona went to her room with a migraine then when she went up after Vickie called, Catriona was gone."

Andy looked around the room. "Catriona! She told must have set it up. Tony found Catriona for Vickie, she's the daughter of his mate, remember? That little bitch, she's set Vickie up, been working for Tony!" He stood up, kicked out at the wall then punched it. "I'll fucking kill her if I get my hands on her."

Johnny looked at him bewilderment and disbelief showing on his face. "Fuck, she was great with the kids and Vickie was good to her. Why would she do it? There has to be some explanation Andy!"

"We don't know anything yet, other than Vickie's hurt, so let's just wait," Jamie said, "the cops will sort it out. Andy, you need to calm down mate, hurting yourself isn't going to do any good. I've got a spliff in the car, come on we'll go out and have a smoke, calm us."

"You can't boys," Colin said firmly, "too many people about. I'll try to get you some pills, Zac probably has some." Colin stood up and left the room.

"Have you called Simon?" Johnny asked the room.

"Yes!" Andy said quietly, "he's on his way here. Lynne's with Chris, I've never seen Chris like that; he always says he's a lover not a fighter."

"I want to kill the bastard," Johnny said quietly. He began to sob in to his hands again. Jamie handed him a pile of paper towels. "He had her chained like a fucking animal; she must have been so scared."

Johnny looked at Andy who stood up, saying nothing he put his hand on Johnny's shoulder, crying with him. "Why didn't we do anything about Dania, Johnny? When we realised what he was capable of we should have made her go to the police."

Johnny moved away and began to pace the floor. He was too shocked to think straight. His mind was going over and over it all, trying to make sense of what he had seen.

They waited for what seemed like hours. Eventually a female

in blue scrubs came into the room. She looked around. "Who's her next of kin?"

"It's technically her father but he's not here yet," Johnny cried. "I'm her ..." He looked at the others. "I don't know what I am."

"He's her partner," Jamie said.

The doctor took Johnny's arm and led him out of the room and across the hallway into an office. She looked at Johnny. "Please sit down Mr Vincent. We're waiting for the forensics team to come but Mrs D'Angelo has multiple injuries." The doctor took a deep breath and looked at Johnny. "She's badly hurt but we don't think it's life threatening."

Johnny took a deep breath and nodded, relief showing on his face.

The doctor continued; her face serious. "However, she has some deep lacerations to her face, her skull is fractured in two places. There is a small fracture to her jaw and some teeth broken. Her right eye is causing most concern. The socket is badly fractured. There's soft tissue damage to her neck and chest, her throat has been damaged through compression. This man meant to kill her." The doctor put her hand on Johnny's arm then handed him more tissues. "My name is Mary Turner; I'll be looking after her just now until we can make decisions about her treatment plan. There's a lot of different injuries. "Her wrist is broken," Mary took a deep breath and looked Johnny in the eye before continuing. "Vickie also has several rib fractures and she has some internal injuries."

"What kind?" Johnny asked, quietly.

"The kind that occur when someone is brutally sexually assaulted. Pelvic trauma injuries, cuts and bruising to her vagina and anus. I'm sorry Mr Vincent but there is no easy way for you to hear any of this. She's conscious now and severely traumatised. I need to ask you something and I need an honest answer. Do you know if Mrs D'Angelo ingested anything?"

Johnny looked at the doctor, ***"Drugs? Vickie?"***

"Yes! She's been swabbed, there's Cocaine in her system."

Johnny shook his head. "No chance, she has never been into coke, and she's breast feeding, she won't even take a drag from a spliff."

The doctor led him back through to the relatives' room and repeated her question.

They all shook their heads. ***"She would never have taken coke doctor,"*** Jamie gasped. "She's been drinking, we all have. Drugs are not her thing. A bit of grass maybe from time to time, not since she was pregnant, she hardly even drinks now."

The doctor nodded. "Unfortunately, it may have been forced on her by her attacker."

"What about Chris?" Andy asked.

"He's doing fine physically," the nurse accompanying the doctor replied. "He's broken a bone in his hand and he has to have a few stitches. He is in the plaster room just now. He's being treated for shock too."

Andy stood up. "Can we go see him?"

"Yes of course. Johnny if you come with me, I'll check if you can get in to see Vickie."

"I need to be with her!" Johnny said quietly. He followed the doctor along the corridor, she paused outside the door.

"She's unable to speak due to the throat damage. I've called for a throat specialist; you need to try to keep her calm and quiet." The doctor put her hand on Johnny's arm. "I'm really sorry. This must be a nightmare for you all after what you've already been through." Johnny nodded and followed the doctor into the room. "Mrs D'Angelo, I have someone to see you."

Johnny looked at Vickie and began to cry, his face showing the horror he felt. He could see the pain on her face. He bent to kiss her head but as he touched her, she shrank from him in terror. "Vickie darling, it's okay. It's me, I would never hurt you, you know that." She pushed him away. He could see the bruising where the handcuffs had bitten in to her. "Oh, my poor baby, we'll get through this," he whispered. "I promise."

He turned as two women entered the room. "Mr Vincent, I

am Detective Inspector Rosanne O'Donnell. This is Detective Constable Sushanna Sharma. We're here to witness the medical examination." Seeing the fear in Vickie's eyes, the police woman addressed Vickie directly, "Mrs D'Angelo, I'm afraid we have to do this because we need forensics to charge the perpetrator. Mr Vincent, we need to ask you to leave the room."

Johnny bent to kiss Vickie, immediately she again shrank from him. Weeping now, not caring who saw him, Johnny walked along the corridor and asked where his brother was. A male nurse showed him into a room. Chris sat the edge of the bed, his wrist and hand encased in plaster. Andy was slumped on a chair talking to him. It was obvious to Johnny that his friend was under the influence of something. Colin was sitting on the bed beside Chris. Immediately on seeing his brother, Chris jumped up off the bed. **"Vickie?"**

"She's . . . she's conscious, having a forensic medical."

"Is she . . . is she going to live?"

"Yes, but she's in a fucking mess." Johnny began to cry again as the full horror of the night caught up with him.

Chris wrapped his arms around him. They stood, not moving for a long time. "Toph, you could all be charged with assault."

"I don't fucking care, let them. I'd do it again in a heartbeat Johnny, he deserved it. I just lost it when I saw her." Chris began to sob. "Chained like some fucking rabid dog. How the fuck could we have got Tony so wrong?"

"Toph, I don't know what to do. "God knows what he's put her through. "She can't fucking speak, he's damaged her throat." He sobbed. "She wouldn't let me touch her."

"Bro it's the shock, she'll be terrified. Vickie loves you. I wish I'd killed him."

Jamie and Lynne entered the room carrying paper coffee cups. **"Jovi!"** Lynne gasped. "What's happening with Vickie, can I see her?"

"The Police Surgeon came to do forensic stuff. I need to go back to her; I'm not letting her push me out." They sat staring at each other, none of them speaking. Andy fell asleep, snoring loudly.

"How can he sleep?" Johnny asked looking around.

"I gave him a couple of blues," Colin said quietly. "Zac had them in the car. Oh, I know he gets stuff for you, didn't think it could do much harm. I've had a couple myself. Want some?"

Johnny shook his head, as did Jamie but Chris held out his hand. He took the pills from Colin and swallowed them.

It seemed like hours before the door opened and the detectives entered. "Oh good, you're all here. Can we take some swabs?"

Johnny shrugged. "Why?"

"Oh, just to rule out DNA from her body that does not belong to her attacker." She looked from Andy to Chris, "just DNA, nothing else. These lawyers will go through everything with a fine-tooth comb when it comes to DNA, just to muddy the waters."

"Can I go back through to her now?" Johnny asked as the policewoman put the swab into a container and labelled it.

"I'll go check. Before I do, can I ask you about Tony Gorman? Did she have any type of sexual relationship with him? I'm sorry I have to ask."

Johnny shook his head. "Purely professional, Vickie was only ever interested in her husband. Her and I, well we got together recently. We've always been close though, she would have told me if he had ever done anything. We think he raped a young singer we know, Dania Phillips, she was in a mess. She'd been drugged and raped."

The policewoman looked at him. "When was this?"

"Just before Christmas but we didn't find out for a few days. According to Dania, she was in a taxi with Gorman and then doesn't remember anything till she woke up next morning. She went to some doctor through a rape help organisation, they did some tests and stuff. She was afraid no one would believe her so she didn't do anything. She was in a real mess though, covered in bruises and bite marks."

"Why would Vickie then go with Tony Gorman? If she knew what he had done to her friend? The CCTV from the venue shows her handing him the keys and getting in the car, Mr Vincent!" the policewoman asked shaking her head, her face showing disbelief.

Johnny sighed, "Vickie is one of these people who tries to find reasons for everything. She thought Tony was taking too many drugs but she didn't believe he hurt Dania. He wrote Vickie a letter telling her that he had got help for a drug and alcohol problem. She never believed the other talk about him either."

"Talk?"

Johnny looked at the policewoman. "There are loads of rumours around the music industry about him. He has a liking young girls and rough sex."

"Why did you keep him as your manager?" the policewoman asked.

"It's hard to get out of a contract; we had been with him for years." Johnny wiped his face with a tissue. "It was hard for Vickie to understand we never knew him." He looked sadly at the woman in front of him, "I'm struggling to understand why she got in the car with him too. The only explanation I have is she called Laura, one of our Nannies, told her Catriona, who is our other nanny, had phoned her and said one of our babies was ill. Vickie is the type of woman who would walk over hot coals for her children. If she was panicking, well, she . . . she must have thought he was straight, or she wouldn't have gone with him."

The police woman put her hand on Johnny's arm, "thank you Johnny, can I call you Johnny?"

"Yeah!"

"I'm Rosie, Johnny. This must be hard for you, you obviously care a great deal for Mrs D'Angelo."

Johnny began to cry again. Rosie watched as he sobbed into a pile of tissues, trying to compose himself. "Yeah, I love her but I let her down big style tonight though, didn't I?"

Rosie shook her head. "From what you've told me, it sounds

as though it was a premeditated, organised kidnap. The nanny could have been working with him. Now come with me, we'll see if you can get in to see her. Whilst we are investigating, myself and Susi Sharma will be your liaison team.

Johnny nodded. "Thanks! Are you going to charge my brother and the others?" he asked as they walked together along the corridor.

"I don't think so, off the record, I would think that Mr Gorman got what was coming to him. Two wrongs don't make a right though. We've no plans to charge them but if the accused makes a complaint we may have to. I can understand why they went for him. You, on the other hand, saved her life by the sound of it."

Johnny was shown back into the room; it was darkened, lit only by the lamp above the bed. Shadows fell across the white starched covers but he could see the bruising and cuts on Vickie's face despite the fact she lay facing the wall. He reached her, sat down and touched her arm. She jumped and moved away from him. "Vickie, please darling, don't shut me out!" Vickie continued to keep her face turned away from Johnny. He spoke directly to her, his voice quiet, pleading with her. "Please don't! I'll be there for you, I promise."

Vickie turned her head to look at him, a single tear falling on to her cheek. She shook her head then pushed his hand away with her good arm.

"Vickie, you won't get rid of me I'll be here waiting." Johnny sat in silence, watching her, trying not to cry, not show Vickie how scared and shocked he was.

The door opened again, a nurse came in. "Mrs D'Angelo, your parents have arrived; can I bring them through?"

Vickie looked at the nurse and then at Johnny, fear apparent on her face, she shook her head. Johnny squeezed Vickie's hand, stood up and walked outside. Arfur, Clinton and Maggie stood in the corridor.

"Johnny what's happened?" Clinton asked, looking at him, "they couldn't tell me anything in reception."

Johnny tried to speak. The words, however, would not come out. Instead, he began to sob. The nurse guided them back into the relatives room where the others waited. "I'll go get Dr Turner."

"Where's my daughter Johnny? Andy? What has happened to Vickie? Where is she?" Clinton cried.

"She's in there," Johnny said. His words came out in fits and starts. "Tony Gorman kidnapped her . . . nearly throttled her, she can't talk; her face is a mess." Johnny's words came out quickly, the fear in his voice apparent to them all. He looked at Clinton and Maggie, tears now running down his face, *"she won't even look at me; I don't know what to do?"* Maggie walked over and wrapped her arms around Johnny, held him as he sobbed.

Clinton looked at Johnny and stood up again. "Where the hell was her security Johnny?" he cried. "Where were you? How did he get to kidnap her? What were you doing to allow him to get to her? You were there when I treated Dania, you fucking knew Johnny, you knew how dangerous he'd become."

Maggie tried to calm her husband, "Clinton, we don't know how it happened, please darling, calm down. Johnny loves Vickie, he would never have left her in danger!"

Clinton pushed Maggie away, too upset to see reason. He turned to the others in the room. *"Where were you lot? Fucking getting drunk and partying no doubt?"* Clinton cried. He began to pace the floor. Eventually he opened the door and left the room. They heard him outside. *"I want to see my daughter, now!"* he bellowed. **Right now!**

"Mr D'Angelo, please calm down and listen!"

"No, my name is Malone, Clinton Malone, Dr Clinton Malone. Take me to my daughter now!"

"She's very distressed Mr Malone. Mrs D'Angelo can hear you shouting, please calm down."

What? You think I am going to make her more distressed?"

A man in blue scrubs came out of a side room. *"Clinton!"*

Clinton calmed down slightly, recognising Richard Mann,

who had been with him as a registrar some years before. "My daughter is through there, Ricky."

"I know Clinton, I'm so sorry. I'm going to be seeing her, to look at her facial injuries."

"If you're involved, it's serious Ricky?"

Richard put his hand on Clinton's shoulder. "I haven't examined her yet. We'll deal with it as we go along but from the x-rays you'd better prepare yourself for a shock. You need to put your professional head on. You know what trauma does. You shouting at everyone won't help her or anyone else."

Vickie lay in the darkened room. She hadn't meant to hurt Johnny but her body felt as though it was on fire. Her skin crawled; she couldn't bear anyone touching her. She could not find any part of her body where there was no pain. She couldn't speak, the pain in her ribs restricted her breathing. She wanted to get in a bath and scrub herself clean.

The lady doctor who examined her had been gentle and kind. Internal bruising, swelling to her vagina, pelvic trauma; damage internally, both in her vagina and her anus. The doctor had put her hand on Vickie's shoulder, told her these injuries would heal. She would need to wait for the facial surgeon to arrive and the throat specialist; they would be the only people able to tell her anything else. Vickie could hear her father shouting at the staff, she knew he was angry. Knew she had let everyone down, by being stupid. Knew she should have listened to the others, they had all warned her about Tony.

The door opened, Johnny came quietly into the room, followed by her father. Vickie looked up, seeing the shock and revulsion on her father's face she turned away. "Vickie please, don't sweetheart." Johnny touched her hair which was matted with blood. He pulled his hand away instinctively. "Darling you'll be okay; we'll make you better, all of us." She shook her head and tried to speak but nothing came out. Vickie stared at him and turned to look at her father, still no tears came.

Johnny sat down beside the bed, Vickie turned away. "Vickie, please don't do this darling, don't shut us out. We love you."

"Please Vickie!" her father cried out. He tried to scoop her into his arms but she physically recoiled, making noises like a wounded animal. She began to gasp for breath. Johnny pulled Clinton, who was crying, back. The nurse looked sadly at them.

"I'm sorry, she really needs to rest; can I ask you to leave?"

"No, you bloody can't," Clinton gasped, "I'm her father. I'm a doctor, a surgeon."

The nurse sighed. "Yes I know who you are but she has to rest for now and you need to calm down Mr Malone."

Johnny and Clinton left Vickie and returned to the relatives room. The others had been joined by Simon Forsyth. He looked shocked, "Johnny, Clinton, I'm so sorry. I can't believe what's happened. How's Vickie?"

"In a fucking mess!" Johnny said. "She's scared of me; she pulled away like a terrified fucking animal when Clinton touched her." He sat down and put his head in his hands.

Clinton looked around the room. "I didn't recognise her; he's left her in a hell of a mess. I'm sorry I shouted at you all, I know it wasn't your fault. I'm a really shit parent when anything happens to my kids. I just panic but her face, oh my God, her beautiful little face!"

The nurse put her hand on his shoulder. "They'll sort the facial injuries; we have the best surgeons available to us. If you know Dr Mann, you must know how good he is? We need to wait until the swelling goes down to see what needs done. We're phoning the hospital you suggested, we'll get her up there tonight."

"Do you have a preference as to who you would like to see her Mr Malone?" Doctor Turner asked quietly.

"Charlie Eskdale for her throat, he's the best there is. I'll call him myself, he's a close friend, Vickie knows him. In terms of the facial injuries, Ricky Mann is who I would have looked for. "Peter Smyth is her Gynaecologist but given what's happened,

I would think his registrar Lizzy Moorhouse would be a better choice. I'll call her too."

Doctor Turner nodded. "We'll see what we can do. Meanwhile, help yourself to tea and coffee and we'll come back once there's news."

Simon waited for her to leave the room. "Okay what are we telling the press?"

Johnny looked up. "We're telling them the truth, surely."

"Vickie might not want that Johnny. They know something has happened, you all rushing off. We also know patients here have put stuff on social media sites. They know something has happened to someone in the band. Do we say nothing? Or just say an incident? There will be a trial, I would expect."

"Surely he'll plead guilty?" Chris asked. "We fucking caught him." He stood up and looked around him. "I need to get out of here, I need drink, more drugs, or fucking both. I'm sorry bro, but I can't just sit here, I need to go home. Andy? Jamie? Lynne?"

"You go!" Jamie sighed. "I'll stay here with Jovi. Marnie's on her way here with the car, she'll take you home then come back for us."

"I'm going nowhere, Jamie!" Johnny said quietly. "I need to be here for her."

Simon's phone buzzed, he went outside to take the call. When he returned he looked worried. "It's out already. They picked it up on the police radio frequency; they know how bad it is too. Christ, poor little Vickie. They also know that Tony Gorman has been arrested, is being held on suspicion of rape and attempted murder. By God, they've been quick this time. We need to get you all out of here and Vickie into the clinic."

CHAPTER

EIGHT

As they pushed the bed into the room Vickie felt sick and began to gag and retch. The nurse took the sick bowl from under the bed and sat her up. Vickie vomited into it, her eyes watered from the vomit, her throat so painful she struggled to breathe.

"Mrs D'Angelo, you're now in the West Wing of St Margaret's, it's very private and safe," the young female doctor said. "We've put you in a suite at the back, which will be quiet and private for you and your visitors. One of your own security staff will sit outside. You are safe!"

Vickie nodded, closed her eyes and lay back.

"Okay let's get you settled." The two females, pushed the bed into place and connected Vickie's drip to a stand. "It's six in the morning Mrs D'Angelo, I'm going to give you something to help you sleep." The doctor took a syringe from a tray the nurse held.

* * *

The doctor led Johnny and Clinton into the darkened room. "She's asleep, we've sedated her. You can sit with her if you like but she won't waken for a while. You should perhaps, go home and get some sleep, come back later."

Johnny shook his head, he looked at Vickie's father, "Clinton, you go, I'll stay here with her. Simon is outside with Rod. I promise I'll call you if there's any change." Clinton began to protest. Johnny shook his head, "we're all going to need rest. This could be a long haul!"

"I'll go upstairs to my office. I have a pull-out bed there. You will come and get me?"

Johnny nodded and walked towards Vickie's room door. Inside the darkened room, Johnny gently kissed Vickie's forehead, then sat at the side of the bed looking at the bruised, stitched face of the woman he loved. Inside he felt as though he was dying. He didn't know what to think, wasn't equipped to deal with this kind of evil.

Exhausted, Johnny rested his head on the back of the large winged chair and wept. Exhaustion took over and he fell asleep. When he opened his eyes, Vickie still lay asleep. Johnny stood up and stretched. Walking over to the door he opened it quietly and looked around. In the corridor, Simon lay across two chairs, his head on his partner Rodney's lap. Both men were sound asleep.

When Vickie woke, it was dark outside. She felt pain from her head to her feet. A nurse sat by her bedside. Vickie pointed at the nurse's watch. "It's 6.30pm Mrs D'Angelo, you've been sleeping for over 12 hours." The nurse took Vickie's blood pressure then left the room.

The door was tapped lightly, Johnny and Simon entered, both still dressed from the night before. Johnny's white shirt was bloodstained and torn. His normally clean shaven face showed a dark layer of stubble. He sat down by the bed. Vickie looked over at Simon then turned away.

Simon moved to stand beside the bed. He spoke calmly. "Vickie, he'll pay for what he's done to you; I swear I won't rest until he does." He took her hand and kissed her fingers before he tiptoed out of the room. Once outside, the full horror hit him. He stood shaking, his back against the wall.

"Are you alright sir?" a passing nurse asked.

"I'm going to be sick," Simon gasped. The nurse quickly

handed him a paper sick bowl, he vomited. He looked up as Clinton and Rodney came around the corner. Vickie's father, the strain of the previous night's events showing on his face, said nothing. He put his hand on Simon's shoulder then knocked on the door to Vickie's room. Rodney sat down beside Simon and held him as he sobbed into a pile of tissues the nurse handed him.

Vickie looked at the door as her father entered. Johnny glanced at Vickie then Clinton, "what about the babies? She needs to express milk to feed them." Vickie looked at him and nodded.

Clinton lifted the chart at the bottom of the bed. He looked sadly at his daughter. "Darling the drugs you've been given would be in your milk. The girls are five months, they're growing well; they've almost caught up. I take it you expressed enough milk for a few feeds if you were going to be drinking?"

Johnny nodded, "there was enough for four feeds. She expressed all day yesterday and fed them before we left."

"My thoughts are Vickie; we need to concentrate on you just now. I'm going to go darling; Johnny is staying with you." He bent to kiss her. She opened her mouth to squeal, only air came out, moving back on the bed, her eyes wide and frightened. Clinton turned and quickly left the room, so she would not see the tears now pouring down his face.

He joined Rodney, holding Simon, who was pale and shaking. Clinton buried his face in the pile of tissues Rodney handed him. "Come with me boys, I've an office here, and a bottle of malt. If we ever deserved a drink it's now. Nurse, can you send Charlie and Ricky to my office when they're finished. I believe they're on their way here."

CHAPTER

NINE

"Hello Vickie, I'm sorry we're meeting again in these circumstances," Charlie Eskdale whispered, taking Vickie's hand in his. Vickie immediately pulled her hand away. Charlie nodded at the younger man accompanying him, "this is Richard Mann. You met him earlier in Windsor."

Vickie nodded, looking nervously at the two men.

"I'm obviously here to look at your throat and Ricky, as you know, is the maxillofacial surgeon. He'll be looking at what needs to happen to your facial injuries. The accident and emergency surgeon and Ricky feel you'll need specialised facial treatment. Shall we let Ricky see you first? I think getting your facial injuries treated will be the most pressing."

Richard Mann smiled at Vickie. "I've had a good look at the x-rays. I'm going to get the scanner in to have a closer look in a few minutes. You'll need surgery Mrs D'Angelo, but I can rebuild you. It will be painful and take a few months but you'll be good as new, facially. Your eye socket and lip will be the most difficult. The socket is fragmented; I need to put a plate in. It may take a few operations to repair but the prognosis is good. The procedures are simple and will be done under general anaesthetic."

Ignoring the fact that Vickie was moving back from him, Ricky came in closer to her. He lifted the dressing from her head and studied the wound. "Your forehead cut is deep but it should heal without too much scarring. The stitching is very neat. Your hair will cover most of the other cuts. Mrs D'Angelo, would you prefer a female surgeon?"

Vickie shrugged, still looking nervously at the two men, her fear apparent to everyone in the room. Johnny took her hand and held it. He raised it to his lips and kissed her fingers, aware of the bruising now coming out and the broken damaged nails which he realised were defensive injuries.

Richard continued to speak directly to Vickie, his voice calm and soothing. "Your right eye is damaged because blood vessels have ruptured. This is due to pressure and lack of oxygen. It should heal through time, with your sight unaffected. We'll get the ophthalmologists to assess you as we go along. The left eye, I suspect we won't know until the swelling goes down. Your lip is fairly urgent, so I'm going to do some work on it tomorrow, along with some wire in your jaw, and the temporary plate in your cheek."

Ricky smiled for the first time. "I'm fairly confident I can do this without problems and leave you as beautiful as you were. If you agree, we'll make you comfortable tonight and operate in the morning. I'm sorry about the circumstances Mrs D'Angelo. I worked with your father for a time as a junior doctor. He's a good man and he loves you very much. He used to have a picture of you as a small baby on his desk." He nodded at Johnny, who had not spoken throughout the time he was there. As I said when I came in, I could offer you a female surgeon Mrs D'Angelo. I realise that your ordeal has left you traumatised but I would rather do this myself." Vickie nodded. She tightened her grip on Johnny's hand.

Charlie Eskdale waited until the other surgeon had taken leave before he spoke. "Okay Vickie, I cannot guarantee your voice will be undamaged but I'll do everything I can to help you get it back. When that monster held your throat, he damaged the soft tissue around your neck. It's bruised and swollen, inside and out. This has affected your vocal chords. It all needs to heal now my dear; we'll do a scan to make sure there's nothing else. It will mean you must rest your voice, at least for the next few months. In other words, it is imperative that even after your voice comes back, which it will in a week or so, you do not speak at all. When the swelling goes down, I'll look at whether anything else is needed. In the meantime, I'll get you an electronic keyboard with phrases you need, so you can communicate."

Vickie took the pen and pad the nurse had given her. "*Will I sing again?*" she wrote in uneven, squiggly writing.

The doctor pursed his lips, looked first at Johnny, then back to her. "Vickie, I don't know my dear, it is just too early to say. It should come back but it might not be the same. You have a very strong voice. I heard you sing Black Velvet last night; it was superb, very soulful. Hopefully, if you do as I say your voice will return." Charlie smiled, "in some cases the voice is even better, although that would be hard in your case. The damage to your ribs could affect your range and breathing for a while. So, I'm afraid I'll not be able to say for now. I've been in this game a few years; I've worked with singers before. I know how much depends on the strength of your voice."

Vickie lifted the pad again and wrote on it. Charlie read it then looked sadly at her. He handed the pad to Johnny.

"*Don't care if I can sing.*" She had written.

"I think once you get over the shock and trauma, you will dear. Your singing didn't do this to you, a very bad man did."

A nurse bustled into the room. "Mr Eskdale we would really like to get Mrs D'Angelo settled for the night. "Are you through for now?"

Charlie stood up. "Yes, nurse for now.

She turned to Johnny. "Mr Vincent, I think you should go home, you have been here since she was brought in. You are going to have to rest, you'll need it. Besides, Mrs D'Angelo will need her things brought in." Johnny bent to kiss Vickie's cheek. She jumped then turned her face away from him.

Charlie Eskdale put his arm around Johnny's shoulder. "Can I speak to you my man?" They walked outside. "Come with me." He led Johnny through a corridor and down some stairs. Charlie stopped at an office with a gold name plate, **Mr Clinton Malone.**

Charlie tapped on the door and entered. Inside Simon, Rodney, Jamie, Clinton and Richard Mann sat. Johnny looked at Jamie, "what are you doing here?"

"I came back with Colin and Arfur; they'll take over from hospital security outside Vickie's room. I want to take you home Jovi, you need some rest. Arfur and Colin are downstairs talking to the hospital head of security."

Clinton handed Johnny a paper coffee cup and poured a generous measure of whisky into it. Johnny took a gulp then gasped as it burnt his throat and warmed his stomach. He had been unable to eat. He sat down in a chair staring miserably into the amber liquid. Charlie took the paper cup from Clinton and rested his hand on his friend's shoulder. "Clinton I'm so sorry my friend, what a terrible ordeal for all of you!"

Clinton looked up at Charlie, "Charlie this is Jamie Connolly, Simon Forsyth, who's the band's manager and his partner Rodney Smart."

Charlie smiled. "We've met before Clinton; I've looked after another of Simons acts. Good to meet you too, Jamie, I saw you play last night, you're a very talented band. Rod, I'm a big fan of yours."

"How is she, Johnny?" Clinton looked at Johnny who put his head in his hands.

Charlie spoke up. "You know how she is Clinton, she's severely traumatised and needs to rest. As your friend I think you all need rest."

"She shrank away from me Charlie; she wouldn't even have me touch her." Clinton shook his head fighting back tears. "I can't even begin to think what he put her through. I want to murder the bastard."

"She's been through a terrible, terrifying ordeal Clinton; she needs you to be strong for her now," Richard said quietly. "I can repair her face. Apart from the eye socket and her lip, most of the damage is superficial. Her mind though, well, that's another matter."

"What about her voice?" Jamie asked. "Is it repairable?"

Charlie shrugged, "I honestly don't know Jamie. Just now she has no fight left in her. She just wants to be left alone. Given what's happened it's understandable. She'll need a lot of strength to recover." He looked at Jamie, then at the other men in the room, "in respect of her voice, I couldn't say whether it will be the same. However, she needs to heal. It could be six months before we know which way the land lies. She's young though, she has good supports. She will, with all your help, get through this."

"She wouldn't see the psychiatrist!" Johnny said, his face miserable, "they tried to get her to at least listen to him but she got upset then just turned her face to the wall."

"It's much too early for that," Charlie said sadly, putting his hand on Johnny's shoulder, "she's still trying to contemplate what's happened. She'll, in time, find a way to let her feelings out. She's still in shock. No one knows the full extent of what she's been through. Vickie must process it in her own mind first, that'll take time. Patience is the key here." He looked around the room, "she's still here, she's alive, stay focused on that fact."

In the darkened hospital room, the nurse adjusted Vickie's drip. "You now need to have a natural sleep. Can I get you some pain medication?"

Vickie nodded, she felt tired. The nurse returned with a glass where Vickie could see tablets dissolving. "Did that man force you to take drugs?"

Vickie nodded.

"Cocaine?"

Vickie nodded again, she motioned to her groin with her hand.

"How awful, that's rumoured to be the quickest way to

ingest some drugs dear. I believe that method is frequently used in sexual pursuits, it supposedly heightens pleasure."

Vickie managed with some difficulty to swallow the liquid and lay back. The nurse checked her blood pressure and temperature then put the buzzer within her reach. "In the morning, we'll get you cleaned up properly Mrs D'Angelo. I know you want to do it just now but we need to hear back from the police forensics that they have everything they need. Right now, you really need to just sleep. We have contacted a nurse specialist in sexual assault injuries; she'll be here in the morning. Tomorrow is another day, Mrs D'Angelo." She switched the light out as she left the room.

Alone in the darkness, the tears finally came.

* * *

The first noise Vickie became aware of next morning was the sound of doors closing and people talking outside her room. She pulled herself up on the pillow and cried out as she felt immense pain in her body. Her face and head felt tight and heavy. Pain in her ribs and body meant she found it difficult to breathe. In fact, it was hard to pinpoint an area of her body that did not ache. She was still attached to a drip. She vaguely remembered wakening during the night, hearing an alarm, someone doing something with the drip. Vickie rang the buzzer. A young pretty nurse with red curly hair entered the room. "Toilet please?" she mouthed. The nurse looked at her chart. She lifted the drip bag from the stand and helped Vickie to get up off the bed. Vickie felt pain rip through her.

"I can take you through, help you?"

Vickie shook her head.

The nurse smiled. "I'll stand outside in case you need me." She handed Vickie the bag. Vickie entered the bathroom and her eyes were drawn to the mirror. She gasped and gripped the basin, dropping the bag on the floor; it burst and splattered the liquid across the tiled floor. She did not recognise the hideous, swollen face staring back. She staggered as the nurse, having heard the noise of the bag falling, rushed in. The nurse helped Vickie to sit on the toilet. However, the pain was immense and she doubled up as the urine burned and stung her. She felt faint and her head spun. The nurse held her then gently helped her back through, to her bed.

Tears ran down Vickie's face. The nurse pulled the bed covers over Vickie then looked at her sympathetically. "It'll be alright Vickie, I promise. It'll all heal, your face, your body and your mind, it just needs time. You've been through a terrible ordeal, you have a long way to go," she said gently. "You've been through so much and for this to happen to you now is beyond comprehension."

Vickie nodded, she looked at the nurse. "What's your name?" she mouthed.

"My name is Mhairi Wilson, I'm a nurse-specialist in sexual assault injuries. I'll be looking after you for the next week or two." She looked Vickie in the eye. "Vickie, this will get better. I'll share something with you, just so you realise I understand. Four years ago I was raped. I was at work, nightshift, not here, in another hospital. I was out having a smoke when this guy grabbed me and pulled me into the bushes."

Vickie stared at her, the nurse nodded. "I wasn't hurt the way you are, in terms of physical injuries. He slapped me a few times and bit me. Biting is quite common, it's about control, but it helps catch and convict them. It leaves a very clear pattern and DNA."

"I had some of the internal injuries you have, they do heal pretty quickly. Mentally it takes a long time but it does go."

Vickie touched the nurse's arm, and for the first time she managed to smile. "Thank-you!" she mouthed. "Thank you for sharing that, it helps."

Mhairi sighed, "I'm glad! It's not very professional to share something personal like that. I know how important it is for rape victims to know they're not alone, so I just wanted you to know,

I understand. It's also very difficult for those who love you, as they're struggling with shock." She looked sadly at Vickie, "we live in a patriarchal society, no matter how you look at it. Men see rape as the worst thing that can happen to a woman. Vickie, what happened to you was awful but you're here, you're alive and you will recover. Your family and friends will find whats happened difficult to cope with?"

Vickie nodded. She reached out and touched the nurse's arm, then took her hand and held it.

Mhairi patted Vickie's hand then looked at her. "This often means the victim is unable to discuss how they feel, for fear of upsetting their loved ones. When it happened to me I felt no one understood, so I freelance now. I did a lot of training and sadly, Vickie, there is always plenty of work for me."

"Thank you," Vickie mouthed. She let go of the nurse's hand.

Mhairi smiled, "you will get better Vickie, I promise. It's not easy but you do get your life back. Now, I'll talk you through what will happen, the technicalities. Your care plan, what to expect. Your obstetrician has been alerted; your dad did that last night. However, they both felt it would be better to change to a female. Doctor Moorhouse, who you met, I believe, when Mr Smyth was on holiday, will be with us later. The lab rang to say all the swabs and forensics are fine so you can have a bath. It hurts by the way but it's worth the pain to start to make you feel clean."

Vickie put her hand up to her face, she touched the padded dressing covering her eye. "Surgery?" she mouthed.

The nurse nodded. "You'll be going to theatre later this morning so you can't have anything to eat or drink yet. You need to have some injections as prevention, and the morning after pill. There is a very low risk of HIV. The blood borne virus test we did was negative. Your attacker was tested as well, and was also negative but you have a three month wait for a second test, for confirmation. We need to discuss your breast feeding, they gave you a little diamorphine last night to relax you while they examined you, that obviously will still be in your system. The coke you were given will be there too, all quite dangerous to babies. You also have quite a lot of damage to your breasts. I believe the outfit you were wearing was taped on?"

Vickie nodded and looked down at her chest. She could feel the pain under the heavy white dressing.

"It was ripped off during the attack. Quite a lot of your skin went with it. So, your breasts, they're raw, they will be painful. I'm sorry Vickie but with the anaesthetic now as well, we think you should stop breastfeeding. If you are okay with it, we'll give you something to dry up your milk."

Tears ran down Vickie's face, she shook her head. Mhairi sat down beside her.

"I won't try to hug you Vickie. I do know how painful this must be but I know you're a good mum and will do what's best for your children." Mhairi sighed and put her hand on Vickie's shoulder. "Your next emotional hurdle will be the police; they'll come in and take a statement. It can last for hours, you think it's never-ending, you have to re-live it all. I trained to help with this, so if you want, I can sit with you through it. They'll wait until you've mastered the speech board though. It's a computer thing. I understand someone will be in from speech and language later. Right, now we need to get your pre-med done!"

Mhairi was there when Vickie came around after the operation. The right side of her face was covered with a dressing and her face and lip felt sore. "Rickie said to let you know it all went according to plan. He's gone to get some sleep now and will be in to check on you later."

A dark-haired nurse put her head around the door. "Mrs D'Angelo your friends are outside; will you be able to see them?"

Vickie shook her head.

The nurse sighed. "Okay I'll tell them."

Mhairi looked at Vickie. "Vickie don't shut out your friends, you'll need them."

Vickie sighed and lay back. The other nurse put her head around the door again.

"Lynne Love is with them. She asked if you would see her."

Tears ran down the left side of Vickie's face, she shook her head and turned away.

The other nurse looked at Mhairi, made a face then left, closing the door behind her.

Mhairi put her hands on Vickie's shoulders and looked into her eyes. "Okay don't get upset. I don't know you Vickie, although I've read a lot about you. I also watched the Brits on TV. I heard what you said, seemed that your group are like family. Don't shut them out, I know you want to try to run away but it won't help. People who love you will be there for you."

Vickie placed her hand gently on the nurse's arm, and nodded.

"Do you want me to go after them?"

Vickie nodded slowly.

"How much do you want them to know about your injuries?"

Vickie shrugged, "everything!" she mouthed.

Mhairi rushed down the corridor. She saw them ahead of her, people she had only ever seen in magazines. Johnny and Chris Vincent, Andy Cowan, Lynne Love, Jamie Connelly who had his arm around a small, pretty, dark haired girl and an older lady.

"Excuse me?" she shouted.

Johnny turned. "Can I help you?" he asked wearily.

"I'm Mhairi, I'm nursing Vickie; she'll see you but can I talk to you first. Come into the day room, Mr Vincent."

"Please call us by our first names," Chris said. "I'm Chris, this is Jamie, Lynne, Andy, Marnie, Johnny and my aunt, Annie."

Mhairi nodded. "Okay here's the deal, as you know Vickie is traumatised. She's in a lot of pain and has had surgery today to start to rebuild her face and mend her jaw. She looks as though she's been in a car crash, you may not recognise her. The swelling is at its optimum and she knows it. You all need to understand, she's been brutally, assaulted, she'll be having flashbacks and reliving it. She has a lot to face over the coming days in terms of her injuries." She looked at the people in front of her before adding, "the emotional impact on her will be significant.

Then there's all the legal stuff. She needs you to be there for her. I understand you witnessed some of the attack?"

Johnny nodded.

"Get help, now. Rape Crisis run a service for friends, relatives and witnesses; I'll get you the number. You need to all deal with your shit before you can help Vickie deal with hers. Now back to Vickie, she is in a lot of pain and discomfort, particularly from the internal injuries. To be blunt mostly when someone is raped they're not aroused so the penetration causes injuries which are extremely painful. This will heal relatively quickly. She can't talk, as you know; which is very distressing because she is unable express how she's feeling. Her breathing is laboured because she has fractured ribs. Her left wrist is broken so she can't write what she is thinking and wants to say easily."

Noticing his distress, Mhairi put her hand gently on Johnny's arm. "One of the most important things for you as her friends is, don't keep going on about the person who attacked her. Make her aware you know it's not her fault." Mhairi paused then looked at them all. "Hate him in private please? Let her come to terms with it. If she thinks you are getting upset, she won't talk to you about what happened, and she'll need to. It will be awkward for a while but it'll pass. One last thing, don't try to hug her or kiss her just now, she may not be ready for physical contact, Vickie will initiate it when she is."

"You sound like an expert Mhairi?" Andy said, smiling sadly at her.

"Unfortunately, I am; I know a lot about how she feels, I've been where she is."

"Oh, Christ, fuck! I'm so sorry, I didn't mean ... "

"It's alright. It was a long time ago." The nurse shrugged and sighed. "It's why I do this job, there are a lot of bad men out there."

They entered the room and Vickie stared at them from the bed. She looked up, away and wiped a tear from her eye.

*"**Oh darling**!"* Chris gasped. He moved towards her, arms

outstretched. Vickie recoiled from him and put the palm of her good hand out.

"Don't touch her, don't you ever fucking listen?" Johnny snapped at his brother. He moved over, sat down and took Vickie's hand. He raised it to his lips and gently kissed it, never taking his eyes from Vickie's face. Annie sat down, her face stained with tears. Vickie looked at her and turned away.

Mhairi returned to the room with an older woman in a white coat. "This is Andrea. She's a speech and language therapist Vickie. She'll give you a demonstration of the speech board then ~~I'll speak to all your friends. Get your~~ most used words and phrases from them."

"She says 'fucking sexist git' a lot," Andy said.

Andrea ignored him and continued with the demonstration. Mhairi made eye contact and smiled.

Andrea put the board down and looked up. "Vickie, you have visitors just now, I'll come back later. Just use it as a typewriter for now until you get used to it. Type the letters, then press this button and they'll come out as words. It takes a while, but I'll come in every day for a few hours and we'll get you talking away in no time. The voice is not too bad but it's a computer and not pretending to be anything else. There's also an app that can be downloaded onto your mobile phone, it's tricky but we can do that later."

* * *

Vickie looked down and typed, the machine said, "okay." She typed into the machine a second time, then lay back down and turned to face the wall. "Please go, I love you all but I'm sorry, I can't do this!" the robotic voice said. She looked at Annie, who burst into tears as Lynne put her arm around her and helped her from the room.

Johnny remained, Mhairi followed the others out. She opened the door of the relatives room and stood back to let them enter. Inside Jamie sat down, crying into his hands. Marnie sat on his knee and wrapped her arms around him, holding him, sobbing herself into his red curls.

Lynne, Annie and Andy looked stunned and tearful. Mhairi watched as Chris pushed Lynne away. He walked to the window then rested his forehead on the glass, tears running down his cheeks.

"I'm so sorry guys, it's all pretty traumatic." Mhairi looked at Chris, as she spoke. "It's even worse from where she is."

"I want to fucking kill Gorman," Jamie sobbed. "That's not our Vickie in there."

"She's still here," Mhairi sighed.

"Will she recover?" Annie asked.

Mhairi shrugged. "With help, probably, but she needs support and understanding from you, her friends. If you don't think you can do that, support her I mean, stay away from her." As she spoke, Chris turned and left the room.

"Lynne, shouldn't you go after him?" Andy asked.

Lynne sighed and shook her head. "He won't want me; he has to work this out himself, he's blaming himself for leaving her alone. He'll go and get wasted; if I go, I will too. I need to be straight, and here, for Vickie and Jovi, Andy."

Inside her room, Vickie turned her face to the wall again. Johnny, still holding her hand, ignored the fact that she had turned away and spoke quietly to the back of her head. "Vickie, I love you baby, and I'm going nowhere. No matter how much you try to push me away I'll be here for you."

Johnny was aware of her struggling to breathe and he could feel the rapid pulse in her hand. He knew she was panicking.

"All that matters to me is you getting well, physically and mentally. I want to help babe, I promise I won't touch you any more than I'm doing now. I want to scoop you up and hold you. I want to take away the pain, fear and hurt."

Vickie could hear the pain in Johnny's voice, her fingers tightened around his. She turned her head around and nodded.

Mhairi entered the room, "Johnny, can I ask you to wait in the relatives room, the police are here to speak to Vickie."

Johnny walked into the room and Annie, seeing the distress on his face, rushed over and wrapped her arms around him. She held him as he sobbed.

Andy shook his head, tears running down his face, "I can't do this!" he cried, "I can't see you like this Jovi, it's not right. I want to kill that fucker and I can't because he's in a cell. What kind of animal leaves a woman in that mess? I can't stand here and accept any of this. I need to get out of here!" Andy opened the door and made to leave, walking straight into Dania.

Dania looked at Andy, her face pale and tear stained, "I went to the house, I was supposed to meet Vickie this morning. Your dad told me what happened Andy, Arfur brought me here. Where is she? Can I see her? She won't blame me for this, will she? Do you all think it's my fault?"

Andy stared at her, pain and revulsion unhidden on his face. "Well if you'd gone to the police at the time, perhaps he would have been in a cell, and not able to attack Vickie."

"Andy for fuck sake!" Jamie gasped, looking at his friend.

Andy threw his hands in the air, looked around, *"I don't understand. Why would she go with him? After all we said to her, all the times we warned her. I want to understand Dania? Why you didn't go to the police? Why Vickie got in that car with him, but I fucking can't. I don't understand any of this. I need to go; I can't stand here and pretend that anything is normal."*

Andy reached for the door and then turned. "She has known us all her life and she's scared of us. I want to understand what happened here but most of all I want to understand why he did it? How he could do that to you Dania, and now Vickie? If you had just gone to the police then this wouldn't have happened."

"You are fucking right out of order here Andy!" Jamie cried. *"The person responsible for all of this is Tony, fucking, Gorman; don't you dare take it out on Dania, or Vickie!"*

Dania looked at Jamie, "it's all right Jamie, Andy's only saying what you're all thinking, and what I'm telling myself. I did go to the police; they were looking for him to arrest him when he attacked Vickie. The DNA was identified as his and two other men, he knew it was closing in on him." Dania began to sob. Jamie stood up and held her. "It was just too late. I need to see her, need to speak to her."

"Dania, she's in a really bad way babe!" Johnny said, breaking away from Annie's embrace and lifting some tissues from a box on the coffee table. He looked Dania in the eye, "physically and emotionally."

Johnny, his voice calm and clear, addressed Andy who was still standing at the door, his hand on the door handle. "When he managed to get Vickie, we were all partying. So, why don't you take some of the responsibility along with the rest of us Andy? Because, we all saw him at that party. Vickie didn't want to believe he was the one responsible for hurting Dania. We knew he was at the party and never checked Vickie was safe. I don't know how to cope with it either Andy, but I'm with Jamie and blaming one person. The bastard, who did this!"

Andy shook his head, tears now pouring down his face. "What would make Vickie go off with him though? I don't get it Jovi? She was there with you, she takes off with him?"

Johnny looked up, his eyes bright with tears. "She most likely panicked. It looks like Tony got Catriona to call her, tell her the wean was ill then he came to the rescue. Why Catriona betrayed us all? I don't know!" But, we do all know Vickie, know she would try to get back to her baby." He looked around the room, his eyes filling with tears, "Tony would know that too, she wouldn't be thinking straight, and, she had my car keys. Vickie would be dead if it hadn't been for that car having a tracker, he would have killed her. As I got to her, I heard him say, 'now no one has you!'"

"But she's not dead; she is lying in a bed a few feet away bewildered and afraid. Trying to make sense of all this, just the same way you all are, trying to work out, why she got in that car." Mhairi looked at them all. "It doesn't matter who did what, or even what happened before! What is important right now is supporting her, and each other. Everyone looking to blame yourselves serves no purpose. This man's punishment will be decided in a court of law. You cannot punish each other for not being there, you weren't. No amount of beating yourselves, and each other about, will change that."

CHAPTER

TEN

In the days that followed, those closest to Vickie stayed away, she refused to see anyone other than Johnny and Lynne.

Mhairi was a great help in talking about what to expect. Vickie, and the others, valued her care and advice. Johnny had brought the twins to the hospital but Vickie, feeling guilty about being unable to feed them, found it impossible to hold them. The babies were unsettled and missing her.

Laura and Annie quickly put the twins on to formula. Vickie refused to see her sons because she did not want them frightened. She was also secretly afraid she would be unable to hug them. Given her own childhood and feelings she was not loved, she was acutely aware of the damage, rejection could do.

Clinton and Maggie helped look after the boys, which freed Laura to take on the care of the babies. Johnny brought the twins to the hospital every day. Vickie eventually managed to hold them; all her emotions went into this. She did not have anything other than superficial conversations with Johnny. Johnny persevered and they did begin to talk, via the machine. She would, however, not allow any physical contact. Vickie could not bring herself out of the black place she was in.

Tony Gorman appeared in court on the charges of attempted murder, rape and kidnap of Vickie. He pled not guilty and was remanded in custody. The police continued to investigate the allegation of rape of Dania as a separate case.

Dania returned to Manchester when it became clear that Vickie would not see anyone. Lynne continued to share visiting with Johnny but they both struggled with Vickie's depressive state.

At Brickstead Manor, the others were devastated. Jamie and Marnie tried to hold them together but Chris and Andy couldn't cope with the pressure. Johnny, too exhausted from looking after Vickie to do anything, tried to ignore the fact that his brother and friend were spiralling out of control. Annie and Doug tried to speak to them, however, they voted with their feet and did not return to the house. Stories of their party lifestyle began to appear in newspapers and they were photographed heavily under the influence of drugs and alcohol.

CHAPTER

ELEVEN

The door opened and Ricky Mann came into the room. Johnny moved away to let him stand by the bed. He was wearing green operating scrubs.

"Ready?"

Vickie keyed in "as ready as I'll ever be."

"This should be quite quick; did my registrar explain it all?"

Vickie nodded.

"Okay, so tell me what I'm going to do?"

Vickie keyed into the machine. "You're going to cut into my face, put in a plate around my eye socket and remove the temporary one. I'll look human again after a few days. Then you are going to do the same with my jaw. I'll be the bionic woman once you've finished."

He moved towards her smiling. "Now Vickie, I'm going to touch you. Brace yourself; I'm going to mark where I need to cut. After this is done you could probably go home, once we're sure there's no infection."

"I don't want to go home," the machine said.

Johnny looked sadly at her. "I want you home Vickie, we all want you home."

Vickie shrugged and keyed into the machine. "Sorry Johnny. I can hide from the world here. If I go home I have to face reality."

"Oh, but you have to face the world," Richard sighed. "Johnny has come every day. It's been nearly three weeks Vickie! You need to get back to some type of normality."

* * *

When Vickie came around after the operation Johnny was at her bedside. "Hi gorgeous," he whispered, looking at her. Vickie tried to smile but her face felt tight and sore. She took his outstretched hand and held it. He leaned closer to her but she pulled away. "Vickie I'm really struggling with this. I need you to try to trust me. I've never done anything to make you feel I would hurt you. I love you, what we have together is wonderful and special. I will love you forever babe, but this is really hard. I need you to come home." Tears welled up in his eyes and he choked. He stood up and left the room. Vickie closed her eyes and went back to sleep. Mhairi followed Johnny out.

In the relatives room Johnny stared at the wall, Mhairi sat down across from him. "Johnny, don't give up on her please! It's early days yet, she'll come around, you just all need to be patient."

Johnny looked at the nurse, "I just want to hold her Mhairi, I love her so much but she won't let me touch her. I can't reach her, what if she never gets over it? She has four young children Mhairi! She's a fantastic mother; her two wee boys are distraught." He began to sob into his hands. Mhairi had to lean in to hear what he was saying. His voice muffled, "James asked Clinton if she had died and they weren't telling him. I can't reach her. I've known her all my life, we were friends before we were lovers. I don't know what to say to her. I want to be supportive, I want to understand but," Johnny looked straight at Mhairi, "I also want to grab her and shake her Mhairi. The counsellor said that it's all normal, but fuck me, I don't know if I can take much more of this. I'm trying to hold it all together. My brother is fucking out of control, staying away from the house most of the time. Him and Vickie, well, they really are like brother and sister. When he does come home, he's out of his face. I don't know what he's taking but it's serious stuff. Andy's my mate and he's been like a fucking zombie for two weeks. He's a bit better since you spoke to him the other day, but Andy's usually sensible, he's in pieces. He's also upset about blaming Dania, she won't speak to him, so he can't apologise."

Mhairi leaned forwards and touched his arm. "Johnny, you're exhausted, go home and sleep. If you need a sedative, I'll get you prescribed something. Lynne will be in later, so let go for a day or so, you're being mother and father to the children and trying to support Vickie. I know you feel you don't want to put pressure on her Johnny, but I'm concerned too. She can't get out of the dark place. I'm also really worried about you. Are you sleeping?"

Johnny shook his head, "I get a few hours, but I wake up and my head won't let me switch off."

"What do you usually do to deal with stress, Andy said you run?"

"Usually I run a few miles a night, I'm not doing it in case she needs me and I'm out running. I also I write but I can't even do that. Everything comes out angry." Johnny looked at Mhairi and sighed. "Is it selfish to just want to see some response from her, just a kiss? She holds my hand, that's her limit."

"It's all she can give at the moment, Johnny." I've tried talking to her about it too, but she just switches off. That's normal behaviour, and you're doing the right things, not pushing it with her." Mhairi shook her head then touched his arm again. "She will come out the other side. Things will be normal again, it just takes time."

"Mhairi we had a fantastic, mutual relationship. We couldn't keep our hands off each other. I know she's been through a terrible ordeal. I understand. I'm not expecting her to want to be intimate with me. I know it will be a long time and I don't care. I just need her to let me hold her. She just pulls away when I get too close. She won't talk about it. She's refusing to speak to a counsellor, so tell me? How is she ever going to get any better?"

"Johnny I'm going to get you some sedatives, I want you

to go home, take one and sleep. She'll be out till morning now anyway."

He looked at Mhairi, wiped away tears with a tissue then nodded.

Johnny, what you and the others are suffering just now is trauma. Just in the same way Vickie is traumatised, you are too, it's called vicarious trauma. Is the counselling helping?"

Johnny nodded, "yeah I suppose so, but I just want to feel I can help her."

"You are helping her Johnny, you come here every day. You and Lynne are helping her through it."

* * *

Mhairi looked at Vickie as she opened the curtains. "Wakey, wakey sleeping beauty, you need to sit up and stay awake. You won't be able to sleep later. It's 8am and you have been out since 6 o'clock last night." She handed Vickie a mug of coffee with a straw. "Can I talk to you?

Vickie nodded.

Mhairi sat down on the edge of the bed. "Vickie!" she said gently, "it's been nearly three weeks now and you have allowed no one to hug you or even touch you."

Vickie shook her head and turned away, but instead of stopping as she usually did, Mhairi continued to speak. "You need to have normal contact. Every day there are a multitude of calls and flowers. Your friends come here and we have to turn them away. If Annie and Clinton hadn't pushed their way in, you wouldn't have seen them either. Vickie, it has to stop; you need to talk them. Your dad says your older children are distressed, they think you've died. Your eldest son asked your step mum if you had died and they were not telling him."

Vickie shook her head, she lifted her speech board, "I don't know if I can do it, hug the children, and what if they're scared of me? I look like Shrek!

"No, you don't, go and take the towel off the mirror in there

101

and you'll see. It's all healing up nicely. Ricky has done an amazing job. Vickie, you are verging on selfishness now; you need to at least see the children. Aren't you missing them?"

Vickie began to cry. She nodded at the nurse, and lifted a handful of tissues from the box on the bedside locker.

Mhairi put her hands gently onto Vickie's shoulders and looked into her eyes. "Please Vickie? You need to see them. It's only just over a year since they lost their father, they need you."

Vickie lifted the machine; she sighed and looked at Mhairi. Typing for a few minutes, she pressed the speak button and sat back, "my dad and Annie are so upset, I can't handle it when they come in. I see the pain on their faces. The kids, Mhairi; what if I'm not able to hug them? What if they're frightened of me?" She looked at the nurse and nodded. "I'll try. Can you call the house and ask if someone can bring them in?"

"Good girl, I think not seeing you might be scaring them more than seeing you will." Mhairi took a deep breath, "Vickie for your next trick," she smiled, "please stop trying to push Johnny away. He loves you and I don't think he is going anywhere anytime soon. Don't lose him Vickie, he's a keeper. Vickie, think about how it was between you and him? How much in love you are with him, not to mention how gorgeous he is." Vickie laughed as Mhairi pretended to swoon. Mhairi became serious and looked straight at Vickie. "He didn't hurt you, Tony Gorman did. Johnny, he saved your life! He tells me what you had before was pretty special. Now I'm going to call your house and arrange for your children to be brought in, whilst you do some soul searching."

Vickie said nothing, but the nurse knew she was thinking about her relationship with Johnny. Mhairi smiled and left the room.

CHAPTER

TWELVE

Marnie put down the telephone. She turned to Jamie who was sitting at the breakfast bar eating a bowl of cereal. "That was Mhairi; Vickie wants to see the children."

Jamie looked up at Marnie, "do you think she'll treat them like strangers?"

Marnie put her arms around him and kissed the top of his head. "For now, it's something at least, hopefully the boys won't let her do anything but be their mother. I'll go speak to Annie. We can take them later today. I really want to see her too, Jamie."

Jamie looked up, his eyes filling. "It was late when Jovi came home last night, I heard him crying Marnie. I went to go and ask him how she was after the surgery, poor sod."

"Jamie, I know it's hard for you all but remember she can't help it; this is not Vickie! She's suffering from the trauma of what happened to her, she'll get better."

"Do you think it's all men?" Jamie whispered, wiping his eyes with the bottom of his t-shirt.

"Well a man she knew and trusted did this to her, Jamie."

"Fuck Marnie, that's heavy. She lived with us, travelled with us for six years, we even shared beds sometimes. She trusted us even when sometimes we didn't deserve it."

"Tony was part of her inner circle too Jamie. Of you all, she was the only one who trusted him. Even when she knew what had happened to Dania, she didn't want to believe he had done it. How many people have you known Vickie to fall out with or let down Jamie? It's who she is, she trusts everyone. I expect, for her, the view she had of people and the world has changed beyond all recognition."

Jamie stopped eating and put the spoon down, "I want to help her Marnie, be there for her. At first when we started out, I really fancied her you know? Now, I love her the way I loved my sister. I just can't stand her being hurt. Like you, Vickie has always been there for me, but it's not like you and me." He smiled sadly and kissed her, before whispering, "totally different type of love. I just can't believe what happened, what he did to her! I feel so fucking helpless. I want to help them babe but what can I do?" Jamie wept.

Marnie held him crying with him. "Well you just need to be there for her now, and for Jovi."

Jamie nodded. "That bastard Gorman should be castrated for what he did to her. I can't believe he pled not guilty, how the fuck can he even think he's not guilty? At least they refused him bail. "You know Marnie? You read about these things and you always try to keep an open mind. The violence, she must have been fucking terrified. God knows how Jovi feels? I mean Marnie, we all love her, but he's in love with her." He kissed Marnie, "I'm going to go back to my counsellor babe! I'm managing mostly to stay of the junk but even with you helping it's fucking hard. Fuck babe, I just don't know what to say to Jovi, and I keep seeing her in that room!"

Marnie kissed Jamie's cheek, "Jamie, you are the one holding everyone together, that's bound to be difficult for you."

"Yeah because I've always been the one who needed the help. You know last night when we, you know. When I tried to have sex, and couldn't stay hard. I kept thinking about the way I've treated you. The way I've behaved, the women I've been with. I love you Marnie, but, I don't fucking deserve you. I keep thinking, you worked for Gorman all that time, it could have been you. I thought I was coping, but I'm not sure I am now."

"I know it's hard, but you're coping better than Chris or Andy." Marnie kissed the top of Jamie's head again. He leaned back and she kissed his mouth.

"What about us Marnie?" he whispered, "should we tell her?"

"No not yet Jamie, that can wait till she comes home. She won't have a problem with it anyway, she's still Vickie. I guess she just needs to heal mentally and physically." Marnie sighed, like everyone in their circle she was confused and hurt. The house was not the same these days, all of them were scarred by what had happened. To make matters worse the media had found out about Vickie having been attacked. Simon, and Jimmy their lawyer, had gone to court and managed to get a press block, but the newspapers were full of a major celebrity having been sexually molested and beaten. Chris and Andy's reckless behaviour was not helping the situation.

Johnny came into the kitchen with Laura, both carried a baby. Johnny's face was pale and his eyes swollen and red.

"Darling you're gorgeous," Marnie said, taking Billie from Johnny, who opened the fridge and poured himself a drink. James came running into the kitchen followed by Denis.

"Good morning boys, I've some news for you. Your mummy's nurse at the hospital has called and you'll be able to see her today." Johnny looked around at her. Marnie rested her hand on his shoulder. "All her special boys and girls," she said brightly.

Johnny poured more juice into a glass and sat down, Denis climbed up onto his knee. "Did Chris and Andy come home?" Johnny asked the room.

Jamie shrugged. "I don't know, I never looked. Lynne's here; her car is outside, so hopefully she brought at least Chris back. Andy wasn't with Chris Jovi. He went out by himself, never said where though. We're going to have to deal with those two," he said quietly. "This can't go on."

Johnny raised an eyebrow. "Hallelujah, who saved you?"

"Marnie!" Jamie said, grinning.

Johnny smiled wryly. "It's amazing what the love of a good woman can do."

"Jovi!"

"What?"

"She'll come back to you, bro."

Johnny sighed. "So, they tell me!" He nodded sadly and sat down at the table. He looked up as Lynne came in to the kitchen; she was dressed in jeans and a sweater, looking sober.

"Auntie Lynne!" James cried, "we're going to see Mummy."

"Where's my brother?" Johnny asked her.

Lynne shrugged then shook her head sadly. "I don't know Jovi, I tried; I'm going to go try again later today. I've messaged him and said I need to speak to him urgently, he just texted me back saying he'll call me later. Andy's upstairs, so I'll ask him to try too. He might respond to him or you, Jamie."

Jamie nodded. "We've had everyone we know looking for him. Pixie Fields saw him two days ago, reckoned he was staying in that hotel at the top of the Kings Road. He hasn't been about though for the last couple of nights. No one has seen him." He hugged Lynne and kissed her, "if he's texted you though, he's alive!"

Annie appeared and placed a full rack of toast in front of Johnny, she kissed his cheek. "You okay love?"

Johnny nodded. "She wants to see the boys Annie."

Denis pulled Johnny's face around. "I want my mummy, and I want you to take me now Uncle Johnny."

"Jovi, we have a meeting with Simon at twelve," Jamie said quietly. "We need to speak to the lawyers about the Australian tour; it has to be put off indefinitely. The insurance will pay out. Marnie, Simon needs you to be there too."

"It's Saturday!" Johnny groaned. "Can't they put it off till Monday Jamie?"

"Apparently not."

Johnny kissed the top of Denis's head. "Aunt Lynne and Granny Annie will take you. I have to go to a meeting Denis but when I get back you can tell me all about your visit with mummy." Johnny gulped and looked at Denis, smiling at him, "then we'll go to McDonalds. Deal?"

Denis thought about this as he moved over to the breakfast bar beside Jamie and began to eat noisily from a bowl of cereal. "Okay deal, but I need ice cream too."

"James, don't you want any breakfast?" Annie asked.

"I'm not hungry; I've got a sore tummy."

Laura sat down beside him. "Is it a missing mummy sore tummy?" The little boy nodded.

"I get that too James!" Johnny said. "The best thing is a big hug, until you can get a mummy hug." He lifted James onto his knee and they clung together. Laura glanced at the others, who had like her tears in their eyes.

Annie, wiping her eyes, opened the patio doors. "Okay boys, let's play outside for a little while, it's nice and dry."

"Laura, Denis is stinking of perfume!" Johnny whispered, watching Annie and the two little boys disappear out the door, "Vickie's perfume."

Laura nodded, "I know Jovi. I caught him in the bathroom yesterday, spraying it." Her voice cracked with emotion, "I was just about to give him a row, when he said....he said....I'm pretending Mummy's just in the shower! Jovi, I sprayed his pillow and his teddy, it settled him. I'm so sorry if it upset you. I cried myself to sleep just thinking about it."

Johnny looked around, tears building in his eyes, and realised everyone was crying.

CHAPTER

THIRTEEN

"Vickie must have missed these two," Lynne said quietly, as she and Annie, both carrying a car seat, and Laura, who had James and Denis by the hand, walked up to the ward doors.

They rang the bell, the door opened and Mhairi met them in the corridor. "Ooh, what beautiful children!" she said as she let them in. "Now boys, your mummy had an accident and hurt her head so she has bandages on her face. She hurt her voice too. She has a special machine to talk to you just now, but she has lots of hugs for you children. She's missed you very much. The doctors are making her better, so she'll be coming home soon. My name is Mhairi. I'm mummy's nurse." She tapped on the door and opened it. "We have some special visitors," she said brightly, looking at Lynne, who had her fingers crossed above the children's heads.

Vickie sat on the bed. The right side of her face was heavily dressed, the left side still badly bruised; the marks now yellowing with age but still vivid. She had her keyboard in her lap. Both boys gripped the adults hands and stared at her. Vickie smiled, tears forming in her eye.

Lynne walked over to Vickie and hugged her, Vickie's body became rigid. "No Vickie, don't you dare pull away from me," she hissed in Vickie's ear. "I'm taking no more of this, I love you, and if you don't hug me right back, I won't let go. We can't go on like this, none of us can. You need to trust us; you need to start living again." Trembling, Vickie relaxed into the hug; she gripped her friend tightly and kissed her cheek.

"I'm so sorry Lynne!" she mouthed.

"So you fucking should be." Lynne broke away, wiping away her own tears and Vickie's. She pulled Denis over. Vickie put her arms out, and Lynne lifted the little boy onto the bed.

"It is you Mummy!" he cried. "I know your smell."

Vickie, still crying, hugged him. Suddenly James launched himself across the room, and bounced on to the bed. Vickie sat sobbing into James blond curls. James reached up and kissed the dressing on her face.

When she and the children calmed down, Vickie showed them the keyboard and keyed in "I love you, I've missed you so much. I can't talk because I've hurt my voice. I tell this machine, and it says what I want to say."

Mhairi opened Vickie's bedside cabinet. "Your mummy got you some books and colouring pencils. Do you want to draw a picture for her?"

"Yeah!" Denis said, jumping down.

James looked up at Vickie, "Mummy, when are you coming home?" he said quietly.

"Soon baby!" the machine said, "very soon." She held him close and kissed his blond curls.

"What's that on your hand?" James asked looking at her left wrist, with its heavy plaster cast. "It's the same as Uncle Topher."

"It's a plaster cast darling," the machine said.

"Did a big, bad, old dog bite you too?" Denis asked, not looking up from the table in the corner of the room where he sat drawing.

Vickie looked at Lynne, who shrugged. "He had to tell them something!" she whispered.

"Your mummy broke a bone," Mhairi told them. "The doctors are making it better. Maybe you can write your name on it."

James kissed Vickie's face again, "I kissed you better Mummy! Please can you come home, I miss you. I thought you had gone away to heaven to be with Daddy."

Vickie's eyes filled with tears. "No James, the doctors are making me better. I'll be home soon, I promise." James moved over beside his brother and Lynne who were drawing pictures. Annie sat down on the bed.

"Vickie, you need to come back to the house," she whispered. "Johnny is devastated he can't reach you."

Vickie shook her head.

Annie put her hand on Vickie's arm. "Vickie, I'm going to send the others away. Please, we need to talk. I don't mind what you are doing to us, but the kids and Johnny, sweetheart. They need something from you."

Vickie sighed, nodded, then reached up and touched Annie's cheek.

James put down his drawing on the bed. "That's for you Mummy, it's me and you, Uncle Johnny, Denis and the twins and Boynancy. Oh, and Uncle Andy; being sick in the bucket." He pointed at the picture, "that's Uncle Topher, he is sleeping on the floor; that's Uncle Jamie, kissing Auntie Marnie."

"Where are Auntie Laura, and I?" Lynne asked.

James thought for a moment. "At Tesco's with Granny Annie!" James jumped up and cuddled his mother. "Mummy, can I just stay here with you? I'll be a very good boy."

Vickie ruffled his blond curls and kissed James's cheek. "I'll be home soon darling, I promise."

"Mummy is your face feeling better because I kissed it?"

"Yes!" Vickie said through the machine, nodding at her eldest son. "I think your kisses are making it better."

Denis came over with his picture. Mhairi helped them to pin their drawings up above Vickie's bed. When it was time to go, James went meekly with Lynne, accepting he would be brought back to see his mother the next day. Denis, however, began to scream for Vickie. He threw himself on the floor then had to be carried out by Annie. Mhairi went with them to help with the car seats. Vickie tried to follow them but couldn't cross the door of her room. She watched them go. Colin, sitting by the door, jumped up and walked towards Vickie. Vickie shook her head at him, returned to her bed and sobbed into her pillow.

When Annie returned, Vickie was sitting on the large window recess, her knees pulled up to her chest. She looked away from the window as Annie sat down on the chair beside her. "Vickie Denis is fine; it was just a tantrum." She took a deep breath and looked at Vickie, "how are you really? We all keep skirting the real issue because no one wants to upset you. Darling this can't go on, you need to open up. Johnny says you won't speak to the counsellor?"

Vickie hesitated and slowly typed into the keyboard. "I'm in bits!" she mouthed then sobbed quietly as the computer voice broke the silence. "I'm broken Annie, I don't want to be, but I don't know what to do. Tony broke me; I was so scared, I thought I was going to die Annie. The last thing I remember was trying to remember everyone's faces." Vickie turned her face to the window and stared out. "I don't know how I can be whole again."

Annie, tears running down her own face, wrapped her arms around Vickie. "You don't need to be alone sweetheart! Vickie look at me, it's all still the same. I'm here for you, everyone else is too, but you need to let us in."

Vickie keyed in to the machine for a few minutes and it began to speak. "I needed to be alone Annie, I couldn't face anyone. The way that Johnny and my dad looked at me that first day. I felt dirty. I was so stupid to get in the car with Tony. Annie, I don't know if I will ever feel clean again. Mhairi told me after she was raped she actually put bleach in her bath because she couldn't get rid of the smell of her rapist. With me, it's his face. I keep seeing it, when I close my eyes."

"Vickie, you can't let that bastard win, don't let him take who you are away. He's an evil so and so, and he's caused so much destruction."

"I was a fool Annie, a stupid trusting fool," Vickie's machine said. Her face crumbled and she began to cry. "I didn't listen and I should have." She mouthed.

"Vickie, it's who you are; don't stop trusting people. There's bad people out there but there are so many good people too. We all love you darling, we want to help; your trust in people is part of who you are."

Vickie nodded. She picked up the keyboard, "I know Annie, but I should have known the boys were right. Billy too, he tried to make me see what Tony was. Johnny did too. Fuck Annie, you all saw it, but I couldn't admit I might be wrong." She began to sob again, "Dania was raped because I wouldn't listen. Then afterwards, I knew she had been raped but I still couldn't let myself believe I'd been wrong about Tony."

"Vickie, stop beating yourself up, stop using energy you need to recover thinking about it. No one thinks you were to blame. He was a lying devious bastard; he never deserved your loyalty. It's done, stop punishing yourself and everyone else. Vickie, you need to let people be there for you, you need to be there for them. It's who you are babe, a lovely, caring, trusting person. You're a strong woman Vickie, but even strong women need to let go sometimes and accept help."

"I want to, but every time I try, I get so scared. Annie I don't know what to do!"

"Vickie what happened to you was brutal, degrading, horrific and it will take a long time for you to recover." Annie looked at Vickie, the pain on her face evident, "I will help you though if you let me. This doesn't just affect you babe, it is killing us all. Little Dania, she calls every day asking to see you."

Vickie looked at Annie and nodded. She began to type into the keyboard. "I never understood rape Annie. What happened to Dania, I thought, because she was unconscious it would be easy to get over. Now I don't know? The pain afterwards, the memories of it happening? At least I know what happened. Annie before I went to America, I met him. Tony, away from the house, because I wanted him to tell me he didn't do it, and he did. He said he knew nothing about it, I believed him." She stopped typing and looked at Annie. Tears poured down Vickie's face and her nose ran, she grabbed a tissue and held it to her face.

Vickie composed herself and lifted the keyboard. "When he raped me, he told me he had sold Dania's virginity to the highest bidder, then he raped her too. He told me . . . he told me what he did. I feel responsible for that happening to her, because I trusted him. I can't give her back her virginity, her innocence."

Annie began to cry with Vickie. Even with the computer voice saying these things it was emotive and distressing. Annie could see the pain and confusion on Vickie's face. "Vickie please just come home, we can make you better," Annie whispered, tears running freely down her cheeks.

"Annie I just wasn't ready to come back to the house. I still don't know if I am."

"Vickie Johnny loves you, he really does. He's thrown himself into looking after the children. You're the centre of our world darling. They're all lost without you, we've been hiding a lot from you. You need to know how they're all reacting, Andy and Chris especially! Chris has been partying, even Lynne can't reach him. He has flashbacks and nightmares. He's been staying in London a lot with a bad crowd and doing God knows what. I'm so scared he is going to end up dead, Vickie. Him and Johnny were constantly fighting. When he does come home now Vickie, it's just to sleep off his hangover, and change clothes. We haven't seen him for over a week now."

"Andy, well he was permanently off his face with Chris for the first two weeks. I have never known him to take so many drugs. It's strange, because by the sound of it, he was the one who coped that terrible night. Doug being there helped, he's really patient with Andy, doesn't do the heavy parenting thing that I seem to do. He's a bit better now. He got talking to Mhairi; he says she helped him put it all in perspective."

"Jamie?" Vickie mouthed.

113

"Well that's the real shocker Vickie. He's been the strongest of us all; he's the one holding us all together with Marnie. I know that they do jump in and out of bed, but since you have been in here they've been together."

A tear ran down Vickie's face. "I'm scared Annie!" she typed. "I just can't face going home. I can't stand anyone touching me. I don't know if I will ever be able to be intimate with a man again. Yet I want to be in Johnny's arms. I'm so scared."

"Vickie I need to tell you something I have never told anyone ever." She paused and swallowed hard. "I was raped when I was thirteen. I let it ruin my life. Please Vickie, don't be like me darling."

"What?" Vickie mouthed, her eyes wide.

Annie put her hand over Vickie's and sighed. "He was a friend of my dad's. I never got help for it. He was my Sunday school teacher, would you believe? He groomed me. Made me feel grown up and important, made me trust him then abused me. It wasn't violent, not what you experienced, he just held me down and did it. Afterwards he made me pray for forgiveness for tempting him, making him sin...."

Vickie stared at her. She shook her head and put her hand on Annie's arm. "I'm so sorry!" the machine said.

Annie looked sad. "I need to tell you all of it Vickie, I need you to know some stuff. I hope it helps you; I've been deliberating over it for a while now. I spoke to Mhairi, she thinks it might. You see, he left me pregnant. I was only a child myself. I never told my parents I was raped. They never knew; they died thinking I was a bad girl. I was thirteen, didn't realise I was pregnant; by the time I did, I was nearly due. My mum pretended to be pregnant then we went away and came back with Connie. That's why we came to Ayrshire and opened the hairdressers."

Vickie stared at her, eyes wide, her hands typing furiously into the key board. "That makes you Johnny and Chris's grandmother? Does Connie know?" Vickie put down her machine. She grabbed Annie's hand.

Annie shook her head, and dabbed her eyes with a tissue. "No I don't think she even suspects. Once she was born, she became theirs, how could I tell them how I got pregnant. I left home at sixteen. You see it was never mentioned again in our house; the day I came back from having her, she became my sister. My dad never really spoke to me again. Mum, well, she just acted as though it never happened. Vickie, I didn't go back until I started working for your mother. That was after my parents died, I wanted to be around for Connie. She had the boys by then. She was only seventeen when she had Johnny."

"You poor thing. You poor, poor, thing," the machine said. Vickie reached out and put her arms around Annie. She held her close, kissing her wet face.

"Vickie, I'm not telling you for sympathy, darling, nor is it emotional blackmail. I'm telling you because I let it shape my life. I see you about to do the same. Please, Vickie, Johnny loves you. Let him in. Let him look after you. He's in a real mess, blaming himself for what happened. Vickie I love you, but I love Johnny and Chris too. I see Chris spiralling out of control through this. I hear, them both crying out during the night." She began to sob, "I know Johnny cries himself to sleep. Please, stop this now darling, just let Johnny in. I'm sure it will be alright, he loves you. I have known you all your life, I love you like my own. In many ways, you are the baby I never got to keep. I have never known you to run away from anything. You need to come home and be with us again, Vickie. I will never let you out of my sight, if that's what it takes. You love Johnny, you know you do. He's in bits, trying to not touch you, or ask you anything, but you're treating him like a stranger. He didn't hurt you darling, Tony Gorman did. Johnny saved your life."

"I love him Annie," Vickie mouthed, tears blinding her.

Annie nodded and sighed. "I know you do! Tell him Vickie, he'll be there for you. Then there's Chris. You and him, you're like brother and sister, you were always close Vickie. You need to open up, talk about it, start to credit them with some trust.

Andy and Jamie too, they are hurting, trying to understand! Your poor dad, he is beside himself because you just have conversations about what you had for dinner or lunch. Although judging by the look of you, talking about food is all you are doing. Then there's me, it's brought it back to me too darling. What I'm trying to say love, is we are a family, and we need to be there for each other. You got hurt, what happened was disgusting, awful and tragic, but they all witnessed it, they are hurting too. I'm not trying to make you feel guilty, Vickie, you need us too. Don't let what happened take anything else from you and us."

"Annie, I don't know what to say to you. You can't hide this. Connie and the boys, they need to know." The machine beeped and Vickie became frustrated. She tried to speak, but her voice was still gone.

"I want to tell them Vickie; this has opened up a lot of old wounds. I nearly told you, when it happened to Dania." She looked Vickie in the eye, "I've decided to go and see Connie, tell her. I've protected a rapist for over forty years. If she hates me, then, so be it! It's a chance I've got to take, and darling, if I can do this, you can too."

Mhairi came into the room, she looked at them. "Am I interrupting anything?"

Annie shook her head. "No Mhairi, I was just talking to Vickie about needing to let people in to support her."

Mhairi nodded. "Especially Johnny. Vickie, that guy really loves you. He's suffering; take a good look at him when he comes in. He looks awful, he's blaming himself for letting you down, leaving you alone that night. Don't drive him away. You'll recover if you let yourself, you'll be intimate again, and enjoy it."

"Do you have sex Mhairi?" Vickie asked, looking at the nurse who in the last three weeks had become a friend and a confidant.

Mhairi nodded, and sighed, "I was engaged when it happened. The relationship broke up after my attack because I let it happen. Like you, I couldn't let him in. Later, I missed him dreadfully but he'd moved on. I've been with a few men since, but no one special."

116

"What if I have aids or something, they said it could take three months."

Mhairi shook her head. "Vickie the three months is just a guideline of the worst possible scenario." She sighed again, and sat down on the bed, looking into Vickie's eyes. "I'm not saying you need to resume your sex life right away. You just need to let Johnny hug you, and move slowly. You'll manage it. What you are experiencing is normal. You also need to consider psychotherapy, that's what helped me move on." Mhairi smiled and looked at the two women, "for now though, I'm going off shift. I have a date incidentally!" Johnny came into the room, Mhairi smiled at him and left, closing the door behind her.

"Hi babe, how're you today?" he whispered. "Sorry if I'm interrupting Annie," he said, seeing Annie wiping away tears.

Vickie took his hand, raised it to her lips and kissed it back. Annie stood up and smiling, she whispered, "Vickie I'm going to go now." She smiled and looked around the room, "Johnny I'll catch you later at home."

"How are you getting home? Do you want to get a coffee with Arfur? He's outside waiting for me."

"I'll get Arfur to take me home Johnny," Annie said, nodding at Vickie, "you'll be here for a while I think." Annie smiled, kissed them both and left.

Outside the room, Annie sobbing held on to Mhairi. "I hope that worked Mhairi, what if it made her worse?"

"I don't think it could Annie, lets just wait and see," Mhairi replied, as Colin and Arfur walked towards them. "I think you are a very brave Lady Annie."

Vickie stood up and walked towards Johnny. She reached him and looked up at the man she knew she loved. "Johnny I'm so sorry!" she mouthed, tears began to blind her and she tried to shake them away.

Johnny came forward and gently kissed her forehead. Vicki tried to stay focused. She put her arms out to him, he moved in and kissed her lips. "Oh, my darling, I've missed you," he breathed.

Vicki typed into the keyboard. "Johnny, I just needed some space, I need to take this slowly. It's only been a few weeks. Johnny, I love you!" she mouthed. She moved away and taking his hand led him over to her bed.

He kissed her cheek and then sat down at the side of the bed holding both her hands. "Vickie, I've been seeing a rape crisis counsellor for a couple of weeks. Mhairi convinced me I should try it. I intend to keep going. I hope you'll speak to someone too. It's helping me understand how rape affects you, and to deal with my feelings. Vickie I hate Gorman, but I don't use up too much energy thinking about it, because I won't let him take you from me. I don't care if you never sing again Vickie, all I want is you me and the kids. The last few months before this happened were amazing, I never thought I could be that happy again." He moved closer, Vickie could see the emotion on his face, "Vickie please don't let what happened take that away from us?"

Vickie looked at him and raising her hand she stroked his hair, he leaned in and kissed her on the mouth. She stiffened up initially and then relaxed.

"That's better Vickie, just a little each day. I'll wait for you to be ready darling, I promise."

Vickie typed into the machine again. "Johnny, do you think you could listen to what happened; what he did to me?" She looked at him, still holding onto him, "If we are going to move on together, I need you to know it all. The police are coming in the morning to take my statement; do you think you could be here?"

"Of course, I can. I do hate him Vickie but he is an insignificant twisted little man. He couldn't have you, so he took you. Vickie, I promise you, no one will ever hurt you again darling. I'll protect you; I'll never let you down again."

"This wasn't your fault," the machine said, "it was mine. I should have listened to Billy, to you, everyone was telling me he was a bad man! Why did I trust him Johnny?"

"Vickie, please don't lose your trust in people. What happened, it wasn't about you, or us, it was about a bitter, twisted, evil little man. Don't let him change who you are babe."

CHAPTER
FOURTEEN

etective Constable Sushanna Sharma, had in the weeks
following the attack, spent a lot of time with Vickie
and Johnny. More than a police liaison officer, she
was a friend. It had been Susi who'd broken the news to them
about Tony's secret recordings of them all. Susi who'd kept them
informed of the progress of the case. Right now, she looked at
Vickie and Johnny and shook her head.

"I'm really sorry but you're a witness Johnny. You cannot be
here when we speak to Vickie; it could lose us the case. I'm afraid,
Vickie, you can't talk to anyone who's a potential witness, about
what happened. Johnny will most definitely be asked in court if
you've spoken to him about it."

Vickie looked crestfallen. Johnny took her hand. "It's alright
Vickie. I'll be there for you afterwards." Johnny looked at Susi,
"how soon will this go to court then? She needs to be able to talk
to me about it all."

"Johnny, we don't know, it's up to the CPS. The quicker we
get all the statements in, the sooner they can act. Vickie is last
because she's been so ill, also because of her voice; we had to wait
until she could use the electronic voice properly. I realise you
two just want it to be over but it would be better if there was a
longer period so you are physically recovered. Don't live your life

120

waiting folks, don't think about it." Susi looked Vickie in the eye, "we'll get him Vickie; he'll go to jail for a long time for what he did to you, and then we'll proceed with the other charges against him. By the time Mr Gorman gets out of prison, he'll be too old to rape anyone."

"Vickie, do you want me to get Marnie to come in and be with you? She's the only one of us who isn't a potential witness," Johnny asked, holding her hand.

Vickie shook her head. "No, Mhairi has already offered to sit with me. I need to come to terms with it all."

Johnny stood up. He wrapped his arms around Vickie and held her, kissing her gently. "I'll come back in later to see how you are. I'm going to stay in town tonight Vickie, I can be there for you quickly if you need me. They think you'll be able to come home the day after tomorrow."

Vickie nodded, and tried to smile.

"Johnny, it could take all day to get this statement," Roseanne O'Donnell said touching his arm gently. Johnny smiled at her, these two police women were almost close friends to them all. In the days after the attack they had provided support, taken statements from everyone. They'd made sure Vickie had been kept informed of every aspect of the investigation.

Johnny didn't return to Brickstead Manor, instead he drove to the Hammersmith flat and slept. When he wakened at five o'clock, he felt refreshed for the first time in the three weeks since Vickie had been attacked. Johnny made himself a sandwich, and sat looking out over the River Thames and the bridge. It was the height of rush hour and traffic streamed onto the bridge. Johnny thought about the thousands of people all going about their business, and wondered about their lives. He didn't stay at the flat often now but he felt at peace there; the solitude, the memories of his life in Hammersmith Heights were mainly good.

Did they have more bad luck than others, he wondered. He knew they had a lot to be thankful for. Johnny did feel the good fortune had come at a high price. Until the crash, Johnny had thought about very little except making music. His creative mind allowed him to write popular songs. It always gave him a buzz when he switched on the TV and a programme, or advert, was using his music. The most popular wedding and funeral songs in the UK for the past three years had been written by Johnny and Andy.

Johnny stared out at river, the picture of Vickie bleeding and broken, came into his mind. Would she ever again be the woman, he had fallen in love with, he wondered. Johnny wanted to hurt Tony Gorman, the anger at what he had done to Vickie, bubbling under the surface. Johnny, looked over at the dining room table, it was littered with paper, his laptop and printer sat waiting. The others were dealing with it differently. Andy struggled to be creative. Whilst stressed, he had been mainly drunk for the first two weeks but appeared to be coming out the other side. Jamie had turned to Marnie, and Johnny was pleased, he could see the difference in his friend. He was deeply worried about his brother though. Johnny sighed. Chris, he felt, was moving further and further away from them all. Johnny realised Vickie had always been the one to moderate his brother's conduct, providing a listening ear and a stabilising influence. Without Vickie, Chris was drowning in his own reckless behaviour. Johnny hadn't seen Chris for over a week. Lynne had, because of her sharing the visiting with Johnny, spent more time with him than Chris. However, concerned about where Chris was, and what he was doing, Johnny had asked Lynne to go find him, with Jamie and Arfur, and bring Chris home if they could.

As he stood under a shower, Johnny wondered if he was strong enough to carry the heavy burden of holding the band together. He suddenly realised he didn't care, he wanted Vickie and their children, all four of them, no matter what happened. He was aware he needed his brother and best friends too, but the band didn't matter. What mattered were the people he loved.

"Well how did it go?" Johnny asked, entering Vickie's room. She was sitting up in bed, her keyboard on her lap. Wearing a nightshirt, her hair scraped back, she looked like a little girl. Johnny knew though, she was tired and emotional.

"It was traumatic!" Vickie spelled into the keyboard. "Very traumatic, but they got it all."

Johnny nodded, "I saw Susi downstairs. I had to sign my statement too, so she just did it all here. How long did it take you Vickie?"

"Five hours, they said I was a good witness Johnny. I remembered everything, I re-lived it all though." She looked at him as she typed into the keyboard, then pressed the speak button and held out her hand, "Johnny would you stay with me tonight? I'm afraid of what I'll see when I sleep. If you're here I think I'll feel safe. Mhairi says it'll be okay."

Johnny smiled and nodded. Vickie looked at him, noticing for the first time how drained and pale he was. She reached up and touched his face. The machine bleeped and the electronic voice said "thank you Johnny, I'm sorry I was so bad to you. I just couldn't imagine anything being normal again for me and you." Her eyes filled up, "I'm so scared Johnny. Can you sit up here beside me?"

Johnny sat gingerly on the edge of the bed and then kicking off his trainers, he shuffled around till his head rested on the pillow beside her. He put his arm around Vickie, gently moving her towards him. She stiffened a little and then, as Mhairi had shown her, she began to take slow deep breaths. Gradually, she relaxed. Johnny kissed her cheek; she rested her head on his shoulder.

Vickie looked up into Johnny's eyes, her own green eyes misted over, "Johnny with you I feel loved but I also feel safe and protected," she mouthed.

He watched her lips carefully then kissed her forehead. Johnny tightened his grip around her. "We'll get through this Vickie," he said, his lips on the top of her head. Vickie nodded, feeling his tears in her hair.

She wakened, startled, several times during the night; each time Johnny held her, talked to her, and calmed her.

CHAPTER

FIFTEEN

Vickie tried to smile as Johnny drove through the gates of Brickstead Manor. He was driving Chris's BMW X5. The police still had his Range Rover. Vickie's Audi was in the garage. Andy had reversed into it outside the house. Vickie had decided not to hide behind the tinted windows in the back but to sit up front, where she knew she could be seen. She wore large sunglasses to hide the worst of the bruising. Cameras flashed from the ever-waiting paparazzi and Vickie turned her face away.

Johnny grimaced. "They're always there, aren't they? Sometimes I just want to go out and tell the world what that bastard did to you."

"Johnny, I probably do need to give a statement to the press . . . I was thinking, maybe we could speak to someone we could trust, like Jimmy Murphy, tell him."

"You need to get a bit better first, my love. Besides, you heard what the cops said, you need to say nothing that will allow the defence to say he was tried in the press." Johnny took a deep breath, looking at her in the mirror, "Vickie, Susi Sharma let me read your statement. You can't tell anyone." He looked at her tears in his eyes. "So, I know it all darling, what you went through." She put her hand over his on the gear knob. Vickie looked out as Johnny drew up to the house; a banner was stretched across the front of it.

"xxxxx WELCOME HOME MUMMY xxxxx."

Inside Vickie looked around the lounge. She couldn't help remembering the night of the awards. The laughter, the fun of getting ready. She looked over at the couch and remembered Marnie taking the photographs of them. The boys making jokes about her breasts and sexual innuendos had always irritated Vickie. They teased her because of it. She had never, for one minute, thought she would be a rape victim, and that the perpetrator would be the one person in her circle who never appeared to see her as a sexual object.

"Mummy! Mummy!" Her sons ran towards her and Vickie quickly sat down and allowed them to jump on to her lap.

"Be careful, mummy's been ill, remember what we talked about?" Laura told them.

"My babies, it's so good to be home. Where is everyone else though?" Vickie asked through the machine.

"They're all in residence, even Chris. He was AWOL but Jamie and Lynne found him last night and brought him home. He's unwell, but everyone else is here and okay. We just thought it might be a bit less traumatic if you saw the kids first Vickie." Johnny put his arm around Vickie's waist and she leaned back against his shoulder. She felt him kiss the top of her head and her eyes filled up.

"Mummy, Uncle Topher was sick in the flower pot this morning. Granny Annie hit him with the brush." Denis laughed. "Granny Annie said naughty words to him."

"Come on boys, let's get some juice and let mummy and Uncle Johnny have a coffee," Annie said as she and Laura herded the two little boys through to the kitchen.

Johnny sighed. Vickie could see the pain on his face. "Chris is either out his face or hung-over. He just won't talk to anyone about it. I can't really say much after the way I dealt with you being pregnant. Andy was much the same, but between Mhairi and I, we managed to get him to see a counsellor. He's been to see her twice; he was really upset last night, but there's been some improvement. The shocker is Jamie. With all his fucked-up life, he's the one who coped with it, and without as many drugs. In the first few days he and Marnie held us all together. Weird though, it's like suddenly Jamie is a grownup. He's even grown a beard and looks older."

James ran back through, his face covered in biscuit crumbs. "Mummy, we are going to have a party. We've been making things with Granny Annie, cakes and jelly and ice cream."

"Lovely, I can't wait." Vickie's machine said.

"Granddad and Grandma are going to come to the party too, Mummy."

"Denis ran through, kissed Vickie, then ran away again. "I made top hats Mummy!" he called as he disappeared through the kitchen door.

Vickie nodded, smiling at the innocence of her little boys. Her heart filling with love, seeing the joy of her being home, on their faces.

"Mummy, can we go out in the garden?" Vickie heard her younger son's voice, "I can ride my bike without stabilisers now, so can James. Uncle Johnny and Uncle Jamie showed us when you were at the hopstipal," Denis shouted from the kitchen.

"Okay, go get your hats and boots; I can't wait to see," the electronic voice said.

"Vickie, are you sure you're strong enough?" Johnny asked. Vickie gave him a withering look and hit him gently with the keyboard. She put it on the table and picked up her own coat and hat. Wrapping her scarf around her face, so only her eyes were showing, she took Johnny's hand and led him through to the kitchen door. The boys were being helped, by Laura and Annie, to put on their boots and coats.

Johnny and the children went outside to the garage to get the bikes and Vickie stood looking at Annie. Moving over, she hugged Vickie and kissed her cheek.

"Great to see you home, and on your feet, chick."

Vickie smiled, nodded then raised her eyebrow. "Connie?" he mouthed, searching Annie's face.

"I'm going to see Connie in a few weeks; I'll talk to you about it later. I'd too much to do with you being in hospital. We haven't hired anyone to help here yet, mainly because we felt that given your situation, we didn't want any strangers in the house. Doug has been helping me, and Jamie and Marnie, Lynne too. We've trained Jamie up to do the washing." Annie smiled and touched Vickie's cheek, "hopefully, once you're a bit better, I can go away for a few days without worrying. Vickie thank you for keeping my secret. I need to tell Connie first then work it all out."

* * *

Vickie enjoyed being outside, watching the boys riding their bikes. After being in hospital for three weeks, it was refreshing to be in the fresh air. Vickie linked her arm through Johnny's. She smiled at him and they walked around the garden following the children. When the rain came on they ran indoors to be greeted by Annie and Doug, with hot chocolate and marshmallows. Doug touched Vickie's arm gently and smiled as he handed her a mug. "Good to see you sweetheart," he whispered, as Vickie sat down at the table.

"You're way too skinny again Vickie," Annie said, heaping fresh cream on top of Vickie's mug.

Vickie pointed to her throat.

"She still has trouble swallowing, Annie; you need to take the marshmallows off." Johnny said quietly.

"I'm going to make loads of soups and stews that can go through the blender. I'll put some meat on you Vickie D'Angelo; that will be my mission," Annie sniffed, wiping away a stray tear.

Laura came into the kitchen with Jamie, and scooped Denis up. "Okay, why don't we leave the big people to their drinks boys? Let's go upstairs and get your swim things."

"Can I hug you Vickie?" Jamie asked. "Marnie said I had to remember to ask you and not just do it." He wrapped his arms around her and kissed Vickie's cheek. "Marnie and I are going to take the kids down to the pool. Their swimming is really coming on now." He sniffed, and wiped away a tear, "I've really missed you, I'm glad you're home!"

"I've missed you too, and I love the designer stubble, you look so grown up. Thanks Jamie, for all you've done when I was in hospital. I'm really grateful to you and Marnie!"

"You're my family Vickie, that's what families do isn't it? Now I'm going to go before I start crying over you. " Vickie kissed his cheek and smiled as he stood up.

Vickie and Johnny were still sitting at the table, when Chris came in. Wearing only boxer shorts and looking worse for wear he nodded and opened the fridge.

"You look like shit!" Johnny said. Vickie nodded in agreement.

Ignoring his brother, he looked at Vickie. "You're looking well Vickie, good to see you home." He lifted a carton of juice from the fridge and took a drink.

Annie slapped him on the back of the head. "That's unhygienic, use a glass."

"No, it's not; I'm going to finish it!" He sat down at the table and groaned. "Fuck my head already hurts, where you hit me with the brush. Fucking evil old cow."

"Hey!" Johnny cried, "don't fucking dare speak to Annie like that."

"Oh, fuck off Johnny, she knows I'm joking!"

"Well you'd better get out there and clean up that mess Christopher," Annie said, taking the carton from him, "because, I'm not doing it. There's a bucket in the utility room. Are you going to be in for dinner tonight? Is Tallulah here too?" Annie asked.

Chris looked at Vickie. She smiled and nodded at him. "Please stay in?" she mouthed."

"Okay; and yes Lynne's staying too. What you making Annie?"

"I don't know? I thought that we would have a bit of a celebration....welcome Vickie home. But it needs to be something she can swallow. I was thinking traditional Scottish fayre, stovies, haggis, and cranachan! Nice soft food Vickie can swallow."

Chris nodded. "Cool, cool, but my stomach is kind of fucked."

Johnny looked at him. "We need to talk Topher?"

"Not now Johnny, don't fucking start lecturing me again! Look after your woman, and kids, leave me alone!" He stood up, pushing the stool back. It screeched on the slate floor making Vickie jump. "Vickie I'll catch up with you later."

Johnny threw his hands in the air. Vickie patted his arm and lifting her keyboard followed Chris from the room. She caught up with him on the second-floor landing.

"Vickie I really don't want to be rude but I don't need a lecture on my behaviour hun."

"Chris, please?" she mouthed, then gestured with her head, asking him to follow her upstairs. Reluctantly, he walked with Vickie into the bright airy family room. Vickie asked him to sit down. "Chris, you look fucking awful!" the machine said.

"I'm okay Vickie. It's not been a great time, the last few weeks. I'm a bit stressed."

"Because of what happened to me?" Vickie mouthed.

He nodded, his eyes filling up he looked away. "It isn't just what I saw Vickie, it was how I felt, and the way it's changed me." Chris stared out of the window. "I wanted to kill him. I've never felt that angry before, it scared me. I didn't know I was capable of it. Johnny is the hothead, not me, yet he ignored that bastard, looked after you. I couldn't stop hitting him Vickie, and it terrified me." He looked down at the plaster cast on his hand. "I've known you most of my life. It was so hard, then I didn't know what to say to you. Johnny, he's my brother, I couldn't make things better for him. Vickie, I spend most of my life not caring about things; not worrying. Suddenly all these fucking emotions are rushing about in my head. I needed to know things were going to be normal again. So, I reverted to partying, that's always my devolved setting."

"Did it help?"

"No! Not really," he sighed and tears gathered in his eyes. "I guess it's easy to be lonely and frightened, even in a crowded room Vick. So, I drank. When the pictures were still in my head I drank more, then I started on the drugs." He looked at the floor. "I haven't been able to perform in bed either, even with Lynne. I've been popping pills." He hung his head and looked at the floor. "I've been smoking stuff too, heroin mostly, Andy and I were both chasing the dragon. It helps you to forget, stops you feeling. You know we've always dabbled. He stopped after a few days." Chris sighed. "I kept going. I realised it was getting out of control when I wakened up in a minging flat and there were two guys I'd never met before, shooting up. I booked into a hotel, and went cold turkey a few days ago. That's why I was so sick this morning, bit of withdrawal, but I couldn't tell Annie! She's worried enough about you. It's bad, the feelings, flashbacks, when I shut my eyes I'm back in that room. I also felt that you'd moved away from me, I feel I've lost you.

"I'm still here Chrissie!" the machine said.

"Vickie, that first day when I tried to hold you, when you recoiled from me, well it almost destroyed me." He looked at Vickie for the first-time, tears pouring down his face.

"I'm so sorry Chris!" the electronic voice said. "I didn't mean to do that, but it's been hard to have anyone touching me. I have to have your friendship back. I need it to be the way it was. I need you. You're one of the most important people in my life. Chris, I'm glad you recognise you need help."

"Vickie, I fucking let him down." Chris cried out, his face wet with tears. He turned away bunching up the throw from the sofa, wiping his eyes, sobbing into it.

"Who? Johnny? Johnny won't think you let him down, he's just worried about you."

Chris took deep breaths, trying to compose himself. He shook his head slowly and looked at Vickie, "no, I let Billy down."

"I don't understand? You let Billy down? What are you talking about Chris?"

He looked straight into her eyes and then looked away. "I once promised that if anything ever happened to him, I would look after you. I thought he was talking shite at the time, but he trusted me and asked me, not Johnny or the others. He knew you and I would always be just friends."

"When?" Vickie mouthed, sitting bolt upright. She typed furiously into the keyboard. "When did he ask you to look after me?"

Chris looked at her, his eyes bright with tears. "A few months before he died, sweetheart. It was the day we came here that first time." Chris stared out of the window again, he hesitated before continuing. "He told me he thought he would die young. I laughed at him, but I promised him I would look after you and the kids if anything happened to him. I don't know why I didn't tell you. He asked me not to tell anyone, I meant to, I think, but it never seemed the right time. Then he died, you were pregnant, then you and Johnny dropped your bombshell. I told myself I didn't want to cause any problems. Oh I don't fucking know why I didn't tell you? Maybe I needed to have something of you and him for me. He said he felt that he was going to die soon Vickie, three months later he was gone."

"He knew?" Vickie whispered, staring at Chris.

"I don't know Vick, how could he? It was an accident! He was so calm about it, said he wanted me to make sure you were looked after." Chris's voice broke again, "he also asked me to make sure I kept Tony away from you, you know how perceptive he was. He fucking knew that Tony could harm you Vick, and I didn't listen. He loved you so much babe. He wanted you and the kids to be safe and happy. Vickie, I fucking failed him and I failed you. I never protected you. I never saw Tony as a threat that way. Like you, I was never sure he harmed Dania. Vickie, the whole world had keys for that flat. He told Susi he kidnapped you because of the remark I made at the awards about the hungry ex-manager." He began to sob. Vickie held him against her and stroked his hair, crying with him. Eventually the sobs subsided and he looked up at her.

131

"I know we joke with you about stuff. Vickie, you are hot; but you're my best friend too! Jamie, Andy and me, well we think of you as a sister, a little sister who we should protect, and a big sister we look up to for support and guidance. I don't know how to take those images of you in that room away. I know I should be there for you but I don't know what to say."

Vickie touched his face; she reached up, wiped away the tears on his cheeks with her fingers then began to type into the keyboard. "I'm okay Chris, it's been hard, and I expect it will still be for a while, but we can't fall apart. I need you to be okay Chris. I lived through it, I'm healing, you will too. The broken mind is worse than the broken body, but we need to get our lives back now. It's going to be a while before we can play again. They think it will be about two months before I can try to speak, never mind sing. But even if we don't play again, I'm glad you're trying to address the destructive behaviour. We could try counselling!"

"What? A shrink?" He stared at her. "Me? The fucking doctor would need therapy if they got in my head!"

"Trauma counselling Chris, for both of us. I didn't think I would be able to talk about it but going over what happened for my statement was almost cathartic. I'm going to try it. If I can, so can you. Johnny says it's working for him, Annie says, it's starting to work for Andy. Look at the difference it's made to Jamie, counselling. He's been seeing someone for a while now. If there was ever anyone who could send a therapist over the edge, it's Jamie!"

Chris shrugged, blew his nose, then lay back on the couch looking up at the ceiling. "I think I prefer vodka Vick!"

Vickie looked down at the keyboard. "It doesn't like you though babe. Will you try for me? I will, if you will!"

"Okay, I'll give it a go! Can I hold you now Vickie?"

She nodded. He reached over and put his arms around her. "I love you Vickie! I think I just needed to know you still remember how close we are," he whispered. "The electronic voice is a bit weird though, maybe I should try it, might make me think before I speak! You and me Vickie, we're so different, yet we're the same, aren't we?"

Vickie looked up, nodded and kissed his cheek. "I love you too, even when you're being a fanny," she mouthed, smiling at him."

He smiled back and kissed the top of Vickie's head. "I promise I'll cut down on the partying. Vickie, this is totally changing the subject, but Mhairi, the nurse, is she single?"

Vickie looked at him and sat up. "Why? You interested in her?" the machine said.

Chris shook his head. "No, but Andy is. He has been talking to her about stuff; he took her out to dinner the other night to thank her. He got on well with her, and really is interested. He's scared to push it too far in case he scares her off."

Vickie laughed and rolled her eyes. She picked up the keyboard. "She's never going to put up with his sexist shit Chris. She's a really strong feminist."

"Well, maybe Andy needs someone like that Vickie. To be honest, I think a lot of the things he says are just to wind you up. Would you have a problem with it? Don't tell him I told you."

Vickie shook her head then smiled. "She won't be impressed by him but it might be fun to watch him try. What about you Chris?"

"Lynne and I are going to be exclusive!"

"What?"

"Well, we need to stop partying and settle down. I'm going to get myself sorted out then we want to try for a baby!"

Vickie gasped, "you're joking, you two with a child, what the hell!" the electronic voice said.

"No, Vickie, it's not funny, we were made for each other. I've known since primary school I would end up with her. I kind of fucked up Vickie. She told me she wanted it to be just me and her. I thought she was kidding. I burst out laughing, then I realised that she was serious. I actually liked the idea but I couldn't say it. I keep thinking, if I had not been trying to avoid her that night I wouldn't have left you out there on your own. Johnny only left you because he was embarrassed."

Vickie shrugged. "If wishes were horses honey. Stop torturing yourself." Vickie looked from the keyboard to Chris and then pressed the speak button. "I know it's what Lynne wants; she told me the night I was attacked about what happened in LA. I'd actually forgotten about it, it's what I'd like to see happening though. You two really do deserve each other."

"She got really upset at me last night, when her and Jamie found me. I was trying to stay away to get clean, I knew Lynne would realise what I was using. Anyway, we talked. As I said, I went cold turkey a few days ago, I'm over the worst of it now. It was a binge Vick, I wasn't using enough for serious withdrawal," Chris groaned and lay back on the couch. "I think my liver is fucked though, Vickie."

"Well see a doctor Chris. You know the answer is stop drinking and using drugs."

"I'm a rock legend!"

"You'll be a dead legend if you don't get a grip." Vickie untangled herself from him. She grabbed his face and kissed him. "You stink!" she mouthed. "Go get cleaned up. Now where is Andy? I need to speak to him."

* * *

Vickie tapped on the door and entered, Andy was lying on his sofa. He wore a pair of sweat pants. Vickie sighed and sat down opposite him. "How're you doing?" Vickie mouthed, looking directly at him.

He looked back at her, shrugged then looked away, "better than I was, I suppose, but still confused. Worried about Jovi, worried about you, feels like the world is upside down."

"I'm okay Andy, so is Johnny, but you appear to have got yourself in a bit of a mess."

Andy sighed and looked directly at her. "It's been a bit of a weird head fuck Vickie. I'm so upset about what happened to you. I couldn't deal with it all. It was even worse than after the crash." He looked away, "I was so angry I couldn't take it out on Tony, which is what I really wanted to do. I took it out on Dania. I'm so ashamed of myself. Vickie, she's just a kid, she came in and asked did I think it was her fault, and I fucking said it was."

"Do you really think that, Andy?"

"No of course not, I was in a state. I couldn't get my head around it all and I lashed out at her. I've tried to speak to her, called her but she won't answer and I feel bad." He sat staring at the floor, when he looked up Vickie could see the pain on his face. "I should have been there for Dania, but I struggled with the fact she hadn't gone to the police. I realise why, she thought she wouldn't be believed, but I just kept thinking if she had, they might have arrested him, and spared you. Then I was so angry at you for getting in the car after everything we had said to you," Andy sighed and wiped his face with his hand. "I think I was angry I didn't protect you, my head was all messed up." He grimaced, "then I got talking to Mhairi, she pointed out the obvious!"

"Which was?" Vickie asked, looking at him.

Andy shrugged, "that you are a wonderful, loyal person. You were always there for your friends! She explained things to me, talked about what happened to her. How she felt, how hard it was to speak to the police, the court case, the fear. She made me understand how frightening and painful it all is. I'm ashamed to be a man right now, but it's what we do now that counts, isn't it?"

"You not cracking up and getting out your face would be a start Andy. That won't change anything, it will make you more confused. I'm glad you feel better. Andy, you all tried to tell me, I wasn't listening. Know what though? I want to be able to trust people again. I don't want to feel the way I did for the first few weeks."

Andy sighed and put his hand out and took Vickie's in his, looking down studying them. He brought his gaze upwards to her face. "I've never had a problem getting laid. Sex is a beautiful thing, but I just couldn't understand what an ugly, violent act, rape is. I couldn't get my head around it being about control and violence, not necessarily sexual feelings. I've been such a sexist bastard Vickie, all my life, I've been selfish sexually. Only thinking about my own pleasure, there was no sexual respect really. I mean, I've never forced anyone but I can think of times when, well I've probably coerced, it was all about me and my needs. What happened to you and to Dania just made me so ashamed of myself because I wasn't a man, I was a horny little boy! This life we lead, it was a bit like being in a sweet shop. What I said to Dania was unforgivable Vickie, but, it's that thing, once it's out, it's out. You can't take the words and the hurt back."

Vickie nodded, "I think what you have done is just a bit of soul searching. You're a decent guy Andy and well, it can only be a good thing if you think about being more respectful towards women. I need to speak to Dania too, Andy. Tony told me what he did, he gave her rohypnol; it was all planned. He'd sold her virginity to the highest bidder, some rich business man, it was really sick. I've been thinking about it a lot. I know mostly what happened to me! She knows something happened but doesn't have any memory of it, that must be terrifying too. Andy, I had such a good experience of sex. I know how it should be, can be." Vickie looked at Andy, "Dania doesn't. She just knows the pain she felt afterwards."

Andy said nothing, Vickie carried on. "I got talking to someone else about it. An older lady, she told me she never ever had sex after being raped at an early age. I don't want that for Dania. I'm going to get in touch with her and perhaps she'll speak to you, let you apologise. If she can't Andy, you'll just have to live with it my friend."

Andy nodded, "I'll message her again Vickie. Hopefully she'll read it and call me. I didn't want to do it that way because I wanted to speak to her. I wanted to apologise to her face, so she would know I meant it."

"Write it in a letter or a song, Andy. Even if you don't post it, or show it to anyone, it'll help to get it out."

136

"Vickie, I love you!"

"I love you too Andy."

"Vickie, all the things I've said to you, the sexual innuendos!"

Vickie smiled. She kissed her finger and put it to his lips. "Andy, don't stop being you, babe," she mouthed.

CHAPTER

SIXTEEN

Vickie felt calm; she looked around the dining table. She realised she was glad to be home. Her keyboard lay in front of her. She swallowed the food Annie had lovingly prepared. Johnny was on her left, the others were spread out. Johnny balanced Billie on his lap. Chiara was sleeping in Andy's arms.

They were drinking coffee when the intercom buzzed. Jamie jumped up and answered it. "Okay thanks Arfur. Your dad and Maggie are coming up the driveway Vickie, and your brother is with them."

"Paddy's here?" Vickie mouthed smiling.

"He's got a couple of days leave," Johnny replied, "he called earlier, said he was with your dad."

The evening was, although difficult because Vickie's injuries were still so vivid, a happy one. Freed from breast feeding and strong painkillers, Vickie enjoyed a few glasses of wine.

Vickie and Johnny went upstairs to give the twins their last feed of the day. "You look beautiful Vickie, sitting there with Chiara in your arms!" Johnny whispered. "It's like Madonna and child." Vickie looked up at him and smiled. Billie lay asleep on his chest, her head turned to the side and her little mouth twitching. "Vickie what are we going to do?"

Vickie looked at him. He looked sadly back at her and shrugged. She reached over and took his hand. "I love you!" she mouthed. Squeezing his hand, she raised it to her lips, and kissed it.

Johnny took her hand and looked into Vickie's eyes. "Do you feel able to sleep in the same bed as me, babe? I'll understand if you can't, if you want me to move back to my old room?"

Vickie shook her head, "no, I want you by my side Johnny. Thank you though, for your consideration."

They settled their daughters before joining the others downstairs. At the lounge door Johnny paused and pulled her into his arms, he kissed her on the mouth. "No matter what happens, remember I love you, never forget that." Vickie smiled up at him, she knew he meant it, he made her feel safe.

The others were laughing at a comedy programme on the television when she and Johnny entered the room. Chris lay asleep on the floor; Boynancy the cat was spread out beside him. Lynne curled up on one of the big armchairs with Denis, whilst Jamie and Marnie huddled together on the sofa beside Paddy. Andy sat on the floor with his back to them, with James in his knee. Annie, Maggie, Doug and Clinton were sitting together on the big sofa.

A picture of normality; a family. Vickie glanced over at the mirror above the roaring fire. The phoenix rising from the flames, she saw the people in the room reflected in it, with her at the centre. In that instant Vickie knew it could all be normal again. Paddy stood up and gestured to Johnny, waving a cigarette packet. Vickie sat down in his vacated space. She put her hand on Andy's head. He leaned back and winked at her as James climbed up onto his mother's lap. Andy stood up and followed the other two men outside.

"How is she really Jovi?" Paddy asked, when they were sitting out on the kitchen steps. "I can't believe no one told me!"

Johnny shrugged, "there was nothing you could have done; she wouldn't have seen you. She just couldn't, besides you were

139

so upset over Dania. We asked Dania not to tell you, and with you being away on exercise, it was easy to keep it from you. It's early days Paddy but she's 100% better than she was!" He gulped, remembering the emotions of the first few weeks.

"I know, Dad told me. He was really upset she wouldn't let him touch her."

"She was so scared Paddy, I tried to hold her, I just wanted to let her know I was there. She shrank away from me like I was some kind of monster, it was heavy going mate. I don't know if our relationship will ever be the same again, but I love her and I'm here for the long haul."

Paddy blew out a stream of white smoke. "I need to go back tomorrow; I've only managed to get a short leave. When I got back to England and saw the newspaper stuff, I realised straight away it was Vickie." He looked at them sadly, "after the way I reacted when Dania was attacked, well, I realised why you didn't tell me. I managed to wangle a couple of extra days. I'd so long off at Christmas, then all the stuff with Dania. Dad needs to be back tonight; he has a patient to see. I just wanted to see her and know she was alright before I go back."

"Well you've seen her," the electronic voice said behind him.

Paddy looked up. "Fuck, sis, it sounds like Siri from the iPhone. Is it weird, that I find it very sexy?" Vickie smiled and sat down on the step beside her brother. Johnny was perched on the kitchen window ledge; Andy was leaning against the wall.

Vickie took a short drag of her brother's spliff and blew out a stream of white smoke before handing Paddy the joint back. Paddy put his arm around her, initially she pulled away, startled, then breathed. Paddy looked hurt. "Sorry!" she mouthed.

"Paddy, Vickie doesn't mean to hurt your feelings, any sudden movement causes that reaction," Johnny said quietly.

"One of the nurses at the hospital explained it as being a flight or fight reaction." Andy looked at Paddy. "Vickie has been so traumatised, her mind's immediate reaction is flight; it's a type of involuntary reflex," he said proudly.

Vickie nodded and kissed her brother's cheek. Johnny smiled. "A week ago, she couldn't have done that Paddy. She's getting stronger every day, aren't you babe?"

"Vickie nodded, "sure am!" she mouthed

"What about your voice?" Paddy asked. "When will you be able to speak?"

Vicki shrugged, she held up her hand, splaying two fingers.

"What! You can't talk for two months?"

Vickie nodded.

"If there is any chance that she will be able to sing again. She has to completely rest her voice," Johnny told him.

"Will you sing again?" Paddy asked.

Vickie looked at Johnny, Andy and then at her brother. "I hope so!" she mouthed. Johnny smiled at Andy, both looked relieved. Vickie stood up, hands clasped up to her cheek, making a sleeping motion. She touched her brother's cheek and he got to his feet.

"Okay sis, I need a hug!" He pulled her close and kissed her forehead. "I'll catch up with you soon. I'll text and e-mail, rather than phone you for now. Love you!"

Vickie nodded, smiled, kissed him back, and then she made her way through to the lounge. Johnny explained Vickie was tired and going to bed. He told James and Denis he would read their bedtime story.

"Darling, I'm so glad you're home," Clinton whispered as he hugged his daughter. "Let's do lunch this week. Are you going to be in town?" Vickie nodded, smiled, and kissed his cheek.

Vickie walked around the room kissing each person there. Everyone knew how much effort it had taken. Annie came through from the kitchen and handed her a mug of coco.

Vickie left the room and went upstairs to her bedroom. The quilt was turned back, there was a hot water bottle in the bed. She slowly took off her clothes, put on pyjamas, then wrapping her robe around her she went out to the veranda. She looked over at the hot tub covered up and switched off. Her mind cast her back to that first night with Johnny. She sighed, remembering how wonderful making love with him, was. Suddenly she saw the image of Tony Gorman's red face above her. Vickie jumped. She dropped the mug she was holding, it smashed into pieces, the milky coco spreading out like blood on the stone floor. The pain and fear of his attack, vivid and alive in her mind. She rushed back through the French doors, banged them shut and locked them, standing with her back to them. She could feel her heart beating wildly in her chest, she struggled to breathe, and her body began to shake violently.

"What's up babe?" Johnny cried, coming into the room. He rushed to her side. She began to cry, quietly at first, then louder, howling like a wounded animal, sobbing into his chest. He held her firmly letting her cry, when the crying subsided, he looked into her eyes and spoke. "It's okay Vickie, you're safe, I promise."

"I'm scared Johnny, really scared." She mouthed.

Realising she was exhausted, Johnny lifted Vickie, carried her over to the bed, put her down and he gently covered her with the quilt. "Vickie no one will ever hurt you again. You can sleep and not be frightened. Have you had a flashback?"

Vickie nodded. Johnny could see the fear in her eyes.

"Vickie, Meg, my counsellor, she says it's part of the healing. To be able to forget, I think you first need to remember." He lay beside her, on top of the quilt, fully clothed, stroking her hair.

Eventually, she relaxed, her breathing became calmer as she fell asleep; Johnny kissed her and stood up. Opening the French doors, he moved out on to the veranda and sat smoking a cigarette.

Johnny, like Vickie couldn't help remembering that first night with her in the hot tub. His heart ached; he struggled to imagine how he could ever have that kind of passion with her again. He was plagued with flashbacks too, seeing Tony on top of her. Her half naked, bleeding body, chained to the bed, haunted his dreams. In the dreams she didn't wake up, he couldn't save her. Sex before, had been a wonderful pleasure for him, Vickie had excited him in a way he had never realised possible. Johnny didn't know if he would ever be able to have that kind of passion again.

"Are you okay, bro?" Chris's voice echoed up.

Johnny looked over the balustrade and down; his brother was hanging over the balcony below.

"How did you know I was out here?"

"I saw the smoke bro, is Vickie asleep?"

"Yeah Toph, she is, she's exhausted. After weeks in hospital being home really took it out of her, she's still really stressed." Johnny watched as Chris climbed over the side of the veranda below, he reached up and grabbed the railing above. His long, slim body dangled for a few seconds before he pulled himself up and over the railing and sat down beside his brother.

"Heavy stuff?" Chris asked.

Johnny nodded. "You could say that! Toph, she lets me hold her on the bed, kiss her, but I can feel her heart racing like a fucking train. She's so scared. There's fear in her eyes all the time. That's not my Vickie!"

Chris sighed. "None of us came out of that night unscathed bro. In some ways, it was worse than the crash. I think because it was Tony, and despite everything that happened before, he was part of our inner circle for so long. Also, we saw it; it's not like being told about something, we've the pictures in our heads now. Then there was Vickie's reaction to us." Chris took a joint from his shirt breast pocket. He lit it and breathed deeply, before passing it to his brother. "She'll get over it bro, she just needs you to slow down, go at her pace."

"Topher, I don't know if I can ever get those pictures out of my head. What he did to her, what we saw."

"You need to, because none of us know what happened in the part we didn't see Johnny."

Johnny blew out a long stream of smoke. "That's the problem for me Toph, I do know. Susi, she showed me Vickie's statement; the bits we didn't see were fucking awful. She must have been terrified. I wasn't there, I let her down."

"Do you want to talk about it bro? I'm here for both of you?"

Johnny, took a long drag from the joint, lifted the glass in front of him. He took a drink of the vodka, put the glass down and looked at his brother. "It's pretty bad Topher; it's better you don't know. I saw that fucker violating her every time I closed my eyes as it was. Now I'm seeing it awake. It's horrific; I honestly wish I didn't know!" Johnny wiped away a tear, looking away he added, "I can't tell her that though. Fucking bastard Toph, he did things to her . . . I can't even bear to think about. I wish you'd killed him; no, I wish I had!"

Chris looked sadly at the plaster cast on his hand. "He'll get what's coming to him bro. They've charged him and his two pervert mates with the attack on Dania. There's young girls coming out of the woodwork. Fucking perverted, paedophile, bastard."

Johnny took the joint from his brother, taking a long slow drag he held his breath then blew out the white smoke. He looked upwards, watching the smoke rise and disappear out into the night. "Apparently, the films from his properties make interesting viewing and we're all starring in them, he's been charged with that as well. Rosie and Susi say he had a library that would have been worth millions in certain hands. How could we not have known what that fucking animal was capable of Topher? All those stories about him?"

"Johnny, stop it, stop beating yourself up. The stories were all about him liking young girls. Yes, we thought there was consenting, sado stuff, but it was never about violence like that. Until Dania, we thought it was consensual."

"Did Vickie tell you about Catriona?"

"What about her? Fucking little bitch!"

"Toph, she's just a kid, Tony was blackmailing her; he was her dad's mate. The bastard abused her when she was really young, then kept it up.

"Johnny! She fucking betrayed all our trust."

"I don't think she had a lot of choice, she was afraid of him. Other girls have come forward; all of them were abused by him at a very early age. He liked them young. Catriona didn't know what he was going to do to Vickie; the police actually don't think he planned it".

"He had fucking handcuffs Johnny, of course he planned it."

"He told Catriona he just needed to talk to Vickie away from us. They think he overdid the drugs and lost control. Chris, Catriona, she tried to take her own life when she found out what happened."

"You can't forgive the little bitch Johnny, surely Vickie is not going to. As for Tony overdoing the drugs! Fuck right off. I have done that loads of times Johnny, but I have never violently raped or tried to kill anyone. You've got to have that in you, to do what he did."

"You beat him up Toph!"

"Not the same thing!"

"It is bro, and what's more, you know it. I fucking hate him Topher. I want to cut him into little bits but I keep thinking, that's what Vickie always said isn't it? About society thinking men have to meet violence with violence. I feel so fucking guilty I didn't protect her."

Chris blew out a stream of smoke and handed the joint back to his brother. "We all feel like that bro. I guess we just need to learn to live with it."

Johnny nodded and sighed. He blew out a long stream of white smoke then looked at his brother. "Vickie thinks Catriona was just as much of a victim as her. She's going to give evidence for the prosecution. Her parents are absolutely grief stricken; she thought she couldn't tell them what he'd done to her. He abused her wee sister too; she's only fifteen, reckons he has been doing it since she was about nine. That's only a few years older than James; it's all pretty grim Toph!"

"That's heavy, but I just can't accept that she took the job, became close to Vickie and then betrayed her. I mean Johnny, if there was ever anyone who you could tell something like that to, it's Vickie isn't it?"

"Don't hate the kid, Toph; you're doing what Andy did with Dania. Catriona, well, she didn't even want to be a nanny, he pushed her into it. Probably so he could have someone spying. They lied about the nanny school. Catriona didn't attack Vickie, Tony did. She wants to bring her back here to work."

"You're fucking joking Johnny, no way. After what she did? Vickie surely can't be even contemplating letting her near the babies? You need to put your foot down too; Vickie is not thinking straight."

Johnny shrugged. "The police have charged her too. I don't agree with it; the girl was in a terrible position. She was afraid of Tony. We know now what he was capable of."

"Johnny no, to be honest I think everyone will feel the same way. Anyway, let's just leave it for now." He took a last drag of the spliff then flicked it over the side of the veranda. Oh by the way, just to add to your problems, Dad phoned, Mum is desperate to come down Johnny. Maybe you should take the twins up to see her; that might help."

Johnny nodded. "I know, thing is I can't leave Vickie just now. I explained to her and Dad what happened but she only heard the bit about them being her grandchildren. The old man was going to work on her. She doesn't know anyone else knows Toph, even you. I thought it might stop her talking about it if she thought it was a secret. I still need to go and see Liz and Bobby and explain to them, I've told mum that. It's all going to come out Toph, Tony knew we slept together, he told Vickie. If there's a trial, he could use it. Mum, she's just not getting it though!"

Chris smiled, and nudged his brother. "Must be killing her if she can't gossip? She was on the phone to Annie this morning. I heard Annie saying the babies were beautiful and the image of Vickie. So, she was asking. Annie is going up soon; maybe you should send Laura and the babies with her, or I can take them. Good old Annie, she and mum are total opposites, aren't they? Mum and Dad love Vickie; they'll be over the moon you're together."

146

"Are we? Together?"

"Of course you are bro, you love each other; the rest will sort itself out. You just need some patience. Johnny, we all love Vickie, but it's a brother, sister thing. With you, it was always something else, there's a different connection between you two."

Suddenly an ear shattering scream came from behind them; followed by a loud smash. Johnny jumped up and, followed by Chris, he rushed through to the bedroom. Vickie was on the floor in the corner; her hands over her head and kicking out. The bedside lamp lay smashed on the floor. Johnny grabbed her and pulled her hands away from her head. The terror on her face was unmistakable.

"Vickie, look at me, focus darling. You're alright, no one will hurt you here. *Vickie! Focus!*" Johnny lifted, the now violently shaking, Vickie up and put her on the bed; he lay down holding her and brushed her hair out of her eyes. Baby you're going to be alright, it was a dream, try to settle. Breathe darling, try to stop the panic, you're safe. I have you!"

"Best I go; she doesn't need me to see this!" Chris whispered, his face showing the pain he felt for his friend.

Johnny nodded, "can you shut the French windows first, please? There's a draught, Toph, thanks, for being here."

Chris nodded, did as he was asked then tiptoed out of the room. The others were outside in the large hallway. Lynne stood up, "we heard her screaming," she whispered. Chris fell into her arms and began to sob.

* * *

After a few minutes holding her, Johnny felt Vickie relax, she slept. This time he lay beside her. Each time she cried out during the night, he reassured her. It was a long night though and neither of them slept much.

After two sleepless nights, and at his wits end, Johnny called the counsellor he'd been seeing. She suggested she contact a psychotherapist who specialised in sexual trauma, and discuss Vickie with her. When the psychotherapist called him back, Johnny explained the situation. She agreed to see Vickie as an emergency private patient.

Johnny peeped into their bedroom; Vickie lay in an exhausted asleep. He studied the bruising on her face and neck which was now fading. He wondered if the emotional injuries would ever do the same.

CHAPTER

SEVENTEEN

They arrived at the Harley Street office of Stephania Van-Swartsnech shortly before the 4pm appointment. Vickie entered the consultation room alone. Johnny handed her the keyboard, she smiled, bent and kissed his cheek. He picked up a magazine, but the lack of sleep from the nights before caught up with him. He quickly fell into deep slumber. He was wakened by a tall blond woman, gently shaking him.

"Mr Vincent, Mr Vincent."

Johnny jumped up. "Sorry, I was so tired. It's been a rough few weeks."

"Mr Vincent, my name is Stephania, could you come through now? I need to go over some of the exercises I've given Vickie for you and her." Inside the consulting room Vickie sat in a chair; she looked calmer, and smiled at Johnny as he entered. Vickie reached over and took his hand as he sat down, entwining her fingers in his.

"Now, Mr Vincent!" Stephania said smiling.

"Please call me Johnny, Mr Vincent is my dad!"

The woman nodded. "I believe the trauma Vickie has suffered can be overcome but she needs your understanding and assistance. I've gone over some exercises with her that I would now like to show you, she tells me she's able to trust you. I will see her twice a week for the next six weeks; you need to accompany her to these appointments. Johnny, Vickie is coping a lot better than she or you think. She just needs help to develop a coping strategy. Not being able to speak is making it worse because she can't easily express her feelings. I believe that within a few months she will be able, with your help, to function again." Stephania looked at Vickie then turned her attention back to Johnny.

"What you have in your life Johnny, is a very strong little lady, a survivor; it's not just the trauma of the rape. It's a build-up of many things, probably starting with her relationship with her mother. The missing father, the attack by her father-in-law, the crash, the shock of the pregnancy and the traumatic birth, and now a violent rape by a man she trusted."

"It's a lot to deal with, isn't it?" Johnny sighed. He tightened his grip on Vickies hand, "can she, do it?"

Stephania looked at Vickie, nodded and smiled. "Vickie can and will deal with it all. She's a strong resilient woman. Most important, from what she tells me, is that she has a wonderful support network who'll be there for her. For the time being you must concentrate on making sure you're both rested. Over the next few weeks I'll work with you on coping mechanisms, and we'll replace all the bad thoughts with good ones. Working on your conscious thoughts will eventually impact on your unconscious ones." Stephania looked at Johnny. "Vickie never got time to deal with one trauma before another hit her. You need to help her, but Vickie, you need to help Johnny and the people around you deal with it too."

"I just want my life back; I want to feel normal again," the machine said.

"You will, I promise, but you need time, Vickie. It's only been four weeks, you haven't even healed physically yet. Mentally, you will take a lot longer to deal with what has happened to you." Stephania looked at them. "For now, I'm going to give you some couple exercises to do. You relaxing is important Vickie but you need to be a couple, relearn how to be intimate. I'll help you use a process called Sensate Focus; it involves, amongst other things, learning to touch each other again. You need to go right back to basics, talking to each other, allowing Johnny to touch you again. We'll work up to intimate touching. Of course, you being able to touch him is as important. Johnny sit in front of Vickie, look into her eyes, touch her face, her neck and shoulders."

Johnny did as he was asked, his eyes locked with Vickies.

"Good, good! Now let's try something else as a contrast? Vickie close your eyes, Johnny, stand behind her. Now Johnny, touch her head and massage it. Vickie, breathe deeply and relax. Enjoy his touch again. Remember when it was pleasurable for him to touch you?"

Johnny put his hands on Vickie's head and under instruction from Stephania he moved his hands through Vickie's hair and down to her neck.

Vickie suddenly opened her eyes. She shook her head. Tears pricked at her eyes and she began to hyperventilate.

"Vickie, breathe slowly and calmly, remember it's Johnny," Stephania said quietly. "Johnny when you do that, and she can't see you, you need to speak to her so she knows it is you." Stephania smiled at them both. "It will be easier when you're alone. Johnny the task is to massage her without it becoming sexual." Stefania looked at Johnny, "you must let her become used to you touching her again. Vickie, you try to do the same, get used to touching him. Just try it for a few minutes each day then add two minutes. When the bad pictures enter your head, replace it with good thoughts of Johnny and you. Johnny you're touching Vickie, making her feel good; put what you saw that night somewhere else. That's your homework for this week."

Johnny took Vickie's hand again; he raised it to his mouth and kissed her fingers. "We can do this babe," he whispered.

Stefania nodded at him then turned back to Vickie. "Vickie I want you to come in twice a week, once with Johnny and once on your own. Johnny, you continue to see your own counsellor. Ask her to call me? We'll synchronise your therapy. As I said, you must accompany Vickie even if you are not coming in for the session. As you've discovered, my waiting room is quite comfortable."

Vickie nodded and keyed into her tablet. "I feel calmer already Stephania, thank you."

"Now can you get your friends to call me Vickie, it sounds as though I could also help them."

"Chris and Andy," Vickie's machine said. "Jamie already has a counsellor, so does Lynne."

Johnny smiled and shook his head. "You'll have your work cut out with that pair, Stephania, they were pretty warped before this happened."

"I love a challenge Johnny."

They left the office, hand in hand, strolling in the spring sunshine. Johnny put his arm around Vickie and pulled her close, kissing the top of her head. "I love you Vickie." She looked up at him. "I love you too!" she mouthed. Back in the car, Vickie looked at Johnny. She lifted the machine and keyed in. Johnny waited, watching the concentration on her face. Vickie pressed the button and the machine began to speak.

"Johnny I've emailed Dania, asked her to come and see me. I need to speak to her about what happened to her. I also need to try to help sort things out between her and Andy. I can't go to Manchester, Johnny. So, I'm hoping she'll come here."

They were in bed when their phone rang, Vickie saw Dania's name come up. She handed the phone to Johnny, he answered and she watched him intently. "Dania, thanks for calling. How are you? Good, good babe, I'm glad." He looked at Vickie and smiled. "Vickie can't speak to you darling, we can't figure out how to link it the speech machine to the house phone. We're waiting for an engineer to come and sort it for us." "Meantime, she's using email and text. She has an app on her mobile, so you can use that but the response is pretty slow. She's doing okay Dania, but she really wants to see you. The others do too. I know Dania, he told me, but we'd all like to see you, it was a difficult time for all of us. Great Dania, thanks, it'll be good to see you.

Johnny smiled at Vickie, "tomorrow night, she's going to drive here. She'll call when she gets near London. She sounds good Vickie; she says it's been hard but she's having counselling and it's helping."

"We'd better let the others know, Andy especially, he really needs to apologise to her for what he said."

"He's done that Vickie, he wrote her a letter. They've spoken today; he's apologised, she's accepted. End of Vickie, it was a difficult time for us all."

* * *

Dania arrived as Annie was putting out the evening meal. Vickie smiled, typed a welcome into the machine, stood up and hugged the younger woman. Dania immediately burst into tears. "Perhaps you and Dania should have dinner upstairs in your quarters," Annie said quietly. "You go up and I'll bring your meals up to you."

Andy stood up, walked around the table and held out his arms to Dania. She moved towards him, he held her, tears in his eyes. "Go with Vickie sweetheart, I'll speak to you later," he said, kissing her forehead.

Upstairs in Vickie's sitting room, Dania looked at Vickie, still crying, she was unable to speak. Vickie reached over and wiped away the tears from the younger woman's face. She motioned to her to sit down then picked up the keyboard. Dania looked at her sadly, "Vickie the police told me what they did to me!"

Vickie nodded. "Dania, do you actually want the details?"

Dania shrugged, "I'm not sure Vickie. I know I was raped by all three of them. I know Tony took money for letting them do it. There's a film, the police have it. They offered to show me it, the film, but I'd be too embarrassed to watch. My counsellor says I should, but I don't think I will. I actually feel a lot better, now I know what happened. There's not really much else to say about it."

Vickie patted Dania's hand, "I think it's probably all about feeling you have control of yourself now. I feel guilty too Dania, they all told me not to introduce you to him and I didn't listen."

Dania shrugged, "Vickie, what I can't get out of my head is that if I had just spoken sooner to the police, you might not have had to go through all this. I blame myself, that's why I was so angry at Andy; he was saying what I was thinking."

Vickie tapped into her machine and then looked at Dania as the computer voice spoke. "Dania no, the only person responsible for this is Tony Gorman, he's the bad man here. There are other victims, mainly young girls. He abused Catriona and her little sister," Vickie's machine said. "Dania don't let this put you off men and sex. In a loving, mutual relationship, making love is a wonderful experience."

Dania smiled shyly, "I've been seeing Paddy again. He's come to visit me. He's so great Vickie. We haven't, you know, done it. I'm not ready for that yet, but when I am, it'll be with him. I hope you're okay with it, I love him Vickie."

Vickie smiled and hugged her friend, "I can't think of anyone I'd rather you were with, but my brother's a lucky guy too Dania," the machine said.

CHAPTER

EIGHTEEN

Vickie and Johnny sat together in Stephania's office. They had been seeing her twice a week for eight weeks. Three months had passed since the attack. Stephania smiled at them, looking from one to the other. "Well how did it go last week?"

Johnny looked at Vickie, he took her hand. "I managed to hold her until she fell asleep, she let me, without her heart beating like a drum. She cuddles me without me having to initiate it; we're sleeping naked again. The night terrors are greatly reduced; it's amazing."

"Still no sexual contact?"

They both shook their heads. Johnny smiled, "I want to again, so that's good, isn't it? Frustrating but good."

"I'm enjoying the massages, Stephania," Vickie said smiling at Johnny. "It's still difficult to lie face down, so I normally sit with my back to him and look up. I know when he's got a hardon though, the thought of it doesn't scare me as much now."

"Have you had your final gynaecological examination, Vickie? Is everything healing?"

Vickie nodded. She lifted her keyboard. "It was on Tuesday, I managed it because Johnny came in with me." She looked at him and smiled, "he held my hand. We did what you suggested

155

Stephania, practiced the breathing with him first. Then I just kept looking at him, whilst they did it. I managed, didn't panic when Lizzie touched me. Everything is good apparently." Vickie looked sadly at Stephania, "I was very tense when they put the speculum thing inside me and it was painful, but I suppose that's only to be expected. They did the anal one with a camera." She smiled at Johnny, "we don't have many secrets now do we babe?" she mouthed.

Johnny entwined his fingers in Vickie's then looked over at Stephania. "We're going to head down to Cornwall for a few days on our own. Vickie's brother is home; the boys are going to be with him and his girlfriend. My aunt is with the twins in Scotland for a few days, they're staying with my parents. We just got back, Vickie and I took them there."

"Did you speak to your parents-in-law?"

"Yes, it was difficult. I got into a right state but they understood." Johnny looked at Stephania and then shook his head, "they were pretty great about it."

"How do you feel now?"

"I feel Stephania . . . kind of feel we have permission to move on, to be happy together. We both still struggle, missing Billie and Ali at times but it doesn't feel wrong to be in love now."

"So, what now? Have you considered the next step? I know it feels clinical but you probably are ready to move your relationship on."

Johnny nodded. "We've borrowed a house in a very remote location, for the two of us. This will allow us to just chill, away from prying eyes. Our life is great. Living with our friends is a blast most of the time. The house, however, can be busy and with the kids as well, sometimes there's not a lot of privacy. Well, not the kind we need just now. We have other houses but we kind of think that we want to be somewhere new, different, special."

Vickie smiled at Johnny, then looked at Stephania, keying into the machine. "We kind of want to resume some kind of intimacy and want to be alone for a few days."

"Good, good!" Stephania said. "Now it's important you don't expect too much from each other, just take it at a pace you're both comfortable with. Talk to each other the way I showed you. Ask permission to touch her Johnny, tell her what you're doing. She'll be able to relax because her mind will keep telling her it's you. Now Vickie, I'll see you when?"

"We should be back in London, Tuesday evening; we have a meeting with my throat consultant and the plastic surgeon in town, first thing on Wednesday morning. Can I come in after that?"

CHAPTER

NINETEEN

"It's beautiful here, I've never been to Cornwall; it's sort of rugged and wild." Johnny drove along the coastal road following the directions on the satnav. He turned off the main road onto what looked like a farm track.

Vickie smiled and tapped into the keyboard. "Billy and I came here about three years ago, with Chris. Not long after we moved down South. We were watching a programme about Cornwall one night, Billy and Chris were drinking. We decided to just go, it was all a bit mad. Billy wanted to paint a sunrise. In the end, the three of us just piled into my car and we came down to Newquay." She smiled at the memory, "we sneaked out without Arfur."

Johnny smiled and looked sideways at her, "you are brilliant with that keyboard now babe."

Vickie nodded and keyed in again, "I know! Anyway, Cornwall, Billy and I fell out because I realised when we got there they had, at some point in the journey, taken acid. He'd promised me after Denis's birth he wouldn't do it again. I was so angry I drove home and left them there."

"I remember that, I didn't realise it was in Cornwall! Arfur had to go and get them. You drove off with their jackets and wallets." Johnny smiled. "You have a very determined nature when it suits you."

158

Vickie smiled remembering, "I went the long way back to London because I realised Tony would send out a search party. I ended up visiting Buckfast Abbey; mainly because I needed to pee." Vickie giggled as the computer voice continued, "would you believe one of the monks recognised me, so they invited me to lunch." Vickie nudged Johnny, as a house came into view at the end of the track. "This looks like the picture Johnny, look there it is, it's beautiful."

"Wow! How did you find this?" Johnny asked looking around him.

"Marnie; she knows the daughter of the owner, Jamie and her came here for a long weekend. When I said we needed somewhere private, they recommended it." She smiled, "its for sale, and Jamie wants to buy it."

The house sat on top of a cliff. The waves of the wild Cornish sea battered against the rocks below. It was remote, miles off the beaten track. Johnny parked his new Mercedes, and they went inside.

Johnny gasped as they walked around the house. "It's fantastic sweetheart, well done Marnie for finding it." The house was large, modern and spacious, with a glass front which looked out over the cliffs to the sea.

Johnny insisted Vickie rested as he made dinner for them both. Vickie sat with a glass of wine watching him unload the groceries and begin to make the meal. He lit a fire in the living room inglenook fireplace and they sat at the dining table looking out to sea.

"That was a lovely dinner Johnny, can't remember the last time I finished a meal," Vickie's machine said. She keyed into the machine smiling, "you should cook more."

"Aye! Like Annie would let me into her kitchen, although it was her who taught me to cook in the first place." He stood up, "let's get a comfy seat." They moved over to the sofa in front of the now roaring fire, and sat down. Johnny wrapped his arms around Vickie, his lips brushed across the top of her head. Vickie stretched, turned around and kissed his cheek. He kissed her lips, pushing her hair back from her face. "You're so beautiful my darling, I want so much to hold you. Can I?" Vickie nodded. He pulled her around so she had her back to him and she rested her head against his chest, her head tilted so she could see him. His arms circled her; she could feel his breath on her neck.

She shivered as he kissed her, she felt relaxed, having consumed a few glasses of wine. His hands moved up, he pushed her slightly forward and began to massage her shoulders through her clothes. Vickie unbuttoned her shirt to allow him access to her bare shoulders, she relaxed against him. He moved his hands gently to her breast over her bra. Vickie shivered feeling her nipples tingle as johnny's hands moved across the thin material. "Can I touch them Vickie?"

She swallowed hard, looked up at him then nodded. He slid his hand into her bra and cupped her right breast. His fingers began to play with her nipple, she shivered at his touch.

Vickie leaned back and put her hand over his. He began to kiss her neck and shoulders, rolling her around so she was facing him. With his free hand he unclipped the bra. Looking at his face, her fingers shaking, she loosened the buttons of his plaid shirt; a few seconds later they lay skin touching skin. Vickie smiled as he kissed her face, her neck, then moved gently down. His lips closed over her nipple and she moaned softly as he rolled his tongue around and then began to gently nibble with his teeth.

"I've wanted to do that for months but I was sharing you with the babies!" he whispered, his voice hoarse. "Now they're all mine. Christ, you're beautiful Vickie." Still with her nipple in his mouth he moved his hand down and loosened the button and zip of her jeans. He looked up at her. "Can I touch you?" She gulped and nodded. He slid his hand down and gently rubbed with his finger, still kissing around her breasts. She felt shivers of excitement, through her body.

Vickie's hand moved to the zip of his jeans. Taking a deep breath, she unzipped them and slid her hand inside. She began to rub his now erect penis and he gasped. "God Vickie, I want you so much but I'm scared I'll hurt you."

Vickie shivered as he touched her, his middle finger moved gently but firmly in a circular motion. He felt her move her hips towards his hand. His mouth left her nipple and moved upwards, finding her mouth he kissed her gently. Vickie, feeling butterflies in her groin, moved away from him and stood up. She pulled him to his feet. Kissing his chest, she slid his jeans down over his hips before removing her own.

Naked, she led him over to the fluffy rug in front of the fire and lay down looking up at him. Johnny groaned and dropped to his knees beside her. "Vickie, are you sure babe? I can wait."

She looked into his eyes and smiled. "I know, you've been really patient with me, but I don't think I can," she mouthed. "I need to know; I want you so much right now!"

Johnny lay beside her and began to kiss her. Still rubbing her intimately, he took her hand and placed it on his penis. "That's what you do to me babe, I'm hot and bothered and I want you." In response, she kissed him, her tongue probing in his mouth. Johnny began to touch her, his fingers gently probed, Vickie gasped, she moved her hips against his hand.

Johnny moved slightly and sat upright on the rug. He pulled Vickie towards him; she straddled him, looking up at him, kissing him. "Stephania said to try this position first." he whispered. He tried to penetrate her, but she cried out in pain.

Seeing the disappointment on her face he kissed her cheek. "Babe it's all right, remember, Stephania warned us this might happen. What did she call it, Vagi something?"

"Vaginismus," Vickie mouthed.

"Baby, it'll be alright," Johnny said gently. "At least you were able to let me touch you. I was sure you would find that more difficult." Johnny grinned. "Now, I have you naked on a rug in front of a roaring fire. You trusting me with your body again, well that's better than sex. Stephania and Meg, my counsellor, they've gone through sexual respect with me. Vickie it'll take time, but we're further than we thought we'd be. I brought the lubricant Stefania suggested but I would rather try something else first."

"Johnny, I have all the desire, but my body won't let me."

He put his finger to her lips. "You do know you said that out loud? It's great to hear your voice again but Charlie said, no matter what, resist until you see him again."

Vickie stood up; she threw another log onto the fire and replaced the fireguard. When she turned around, Johnny was placing cushions on the floor. She lay down beside him. He pulled a soft velour throw from the couch and covered them both, the material soft and warm against their skin. He began to kiss her again, his tongue probed as he did. "Can I go down on you Vickie? I'll stop if you find it uncomfortable. I have to try to give you pleasure again. Make your mind and body remember how good it feels when we're together." She nodded and lay back. He kissed his way down her body, using his tongue in feather-light movements. His right hand reached up and he rubbed her nipple between his finger and thumb, his left hand parted her legs.

Vickie focused on his right shoulder watching his distinctive tattoo sleeve. She relaxed, enjoying the sensation. Initially she thought nothing was going to happen. Johnny persevered, gradually Vickie felt a familiar stirring in her groin. Her head telling her this was Johnny, her eyes on the tattoo, she began to respond to him. Arching her back she cried out, moaning and gasping as she began to climax. She grabbed his head with both hands, holding him to her, as she let herself feel the pleasure of her orgasm. Her body tightened as she relaxed into the sensation, crying out again as the next wave pulsated through her.

He held her afterwards as she sobbed, gently stroking her hair and kissing her. "I never thought I would ever get you to orgasm like that again." Johnny moved around so he was looking at her, "I could feel it in my mouth; it was like electricity surging through you." She nodded and held on to him, tears running freely down her face. Johnny pulled up the throw covering them both. They lay not speaking, neither of them wanting to break the spell.

Together they watched the dying embers of the fire. "Vickie!" Johnny whispered, "I love you darling, will you marry me?" She looked up at him and nodded. He kissed her forehead. "I'll never let anything or anyone hurt you, or come between us again Vickie." He smiled as he realised she had closed her eyes and was already drifting towards sleep.

Johnny wakened before Vickie, still on the rug, still with her in his arms. She had turned around during the night, her head now rested on his chest, his arms wrapped around her front. He stretched his neck and looked at her face; she looked more content and relaxed than she had done in months. He kissed her gently, moving away from her. Vickie rolled over, still asleep, she moaned softly and relaxed.

Johnny stood up. Taking a throw from the chair and wrapping it around himself, he padded through to the kitchen, shivering as his bare feet touched the cold slate tiles. He switched on the kettle then made coffee, taking the mug outside to the patio where he lit a cigarette. He exhaled deeply, blowing out the smoke, watching it rise above him and disperse.

It was a beautiful, early summer morning. At peace with the world, Johnny listened to the sound of the waves crashing off the rocks below. For the first time in three months, it felt good to be alive. He looked up smiling, as Vickie came out onto the patio wearing his discarded plaid shirt and her suede Ugg boots, her hair tousled and sticking up. "You look like a hippy, surfing chick! You just need a pair of denim cut offs." She sat down on his knee and kissed his lips. Johnny smiled. "Good morning wife to be!" he whispered. She grinned at him and held up her left hand pointing at her ring finger.

"Oh, so you want a ring, do you?"

Vickie nodded.

"Well we better go do some shopping then. Truro or Newquay?"

Vickie shook her head and raised her hands. "London!" she mouthed. "Bigger diamonds there!" Vickie stood up and disappeared through to the kitchen, she returned a few minutes later with a mug of coffee and her keyboard. Putting the mug down on the small table, she carefully typed into her keyboard and pressed the speak button.

Johnny smiled at the concentration on her face, her tongue poking out from her lips. The electronic voice began to speak. "Johnny, I love you so much. I want to be your wife more than I've ever wanted anything. I don't really need a ring, it doesn't matter. I know, and you know, this is the real thing. I want to be with you forever. Let's just enjoy the moment and be together. By the way, you're a fantastic lover. But, if you ever lose your tongue in a weird accident, then I'm leaving you." She looked at him and grinned as the voice continued, "I never thought I could be this happy again, ever, thank you." Vickie stood up and knelt in front of him, moving the blanket away to expose his body. She began to stroke his penis, bringing him to climax a few moments later, never taking her eyes away from his face.

They spent the day walking along the beach, collecting shells, running in and out of the water. They ate dinner in a little restaurant by the harbour of the nearest village. The elderly couple serving in the restaurant didn't recognise them. They sat by the window, comfortable and content, watching the boats bobbing about within the sheltered cove. When bedtime came, they slept soundly in each other's arms.

The next few days passed quickly, they travelled around the area slipping in and out of attractions unnoticed. Although they made a striking looking couple, sunglasses and hats helped them to mingle unnoticed in the crowds in the Eden Project. They wandered around the Lost Gardens of Heligan and walked along the cliff top at Newquay watching the surfers. They ate ice cream in little parlours along the coast, and drank hot chocolate by roaring fires. Vickie left the keyboard in the house; she refrained from speaking but did not need words to communicate.

At night, they lay in bed, content to be together. Vickie managed to sleep without a light for the first time since she was attacked. On their last night, they lit a fire in the pit behind the house, and sat in front of it. Johnny pulled Vickie close, his arms around her. She rested her head on his chest, looked up and began typing, the machine spoke. "Johnny I don't want to go home!"

"What?"

"I want you to go get the children, we'll stay here."

"Vickie I'll do anything you want; live anywhere with you. Nothing matters anymore, not the band, the house, the money. Nothing matters, except you and our four kids. Vickie, we don't need to go back home sweetheart. Why don't we look for a house here, or buy this if that's what you really want?"

She smiled and nodded, the keyboard spoke. "That way we can escape whenever we want to and still keep Brickstead too." She smiled and spoke to him. "Johnny I don't want to leave the band; I want us to carry on. I just needed to know you would go anywhere with me, if I asked you. The band has always been your dream."

Johnny looked back at her. "Not as much as you are babe. Nothing will change when we go back Vickie. I love you, and I want us to go into town to look for an engagement ring on Wednesday. We are going to be engaged Vickie, and we are not going to keep it a secret either. We've done nothing to be ashamed of, now Liz and Bobby know about us we don't need to hide." Johnny stood up and motioned to her with his head. He poured her a second glass of wine and carried it through to the bathroom. Vickie followed him, candles lit the room and the spa bath bubbled. Johnny pulled her into his arms. "I thought it might be fun to just chill in the bath." Vickie nodded, her robe dropped on to the floor, and she stepped into the tub. "Your body is exquisite Vickie," he whispered, as he removed his own clothes then followed her. "You have beautiful little dimples right on the cheeks of your arse."

The water bubbled all around them, they finished their wine; Vickie poured them a third glass from the ice bucket beside the bath. As Johnny sipped from the glass, she leaned back against his chest.

Vickie shivered with delight as Johnny kissed her neck and shoulders, running his hands over her upper body. She pulled herself around to face him. Straddling him, Vickie began kissing his face, her tongue explored his mouth, and her hands gripped his head as he pulled her towards him and took her nipple in his mouth. Vickie reached down and held his now erect penis in her hand. Taking a deep breath, she moved forward and pushed down. Johnny gasped as he felt himself slide inside her. "Vickie, babe, we've done it." He began to kiss her passionately. She responded, pushing her hips down onto his lap. He gently held her face in his hands, as his lips met hers again his arms wrapped around her holding her to him. "It's over; babe it's over, we did it. God, I love you, I love you, Vickie."

Excitement mounting, Vickie began to tremble. She gasped as she climaxed a few seconds before him. The water bubbled around them; she remained sitting on his lap, their arms wrapped around each other, his penis inside her, enjoying the sensation. "It's been too long," she whispered in his ear.

CHAPTER

TWENTY

C harlie Eskdale smiled as Vickie sat back down after her scan. "It's looking good Vickie, you've done well. Have you tried to speak?"

Vickie and Johnny nodded.

"Was her voice the same, Johnny?

"Yeah pretty much, maybe a bit huskier, still really sexy though."

Charlie put his hand on her throat, Vickie jumped to her feet. "Vickie I forgot, I'm so sorry. You're so calm now, it's easy to forget what you've been through."

"Sorry!" she mouthed.

"It was totally my fault Vickie. I need to put my hand on your throat and upper chest to try this. I want you to say something, when I do that."

Vickie smiled, looking at Johnny then back at Charlie. She nodded, and taking a deep breath she relaxed, as Charlie put his hand on her upper chest.

"Okay Vickie, now!"

"Sorry I jumped Charlie. I still get a bit of a fright, when someone touches me without warning. Good old fight or flight is still in there. Tactile people are my worst nightmare now."

"Wonderful, wonderful, Vickie, you're going to be healed a

lot quicker than we thought. I can't see any scar tissue on the scan either; you've been a very lucky lady. I would like you to rest your voice for about twenty hours a day now. I'll still see you every couple of weeks. No singing for a month, then practice an hour a day max, for about four weeks."

"What about going on tour?" Johnny asked.

"When?"

"Last week in October and all of November. Fifteen dates over five weeks."

Charlie made a face. "Ideally folks I would like to see you do half that amount in the timeframe? I would also have recommended you wait till into next year. Are you playing indoors?"

"No stadiums. All outdoors, why?"

"Air conditioning inside could do damage. If you're outside and can cut down, ideally one venue a week and rest a lot, you should be okay! Do you want me to speak to Simon?"

Vickie shook her head. "Simon leaves the decisions up to us. We want to do Australia and New Zealand this year if we can, even if it's limited. Johnny and I are getting married. We want to end this year as husband and wife. Then we're going to take a break for a while. Stop touring for a few years, concentrate on the family. I missed so much when my eldest two were small, due to work. It's going to be different with the twins. We haven't told anyone yet, but we will soon."

"I'm really happy for you both." Charlie looked at the young couple, "you've come through so much to get here."

"I never thought I could ever be this happy again Charlie."

"But you are, happy?"

Vickie nodded, "I sure am." She looked at Johnny, took his hand, smiling up at him.

He smiled back and then grinned at Charlie, unable to stop smiling. He took the doctors outstretched hand and shook it.

"You are a very lucky man, Mr Vincent,"

"Oh, I know!"

"Vickie, use the machine the rest of today," Charlie said

smiling, "your voice appears to be fine on all the readings, but let's just ease in gradually. It's still only thirteen weeks since it happened, so you've lots of time. You'll need a voice coach. I would suggest Evie Green, she's worked with my patients before. She's not cheap but the results are worth it. I would have you start singing around the start of July and then build up. October should be doable if you take care. Rest your voice in between rehearsals and see me weekly again once you start, so I can monitor you. Your face looks as good as new Vickie. Ricky has done a great job." He looked at her closely. "You can't see the lip ones, unless you are up close and look for it."

Vickie smiled. She reached over and hugged Charlie, he smiled back at her.

"Where are you off to now?"

"We've an appointment with Ricky, then the psychotherapist," Johnny said quietly.

"Is it helping, the psychotherapy?" Charlie asked.

Vickie nodded.

"Great Vickie, you're a young woman and you need to get your life back." She nodded again and smiled.

"Well?" Stephania asked, as Vickie sat down. "Your few days away have obviously done you some good."

Vickie blushed, Johnny took her hand.

"Johnny?" Stephania said, looking at Vickie and smiling.

"We managed to be intimate; she did have that Vagi thingy."

"Vaginismus! Did you overcome it?"

"Well we didn't at first really, we improvised." He poked his tongue out.

Vickie's blushed scarlet and Johnny laughed. Stephania looked at Vickie as Johnny kissed her cheek. "Sorry babe, I was just so pleased I was able to give you pleasure. She slept all night that night without any night terrors too Stephania. In fact, there was only one bad night each the whole time, and on the same night. I'm sure it had something to do with the oysters we ate that day though."

169

Stephanie looked at Vickie and sighed. "We need to talk about these things Vickie. Did she get embarrassed before Johnny?"

He looked into Vickie's eyes, as he answered. "Sometimes but usually not."

Vickie lifted her keyboard. "Making me feel like an experiment, thanks Johnny!! I didn't get embarrassed about sex before I was raped Stephania, it was the most natural thing in the world to me." Her eyes filled with tears.

Stephania looked at them both. "Your perception of sex as being something you controlled has changed Vickie because of what happened to you, it will take time. As time passes, you'll find it natural again. Oral sex is a great compromise; it requires more intimacy than intercourse actually."

"It's also the one thing the rapist did not do to me," Vickie keyed into her board. "I appear to be fine, and able to relax, if I can see it's Johnny doing things to me. When he went down on me," she blushed, and looked at her feet, "I focused on his tattoo."

"Did you try to have intercourse again?" Stephania asked.

Johnny nodded. "Not right away. We just did all the exercises, the massage and stimulating. We did normal things, a bit of sightseeing, ate some lovely meals, just relaxed. We didn't do anything else intimate for a few days, well there was a lot of kissing and touching and she wanked me." Vickie looked at him and made a face. "Sorry Stephania, I'm not good at the technical terms. She masturbated me!"

Vickie's machine spoke, "I couldn't perform oral Stephania. I panic when I try because I can't see it's him. The first thing the rapist did when he got me in that room was put his penis in my mouth." Tears welled up in her eyes, she looked at the ground. "He was not gentle; I thought I was going to choke. I was so scared; does that make sense? When I tried to do it, you know? Give him oral, well it all came back!

"That's a common reaction, after the type of trauma you suffered, you're focusing on the start of the attack. Believe it or not that's a good sign, you're working through it. How does that make you feel? Hearing that, Johnny?"

"Great actually, if I'm honest. I know she trusts me. It's the not being able to see it is me that frightens her, I get that."

Vickie sighed, "I so want to be totally relaxed, able to just do everything I could before. We had a very active sex life, but we had only been having sex for seven weeks when it happened." She looked over at Johnny and then at Stephania. "It was all fairly new, but oral was something we both enjoyed."

Johnny squeezed Vickie's hand and smiled. "I can wait for that. Someday, you'll manage it. You'll know when you're ready."

"Did you have intercourse, then?"

"Oh yes!" Johnny said, smiling as he remembered. "On our last night, we got in the Jacuzzi. She made the first move and we did it!"

"You had full intercourse? Was it girl on top? Was it enjoyable?" Stephania asked.

They both nodded.

"It was maybe not as intense as it has been before, but, it was lovely. We both enjoyed it." Vickie smiled shyly, still holding Johnny's hand, "the oral, however, nearly blew my brains out when I climaxed. It means we know it can happen the way it was before. Johnny and I . . . are, such sexual beings."

Johnny, wrapped his arm around her, pulled her close kissing the top of her head. "I don't care babe. I'll be there, no matter what!"

"Vickie, you're doing great; you are definitely my star pupil." Stephania laughed. "Johnny for such a young man, you have a great grasp of Vickie's needs, well done you. I'd like to make a change in the next appointment. I want to see you both, but separately! Are you okay with that Johnny?"

"Yeah, are you going to teach me how to say proper words?"

"No, I was going to teach you how to be intimate with someone who has Vaginismus! But you appear to have worked that out for yourself. It will, however, come back. It most definitely will be a feature sometimes. So, there are other techniques."

"If you don't mind, I would still want to learn that." He grinned, "I want to be a sexpert!"

Stephania smiled. "We're going to talk about how you feel. I'm impressed by your reactions Johnny, but this must be frustrating for you. I know you're still seeing your counsellor, but I'd like one or two sessions with you on your own. On your way out folks, can you remind my receptionist that Tuesday's appointment is a double one?"

"How's it going with my brother Stephania?" Johnny asked, as he stood up to leave.

"I couldn't possibly comment."

"We're very different."

"Are you? I think you want the same things, but just come at it from different angles. He's doing well Johnny, him and Andy, they both make me laugh." Stephania smiled, "I asked them to come in together, and they brought Jamie with them, it was surreal. I don't remember when I have ever laughed so much."

"They're murder together!" Vickie said, smiling and shaking her head, "you should have seen them before. They've all grown up in the last year or so."

"They're lovely boys," Stephania replied, "so not what I expected."

Outside in the sunshine, Johnny put his arm around Vickie. "Now I want to take you for a late lunch, then shopping."

"Where are, we going?"

"Vickie, Charlie said rest your voice, so shut up!"

"But!"

"No buts, babe, do as you are told, just for once!"

Vickie smiled and held up her left hand.

"Oh yes, we have an appointment at Cartier too!" They got into the car. "Vickie what are you doing?" Vickie put her finger to his lips. She slid her hand inside his t-shirt, pulling it back, to expose the elaborate tattoo on his chest and upper arm. Then she took his hand and pointed to his ring finger and then hers.

"Oh, I get you! You want us to get a ring tattoo." She nodded. "You sure?"

Vickie smiled and nodded.

"I'm a traditionalist Vickie. I really want to buy you a ring and I want to wear one too."

Vickie smiled and then spoke, "well what if we do rings as well? I want a permanent sign of our relationship. One that's just yours and mine!"

Johnny looked thoughtful. "We can go visit Sid the Needle. You need to stop speaking Vickie. You heard what Charlie said. Let's agree on a compromise? You stop speaking for at least today. I'll take you to Sid's, but we need to get the rings first!"

CHAPTER
TWENTY-ONE

Everyone was around the breakfast table, Andy looked up from his newspaper as Johnny and Vickie joined them. "Thought you two were at hospital appointments yesterday?" You were very late back."

Vickie smiled, and keyed into her machine. "We went out for dinner then went to Ricci's. We were celebrating."

"What?"

"We were celebrating," Vickie's machine repeated.

"He means, what were we celebrating Vickie? Well, tell them." Johnny folded his arms watching her grinning.

"I came."

"Came where? Fuck! I get it!" Andy laughed.

Johnny shook his head. "Fuck sake Vickie, you are worse than them, is nothing sacred? You didn't get embarrassed there though! Tell them what we were really celebrating."

She looked at him and smiled. *"You came!"* the machine said.

Annie bustled through with a plate of bacon and eggs, she placed it in front of Andy. She pulled the newspaper and threw it away, "I've told you before about reading at the table, it's rude!" Doug, a slice of toast in his hand, came through behind her and sat down. "Do you two want a cooked breakfast?" Annie asked Vickie.

Vickie shook her head. She lifted the coffee pot and poured some in a mug.

"What was that about celebrating?" Doug grinned at Johnny, "not sure I want to know from whence you arrived, so let's stick to a safe subject!"

Johnny put his arm around Vickie. "I asked her to marry me, she said yes." He put a small leather box on the table. "What can I say I'm old fashioned; she can't wear it yet!" He opened the box and passed it to his brother. Andy and Jamie leaned over and looked in.

Andy let out a long low whistle. "Is it a sapphire?"

"It's a strange shade of blue, what is it?" Annie asked, sitting down next to Vickie and looking at the ring.

"It's a blue diamond set in platinum, quite rare, and very expensive. Well he's worth a few million, he can stretch to an expensive engagement ring, I'm worth it," Vickie's machine said. She raised her head smiling and looking around the table.

"Fuck it's big!" Chris gasped, smiling slyly. "Must have been some shag you got bro."

"This is mine," Johnny said, opening a second box with the same colour stone set in a signet ring.

"What's wrong with your finger?" Chris asked, pointing at the white dressing covering Johnny's ring finger. Vickie held up her left hand. "You too? What have you been up to? Some tribal initiation thing?"

"We went to see Sid, got these." Johnny gingerly pulled off the dressing. Andy squinted to read it. Victoria was tattooed in a spiral around his finger.

Chris lifted Vickie's hand, pulled off the white bandage and looked. "Jonathon," he read. "Your fingers are freakishly small, but it's beautiful, and it's what it means that's important."

"Wow, it's great guys!" Jamie said smiling. "Very original Sunday names too. How did Sid manage to fit you two in? He said he couldn't do mine until next month."

"We're special clients, it didn't take long. He was so stoked at Vickie coming in with me, he let us come back after he closed the shop. It's actually our own signatures and he just traced them and did them. He filmed it for that TV programme he's involved with. It won't go out until next year anyway. Vickie's going back to get the marks on her breasts tattooed over. Ricky reckons it will be less painful than anything he can do."

Jamie grinned at them. "You're going to let Sid touch your tits Vickie? He'll love that, he's a wee bit obsessed with you. He said he drew you for a tattoo some guy asked for. He liked it so much he did it on his own thigh."

"He showed us Jamie," Johnny said grinning, "he's going to do that one on me too." He put his hand over his heart, "right here."

"You're a fucking big sap," Andy sniggered.

"Does it hurt?" Marnie asked, "I want a tattoo, but I'm scared I won't be able to take the pain. I love the one on your thigh Vickie. I think I'd like something like that. Was it sore?"

Vickie turned her hands over, smiled and shook her head.

"So, you're getting hitched?" Jamie asked grinning at Vickie. "Can I come too?"

"Marnie slap him!" Vickie's machine said.

Chris nudged Johnny, "Mum and Dad are here by the way; they came back with Annie. They've gone into town to the soft-play with Laura, Arfur and the kids."

"Is she still angry at me, Toph?"

"I'm sure you will find a way of placating her bro, you always were her favourite son."

"Only because I'm the sensible one, Toph."

"Oh aye, I think getting someone pregnant, not knowing you actually pumped her because you were out your face, then not telling Mum she's a granny for six months, is right up there with my worst behaviour."

Annie stood up. "If she ever finds out how long I knew about the babies being yours Johnny, I'm in deep shit! There's something I need to talk to you two boys about before her and your dad come back." Annie looked nervously at Vickie and nodded.

"I'll go and make a start on the washing up!" Doug said,

standing up and gathering up the breakfast plates. Vickie noted he winked at Annie as he did, and Annie blushed.

Vickie looked up and typed into the machine. "No time like the present Annie, go up to our sitting room, there's no one up there."

"What's going on Vickie?" Jamie asked, after the door closed behind them.

Vickie shrugged. "Just wait and see, all will be revealed," her keyboard said. "Now come down to the studio and play me your new song Andy, Johnny says it's great."

When Johnny and Chris came into the studio, they looked emotional. Johnny looked at Vickie. "Did you tell them?"

She shook her head. "Not my tale to tell Johnny," the keyboard said.

"Fuck Vickie, I never saw that one coming. She says she told you while you were in the hospital. Thank you for supporting her."

"You're not angry at me then, for not telling you about it?" Vickie asked. She hugged Chris and kissed his cheek, before wrapping her arms around Johnny and holding him. "She had to be ready emotionally, to speak to you two; she and Connie had to work it out first."

"Of course not! Poor Annie; what a terrible thing to happen," Chris said sadly, "I always wondered about her, you know? Why there was no man, she's a really attractive woman isn't she?"

"What?" Jamie cried, "what's going on now? It's like fucking East Enders in here."

Chris smiled, his eyes moist. "Annie isn't our Auntie, she's our Grandmother. She had our Mum when she was 14, the result of a rape apparently. She only told Mum the truth after it happened to Vickie. She got talking to Mhairi at the hospital and decided it had been a secret too long."

"Fuck how many more women are going to admit to being raped? There are dirty, bastard, men out there," Jamie gasped. "I didn't think I knew any women who it had happened to them, and there are three just in our circle, and your Mhairi too Andy. It happened to her, didn't it?"

"Three out of four women will be sexually abused or assaulted, in some form in their lifetime Jamie," Vickie's machine said. "Not a lot of people want to know that. I want to do something to raise awareness of sexual assault. When the trial is over, I think we should start organising a benefit concert."

"We can consider it when we come back from down under," Johnny replied, watching her.

"We're going to Australia then?" Andy asked.

"When?" Jamie sighed, "hope it's not in their summer, I hate the sun! Might as well just toss me in butter and put me on the hotplate."

Johnny smiled and wiped away a tear, he looked at Vickie. "Well, Jamie mate, you'd better invest in some Factor 50, I'm sorry but we reckon about mid-October if Vickie's voice keeps healing. It was provisionally booked when we cancelled in February. We saw Charlie yesterday; he says Vickie's throat is almost back to normal. He thinks by July she'll be able to sing again in a limited way and then by August, it should be alright for her to begin rehearsals. By the autum we'll be able to work again we reckon, if we did just eight concerts over six weeks."

"That's quite a long drawn out tour, Johnny!" Andy observed, "but at least we won't be doing the usual four planes, two cities same day, thing."

Vickie nodded, "Quite a bit of travel but a lot of downtime. One a week mostly: Wellington, Christchurch, Darwin, Perth, Alice Springs, Melbourne and then two in Sidney probably." She grinned, "we can just make it like a big holiday. Financially we will just about breakeven but we will have fulfilled our obligations."

"It means Vickie won't over-stretch her voice though." Johnny looked at the others. "We saw Simon and Sam whilst we were in town. Simon called the promoters; they are just desperate to get us out there. It's up to you lot though. We need to talk about it together first.

Vickie smiled and pressed her machine. "We are also looking at two weeks in Dubai to rehearse guys. So, we'd be away most of October and all November. When we get back, we have a break for a few months from recording, and a big break from touring."

Johnny smiled at his friends, "Simon reckons we'll rehearse better away from here."

"Be good to get back on the road!" Andy said smiling.

Johnny gasped. "You were moaning you didn't want to tour again, Andy."

"I always forget how much I hate it when we're not doing it," Andy laughed, "but this sounds more like a holiday."

"After this, it needs to be a couple of years before we do it again. You were right Andy, we've been over exposed," Chris sighed.

"I'm actually looking forward to this one. It's like a comeback and farewell tour." Andy put his arm around Vickie and smiled, kissing her head. "It means, folks, we are all going to be okay."

"What you going to do about the boys Vickie? I thought you didn't want them missing school?" Chris asked.

"Tutor!" Vickie mouthed.

"School says if we pay for a tutor, we can take them out. Vickie has arranged to take one of James teachers, and pay for her and her replacement for five weeks," Johnny said smiling.

You two have been busy," Jamie said smiling, "I'm impressed. What are you going to do about getting married? Are you having a wedding?"

"Ah well, we are just going to fuck off for a few days, do it. We don't want a big deal, just me and Vickie and a registrar some-where." Johnny looked at Vickie, who nodded.

Andy stood up, he looked at Vickie, "I'm going to go upstairs and see Annie. What the counselling has done is make me face things head on. Any more news you want to share?"

Vickie smiled. "Best news is that I can speak for four hours a day from now on."

"Vickie, you spoke! God, it's great to hear your voice again, although I quite like the Siri thing too, very sexy," Jamie sighed. "Can you give the machine to Marnie when you are finished with it?"

Johnny started keying in to the machine. "Fuck me Jamie, you ginger stud! Fuck me big boy. Ooohh Marnie you're hot. Marnie, you are so out of my league," the electronic voice said.

"Like you can talk about a woman being out of your league! I'm sure Vickie got a bump on the head or something when you got together Jovi," Jamie cried.

"She was fucking drugged, and thought he was someone else," Andy gasped.

CHAPTER

TWENTY-TWO

"They say this is definitely the best time of year to see Australia, it's not going to be too hot, it's spring and early summer," Marnie said, as she brought Vickie and Lynne a drink. Vickie looked around, "where did Dania go?"

"We met your brother at the bar, she went off with him. Some story about a missing bangle," Marnie laughed.

"Sounds awfully like one of the stories you and Jamie used to tell us. When you didn't think we all knew you were doing it Marnie," Lynne said grinning.

Vickie smiled and sighed. "His leave finishes tomorrow; he's flying to Cyprus tonight. She won't see him for eight weeks. So, I would imagine they will have a lot of goodbyes to say. I used to be like that when I was going on tour without Billy. We once did it in the hall of the Chelsea flat, while the car was outside waiting for me."

"Where were the kids?" Marnie gasped, "was that the time we were going to Japan? You said you got caught short, with a dodgy tummy?"

Vickie shrugged, "don't know, might have been. It's strange; we used to do things like that all the time. When he was leaving Vegas, I was pissed off with him over something silly, we didn't. I went out to rehearsal and just . . . if I'd known it was the last time I'd see him? Oh, I need to stop thinking bad thoughts. Johnny's the same. He fell out with Ali just before he left because she didn't want to travel. Then argued with her on the phone the week before the crash, for the same reason."

Lynne moved over and put her arm around Vickie. Wiping a tear from her friend's cheek, she whispered, "we all miss them babe but we've got to get on with life. Now stop all this maudlin stuff, you and Jovi have something special now! You both need to look to the future."

Vickie nodded, "we just don't want them to be forgotten."

"They won't be. You know that. Happy thoughts Vickie, think them now!" Lynne moved over to her own bed and picked up her Kindle.

The three women were lying on the beach in Dubai, Vickie rolled over on to her front and picked up her glass. Lynne looked over at her. "The tattoo looks beautiful Vickie, when you said you were getting the marks covered I had doubts."

Vickie smiled and looked down. Sid had made the tattoo a feature, with lilies joined together by intertwining delicate green stems. It stretched from her breasts on both sides, joined together around her back, then wound around her lower abdomen where a small but colourful phoenix, copied from Billy's painting in their lounge, rose out of the leaves covering her caesarean scar. "It was painful but I love it. Poor Johnny had to sit through it with me for all those sessions, holding my hand, letting me see his face so Sid could work on me."

"Marnie giggled, "Jamie and Andy kept asking Sid what your boobs were like." Chris was trying to pretend he wasn't interested."

"What did Sid say?"

Marnie and Lynne giggled. "A work of art!" Lynne laughed.

"You really do look good in a bikini Vickie!" Marnie added. She looked down the beach, "this is a fantastic place. I've always wanted to see Dubai, so that's two things off the wish list; Dubai and a tattoo."

"Vickie sighed. "I still can't believe you all got tattoos.

Especially you two, Lynne you always said it would limit your work potential. Marnie, you were scared!"

"Ah, it was quite easy actually," Marnie replied. "And, because we are here on the beach, I get to show it off!"

"Two weeks here for rehearsal," Vickie lay back on the bed. "I think I love Simon, fantastic setting."

"Well, you'd better start rehearsing!" Lynne said, pushing up her sunglasses and lifting her watch. "The boys said you'd to meet them at two, and it's ten past one now."

"They'll be late, they were having a poker competition. We've two weeks to rehearse anyway." Vickie stood up and lifted her sarong. "I suppose I'd better move myself, although they always need more rehearsal than me anyway."

"Look, speak of the devil!" Marnie laughed pointing across the beach. Vickie turned to see her band mates and crew coming towards them.

"Jovi is actually quite fit Vickie, when you see him bare-chested and in shorts. Wow, that six pack is very defined now," Lynne said, lifting her sunglasses onto her head again. "Think I might be with the wrong brother, chick."

"No, you're with the right brother even if he is skinny."

"I suppose so; Chris does have . . . "

"A big knob, we know!" Vickie and Marnie said in unison.

"Actually, Johnny is well endowed too Lynne," Vickie said, looking from one friend to the other, "and he knows how to use it."

Marnie smiled. "Jamie doesn't actually fall short in that department either, as you well know Lynne! I've heard rumours about Andy. I think that's why they all get on like brothers! No penis envy."

Lynne made a face. "I've seen Andy's too! Long complicated story best forgotten, we fooled around a few times. Has Jamie still not admitted it to you Marnie?"

"Nope, I'm waiting for him to do it. I must get something out of it. I keep feeding him opportunities to say it, but he must be shitting himself," she grinned at Lynne, "I'll pretend to be suitably shocked of course."

"You've been with both Jamie and Andy? You told her but not me? Thought we had no secrets?" Vickie gasped looking from Lynne to Marnie, then she grinned. "Billy told me about it when Frankie and Andy split up. So, I suppose I'm as bad."

Lynne looked at Vickie over the top of her sunglasses, "part of my misspent youth, so no regrets. Marnie and I talked about it and we can laugh now, as friends. Jamie and I did it early on; we were both horrified after it, actually. Chris was always going off and it was just sex, nothing more. I told Marnie because I felt I had to when her and Jamie started getting serious. We're friends and she slept with Chris once too. So, we're quits aren't we Marnie?"

"Yeah, I'm waiting for Jamie to tell me about Lynne, he knows about Chris and me." Marnie smiled and looked at her two friends. "I think I was just curious as to what the fuss was about. He was good but there was no chemistry, same as Lynne with Jamie."

"Do you lot have any morals at all?"

"Well Vickie, you were born aged thirty and we all love you, but there are some things . . . " Lynne laughed, looking at Marnie.

"We would have told you, but you'd have done that moralistic thing you do. You're doing it now, the disappointed look. We were all young and stupid, Vickie." Marnie smiled as she looked over at the group who had stopped to sign autographs.

Lynne shrugged, "Chris knows everyone I've slept with and doesn't mind. Me and him, it's just special. Chris has a beautiful knob. I know now I'll never need or want sex with anyone else. What can I say? We both had to experience everyone else, to find out that what we both needed was right there all the time. Chris and I in bed, wow, wow, wow."

"You tell us every day Lynne. It used to be a feature of the gossip columns before you captured him."

"No one will ever capture Chris Vincent, Vickie."

"Oh, I don't know, that little pot belly of yours seems to have him enthralled, Lynne."

"Yeah, can't believe we're having a sprog. At least it's just one though. I was shitting myself when Connie said the multiple birth thing had come from Martin's side. I thought I might end up with triplets or something."

Vickie laughed, "she's talking nonsense. The girls are identical, the egg splits. It's fraternal twins who run in families, they're the non-identical type. But there's a grain of truth that fraternal twins can run through the male line. The reason you sometimes get triplets is that two eggs are fertilized and then one splits, so you get identical twins, and a third baby."

"Well, whatever, she is going to be there right from the start, fucking interfering you know, thanks to you and Jovi not telling her about the twins for months."

"You really should try not to swear; the baby can hear you in the womb," Vickie said sternly.

"You've met Chris Vincent, haven't you?" Lynne laughed. She looked down and rubbed her little bump, "you need to learn to ignore bad words little man."

"I was just coming to meet you lot," Vickie said as Johnny reached them and sat down on the lounger beside her.

"No need, there's a problem with the air conditioning needing a repair. Our studio is not available until five now. So, sexy lady, we thought we would just join you for an hour or two." Johnny lay back then pulled Vickie into his arms.

"Jamie, you better lie on a towel!" Chris laughed, sitting down beside Lynne. "If you lie on the sand we won't be able to see you. It'll be like a fucking chameleon with that white body. It's just as well you have all those lurid tattoos mate. Why do you have you so many on your arms and hardly any on the rest of you?"

"I have got some on my body now; I just don't usually show my body in public."

Vickie looked over at him, "I hope you have sun screen on Jamie. You'll burn really quickly in this heat. I have the kid's stuff on my face, in case my scars show. Nicky was freaking out at me."

"Factor 50. I used the kids' stuff on him too," Marnie laughed, sitting down on the sand beside Jamie. "He always comes back from holiday with a bar room tan, or a t-shirt one, don't you sweetie?"

"It's alright for you lot!" Jamie cried, "with your boring, tan easily skin. I'm a natural redhead, with milky skin." He squinted and pointed over at the wall beside the beach. "Fuck here we go, look it's Rat-fink." Vickie turned around to a camera pointed at her.

Colin and Arfur despatched themselves from the group and walked towards the two men, one with a notebook, the other taking pictures. "Come on Helmut, give them some privacy, you're far too close."

"Vickie, nice artwork. What have you got to say about Tony's trial?" Helmut Ratzinger shouted.

"What?"

"Tony's trial date being set for January, Vickie. What do you think?"

"Why would I have an opinion?"

Johnny, feeling her beginning to shake, put his arms around her and glanced over at Arfur, motioning with his head. Arfur smiled and nudged Colin, who moved closer to the big German reporter.

Helmut laughed and shook his head. "We know it's you Vickie, you're the so-called 'celebrity victim', what about a comment? Is it true it was a sex game gone wrong? Come on Vickie, what about an exclusive? Or you Johnny, what's it like to be doing Vickie? Doesn't it bother you, Tony had her first? What about a comment?"

"I have one, it's fuck off, fucking heartless bastard," Jamie shouted.

They watched as Colin took the camera from the photographer. "Oops, clumsy me!" he said as he dropped it on to the ground, smashing the lens from it.

"Oh dear!" Arfur sighed. He pretended to trip and kicked the camera into the nearby kids paddling pool. "Now clear off, if you had an ounce of decency in you, you would leave them alone." Arfur looked the reporter in the eye and growled. "Stay away Helmut, you know what the truth is. If you don't leave them alone, you might not make it back to the UK to collect your writ for slander."

Chris stepped over and pulled out his wallet. "Here!" he said. "I'm so sorry my clumsy friend here appears to have damaged your camera." He threw a wad of notes at him. "Get yourself a new one." He leaned closer. "Then fuck off and annoy someone elseh" He said through gritted teeth. "Vickie has had enough to cope with."

Johnny tightened his arm around Vickie, who was shaking violently. She knew he was angry, but containing it. "You knew the trial was going to be in the New Year honey. We'll finally get some closure," he whispered pulling her closer and kissing the top of her head.

"I really hope so Johnny, but what if he gets off with it? Johnny! I can't breathe . . . how can I?......oh God Johnny, he's going to get away with it! I'm going to pass out in the witness box. He'll get out and no one will be safe."

"Vickie, stop it! Stop panicking, calm down. Come on babe, breathe; that's it, slow and easy." The others looked on, sympathy on their faces. This had happened a lot in the early days. Johnny looked at the group, "someone get us a drink please? Brandy for Vickie. Get me a vodka; doubles."

"We'll get fucking arrested if we drink on the beach Johnny!" Jamie hissed looking around him.

"Just do it! You three have carried drugs into every fucking country in the world, improvise!"

Ten minutes later Vickie sat, calm and drinking from a paper cola cup. "Sorry folks, I kind of lost it there. I'll be fine, it's been a while."

"Yeah, well you got it under control pretty damn quick,

sweetheart," Andy said smiling, "you're doing great, we'll all be with you for the trial."

"Once the rapist is locked up for good we'll have a big party. Tell the fucking world how brave you are Vickie," Marnie said smiling.

"What if he gets off with it? We haven't even considered that as an option, what if . . . ?"

"He won't Vickie, don't start getting paranoid." Johnny smiled. Everyone knew he was putting on a brave face for Vickie's sake. "We've two weeks here, then five weeks, and we'll be home safe for Christmas." He reached over and pushed his brother. "Then we get to watch these two trying to be parents, should be good for a laugh. Let's not even think about the rapist, he's where he should be. Come on, let's go for a swim." He pulled Vickie to her feet, scooped her up and ran down the beach carrying her.

A stream of photographers detached from the crowds on the beach and ran after them. "It's freezing!" Vickie gasped as Johnny dropped her into the sea.

"No, it's not; you've just been lying too long in the sun. Bet you haven't moved since the kids went back to the hotel." He pulled her to her feet and wrapped his arms around her, kissing her on the lips. "You look beautiful darling. You'd never believe you're a mother of four."

"Ooh, the photographers."

Johnny pulled Vickie towards him. "Fuck them, let's start filling the gossip columns." He turned her around so her back was to the cameras, placed his hand on her hip, sliding it into her shorts. He grabbed her bottom and squeezed.

Chris sidled up, following Jamie, who was tying back his hair. Johnny kissed Vickie and they moved over towards them.

"Get away from me Jovi," Jamie shouted, "you make me look skinnier, and he's making me look whiter."

Vickie giggled. "We should have got Nicky to give him a spray tan before we let him out."

"Fuck off Vickie, I'm pale and interesting."

Vickie moved away as the boys went out to swim, racing up against the waves. Ignoring the photographers, she sat down on the shore with Lynne, letting the waves gently wash over her. Andy moved over and sat down between them.

"You really are up the duff then?"

"Of course, did you think we were kidding? I'm six months Andy, it's due in February." Lynne looked down at her stomach, covered by a long shirt. "We're going to have to announce it soon; we wanted to get the tour over with first!"

"I don't know? I just can't imagine you and Chris with a kid."

"Why?"

"I don't know, it's just weird, us all grown up and doing big people stuff. I suppose it's how it is now though."

"Speaking of grown up things, how's it going with Mhairi?" Vickie asked.

Andy grinned, "she's great Vickie, a bit like you really, tough, with a soft centre. I asked her to come out on tour with me. She said she couldn't get the time off. She's agreed to meet me here on the way back though." He smiled and rolled his eyes, "she insisted on paying her own fare, but I've booked her an upgrade and am getting them to say it's just because she's travelling alone."

"You're still keen then?"

"Uh huh, it's early days but no doubts, she's the one. She's beautiful, with all that red hair, what can I say, it's love." He nudged Vickie, "It's in the way she looks at me, and I haven't looked at another woman since I met her."

"And you think Chris getting me pregnant is strange? You settling down? With someone who has the same hair as Jamie too, hmm think this tells me something! Unrequited love, I think," Lynne giggled.

Andy laughed. "He does have lovely hair too; I've always had a thing about redheads."

Lynne looked over the sea, where Johnny and Chris were throwing Jamie into the waves, playing to a group of photographers who had gathered around them. Marnie stood taking pictures of the scene.

The photographers, spotting a British Soap star and her boyfriend, went off down the beach. The three men came back and sat down beside the others. Marnie walked towards them with a camera in her hand. Jamie stood behind her and wrapped his arms around her, kissing her cheek. Vickie grabbed the camera and took some snaps. "You actually make a lovely couple, you two."

"Yeah it's like beauty and the beast" Andy said grinning.

Vickie handed Marnie the camera, then sat back down in the middle of the group, between Johnny and Andy as Lynne stood up and moved over to Marnie's side.

"Okay guys, some tour publicity shots. Johnny, take your hand off her boob. Andy, tongue out of her ear please." Marnie shook her head, "Chris that is disgusting, we all know you have a big whopper, it's getting boring, over exposure mate! Jamie bunny ears, *really*! It's bad enough him feeling her up, it will be all over the papers tomorrow."

Vickie looked around and smiled. "It won't matter anyway. The press is convinced Chris and I are an item, despite all the speculation about whether Lynne is pregnant." She leaned back against Johnny and looked up. Marnie zoomed in and clicked the camera. Johnny bent forward and kissed her on the mouth.

"Okay someone throw a bucket of water over those two, please?" Andy giggled.

As Marnie stopped clicking, Johnny stood up and pulled Vickie to her feet. "Come on we really need to get to rehearsal soon. We have to get showered and changed."

Back in the hotel, Vickie showered and dressed in denim shorts, a vest top, and sneakers. "You really need to wear heels honey!" Johnny said, coming up behind her as she put make-up on. "Look! You just come up to my chest," he said, smiling at her in the mirror. She turned around and put her arms around his neck. He bent down and kissed her. "I love you babe."

Vickie kissed him back and smiled. "I never thought I could feel this happy again Johnny, life's perfect."

Johnny breathed against her neck then looking her in the eye, he sighed. "Tempting as it is, we'd better not stop now to let me show you just how perfect babe. We need to do this rehearsal, are you still nervous?"

Vickie nodded. "I'm really scared, my voice Johnny? What if it's not as good as it was?"

"Vickie it's the same, maybe even better."

"You sure?"

"Yes, I'm sure! I was there when you were working with Evie, sweetheart! Once you found your range again, you didn't need much help. You were always a natural, Vickie. You've lost your confidence, not your talent. Now we have two weeks, let's go," Johnny grinned and kissed Vickie, "before I throw you on the bed, and we don't make it to the first rehearsal."

They walked out to the foyer, the others were waiting. "Just us, Evie and Sam; Jovi reckoned you would be nervous about singing again." Andy smiled at Vickie.

"Vickie, Jovi, Andy, come look at this!" Jamie shouted, beckoning them over to where he and Chris were standing with Marnie, looking on an iPad at the photographs she had taken. It showed Vickie leaning back, looking up at Johnny.

Johnny leaned over Marnie's shoulder. "That's the photo we'll release when we get married." He kissed her cheek. "Now Marnie fuck off, and you lot, let's move it."

"Hey hold on!" Patrick shouted, walking towards them. "Sis I need to leave in an hour, I got caught up in something!"

"Yeah, a nice little blond singer, Paddy," Johnny said, shaking Patrick's hand. "See you at Christmas mate."

Patrick wrapped his arms around Vickie and kissed her. "Knock them dead sis, you'll be great. Thanks for everything you've done for Dania. You will look after her, won't you?"

"You know we will. You take care of yourself Paddy; we'll all be fine."

"Vickie I'm really, really proud of you, the way you've coped with all the shit you've been though. You're an inspiration to me, and to everyone around you. Me and Dania both admire you so much. I'm not going to say good luck, because you don't need luck Vickie, you'll be great." He grinned, "apart from Dania, obviously, you're the most talented artist around these days. Wish I could stick around for the tour, but that's the life I've chosen. Hey no tears sis, I'll see you at Christmas, I'm really looking forward to it."

CHAPTER

TWENTY-THREE

"That was a stroke of genius Evie, starting with Black Velvet! It was the last song she sang in public, it should be the first she sings as her comeback." Sam clapped his hands as Vickie lowered the mike.

The others cheered and Johnny swept Vickie into a hug. "Great stuff, Vickie," he whispered in her ear, then kissed her on the mouth.

"That was amazing, pitch, note and word perfect. If it's possible, your voice is even better than it was. More than I can say for you lot." Sam pointed at Chris. "What the fuck were you doing there? You were in the wrong key, and Andy, fuck me, are you sure you can play those drums? You were way ahead of everyone else. You two seriously need practice."

"Maybe if you had done less partying, and took things seriously," Jamie laughed.

"Don't you fucking get me started on you Jamie, you weren't even playing the same tune as them. Vickie let's do another couple, see if your professionalism rubs off on this lot babe."

They played a few numbers. "Vickie that's enough for now, you're fine," Sam said smiling at Vickie. "Go and get yourself a drink darling. You lot, take it back to the beginning; let's get it right, before we add the vocals. You'd better be ready; if you don't get your acts together, I'm bringing in extra sessions. You've got fat and lazy whilst Vickie was ill. Jovi, we all know you are loved up; but take your eyes off Vickie and look at your guitar please? You wrote the song; I expect you to be able to fucking play it."

Chris put his guitar down. "Sam, can I do a solo?"

"What?"

"A solo? You know, a song that I sing by myself."

"I know what a fucking solo is, I'm just not sure that you do? You actually have to put some work in, you know? That thing you and Jamie avoid like the plague!"

Chris looked around the room, grinning at the expressions on his friends faces. They all stared at him.

"Why?" Jamie asked.

Andy looked up from his drum kit. "Can you actually sing?"

"Oh yes, and he's good Andy, but he's just too lazy to practice." Vickie laughed. "We were in quite a few musicals at school, he was great. He's got a really good voice. Can I play this Chris?" she said lifting his guitar. "Okay, Chrissie, let's show them. I think I can still play our song."

"How did you know?" Chris asked, smiling.

"Just a good guess." She began to play, and Chris sang 'In the Arms of Mary'. One by one the others joined in and Sam and Evie stood watching, their arms folded.

"Fuck sake Toph! You are actually good at that." Johnny shook his head, "it's one of Annie's old records. She used to play it when we were wee boys."

"He used to sing it about Lynne, didn't you?" Vickie said remembering.

"Yeah or you!"

"I never taught you about sex!"

"Oh, you did Vickie; you just didn't know you were starring in my adolescent fantasies. Especially when your tits sprouted. I was a 14-year old boy with raging hormones."

Jamie laughed. "I can imagine. I used to have a lot of those impure thoughts myself when we started out."

"No, you had to be there Jamie," Andy said grinning, watching

Vickie out of the corner of his eye. "She went from having two backs, to those puppies, in one summer. We thought she'd been for a boob job. Billy said they were hand reared. You remember Jovi, don't you?"

"Oh yes!" Johnny smiled and rolled his eyes. "It was like, where the fuck did they come from? My Mum and Annie, they had to take her to Glasgow for a bra, cos they didn't do training bras big enough in town!"

"Sam, do you think we could get the licence for him to sing it in the gig?" Vickie said, ignoring them.

Sam looked over at Johnny who shrugged. "Don't see why not, he's good enough. And it's an easy tune to pick up on."

"Two covers, Jovi? You're getting commercial son."

"Don't read too much into it." Johnny laughed. "I've just never seen my brother actually take an interest in anything but having a good time. Must be the effect of impending fatherhood."

"Can't believe he can sing!" Jamie said shaking his head.

"I never knew that she could play guitar either," Johnny said, looking at Vickie. "Impressive babe, but you play right-handed guitar upside down, that's pretty unusual."

"It's because Chris taught me; you would never let me touch your guitars, he's right-handed. Then we found out Jimi Hendrix did it, just turned the guitar around. We used to play years ago. Lynne can too, she's better than me because she's right-handed."

"That's what I used to do in my bedroom with them." Chris sighed. "They told me everything I needed to know about girls. I taught them to play guitar, because she's left-handed that's the only way I could teach her."

"Then I used to keep edgy, whilst he and Lynne snogged," Vickie laughed. "If Connie had found out he wasn't gay then we had nowhere to go on cold nights. By the time she did find out, I was with Billy and we had Gillian's hayloft."

"I can't believe it never bothered you, everyone thinking you were gay!" Andy said shaking his head.

"Chris shrugged, "I knew I wasn't! What can I say? Stephania, she reckons it was because I was dead confident. Unusual in the younger brother of an over achiever apparently. Mind you, I could have just been a late developer!"

"Okay folks, fascinating as this conversation is, let's do a run through of everything," Sam shouted, "Vickie you open with Black Velvet and we'll put Chris in halfway through, he might stay sober that way."

"Ye of little faith!" Chris said, taking his guitar from Vickie, "I'm off the drink; if Lynne can't, I won't."

Johnny sighed. "Toph, you don't need to completely stop, just don't do it to excess."

Chris grinned. "I fucking can't. Once I start, I forget to stop, and I promised Lynne I'd stop for the pregnancy. She doesn't think I can do it either. Stopping the drugs was easy. I actually had scared myself off them, but alcohol was my first love." He lifted a bottle of beer from the cool box on the floor. "Know what folks? She's probably right." He grinned, "we might be grown-ups but once she spits out my son we'll be going on a bender, she misses it too." He turned around and opened his bottle on the table.

"What if she breast-feeds?" Vickie asked.

Chris winked at Jamie then turned back around to Vickie, his face straight. "Nah, she won't do it, she says it makes a woman's tits saggy, and she still wants to work. Victoria's Secret shows a lot of flesh."

Vickie looked indignant, "I breast fed twins and mine are fine!"

"Prove it!" they all said at once.

"Fuck off, and grow up!"

"Hook, line and sinker, you're like a fish, Vickie," Andy laughed, putting his arm around her shoulder. "There's actually no sport in winding you up." He nudged Chris, "and you didn't think it would be a laugh being sober."

Vickie looked around her, "you all look better because you've cut back on the partying. See what the love of a good woman does? I suspect that that is why Simon chose Dubai for our rehearsal, to dry you all out before the tour. I can't believe you have to get a licence to have a beer here," Vickie said, opening a bottle on the side of the table. She looked at Chris. "A beer is fine, especially in this heat. It's the vodka and tequila you need to stay away from."

"You know, funny you should say that, I think I've actually managed to sicken myself off vodka. I just don't want it," Chris said grinning.

Jamie laughed. "Yeah, right."

"I'm serious, the last bender scared me off vodka. I was fucking hallucinating, I thought you got a round in Jamie."

"That wasn't a hallucination that was a miracle." Andy laughed and nudged Sam. "You do know that Jamie is the richest of us all, he has all his dad's share of his bands royalties. He actually tops the young British musical rich list. He is up there, quite a few million ahead of the rest of us but as tight as a drum."

Jamie grinned. "Yeah more money than a cow can shit folks. I'm the original Richie Rich."

"Right folks," Sam shouted, "drink your beer and get back up. Okay let's do a run through and then I'll tell you what you need to work on."

Vickie was perched on top of a speaker with a beer bottle in her hand when Simon arrived. "How's it going my love?" he asked.

"Not too bad.

"What's the story behind the camera?"

"What camera?" Vickie asked, looking innocent.

"On the beach Vickie. Colin and Arfur broke a camera."

"That was an accident, but Chris paid for it."

"Liar," Simon said, smiling.

Vickie grimaced. "They were taking pictures of us."

"That's okay, it was a public beach."

"It was Helmut Ratzinger, Simon! He was Tony's company's press contact. His mate, his sidekick photographer worked for

Tony too." Vickie glanced at Simon and looked angry. "They were five feet away from us. The camera was pointing at my tits. They knew about me and Johnny. Then Ratzinger started to ask about Tony's trial. They were trying to provoke us, saying that it had all been some kind of sex game gone wrong. Did you know the date is set?"

Simon nodded. "I got the call this morning love. I'm sorry, I didn't know anyone else knew. They said it would not go on the court website till tomorrow. I didn't want you worrying today, when you were so stressed about the rehearsal." He sighed. "That's what I'm here to tell you; 5th of January. CPS is ready to go with all the other charges too, but they want the rape, kidnap and attempted murder of you as a separate trial."

"5th January?" Vickie felt herself begin to shake, "what do we need to do?"

Simon laid a hand on her arm. "You've got Anita Robinson, who is a top-class barrister by the way; we have a meeting with her when we get back. The CPS are adamant, because yours is the strongest case it's going to stand alone."

"Won't there be a public out-cry at the cost?"

"No, the public will get it once they hear the evidence. We have a news blackout at first but it will get out Vickie."

"Why the blackout? I want people to know Simon, I want it to be heard, what he did to me! Why should I have to feel ashamed?"

"The CPS lot are still worried his lawyers will claim he was tried in the press. It could mean a miss-trial, or grounds for appeal. After he's found guilty, we can release a statement, if you still want to. I think they feel, if they lump them together, he will get a lesser sentence. If they get a prosecution with you, it strengthens the other cases, makes it more likely he abused those little girls. There's also all the films, apparently he edited hours of coverage from the houses he owned. He had cameras everywhere. It's going to take a while because everyone in the films needs to be identified and spoken to." He looked over at the band, then shook his head and looked at Vickie. "Apparently, there was a lot of action with those three, and Lynne, so it could take some time and effort! With Dania, there's two co-accused, so it needs to be separate but we don't have a date for that either. Fuck he's a perverted, dirty bastard Vickie."

"You don't say!" Vickie lowered her gaze. "Some days It feels like it happened to someone else Simon." Her eyes clouded over. "Other days, it's there from the moment I open my eyes until I go to bed, and then I dream. It's the same for the others. I might have been the one who was attacked but we were all left damaged by it. Stephania has been great though, worth every penny. She's doing voluntary work, training counsellors for rape crisis too, now. She's amazing!"

"You're pretty amazing too Vickie, can I put my arm around you?" Simon asked.

Vickie nodded and smiled.

"Vickie, I just want you to know, I think you're an amazing, brave lady. I've never met anyone with your resilience and strength, you're an inspiration. I think however, you need to speak out and use what you've been through to help other people. Why don't you sell your story and donate the money to charity? You'll be able to do it once he's convicted."

Vickie nodded. "We're thinking about it!"

"I'm so glad you're back on the bike Vickie. You're incredibly talented. I was listening to you singing from out there in the corridor, your voice is better than ever." Simon shook his head sadly, "I'm not Tony Gorman darling. I'll never ever try to control you lot. I'll do what you want me to do, not the other way around. I couldn't believe how much control you gave him! Then I realised how young you all were when he got his claws into you, you were just children. When I think about all the shit you've experienced, I can't believe you're all as strong as you are."

Vickie looked at him, tears welling up in her eyes. "I had just turned 17, Jamie was the oldest, only 19. It was a pretty big deal; Tony Gorman being interested in us. Then after that magical first year, we were so grateful, star struck I suppose. We were, we thought, living the dream! We just didn't realise what we were signing up to. We're all victims Simon, all damaged by what has happened to us over the years, but we still have each other, that's what is important. I only started to think about it when I saw the psychotherapist, that's why I talked the others into going. They had traumas; I thought mine were worse. But all of us have been through so much. Tony's attack on me changed us all though. Know what? This is going to sound crazy, it's so much better now than it was a year ago! Johnny is everything I could have hoped for. After Billy died I never expected to be able to love again. You know the painting of the phoenix in our lounge?"

Simon nodded.

"Well that's what inspired me to carry on; out of the ashes the phoenix rises! That's why I got the tattoo, the one on my stomach!"

Simon lifted her left hand, and looked at her ring tattoo. "I really like it too, Vickie. Are you two going to get married?"

"Yes, as soon as we get back. We're probably just going to slip off and do it quietly."

"Why don't you do it in Australia? I can help you arrange it; you should be able to get a special licence. Years ago, Elton did, he married a woman in Australia and they were granted a special licence because he was on tour. They can issue it in hours. You don't need to publicise it; you can just go off and do it quietly.

"Hmm, I'll talk to Johnny about it. I'm not sure if I really do want to just disappear and get married. It feels like we are always having to hide stuff." Vickie wiped away a tear, "can we change the subject Simon, before I start snivelling?"

Simon squeezed her shoulder and nodded. "Are the kids settled alright? How's the new nanny?"

"She's good. She didn't go to any fancy nanny school, just the local college. Katie is Andy's cousin and she's great with the boys. It means Laura can spend more time with the twins, now they're on their feet. It was a stroke of luck too, Annie being able to come with us; four kids take a lot of planning." Vickie smiled. "She's the twins Great Grandmother; we're all calling her Granny Annie now."

"I'm glad you decided not to let Catriona come back! I think it was the right decision Vickie. I kind of understand how you felt but you would always associate her with that time, wouldn't you?"

Vickie nodded, "I just felt so sorry for her. It's a different type of control, isn't it? What he did to her? I think the boys get it. Chris got her a job with an actress he knows, as a companion, so we know she's okay. I had to forgive her Simon, I couldn't carry that kind of anger about; she was as much a victim as me. I know the others didn't get it at first, but they do now."

"Vickie what's the story with Annie and Doug?" "I know he and Andy are trying to spend time together whilst you're here, but I saw Annie and him last night, they looked pretty comfortable together."

Vickie smiled, "they knew each other before. He was ten years older than Hannah. He's the same age as Annie and knew her from school, always fancied her apparently, but Annie was so traumatised by being raped, she didn't ever have a boyfriend. She went for counselling after she told us, then I linked her up with Stephania. I think Doug just might be her homework."

"My God Vickie, it's getting very incestuous here, isn't it?

Vickie shrugged, "again Simon, I think it's what we have all been through together." She looked up at him, "Annie looked after Doug when Hannah and Jake died, but they were just friends. I think it just grew from there. Andy is fine about it, just happy for them. Annie is like our mother anyway."

Simon looked over at Chris, who was discussing the chords for a number with Johnny and Sam. "Are you all really going to continue to share the house, even after you and Johnny are married?"

"Yeah, for the time being. Apart from Andy they all have their own homes in the UK anyway but they stay most of the time at Brickstead. We've got the new staff looking after us now. So

Annie's not doing it all. She is loving being the boss though, ordering everyone about. The others do move around a lot, but we'll always keep their rooms for them. Chris uses Johnny's flat in Hammersmith but Lynne has a couple of homes. Brickstead is huge, much too big for just Johnny, me and the kids. Billy and I were a bit ambitious when we bought it. It is however, perfect for bringing up kids, so I think Lynne and Chris are going to make it their main base. We're going to do some conversion of the second floor, there's no point in them buying somewhere just now when we have all that space. We also have two nannies and the boys are both at school now."

"What about the others?"

Vickie sighed. "Trouble is, if Jamie goes, I lose Marnie too. I think over the next couple of years they'll all move on anyway. I'll be like a parent losing her kids if they do go. I know it's kind of weird but I miss them when they're not there. We moved in together at a time when we needed the support, all of us were grieving. They all rallied around me when I had the girls, and again when I was attacked. We're closer than most siblings because of it all."

"What about your relationship with your brother Vickie, does it bother him? What about Andy? His girlfriend?"

"Dania being there too, means that Paddy is also around a lot. He's always got on with the boys. Andy is still trying to get Mhairi to agree to go public about their relationship. She's been so good for him, he's really in love, I think."

"Sometimes though Vickie, you sound like a mother talking about her children."

"Well, it's not as cut and dried as that, we all look after each other. We were always close but the crash just kind of pushed us together."

"It's pretty amazing how long you've managed to all live together."

"Yeah I suppose so Simon. They behave differently when we're living together. It kind of tones them down, a bit less of the rock star life. Mind you, to be fair, they are all fairly settled and stable now. They have always been there for me. When I was pregnant and after I had the twins, they were even doing the school run, to give Laura a break."

Simon laughed, and shook his head. "Vickie, it made the nationals. They were doing more than the school run, they were doing the school mums."

"Well, I didn't say they were perfect."

Johnny looked over, and motioned to Vickie.

"Vickie, I think they are ready for you again," Simon said, kissing her cheek.

"Andy thinks he is fucking Beethoven, directing his musical prowess," Johnny said as Vickie walked over.

"Beethoven was fucking deaf, Jovi! He wouldn't have heard your fucking dud notes."

"You don't know your arse from your elbow Andy."

"Boys, boys, please?" Vickie cried. "Let's just get this finished. I'm starving."

"Vickie!" Andy shouted.

"What?"

"You're a beautiful talented woman darling; you can have any man you want. What the fuck are you shagging him for?"

"Tosser!" Johnny said, through gritted teeth.

Vickie smiled. "God, I'm so glad things are back to normal boys!"

CHAPTER
TWENTY-FOUR

"Vickie, come out and have a look at this view honey?" Vickie walked up the stairs to the roof terrace of their hotel suite and stood beside Johnny.

"Wow!" she said, rolling her eyes and nudging him, "it's worth the £10,000."

Johnny laughed and handed her a glass of wine, "Yeah, beats a Travel Lodge, doesn't it!"

Spread before them was the amazing sight of Sydney Harbour bridge and the Opera House. Johnny wrapped his arms around Vickie and pulled her back, her head resting on his bare chest. "Are the twins settled now?"

"Yeah, Billie's still a bit fractious but I think it's the travelling. The boys were the same at that age; still we're on the home run now. Chiara went down no with no problems but it took a while to get Billie settled."

"The boys went out like lights!" Johnny whispered. "They are absolutely done in. Why on earth did you allow everyone to have the night off on our first day in Sydney?"

"So we could be alone. There's some stuff I want to discuss."

"Vickie, we have four children; without the Nannies, we're never alone."

"Only one more week and we'll be finished. I need to discuss us as a family . . . " She stopped and looked up at Johnny as he kissed her neck.

Johnny whispered in her ear, "Vickie I really want to adopt all the kids after we're married. The boys will always be Billy's sons; I'll never let them forget him. I just want them and the girls to be legally mine."

Vickie looked at him sighed. Breaking away, she walked through to their bedroom and returned carrying a large white envelope. She handed it to Johnny. He opened it, looked at the contents then gasped.

"When did you do this?"

"At the time, I just never told you. I don't know why Johnny. Oh, if I'm honest . . . I thought you might freak out. Time passed so quickly, everything went pear shaped, and then I never knew how to broach it with you." She looked at him and shrugged. "I still hadn't registered them when we found out. I had to pay a £200 fine too. I think somewhere in my head I knew. When I did register them, I put your name as the father. Jimmy and I got you to sign that paper saying you were their father!"

"Yes, for your will, and to give me guardianship of them and the boys," he looked at her, narrowing his eyes, "in case anything happened to you, so your mother didn't get them. I only agreed because you were making such a fuss."

"Well that was why I was able to do it, because I had a signed legal declaration from you."

Johnny's eyes narrowed and he glared at her "Fuck sake Vickie, that was a year ago, you could have said."

"I didn't mean to do it. It was an impulse thing. Maybe it was hormones? Then I forgot."

"You forgot?"

She put her hand on his arm and smiled up at him. "It means nothing. I agree with you adopting the boys; they're so young, they need to feel they're part of a family. Jimmy and I have the papers done; as soon as we're married they're ready to go." She looked him in the eye before continuing, "Johnny, I want to tell the truth about the girls."

"Vickie, I'm really angry you told Jimmy you had registered them in my name, but not me. We also agreed we'd say nothing until after the trial, in case they use it against us."

"Johnny, they'll find out anyway. The rapist knew, he told me; even if he didn't, anyone can buy a birth certificate. I discussed it with the senior registrar and she assured me no one else would see it. She did the registration herself but she warned me that it could become public knowledge."

"What did Jimmy think? Surely, he didn't think it was the right thing to do?"

"Oh, you know what lawyers are like? He tried to talk me out of it, told me to tell you. I meant to Johnny, I really did."

"Vickie, you think this could all come out at the trial! Don't you?

"When he had me in the car, the rapist told me that he was going to say he and I had been having an affair. He said that he would expose me sleeping with you and others. I just don't want to lie anymore. The girls are your daughters and they are beginning to look like you. Someone is going to realise and it will make it look worse."

"Vickie they're your image; I suspect I just provided the sperm for them."

"That's a horrible thing to say."

He wrapped his arms around her. "It's true babe, I look at them and all I see is beautiful miniatures of you. Vickie I'm angry, but for some reason I'm aroused. I really want to make love to you, right here right now."

"You're becoming like your brother! Is that your answer to everything these days?"

"Pretty much. Topher always says everything looks better after an orgasm." He unbuttoned her dress and moved his hand inside her bra.

"Johnny!"

"What?"

"I love you!"

"Yeah, Yeah! Doesn't make you do as you're told though, does it? Are you going to promise to love, honour and obey when we get married?"

"Are you Johnny? Going to obey?"

"Of course, I am! Just tell me, how you want it right now and I'll obey."

Making love was easy, neither of them held back, and it felt natural again. They both still saw Stephania monthly and sometimes struggled with flashbacks. At times, they couldn't make love but accepted it as part of their relationship. They knew each other's moods instinctively now. The intensity of their lovemaking when conditions were right, more than made up for any setbacks. Tonight, the conditions were perfect; they found the height of passion quickly and easily. Vickie clung to Johnny as he moved against her, they reached climax simultaneously; she cried out, her own hunger slated as she felt him explode inside her.

"Christ it's warm in here." Johnny rolled out of bed; he turned up the air conditioning.

Vickie lay watching him, a smile playing on her lips. "I love your body Johnny; I could just bite your bum after we make love and you stand up. I always think I'm satisfied until you turn around. I see your arse and want to do it all again."

Johnny turned around and shook his bottom. "I wouldn't be averse to going again Vickie." He sat back down on the edge of the bed. Vickie began to touch his penis. As it became hard again under her touch, she rolled over and took it in her mouth. Johnny gripped her head as she rolled her tongue around.

He lay back and grinned, his hands firmly on her head. Within minutes he began to shake, his body tensed, he cried out her name as he climaxed. Afterwards she crawled up beside him. He held her in his arms and kissed her on the mouth.

"That was record time, Johnny!"

"Babe that's the first time you've had my cock in your mouth, since . . ."

"Since I was attacked!" she finished for him. "Every time I tried, I saw that bastard, Johnny, suddenly it's gone. I've owed you that one since Cornwall." She smiled, "the roaring fire, you going down on me, the amazing orgasm that told me I could be normal again, still makes me horny thinking about it. Now I can reciprocate, I feel better about receiving."

"The tattoo worked then?" Johnny whispered, pulling her closer.

Vickie smiled and nodded, "Yeah I'm glad you thought of it, even if everyone did laugh about it. Why on earth did you tell Chris of all people? He can't hold his own water!"

"I wasn't going to tell anyone but he heard me say I was going to Sid's, he insisted on coming. I thought I was being so original too, now thanks to our Topher it's all so common." Johnny chuckled. "Sometimes I think he doesn't come from the same loins as me."

Vickie laughed. "Still the result was worth it, wasn't it? It was weird though, going down on you with my own face staring back at me."

"Thank fuck. It was really painful, Vic."

"I want to get married Johnny!"

"We would need to get dressed first babe."

She slapped him playfully. "I'm serious."

"Really?" he said, rolling onto his side. "I'll marry you tomorrow Vickie, you know that. You're the one who didn't want a fuss. I want to shout it from the rooftops, reckon I'm punching well above my weight here."

"Johnny, remember I told you Simon said that we could get a special licence in Australia and marry in 24 hours?"

Johnny smiled, "you want to do that?"

Vickie nodded. "That's why I have all the certificates; I got my dad to send them out by courier." She looked at him a sad expression coming over her face, she swallowed hard. "I needed

Billy and Ali's death certificates too. I want to do it now, and I don't want to hide it. I don't want to sneak away; we've hidden for too long Johnny! We've done nothing wrong. I want to come out and say, *'I love this man,'* I don't give a toss who knows or what anyone thinks."

"Vickie, we have two concerts to do, when can we fit in a wedding?"

"Let's do it on stage!"

"What! Are you crazy? You want to get married in front of 80,000 people?"

Vickie shrugged, "you can't get more public than that."

He looked her in the eye. "You're fucking mad Vickie."

"I know but you love me anyway."

"I actually like the idea Vickie. Could we arrange it on time?"

"Don't know, but we can try."

"People will think it's a publicity stunt."

"So? It probably is, after the trial, our whole lives could change. People are going to know about you and me, our lives could be under a microscope. I want to say publicly I'm with you.

Johnny looked at her, you want to arrange a wedding in four days, how on earth could we do it?

We have a venue, guests, and most of our loved ones here Johnny. You have your kilt, I'm sure I'll be able to find a dress to wear. We could do it on the, last night then fly out next day as Mr and Mrs Vincent."

"Are you going to take my name then?"

"Of course I am."

"Vickie Vincent, nice!"

"Victoria Margaret Vincent, if you want to be precise, Jonathon Allan Vincent." She looked at him. "I'm going to change the boys names to Vincent, we need to be a proper family."

Johnny looked thoughtful, "Why don't we compromise and double barrel it? D'Angelo-Vincent or Vincent-D'Angelo! That way we kind of honour Billy's and Ali's memory too." He chuckled. "An added extra is it will really piss your mother off."

Next morning, Johnny got up early and left the hotel. Laura came through as Vickie and the children sat on the roof terrace eating breakfast. "How's Billie?"

"She's fine this morning, Laura."

"It must have been a bug or something," Laura sighed.

"I think it might just be teeth, she looks as though she is cutting a back one judging by the way she is chewing that toast," Vickie said laughing.

"Where have Jovi and Marnie gone?" Laura asked, "I saw them leave in a taxi."

Vickie smiled. "Can you keep a secret?"

"Of course,"

"They've gone to meet Simon, to try to get a special licence for us to get married here."

"Wow! Congratulations. Why didn't you go? Why send Marnie?"

"We thought that we'd better avoid being seen together, in case anyone picks up on it, and Marnie is, as my assistant, my organiser."

Laura hugged Vickie and smiled.

"When? Where?"

"Not sure, we'll tell you later when they get back."

"What are you going to wear?" Laura asked, frowning.

"I don't know; I suppose Nicky will have something."

"It's your wedding we are talking about Vickie. Nicky's a few doors away, I'll go and get her and then take over here."

"No, not yet. I'd better wait until they get back, see if they have got the licence; it apparently has to go to the Australian Prime Minister."

"Well he's a big fan." Laura grinned, then stretched out her legs and looked over at Vickie.

"Can you keep a secret too, Vickie?"

"You know I can."

"I've been seeing someone."

"Oh!"

210

"You don't look surprised."

"I'm not. It's Nicky, isn't it?"

Laura gasped. "You always know these things! How do you do it?"

"I kind of knew you were gay; you just don't respond to our boys the way other women do." "Everyone has a type; the guys are so different, there is everyone's type of man in there, you never ever reacted. Then I watched you and Nicky. I actually noticed when we were having the pre-tour meeting."

Laura smiled, "does anyone else know?"

"Not as far as I'm aware Laura, no one's mentioned it. If they had noticed, you would be getting teased. I never even said to Johnny, figured you'd tell me when you were ready."

"You don't mind?"

"No, why would I mind? I love the fact that everyone has someone special, and I think you and Nicky will make a great couple." Vickie grinned, "it's time she settled down. You'll certainly make a striking looking pair. When did it start?"

"It was when you were in hospital. I was already thinking I might be more interested in women, and when I heard the state you were in . . . " She sighed, "Jovi took the babies to the hospital and the boys were with your dad. Nicky came over to see how you were. She was in a real mess because she thought it was her fault. You know, making you wear that dress when you hated dressing up." Laura's face clouded over, remembering, "I was in a right state. As you know, I felt guilty I never twigged what Catriona was up to." Laura smiled, "we did the Chris Vincent method of seduction, got drunk, ended up in bed. It's been on ever since. I wasn't trying to deceive you or anything; I just wanted to be sure. We've told my family now and I've met hers."

Vickie stood up and hugged her. "I'm really happy for you, I won't say anything until you and Nicky do."

* * *

"Well? Don't keep me in suspense," Vickie cried, as Johnny came out on to the patio, where Vickie was sitting with her feet in the kids paddling pool.

"Everything's done!" Johnny said, sweeping her into a hug. "On stage at the stadium, 9pm Sunday night; in front of a record crowd of 81,000 people. The Prime Minister wants to attend too, he's flying in for it. Thank fuck you shook your tushi at him, Vickie."

"No one else knows?" Vickie asked, as she put her arms around his neck.

"No, the PM actually spoke personally to the man marrying us. Then assured us it would be our surprise; you are sure you want to do this babe?"

Vickie looked him in the eye. "What do I need to do?"

He kissed her, and sighed. "We need to go later and sign the paperwork; it should be ready about 2pm. I quite liked him, the PM, even if he does fancy you."

"Listen to you, the PM, ooohh," Vickie smiled. He got a lot of stick in the press that night, watching my ass, not Kylies."

Johnny put his hands out doing a balancing act. "You? Kylie, gorgeous older woman?" He hugged her and kissed the tip of her nose. "You know it will always be you with me. Now come on let's see if you can thank me properly. What did Jerry Hall say? You can hire someone to do the housewifely tasks, so you can be a seductress in the bedroom."

"You want me to seduce you?"

"Hell yes, as many times as you like!"

* * *

"What's the big problem bro? What's with all the mystery? You said be here at 4.30?" Chris called out, coming out on to the terrace with Andy. "Hi kids!" he said, catching sight of the children splashing in the paddling pool. Marnie was perched on Jamie's knee beside the pool, with Dania. Arfur, Colin and Zac sat with their feet dangling in the pool; Simon was deep in conversation with Sam and Rory at the pool-side table.

"Wait till everyone else gets here?" Vickie looked around, "where's Lynne?"

"Sleeping, I thought it was a band meeting?"

"No, it's everyone's meeting, go get her and hurry up. Oh, never mind! Johnny, phone Lynne will you? We have something important to tell you all."

"You up the duff again Vickie?" Andy asked, watching Johnny speaking to Lynne on his mobile.

"Not as far as I know Andy."

"So, what is it then?"

"Come out on to the terrace mate, get a drink," Johnny said, laughing and putting his arm around Andy's shoulder. Simon walked towards them as Vickie called Johnny back over.

"Andy, have a beer, chill out mate," Simon said. "Why are you looking so worried anyway?"

Andy took the beer and watched Vickie walk away with Johnny, his eyes narrowed. "Her dad said another pregnancy could kill her Si! Surely they wouldn't risk it again?" He looked away, distracted as Lynne padded in barefoot, wearing a cropped top with 'bite me' emblazoned on the front and shorts sitting under her little baby bump. Her hair was tousled and sticking up, her eyes panda like with mascara. "How the fuck did you ever become a Victoria's Secret Angel?" Andy said looking at her. He held up a bottle of beer.

"Just the one," Lynne said, taking it from him.

"Okay everyone's here!" Vickie shouted. "Right folks, we have some news."

"Good news?" Jamie asked.

"We think it is." Vickie said, moving towards Johnny. Johnny, smiling broadly, pulled Vickie into his arms and kissed her.

"I told you, she's bloody pregnant!" Andy nudged Jamie.

"She's not pregnant Andy." Johnny said, unable to stop smiling. "We're finished with babies. Our family's complete, you lot can make the rest of the next generation. We wanted to tell you we're getting married."

"Is that it? You told us that ages ago, Jovi. Soon as you get back; we're not invited," Jamie said, shrugging his shoulders.

"No, we're doing it Sunday night; we're getting married on stage. At the end of the gig, special licence, signed by the Prime Minister this afternoon."

"Well he would, wouldn't he? Liked Vickie a bit too much," Andy said smirking, visibly relaxing, "he was watching her arse when she walked away, there was a picture in the papers of him. They had drawn in a chalk line from his eyes to her arse."

"Makes a change from them looking at her tits," Jamie said smiling. He shut one eye, tilted his head and looked at her. "I prefer the tits Vickie." He grinned. "So, on stage in front of everyone?"

"Fuck if that's your idea of a small intimate ceremony, we need to talk!" Chris said laughing and shaking his head.

"We decided that we needed to do it publicly, put all the rumour mongers to rest," Johnny told them. "We don't want to hide our relationship."

"What about a honeymoon?" Chris asked.

"Every day with your brother is a honeymoon; we're not going to bother." Vickie giggled, as Johnny wrapped his arms around her, and nibbled on her ear.

Nicky stepped forward, a frown set on her face. "You need a wedding dress Vickie. I need to go downtown. Fuck, how could you do this to me? Three fucking days notice to organise your wedding outfit, and in front of 80,000 people. The world will be watching. We'll lose you tomorrow for the concert. I'll need Marnie, Vickie, to search."

"Nicky, stop panicking, you're a stylist, you'll find something. It's better you do it so no one finds out. Laura can help you; she is much the same size as me." Vickie looked her in the eye, and grinned.

Nicky raised an eyebrow and looked at Laura. "You up for it Laura?" she asked.

"Of course she is. Marnie and Annie can manage to look

after the kids with Katie. Don't worry if you can't find a dress." Vickie laughed, "I thought I'd just wear my stage clothes. We just want to be married, what we wear is kind of secondary to the commitment."

"You cannot get married in jeans, Vickie," Nicky gasped.

"Well find me something to wear then, erm . . . you'll need to find outfits for the kids."

"I guess I owe you one," Nicky laughed, shaking her head. If you end up getting married in a dress from Marks and Spencer, don't blame me."

"Who's your best man?" Chris asked, looking at Johnny.

"You are, you tit, you're my brother."

"What about a Stag Night?"

Johnny shook his head. "No Stag Night Topher; sorry, we just don't have time. Well maybe this can be it. Or we can have a poker game after the show tomorrow."

Andy looked at Vickie and Johnny, "When are you going to announce it?"

"Sunday night," Vickie said, laughing.

"What?"

Johnny grinned at his friends. "We're just going to announce it and do it."

"What about your mum Johnny?" Annie asked frowning, "she'll never forgive you for doing it again without her there, and I'll never hear the end of it."

"Sorted, we called her, Marnie sorted out the flight; we borrowed a private jet. She's on her way with Dad and Vickie's dad and Maggie. She's even got an outfit, Marnie arranged a Harrods personal shopper for her and Maggie." He made eye contact with Dania. "Paddy's going to be here too, I asked to speak to his CO and got him special leave. It's cost us a gig for Help the Heroes but he is on his way, along with the Prince would you believe?"

Vickie looked at Andy and grinned, "Mhairi is also with them; after everything she did for us, we couldn't do it without her here."

Johnny put his hand over his mouth, "Vickie we forgot to call Jenny."

"Fuck off."

"Nice! Hope you are going to remember you're the bride using language like that."

* * *

The party went on into the night. Vickie and Annie put the children to bed. "Annie you'll be my Granny too after Sunday," Vickie whispered.

"Vickie, I've always been your granny. I'm so happy for you, you've been good for Johnny, he loves you, and I know you love him."

"What about you and Doug? I'm not going to lose you now, am I?"

Annie blushed but she smiled. "He asked me out when I was 16 you know? He was always hanging around; it was just before I went to London. I couldn't Vickie; I just was so scared of men. I'm not sure I fancied him or anything then, I do now though! He knows everything, so it's all good. Vickie, as your Granny love, I can't talk to you about my sex life but let's just say Stephania's help worked and, well, it's all moving along nicely."

"Annie, I'd hate to lose you but you need to know I won't stand in your way if you want to move on. You of all people deserve to be happy, Doug's a lovely guy."

"Vickie it's early days yet. Doug wants to spend more time with Andy. With you slowing down they can. If anything, he'll consider early retirement; you think I'm going move away from my great grandchildren?" Annie burst out laughing, "besides, there's Chris and Lynne about to have a baby! What on earth will those two numpties be like as parents, without me there?"

"I'm so lucky to have you in my life Annie, where would I be if I hadn't had you?"

"Here with four beautiful children and still the lovely, honest person you are. What about the twins, Johnny and you? What happened wasn't your fault, you were drugged. Now they're investigating the doctor who gave you all the drugs. Why don't you just announce Johnny is Chiara and Billie's Dad?"

"I wish we could go public about the twins but everyone thinks it would be a mistake just now, before the trial."

"What about your mum, Vickie, shouldn't you just let her know about you and Johnny?"

"No, why should I? You know what she was like Annie, only there for me if I fitted into her idea of what a daughter should be."

"She does love you Vickie, she just doesn't know how to show it. You have such capacity for love and are so forgiving darling. You shouldn't be carrying all that bitterness. You're such a loving, great mother, you did it all instinctively."

Vickie shook her head, you know when I found out I was pregnant with Denis, I worried about how I could love him as much as James. "But you love your children unconditionally. You just fit them in somewhere; your favourite child is always the one who needs you most, at a particular moment. She should have been able to love me Annie, I was all she had." Vickie wiped away a tear. "She never said it, Vickie I love you, it was Victoria, your face is dirty, your dress is torn, I'm busy, you little bitch ruined my life. You know just little endearments like that. You're supposed to nurture your children, be there, love them. You loved me I knew you did, always there for me, always putting me first. Despite what happened to you with Connie you loved her and the boys didn't you?"

"Hm, my mum and Dad loved Connie, they really did, I was traumatised the rape, the birth then having to hid it all." Annie sighed a faraway look in her eyes. "With me it was my grandchildren, it was like an instant thing, with you and them. When I saw Connie with Johnny in her arms it was just instant. The way it should have been with her. So, I became the Auntie trying to guide them, be their favourite Adult. With Johnny, it was easy; he was always more sensible Vickie. Chris was such an interesting child, into everything, with all that energy but with such a huge capacity for loving people. He needed to be guided, still needs it. I worried about him constantly but I always knew Lynne and him would work things out."

"They really have, haven't they?" Vickie said, shaking her head.

Annie smiled. "You will always be my Golden Child Vickie. You were such a sad little thing, always looking for Jenny to love you. She's missed out big time because you are the single best thing she's ever done and she can't see it. Sweetheart, I'll always be there for you and the children, all of them."

"I know Annie, you always have been," Vickie said, gently touching Annie's face.

CHAPTER
TWENTY-FIVE

"**O**kay folks!" the master of ceremonies said through the public-address system, as Dania left the stage. "There's been a slight change of plan. The second support band has been moved and Black Velvet are coming on next. If you came to see the Belafonte, hard luck, they're now on last. We need to have the main act in the middle for reasons that'll become apparent later. Don't disappear after Black Velvet though, there's a surprise in store."

"Vickie, fuck, I want to just pick you up and run with you, I have a fucking hardon!" Johnny whispered in her ear, as they stood waiting to go on. Grinning, he pulled Vickie behind a huge speaker and began to kiss her, his hand slid into the front of her shirt.

Vickie giggled, "stop it, you're a mad, horny bastard. You'll get me going if you don't leave me alone. Just wait till later. I hope you've organised the kids to be somewhere else tonight because as your wife I'll be required to give you your conjugal rights." She kissed him, grabbed his groin and squeezed. Looking down, she laughed, "you'd better start thinking unsexual thoughts because your erection is showing through those trousers babe!"

Jamie stuck his head around the side of the speaker, "unhand that man Victoria . . . Christ you two don't need Oxytocin, do you? We need him and his parts on stage!" Jamie glanced down at

219

Johnny's groin. "Better sort out your hardon, mate, and Vickie, your tit is showing."

An hour later Vickie came off stage, Marnie threw a towel around her. Vickie kissed Johnny. "See you at the altar, Mr Vincent-D'Angelo!"

"I'll be waiting for you, Mrs Vincent-D'Angelo!"

Leaving Johnny, she headed to her dressing room. Inside she peeled off her sweaty stage clothes, covered her hair with a clear plastic shower cap and stood under the shower. The door opened and Johnny stepped into the cubicle. "Johnny! No! We have to be back on stage. It's bad luck for you to see me before the wedding...."

"Vickie we've had our share of bad karma, my love; it's all good now. So, nothing will give us any worse luck." Johnny pulled her into his arms. "I got so horny tonight on stage. I just must have you, I can't wait until later. This is how it all started anyway babe, under a shower."

"But, we were out of our faces that night," she breathed.

"Love the shower cap." Wrapping his arms around her, he lifted her up and pushed her against the cabinet wall. She cried out as he guided his penis inside her, his strong arms holding her slight body easily against the glass. Within minutes, Vickie was gasping and writhing along with him. Holding on to him, she climaxed. Johnny shuddered, gasped and joined her, his legs shaking, his body tense. The water poured down on top of them. Oblivious to anything other than the sensation engulfing them, he held her against the cabinet, kissing her and milking the last remnants of his orgasm, before lifting her back on to her feet. When Johnny eventually caught his breath, he held her whispering in her ear, "God you're amazing Vickie, that really was a quickie, just wait till I get you alone later."

She kissed his mouth. "Can't wait, I love you so much Johnny Vincent-D'Angelo, now get fucking out, so I can get dressed. Leave me something to surprise you with. Can you find Nicky and send her in; she'll probably be helping Laura and Katie to get the kids dressed." She slapped Johnny playfully, "I'm going to need my hair redone, thanks to you. Are you going to be this horny, after we're married?"

"Hey, you and I are going to still be doing it over the Zimmer frames, babe. Just you wait!"

As Johnny left Vickie's dressing room, his father and Clinton came around the corner. "Great you made it, how was your flight?"

"Long! Your mother and Maggie are with Nicky having their hair and makeup done, we thought we'd find the green room and the alcohol. Your mother and I are of course delighted, but what on earth made you do this so quickly?" Martin Vincent asked his son.

Clinton looked at Johnny over the top of his glasses, his face anxious. "She's not pregnant, is she? Her body won't take another pregnancy Johnny."

"No Clinton, we've all the kids we need, as I said to you both on the phone. We just don't want to keep hiding."

* * *

Johnny entered his dressing room. Everyone was in different stages of dressing. "Have you had a wet dream by any chance, Jovi?" Andy asked, as Mhairi tightened his kilt around his waist.

Jamie, in full highland dress, was sitting on the couch, his arm around Marnie. He raised his beer bottle. "Impressive speed shagging, mate." Johnny looked around the room.

Marnie stood up and motioned to Mhairi, "interesting as this is, come on Mhairi, let's go find Vickie, I really want to see the dress." The two girls left, closing the door behind them.

Johnny grinned at the others, "how did you know?"

"We had a present for you and Vickie. We came into her dressing room looking for you." Chris, wearing shoes, socks and a shirt, shook his head and grinned. "I'm fucking traumatised. If you are going to do that, please at least lock the door, you fanny. I thought I was the stud in the family. You had her fucking coming

221

five minutes after you left here, that's a real quickie. Here was me thinking you learned nothing when we were doing the pub circuit."

Jamie smiled. "Still, at least it was Vickie's arse we could see and not your big hairy one. What's the tattoo on her bum, mate? When did she get that? It wasn't there before. I saw her change her trousers when they split in Christchurch, she had a G-string on, it wasn't there then."

"You're a perv Connolly, looking at my woman's arse!"

"WHAT!" Jamie cried, grinning, "like the rest of you don't look at other women? You think because you sit there with a book in your hand and shades, no one notices. They discuss our cocks too; it's what people who are comfortable with each other do. I don't want to shag her but if a beautiful woman's arse or tits are in front of me! I look . . . it's not sexist, it's studying an art form."

"You are so a perv, Jamie, and you know it," Chris laughed. "And we are not normal, any of us, we live in a fucking bubble sometimes." He grinned, "but it's a great bubble, isn't it? What is the tattoo Johnny?"

"Private! That's why it's on her bum. She got it in Auckland; Sid flew out and did it but it's not fully healed yet. She may show you when it is, but she probably won't."

"You flew Sid out and didn't say anything; that's what those three days away from us were?" Andy gasped. "Why Sid?"

"Because Vickie trusts him. His sister lives in New Zealand" Johnny said smiling, "so we gave him a holiday as his fee. It's linked to your stunt Toph, that's all I'm telling you."

On stage the support act finished their last number. Simon Forsyth walked on with Chris, Andy and Jamie, all looking resplendent in full highland dress. The crowd began to cheer. "Okay!" Simon announced. "We told you that tonight, our last night in this beautiful country, was special and that we had an announcement. I'm Simon Forsyth, I'm part of the band's management team. Chris here, has something he wants to tell you, so can we have some quiet?"

Chris took the microphone. The stadium hushed in anticipation. "Okay, here's the deal; you're probably wondering why we're dressed like this. Well, we've been keeping a big, big secret. Some of you may be aware of the rumours of a romance in the band. You're all about to be guests at a wedding. It's not mine though, straight up, no joke. I'm a very happy man tonight, my brother and my best friend, well my BFF really, are about to get hitched."

"When?" Someone in the press box shouted.

Chris smiled. "Right now, here on stage in Australia, and you're all invited." The crowd roared and white flashes blinded him. Chris waited a few moments, smiling broadly, before calling for quiet, "your Prime Minister very kindly signed a special licence for them and kept it secret. He also agreed to be here as guest of honour. For Andy, Jamie and I, it's a relief we can tell people because it's been a great big secret for a while now. We're just not comfortable with secrets, especially when they're not ours." He grinned then nodded to the press box. "You lot were so focused on thinking it was me, you missed it boys and girls."

"Lately, it's been staring you in the face and you all ignored it, thinking it was a smokescreen," Jamie said into his mike, as a photo of Johnny and Vickie's tattooed fingers flashed up on the screen behind Chris. "Honestly, we are absolutely delighted for them. If you could see how happy they are together, after all they've been through. You would understand why we're all over the moon."

The picture Marnie had taken on the beach came up on the screen. Andy turned and pointed at it. "Well maybe that says it all, guys. Have you ever had a woman look at you like that; ladies do your men look at you with that much desire in their eyes? So, without further interruption, if you could hush please, we can go ahead."

The crowd roared louder still as Johnny appeared on stage and stood beside his brother. Laura and Dania came into view carrying the twins, who were dressed in little white organza dresses, with tartan sashes, and pink ear defenders. Andy and Jamie reappeared with James and Denis, who were also wearing kilts. The crowd roared again and lights flashed, as Chiara held her hands out to Johnny. He took her from Laura to stop her crying. Finally, Clinton and Vickie walked on, followed by Lynne.

"God, you're as beautiful as the bride!" Chris whispered, as Lynne moved over to stand beside him. He kissed her cheek and put his arm around her waist. "Let's do it too!"

Vickie wore a white silk, floor length, strapless dress with rose patterned lace overlay, and a matching bolero jacket. Nicky had carefully pleated flowers into her hair. The dress had been made by Nicky in two days, from two shop-bought dresses. Vickie stood beside Johnny, who was still holding Chiara, at the front of the stage whilst they were married. Vickie looked into Johnny's eyes, smiling as they repeated the vows the registrar read out. When the registrar finally said, "you may now kiss the bride!" Johnny handed Chiara to Chris and swept Vickie into his arms as the crowd went wild.

Jamie and Chris stepped forward. Andy sat down at his drum kit lifting James, who was carrying drumsticks, onto his lap. Chris passed Chiara to Laura, then brought a small guitar from behind the set and handed it to Denis.

Jamie called for quiet. "Ladies and Gentlemen, we've only had a few days to practice this! It's a song Andy wrote for the happy couple. We thought that they should have their first dance here." They began to play; to Vickie and Johnny's amazement, Jamie sang. The crowd roared and whistled as James and Denis played along with the band. Johnny took Vickie in his arms, moving her around the stage.

Vickie however, could not take her eyes off the band, "I can't believe Jamie's singing; he's fantastic! Involving the kids, I knew they were doing well with the music lessons but I'm flabbergasted Johnny."

Johnny nodded then looked into her eyes, kissing her as the crowd roared encouragement. "You look beautiful Vickie!" he whispered, "but I can't wait to take this dress off for you."

"Wait till you see what's under it," Vickie whispered in his ear, "I shopped for the underwear myself yesterday. Okay, I'm lying, Nicky got an upmarket lingerie shop to bring samples to the hotel."

The flashing of cameras blinded them and they knew they were the front page of newspapers all over the world. Britain would wake up to the news that they had married; America would have it on their evening news.

As they came off stage Clinton, swept his daughter into his arms. "Vickie I'm so happy for you. So very, very happy. I called your mother by the way. I didn't want her reading about it in the papers. She sends her love."

"Dad, it doesn't matter anymore, nothing that woman can do, or say will affect me."

"Vickie, just go see her when you get back from your honeymoon. I had a long talk with her on the telephone, told her a few home truths." He grinned, "she started saying to Stan, *'do you know what he's saying?'* you know what she sounds like?" Clinton began to laugh. He kissed Vickie before continuing, "Stanley, God help him, must have grown a set because he told her, 'I heard him.' He told her she should listen to me. It was her fault, she had a beautiful family she was ignoring. When you get home from the honeymoon, go see her."

"We're not having a honeymoon, Dad."

"Oh, we are sweetheart." Johnny grinned, glancing at Andy, who was shaking his head. "The guys were coming in to tell us they had booked us a honeymoon as a present; they saw us in the shower."

"They saw us!" Vickie gasped. "When we were....?"

"Oh yes!" Jamie laughed. "By the way, what's the tattoo on your arse? He won't tell us!"

"Private!" Vickie hissed.

"Whatever," Chris said, shrugging, "you know we'll find out anyway. For now, we have got you ten days on Musha Cay; it's a private island in the Bahamas. Whole island, luxury accommodation, just the two of you; you leave in about two hours. No one else there, just a few staff, white sand, clear blue sea and lots of sex."

Johnny looked at Clinton and smiled. "I am so going to ravish your daughter Clint."

"Just make sure the eggs remain unfertilised then."

Vickie kissed her father on the cheek and smiled, "no more kids Dad, we promise. You can stop stressing, we've all we need, two boys, two girls."

"Vickie I'm glad. I don't want to be a prophet of doom but another pregnancy could kill you. I couldn't go through all that again. If he is shooting doubles, it could be multiple births."

"Dad you're a paediatrician, you know fine well there's no evidence identical twins are genetic."

"I know but with your luck the research will be wrong."

"Please Dad don't worry, I'm a bit old for you to become an anxious parent." She nudged her new husband and laughed, looking at Clinton. "I'll have him done Dad, we did speak to someone but they're not keen because of our ages."

"I'll sort it out for you." Clinton laughed nudging Johnny. "I could do it myself if you like."

"Ha-ha Clinton. Like I'm letting my father-in-law near my crown jewels."

Vickie lay in a hammock, looking out at the miles of sandy beach and sea ahead of her, her head resting on her husband's chest. "Johnny, life doesn't get much better than this but I still can't believe how much this cost," she sighed.

Johnny smiled; his hand slid into her bikini top. "It's great here, three more days, and there's no one for miles, sweetheart. Ever had sex on a hammock? We've done it everywhere else now."

Vickie kissed her new husband and sighed. "I don't know, we could try but I think we might end up on the sand anyway. Sand isn't romantic; I had it in all my bits after yesterday. Sex in the surf might seem romantic but it's not, is it? Don't dare say it is. May I remind you, you were crying last night about the sand in your foreskin."

Johnny rolled over, the hammock swung around and he bounced out, Vickie landed on top of him. "Ouch fuck that hurt! Vickie, stop laughing please? I'm serious, it really hurts."

She glanced down, and gasped, "Johnny I think you might have broken your wrist."

"You don't say!"

CHAPTER
TWENTY-SIX

Vickie and Johnny came out of arrivals. Chris, Andy and Jamie stood waiting. "We had to come when we heard," Chris laughed, pointing at the heavy white plaster cast on Johnny's right hand. "At least it wasn't your left hand, bro; you'll still be able to play your guitar."

"No I won't, we're having a rest until after Easter as planned. No playing, nothing at all."

"The press is here, folks," Andy said pointing to the door. "You having to be airlifted to Nassau for treatment made international news. There are all sorts of rumours flying around, one of them was she broke your cock. Anyway, we didn't bother to respond. We just practiced looking concerned, thought if we all came to collect you it would stir it up a bit. They're in their hundreds outside, so be prepared."

"You look ravishing Vickie," Jamie whispered, as he kissed her cheek, "marriage obviously suits you."

Chris grinned at them. "Well? Mr and Mrs Vincent-D'Angelo, are you ready to face your public? The single went straight in at number one here, America, and Australia, by the way. Stroke of genius to release the cover of Black Velvet, just in time for us coming back off tour."

Andy nudged Johnny, and rolled his eyes upwards. "The video is amazing. It's just as well you got married publicly, because the

228

film taken from the Perth gig captured you touching Vickie's arse and kissing her before we went on." He giggled. "They had to Photoshop some of it too, because of the obvious bulge in your jeans when she was on her knees in front of you in Sydney. Mate, that is so going to end up on one of those outtake shows."

"Stirred, a 'who has the biggest cock in Black Velvet', debate in the tabloids, it did," Jamie said smiling at Johnny. "Lots of kiss and tell stuff, you've no chance mate, with no one who has kissed you and can tell. Chris is winning we think, we announced Lynne's pregnancy. Someone did a mock of a scan; picture a baby with a huge dick. It did the new single a mountain of good though."

"Here goes!" Johnny put his good arm around Vickie as they walked through the doors, out into the main airport. Cameras flashed, there was a buzz of voices as the journalists vied for their attention.

"Johnny, how's married life?"

"Vickie, is it true you're pregnant again?"

"Johnny, how did you break your wrist?"

"Well he didn't do it wanking, did he?" Chris laughed.

"Chris that's disgusting," Vickie gasped. Shaking her head, she smiled at the journalists. "Married life is everything we thought it would be, and more. I'm definitely not pregnant."

"The wrist?"

Vickie smiled and winked. "How could a man break his wrist on his honeymoon? I'll leave that to your imagination."

Johnny smiled, leading Vickie away from the crowd. "Thanks folks, we're tired and want to get home to the children."

"Johnny, what're you doing for Christmas?"

"We're going to have a very quiet family Christmas, just Vickie, me and the kids." Johnny grinned and looked around at his friends, "and the four ponies, two horses and complete stable block these three idiots bought for our present!"

"I said £100 limit for the kids!" Vickie gasped.

"We bought two legs and a tail each!" Jamie said, grinning back at her. "You actually didn't stipulate how many hundred pounds we could spend."

CHAPTER
TWENTY-SEVEN
January 2013

"Can you state your name, age, and occupation, please?"
"Anthony William Gorman! I'm fifty-four, and I'm director of a music management and promotions company."

"Mr Gorman, you have pled not guilty to the charges against you in relation to the kidnap, rape and attempted murder of Victoria Vincent-D'Angelo. Could I take you back to the night of February 27th 2011, when these offences are alleged to have taken place? Can you tell the court where you were?"

Tony looked around the packed courthouse, he knew this was his day in the spotlight; he was not going to waste a moment of it. His legal team had advised him on how to look in the witness box and what to say. Tony knew however, he didn't need their guidance, this was revenge.

"Mr Gorman, could you tell this court what happened that night?"

"I had just arrived at the venue in Hammersmith and I met Vickie outside."

"She asked me if I had any coke, which I'm ashamed to say I had. As it was raining we went to her car to do a line."

"That is, take cocaine, Mr Gorman?"

"Yes!"

"Had you taken cocaine with Mrs D'Angelo before?"

"Yes, many times, she and I, well we had an arrangement." He looked at the public gallery. "She was my lover for many years."

"So, you were intimate with her?"

"I was!"

"Did you also have a professional relationship with Mrs D'Angelo?"

"I was her band's manager for six years; however, we had recently parted company. Vickie was upset about this. It had been the other four band members who wanted the split, not her."

"Mr Gorman, what was your sexual experience with Mrs D'Angelo like?"

Tony smiled and looked around the courtroom. Marnie, Annie, Patrick and Clinton sat in the front row of the public gallery. Tony could see the shock on their faces. The court buzzed with anticipation. "We had an arrangement; she liked rough sex. I indulged her, had done for many years behind the back of her husband."

"Mr Gorman, were you upset that night?"

"Yes, I had been sacked by the band! I felt it was because Vickie had got into a relationship with Johnny Vincent. He suspected she and I had something going on, he wanted me out. Vickie and I had been meeting up in secret to have sex."

"Did you have sex with her that night?"

"Yes, she had fallen out with Johnny and he had gone off. She was alone and she asked me to take her somewhere to have sex. I suggested we go to my house in Windsor, where we had gone before. Vickie decided to call home first, tell her children's Nanny she had met a friend. However, she was very drunk and had taken drugs. We stopped in a layby because she felt sick; she fell out of the car. She hit her face on the door on the way out then she vomited. I cleaned her up. She insisted on giving me a blow job."

"A blow job?"

"Oral sex, she performed this, I sat on the passenger seat, she stood outside the car."

"Then what happened?"

"She asked me to finger her; put my fingers inside her! Then she took a photo with my phone and sent it to Johnny and Chris Vincent!"

"What happened next?"

"We drove to Windsor, and went to the bedroom. We had used handcuffs many times, it wasn't unusual for Vickie. So, I chained her to the bed and we had sex?

"You had consensual intercourse with Victoria Vincent-D'Angelo? Did you do anything else?"

"Yes, we did more cocaine together; she asked me to put it inside her vagina as she liked it this way. We had done it before; she said that it enhanced our love making."

"Then you had intercourse with her?"

"Yes, she liked it rough," Tony said looking sadly around him. He glanced at the jury, "she liked me to hold her throat when she was climaxing. We had done this before. Vickie reckoned it made her orgasms deeper." Tony began to cry, he looked around, tears falling on his cheeks. "I never meant to hurt her but I had been drinking, I had taken a lot of drugs. Vickie was demanding; I needed Viagra and coke to keep up with her. I don't know what happened," he sobbed, "I don't remember anything else. I think I was hallucinating or something, next thing I knew I was in a police cell."

"Do you know what you did to Mrs D'Angelo?"

"Yes, I've seen the police statements. I never meant to hurt her. I love Vickie. I believe she cared about me. It was the amount of alcohol and drugs we took that night." Tony looked around the court, he had tears running down his face, and he looked upset.

His barrister turned to him. "How do you feel now Mr Gorman?"

"Ashamed, remorseful, I just can't believe it happened. I've been having treatment for addiction in prison." Tony looked directly at Clinton and the others. "I never really took drugs before I signed Black Velvet, they introduced me to it. Can I be excused please? I don't feel at all well; I need a break."

The court was adjourned till the following day. Clinton, who was white with anger, spoke to Anita outside the courtroom.

"He's a liar, a fucking lousy, rapist, liar. She would never have done anything with him. Yes, she trusted him, but that wasn't Vickie he was talking about."

Anita nodded, "I know Mr Malone, but now we know what his defence is, I can build the case around it. He had already told the police he did it." "He knows he's going to be convicted, he's just trying to muddy the water a bit, condone his actions."

"I hope you are going to discredit him? Show him for what he is?

"Not yet Mr Malone, I'm going to play along with his show of being too unwell to carry on." Anita smiled and put her hand on Clinton's shoulder, "it gives me a chance to build our attack. We'll play along with this; I'll ask for the right to cross examine him later in the trial. I'm going to call the medics, police witnesses and the psychologist, then Jamie and Andy. Lynne will give us an account of what happened when she and Johnny got into the house. My guess is, they'll be honest, and this will shine through." Anita smiled and put her hand on Clinton's arm, "the truth will out Mr Malone, and Tony Gorman will get what's coming to him. Christ he's a convincing liar, isn't he?"

"A psychopath with sociopathic tendencies, really quite unusual. If you get him convicted, he will keep the psychiatrists in Broadmoor in business for the next few years." Clinton sighed and looked at Anita, "that's my little girl's reputation he is destroying in there! None of it is Vickie, and the boys, they aren't at all like he is making out. They were real innocents abroad, when this all started." He shook his head, "that's why he was able to manipulate, and control them."

"Mr Malone, Tony Gorman will hang himself in there, we

just need to give him enough rope." Anita smiled wryly, "I've spent quite a bit of time with them all recently. I am in awe of them all, the way they cope, especially your daughter. She really is amazing. Strong women come in all shapes, sizes and ages, don't they?"

CHAPTER
TWENTY-EIGHT

ndy stood in the witness box. He was wearing a navy blue suit, pale blue shirt and navy blue tie. The room was crowded and there were many young females in the court, both in the public area behind the dock and in the gallery above the court. There were shouts and sexual connotation.

"Order in the court! Order in the court!" the usher shouted, as Andy was sworn in. The court had heard all the medical and police evidence first, and was now ready to hear from the band about what they had witnessed.

Colin had been called first then Laura. Jamie had been called the day before, however after giving evidence for the prosecution, the defence had concentrated on whether Jamie could remember anything useful because of his drug use.

Rather than speaking about the attack, the defence barristers had focused on Jamie's lifestyle. Jamie however, to his credit, had remained calm. His eccentricity had been amusing, rather than condemning. Jamie played to the crowd; the barrister had eventually given up. Jamie had warned the others, the defence were not interested in the attack but were merely trying to discredit him as a witness.

They had repeatedly asked Jamie about his relationship with Vickie and whether they had ever been intimate. Jamie had admitted to having been attracted to Vickie in the early days but denied any other relationship with her.

Anita Robinson stood up. She nodded at the judge. "Good morning My Lady." She turned to Andy, "good morning Mr Cowan, can you state your full name, age, and occupation to the court please?"

"Andrew Douglas Cowan, I'm 24 and I'm a musician."

There was a cheer from the public gallery and the judge looked around and said sternly, "please refrain from shouting out! Or the court will be cleared."

"You are, I believe, a drummer with the band Black Velvet?"

Andy nodded, "I am!"

"Can you tell me where you were on the night of the 27th of February last year Mr Cowan?"

"I was in London attending an awards presentation."

"Who were you with Mr Cowan?"

"The other members of Black Velvet and our management team!"

"We've heard from your bandmate James Connolly about the events where your vocalist Victoria Vincent-D'Angelo went missing, and the search for her. Could you tell me in your own words what you witnessed when you entered Poachers Cottage please?"

Andy's voice sounded emotional as he recounted entering the room and what he had witnessed. He admitted that he did not see Vickie being attacked. He was asked about Tony and the band's relationship with him. Anita thanked him. She turned to the defence barrister, "your witness!"

"Good morning Mr Cowan!" The young female barrister looked at Andy, "how are you this fine morning?"

"Good morning, I'm good, thank you."

"You seem very nervous, for someone who lives his life in the spotlight."

"Objection!" Anita cried, jumping to her feet. Addressing the judge, "my learned friend is making an assumption. She's

deliberately trying to undermine the witness. Like many people, Mr Cowan has never been a witness in court before."

"I was merely stating an observation My Lady," the female defence agent said, looking at the judge and then the jury.

The judge looked at the defence barrister over the top of her glasses. "Sustained, counsel please keep your observations to yourself. Mr Cowan, would you like some water?"

Andy shook his head, "no thanks, I'd probably spew . . . sorry, be sick, Your Honour." Laughter could be heard in the courtroom.

The defence barrister resumed her questioning of Andy. "Mr Cowan, we have established that by the time you arrived in Mr Gorman's home, Mr Gorman was being restrained by police. What exactly you can contribute to this part of the prosecution is beyond me; however, I am interested in the dynamics of your band. I believe you all live in the same house?"

"We do!"

"What is your relationship to Victoria D'Angelo?"

"It's Vincent-D'Angelo, she's my friend."

"How long have you known Victoria Vincent-D'Angelo?"

"Over 20 years, we were at the same nursery, primary school and secondary school."

"You were a friend of her late husband, Mr Cowan?"

"Yes, both her first husband and her present husband."

"What did you think of Victoria Vincent-D'Angelo taking up with her late husband's friend only months after he died?"

"I was surprised, but happy for them. They were friends, we all were but they fell in love!"

"Were you jealous?"

"No not at all, we were all happy for them."

"Did you ever have a sexual relationship with Victoria D'Angelo?"

"No and it's Vincent-D'Angelo now."

"Did you ever want to sleep with her Mr Cowan?"

"Yeah, I would have, most men would, if she would have let me. We all would have, but she was married to Billy and," Andy looked around the court then at Tony, "100% faithful to him."

The barrister moved closer and stood in front of Andy, blocking his view of Tony. "Did you ever sleep in the same bed as Mrs Vincent-D'Angelo? This woman who wouldn't sleep with you!"

"Yes, a few times when we were on tour, and on buses, we . . . we're close friends."

"So, you admit you slept in the same bed as a woman you wanted to have sex with, and did nothing! The wife of your close friend, did she lead you on Mr Cowan? Letting you see her, teasing you? In the manner, she adopts on stage?"

"Objection!" Anita cried, jumping to her feet, "my learned friend is making subjective assumptions about the character of the victim here."

"Sustained!"

"Did you ever have fantasies about Victoria D'Angelo? She's a very attractive woman, who dresses seductively and gyrates on stage in front of you. Like this. Can we show Exhibit 19?" Andy looked at the screen as a picture of them on stage, Vickie kneeling in front of him, flashed up. "This is very seductive, Mr Cowan, it is a very intimate pose!"

"What? No! You've been watching too many porn films, Mrs. We're as close as brother and sister, that's as far as our relationship goes."

"You tour a lot, Mr Cowan, you and the band. In the last five years, how long were you away from home?"

"On average, we were away six out of twelve months for the first three years, not so much the last two."

"How often did Mrs Vincent-D'Angelo's first husband tour with you?"

"In the last year of his life, not at all, he flew out and joined us for a few days."

"So, she toured and lived with four bandmates and a mainly male entourage. You admit you were all attracted to her, shared beds, and were close, but that was it?"

Andy shook his head, "we, the band and our crew, we looked

after Vickie and the kids when Billy couldn't be there. Vickie has always looked after all of us, as a friend. There are other females in our group; our P.A, stylist . . . "

"Did the other males in your entourage feel the same loyalty to Billy D'Angelo? Johnny Vincent obviously is now married to his friend's widow.

"She was our friend's wife. Johnny and Vickie got together through shared grief. There was nothing before Billy and Ali died. We all get on but there was a line none of us would have crossed."

"So, there are boundaries with a friend's wife? What about unmarried couples, are there boundaries there? Have you slept with other men's wives, girlfriends?"

"Objection!" Anita shouted again leaping to her feet."

"Denied, answer the question please Mr Cowan."

Andy shrugged and looked around, "probably, but not with Vickie. I think of her as my sister."

The barrister looked at him, "who are your best friends Mr Cowan? Perhaps your bandmates?"

Yes, Johnny and Chris Vincent, Jamie Connolly and Vickie are my friends."

"So, Christopher Vincent is your friend?"

Andy nodded, "yes!"

"Does Mr Christopher Vincent have a partner?"

Andy's face coloured, suddenly realising where the barrister was heading. "Yes, he does."

"What is this partner's name Mr Cowan?"

"Lynne Love!"

"Have you ever had sex with Lynne Love?"

"No!"

"Are you sure?

"Objection!" Anita leapt to her feet and addressed the bench, "who this witness may or may not have slept with has no bearing on this case, My Lady. Mr Cowan has already denied this allegation, my learned friend,is badgering the witness." Anita cried.

The judge looked at the defence barrister. "Is this relevant to the offence being tried here Counsel?"

"It is My Lady; this man lives in the same house as the alleged victim. It is important to establish the life style and character of the victim and all witnesses."

"If it does not become clear in the next sentence where this is going Counsel, I will be sustaining the prosecutions objection. Mr Cowan please answer."

Anita sat down, watching Andy she nodded at him.

Andy looked at the barrister, "I've never had intercourse with Lynne!"

"I put it to you, you are lying. There were concerns about you sleeping with her, and other bandmates girlfriends. In fact, you all share girlfriends don't you?"

"Not anymore."

"So, there have been females you have shared?"

Andy shrugged, "there could have been, but it was always consensual."

"What about Francesca Middleton? There are newspaper stories of her being with you, James Connolly and Christopher Vincent."

"I can't comment on that; I wasn't there!"

"Mr Cowan, do you and the other male band members discuss sexual goings on? Is it not true you share information, have had competitions within the band, about how many women you have slept with?"

"Well, yes, we did when we were younger, not any more though. We are all very close and trust each other. We did have a lot of relationships with different people, part of growing up I suppose."

"What about Victoria Vincent-D'Angelo? You say you have never had anything but friendship with her? Were you aware of her having any extra-marital relationships?"

Andy shook his head, "No, never! Because it never happened."

"What about her relationship with the defendant, Anthony Gorman? Were you aware of that?"

"The only relationship she had with him was professional. She defended him, even when she knew he was in the wrong!"

"How do you know their relationship was professional? Would you have known if it was a sexual relationship?"

"No chance, Vickie would never have cheated on Billy, and certainly not with him, that's all in his head." Andy looked over at Tony.

"You said you were shocked about the relationship between Mrs Vincent-D'Angelo, and her now husband Johnny Vincent.

"I said I was surprised."

"So, you didn't know until they told you?""

"No!"

"So, in theory Mr Cowan you could have missed her and Mr Gorman having a relationship?"

"I know she didn't have a sexual relationship with him, there is just no way."

"Did you ever argue with Victoria D'Angelo, about her relationship with the defendant?"

"Yes, but only because she wouldn't listen to our suspicions about him. Vickie was loyal to him; she felt we owed him something!"

"So, Victoria Vincent-D'Angelo was grateful to Anthony Gorman?" She looked over at the dock. "The man you owe your success to, is that not true?"

"What, that Vickie is a loyal person? Yes, she is, once you are her friend she trusts you."

"I put it to you, you knew Victoria Vincent-D'Angelo was not faithful to her husband. I put it you, she was sleeping with Anthony Gorman, wasn't she?"

"No, she wasn't, he's a fantasist and a liar," Andy said looking around him, shaking his head. He looked Tony in the eye, "he can't go any lower than to tear Vickie's reputation apart. It's all nonsense."

The defence barrister smiled then looked at Andy, "I put it to you, Mr Cowan, that there was a blurring of boundaries, both professional and personal, within your circle. You, yourself, made comment on many occasions about Victoria's relationship with the defendant. I put it to you, you were jealous Mr Cowan. You have admitted in this court that you wanted to sleep with her yourself. You have also admitted to sexual relations with women who were in relationships! You knew of rumours about Mrs D'Angelo and other members of your band?"

Anita leapt to her feet, *"Objection,* the defence are badgering the witness, who is not on trial here My Lady! They are introducing subterfuge, and hearsay."

"Sustained, defence agent, the witness's private life has no bearing here. Please either bring this to a close, or ask pertinent questions."

The barrister nodded at the judge before turning to Andy. "No more questions, thank you Mr Cowan."

Andy stood down and left the court. Jamie, sitting at the back, followed him out. Andy staggered and Jamie took his arm and led him into the toilet. "Did you shag Lynne?" he hissed in his friend's ear. "You denied it to Billy and me when we asked."

Andy shook his head and then shrugged, "I don't think so, but we came close a couple of times I think. I was out my face Jamie, I don't fucking know, we were playing a game one night, it went too far. I wakened up one morning in bed with her. I might have, we can't remember."

Jamie opened the cubicles, making sure they were empty before speaking. "I did it with Lynne, years ago. Chris was on holiday with some bird. Lynne and I went to a party, we got wasted and did it, but no one knew. It wasn't good, we both realised that we shouldn't have and never did it, or wanted to again. Fuck sake Andy, I've never told Marnie. She slept with Chris once, years ago. "She told me when we first got together. I should have told her then but didn't. How the fuck did they find out about you and her, and not about me?"

"I don't know Jamie; Chris knows about it."

"WHAT?"

"Oh, we were trying a threesome but we didn't do it. Fuck, the camera in the houses! We were in the house in Fulham when it happened the first time! I'd forgotten about it."

"Fuck sake, you did it more than once then?"

"We didn't do it. Well, actually I'm not sure! You know what we were like. We were fucking wasted a lot.

"We'd better do a bit of talking about what we did in that flat Andy. Cos I fucked my way around it, so did you and Chris! We'd better get back in to court and see who they call next, hopefully it's not Lynne, and we can warn her."

However, when they re-entered the court, Lynne stood in the witness box. She was dressed in a black maternity dress, her baby bump looking huge on her slender figure. She sat down at the judge's direction. As she did, she caught sight of Jamie and Andy out of the corner of her eye. Lynne knew it was going to be tough. She knew Jamie had been left traumatised, mainly though, by the personal nature of the defence questions. Andy had been in the witness box just before her. Anita had whispered to her, warned her to be on guard. Jamie made eye contact with her and shook his head, *"be careful!"* he mouthed.

CHAPTER
TWENTY-NINE

Anita addressed Lynne, "Miss Love can you tell the court how long you've known Mrs Vincent-D'Angelo?"

Lynne smiled. "I have known Vickie since we were in Primary One. We were four years old when we met. We've been best friends since then."

"Do you share personal things, Miss Love?"

"Yes!" Lynne replied, nodding her head, "we talk about most things, even things we don't share with our respective partners. It's what best friends do."

Anita asked her about the night of the awards. Lynne told how she had been speaking to Vickie shortly before she disappeared. She told how Vickie had said she was returning to Johnny's Hammersmith flat, to spend the night.

"Did you get the impression that she was unhappy with Mr Vincent?"

Lynne shook her head. "No quite the opposite, she said she just wanted to go home and into bed with Johnny. It was a very new relationship at the time; they were not declaring it publicly. She said she couldn't keep her hands off him."

"So, it's a good relationship in your opinion?"

"It's a fantastic, mutual relationship."

"Miss Love, did you ever think Mrs Vincent-D'Angelo was having a sexual relationship with Mr Gorman?"

Lynne looked over at Tony and laughed. "I'm sorry but Johnny Vincent, Billy D'Angelo and Tony Gorman?" She rolled her eyes, "in his dreams! She was nice to him; Vickie is nice to everyone, but there's no way she would ever be interested in Tony." Lynne looked at Anita, and shook her head. "Not while there are dogs in the street!" The court erupted in laughter. "Sorry!" Lynne said, making a face "that just slipped out."

"Well, make sure nothing else derogatory slips out Miss Love! Or you will be held in contempt of court," the judge said sternly.

Anita smiled, despite herself, straightening her face, she addressed Lynne. "Miss Love can you now tell me about what happened when you discovered Mrs Vincent-D'Angelo was missing?"

Lynne then told of the shock of discovering Vickie was gone. The realisation she had gone with Tony. The images sent on the mobile phones to Johnny and Chris. She told the court of the chase across London, following the tracker signal. The court hushed as Lynne told of the scene that met her in Tony's bedroom. She began to cry.

"So, it was traumatic?"

Lynne nodded. "It was very traumatic; I still have nightmares.

"Can you describe for the court, what Mr Gorman was doing to Mrs Vincent-D'Angelo?"

"He was on top of Vickie . . . " Lynne began to sob. "He has holding her down by the throat, he was coming."

"Coming?"

Lynn took a deep breath, trying to compose herself. The court hushed in anticipation. When Lynne finally managed to speak, her voice was almost a whisper. "Climaxing, having an orgasm!"

"How did you know this, Miss Love?"

"He was making groaning noises; his face was contorted." Lynne took the wad of tissues the usher handed her and buried her face in them.

"Miss Love, do you need a break?" the judge asked, looking concerned.

Lynne shook her head, refusing the judge's offer of an adjournment. Anita waited until Lynne had taken a drink of water before continuing. "Can you tell the court what happened next?"

"Chris, he pulled Tony off her, threw him onto the floor."

"That would be Christopher Vincent?"

Lynne nodded. "Yes." "Vickie wasn't breathing." She looked at the ceiling and then at the judge, "Johnny and I did heart massage and the kiss of life. It seemed like a lifetime. I think though, it was probably only a few minutes. I thought . . . she was gone. I thought we had lost her." Lynne's face crumbled and she began to cry softly, "then she kind of coughed, and started breathing again."

"Miss Love did you think this was a scene of consensual intercourse?"

"No, absolutely not, it was a scene of extreme violence." Lynne buried her face in her hands and began to sob.

"Thank you, Miss Love, do you need a break?" Lynne shook her head, "No I'm fine. I see that scene in my head a lot."

Anita turned to the defence team. "Your witness!"

The defence barrister stood up. "Miss Love, you are obviously pregnant."

Lynne looked down at her bump. "Yes, it would appear I am."

"Who's the father of your child?"

"Chris Vincent."

"Where was he when you say you were rescuing Mrs Vincent-D'Angelo?"

"I don't know; I was preoccupied trying to get Vickie to breathe."

"Did you see Christopher Vincent hitting Mr Gorman?"

"No."

"Did you see anyone hit Mr Gorman?"

"No!"

"Are you sure?"

Lynne looked at the barrister then sighed. "Look, my best friend was dying in front of me. I concentrated on trying to save her. There could have been a brass band in that room and I wouldn't have noticed."

"Miss Love how much alcohol had you drunk that night?"

"Not a lot, I had one glass of wine. I had only just arrived when Vickie went missing."

"You were not at the awards?"

"No I was working. I had also fallen out with Chris, we weren't talking."

"You did go to the party though?"

"I did; I was invited to the record company party."

"Had you taken any drugs?"

"Yes, I had some cocaine."

"Why did you take cocaine, Miss Love? And how much?"

"Only a little, about half a line.

"Why did you take this drug Miss Love?"

"I took it because I had some in my bag. I needed some stimulation. I don't know I just did."

"So, you took cocaine, an illegal substance, and you expect us to believe you are a reliable witness? You could have imagined the situation in your drugged state?"

"I was very alert actually, that's what coke does."

"When did you last have cocaine?"

"That night! When I heard how much cocaine featured in the attack on Vickie, well after that, I never did it again. Chris and I got back together and we decided to stop using it."

"So, Christopher Vincent used too?"

"Yes, it's well documented he used cocaine! He and Jamie are the poster boys for the government's STOP campaign." Lynne looked over at Jamie and Andy then smiled. "We've both cleaned up our acts, and are about to be parents."

"Did you ever do drugs with Vickie Vincent-D'Angelo?"

"No never, she doesn't do it, never has."

"What about Jonathon Vincent?"

"Yes, many years ago, he hasn't used drugs for a long time. He's a bit of a fitness freak now."

"Did you use drugs with William D'Angelo?"

"Yes, a few times."

"So, he was a drug user?"

"He was an occasional recreational drug user. In the last couple of years of his life, it was very occasional."

"*Objection!*" Anita cried, jumping to her feet. "William D'Angelo has been dead for nearly two years. Whether or not he took drugs has no bearing on the offence being tried here."

"Sustained, counsel for the defence, please stick to the offence being tried," the judge said sternly.

The barrister nodded. "Sorry My Lady." She turned back to Lynn and asked, "Miss Love, is your relationship with Chris Vincent exclusive?"

"It is."

"But, you both had a lot of different partners didn't you? When did you decide to stop sleeping with other people?"

"It has been exclusive since the night Vickie was raped and beaten."

"Mrs D'Angelo-Vincent 'alleges' she was raped and beaten!"

"Whatever," Lynne said, glaring at the barrister.

"Before then, did you have a lot of sexual partners?"

"I had a few."

"Did you sleep with any of the other Black Velvet band members."

"No."

"Are you sure? Did you sleep with Andrew Cowan?"

"No!"

"Jamie Connolly?"

"No."

"Are you sure about this? My client would say under oath, he saw you, and these two men, together."

Lynne looked up, and sighed. "He might have."

"What do you mean, he might have Miss Love?"

"We used to drink a lot, wake up in strange situations."

"Miss Love, did you like Tony Gorman?"

"No I didn't. From the moment I met him, I thought he was creepy and a parasite."

"Did you ever sleep with him?"

"No, of course not!"

"Are you sure?"

"Absolutely!"

"So, you are sure you did not sleep with Mr Gorman but you are unsure about others."

Lynne looked around her then sighed. "Jamie, Andy and I did a lot of drugs together." She looked over at Andy and Jamie who were sitting in the front row. "We might have messed around, but we never had intercourse."

"Where was Christopher Vincent, when you think you might not have slept with his friends?"

"He was there too most of the time, he can't remember either. We used to take cocktails of drugs and alcohol, it affects your reality. You do stupid things, you hallucinate, that's why we all stopped."

"Did you ever indulge in these orgies in Vickie Vincent's home?"

"God no, never! Vickie and Billy would have thrown us out if they had caught us using drugs in the house. Never mind anything else. All of this was years ago, when they first moved to London. The four of us house shared for a while. Johnny and Vickie were still in Scotland, with their respective partners. We were teenagers, I was eighteen, very young and very stupid."

"I put it to you Miss Love, you and the five people in the Black Velvet band indulged in many forms of sexualised behaviour."

"Look Chris, Andy, Jamie and I, we did a lot of drugs back then. Johnny and Vickie, they don't, they never got into it, well not the way we did. They were both in stable relationships." She looked at the judge. "This is unfair. It has nothing to do with what happened to Vickie."

"Where is this line of questioning going counsel?" the judge asked.

"The defence will show there was a blurring of sexual

boundaries within this group of people Your Honour. We have heard both Miss Love and Mr Cowan say there was sharing of partners and sexual games."

Lynne turned around, the shock evident on her face. She looked at Andy, who grimaced.

The judge shook her head. "The witness is not on trial here counsel. You have made your point. Please refrain from this line of questioning."

The barrister nodded at the judge before continuing. "So, you say you saw my client having sex with Vickie Vincent-D'Angelo. On his bed, where she had gone, apparently willingly. Please show Exhibit 21!"

The court was shown a video of Vickie handing Tony the car keys and then getting into Johnny's car with him.

"Would you say Mrs Vincent-D'Angelo was leaving with Mr Gorman of her own free will?"

"You can't hear the dialogue, she was told lies. She was . . . "

"Miss Love, does it appear she was leaving of her own free will? Please answer the question!"

"From that video, yes, it could appear so. But it wasn't!"

"So, you entered the house, saw them having sex. How do you know it wasn't consensual?"

"She was unconscious, beaten to a pulp covered in blood. He was having sex with her."

"You've already said that people in your circle indulged in sexual gratification from various sources. So, you don't actually know if it was consensual or not do you?"

Lynne began to cry and was unable to speak, she looked at the judge. "I need a break My Lady, I have nightmares about what I saw."

The judge looked over at the defence barrister and banged her fist on the table.

"Counsel for the defence, you are not only badgering the witness, but you are now asking her opinion to suit your own needs. We will adjourn and ask this vulnerable witness to stand down for the day. Miss Love, may I remind you, you are still under oath."

Lynne stood down, she caught Andy's eye as she walked away. He made a face.

CHAPTER

THIRTY

Lynne sat at the kitchen table in Brickstead Manor with her friends around her. She had waited in town before travelling home. Waiting until she knew Vickie had put the children to bed, and retired herself. Johnny had gone out running. "Look, we really need to discuss this! I know it was years ago, but you all better think about what you did in the Fulham flat." She looked around the table, "there could be video evidence around. They'll know we're lying. Chris hasn't been called yet, and I've got to go back there tomorrow."

"Fuck sake Lynne we did some really stupid things in that flat," Jamie gasped, "all of us, Chris, Andy and I screwed half the world. Shared women, did threesomes. There were more fucking drugs than there is in the London hospital."

"Chill out guys, stop fucking panicking," Chris said smiling, "I spoke to Anita about it after you all rushed off. She reckons they can't use any of the stuff Tony gained from the cameras. Think about it; the films, they were illegally gained. Folks, they are trying to put the wind up you. Jamie, Andy, you'd better tell your women some of the stuff that you did back then, in case it comes out." He looked at Jamie then Marnie and smiled, "Marnie knows what we did Jamie, she was there a lot of the time. Andy, the fact that we all went out with

Frankie, was common knowledge; who gives a fuck, it wasn't at the same time."

"Chris how can you be so calm about this?" Jamie gasped.

Chris looked at Jamie. "We were what, 18,19 and living the dream? Shit who doesn't in our circle, it was all there on tap. We've all grown up now, and don't." He grinned, "well, not as much." Chris put his arm around his girlfriend, "stop worrying Lynne." He kissed her and smiled, "I know everyone you've slept with, so it makes no difference. I was as big a tart as you were. You and me babe, it's all we want now, isn't it?" Chris looked around the table, "it's all in the past, that lifestyle, we're all settled, not likely to stray. I know I don't want to, too much like hard work."

"Jamie, he's right!" Marnie sighed, "they're trying to tie Vickie into the stuff you all did. We all know she didn't get involved in it. Johnny, Ali and Billy never got into the sex stuff, and you have never hidden any of it really."

"But Marnie . . . I never told you."

Marnie looked at Lynne and Chris, then smiled. She patted Jamie's arm gently. "I know about you and Lynne, Jamie, she told me two years ago. I slept with him, you slept with her, the chemistry was wrong and it was a one night thing." She grinned at Jamie's shocked expression, "can we all grow up, and put it behind us?"

"Do you know how much I've worried about that Marnie, you knew and never told me?" He glared at Chris, who was grinning at him, ***"and you Vincent, you let me fucking squirm, knowing she knew?"***

Marnie looked Jamie in the eye, then shook her head, "Jamie, do you really want to get into who should have told who, what, in this house? It was a long time ago, you and I are together now. What happened to Dania and Vickie changed how all of us see sex, didn't it?"

"Fuck sake, we've all lived here for two years, and haven't ever done anything, but be friends!" Chris said smiling, "I think that's really grown up, don't you? None of what those lawyers are trying to prove is about us. It's about proving that Tony Gorman is not a fucking, paedophile, violent rapist. Which we know he is. Tony knows Vickie and Billy were never into swapping, or casual sex. Just like he knew Johnny and Ali weren't, but he's told the lawyers enough to make it look as though we're still living like that."

Jamie looked thoughtful, "I was watching the jury when Lynne said about us being young and stupid, doing daft things." He added, "I think they believed her."

Lynne nodded, visibly calming down, "Vickie and Johnny are going to write a book." She looked up at Chris standing behind her, his hands on her shoulders. "You're so right babe, I'll just tell the truth." She smiled, Chris bent down and kissed the top of her head, "apart from the drugs, we've done nothing illegal, immoral, perhaps, but the sex was consensual." She looked around the table, "we're all still friends. It's Rock and Roll! We're all suitably ashamed of it all, and doing stuff to educate young folk on the ills of drug and alcohol misuse! So, what the fuck, guys."

Andy still looked worried. "What about me and Mhairi folks? You all live in this circle, she doesn't," he sighed.

Chris snorted. "She would need to have been living in a fucking remote village, in the Amazon rainforest Andy, to not know what you're like mate! You were never out the papers before you met her. Frankie and you, that sex tape went viral. I reckon you fess up to the stuff with Lynne, then let Lynne and Marnie talk to her about it."

"Actually, we didn't Andy!" Lynne said smiling, "you fell asleep. When you wakened up and panicked, I just let you think you had. You ran straight to Chris; it's okay, I didn't tell him either. It was great; you couldn't look me in the eye for weeks!" She looked around the table. "By the sounds of it, we're all starring in sex tapes now. Can you imagine what the police who had to watch, to charge him, thought?"

"Suddenly what felt like an exciting time, now feels so wrong! It all seems sordid and dirty folks!" Andy said grimacing.

Chris laughed, "fuck sake you're a grown-up Andy, how fucking strange is that? First Jamie, now you! Vickie will be so proud; her work is done."

Andy, still looking uncomfortable, shook his head, "you two, Sid and fucking Nancy! You're having a baby, haven't touched drugs in a year. So if there's a Vickie prodigy here, it's got to be you pair." He looked up and smiled as Vickie came back into the room, she was wearing a dressing gown and slippers.

"What? Who's my prodigy?" she asked, pouring a drink, she moved towards the table.

"We were just talking about the past, some of the daft things we did, thinking we were cool. You know sex, drugs and rock and roll. There's things coming out in court. Stuff you don't know about." Jamie sighed, looking around at Vickie, then making eye contact with Marnie, who smiled.

Vickie looked around the table and laughed, "you lot think you have secrets? All of you told Billy about your exploits, he told me." She sat down in the empty chair between Jamie and Andy. "We used to piss ourselves laughing about some of the things you lot did! There won't be much I don't know folks." She smiled at Chris, "anyway for what it's worth, I'm really proud of you, and grateful to you all. Billy and I used to learn from it, try things, because you all blabbed to him about what you got up to. Learned everything I know from you lot, without you even being aware of it! Well, there was also the Kamasutra. I put it all together with my gymnastic talent. Johnny now benefits from that learning." Vickie grinned and looked around the table at the shocked faces of her friends, as Johnny came into the room.

"Oh, you lot have no idea how talented my wife is, and for someone who has had two sexual partners, wow!" Johnny grinned, dropping a kiss on Vickie's head. "You lot blab to each other about everything, she's right."

Vickie grinned and put her hand out to Johnny who high fived her before sitting down across the table from her with a bottle of water. Vickie looked around her. "So, it's all good, no experience is wasted, a secret is only a secret if you don't tell anyone. Besides, it's all going to come out in court by the look of it." Her face sad, she put her hand on Andy's shoulder. "I'm sorry you have to go through it, but I doubt if it will do any real harm to your reputations. Because, you don't have reputations, and it's all stuff that's been in the papers anyway."

"Vickie, it's going to be quite rough in court babe," Lynne said, "they are trying to make out you were involved in some of the stuff we did."

"Anita told me Lynne, she said that you are all getting your past lifestyles brought up." Vickie looked around the table, "they don't have anything on me, thank you for defending my honour by the way. I love you all, I really do. Everyone needs friends like you lot."

Johnny reached out and took Vickie's hand, he smiled at her. "They are painting them as being real sexual deviants."

Vickie smiled again, "they are Johnny, I'm really looking like Snow White here, with you as the knight in shining armour." She glanced at the others. "All we do different from you lot, give or take a few hundred partners, is . . . we're discreet, and that's something Billy taught me." Vickie smiled sadly and patted Jamie's hand, "I'm so sorry you're all having to go through this because of me though. I'm really grateful to you all for that too."

"You really are a dark horse Vickie!" Jamie gasped.

CHAPTER
THIRTY-ONE

The court hushed as Vickie was called to give evidence. She was sworn in, and sat down. She looked around the packed court; Andy, Lynne and Jamie were sitting across from her. She smiled, calming slightly as Andy blew her a silent kiss, and Jamie winked at her. Their barrister stood up. "Mrs Vincent-D'Angelo, could you state for the court, your full name, age, and occupation?"

"My name is Victoria Margaret Vincent-D'Angelo. I'm 23 years old and I'm a singer."

"Who do you sing with?"

Vickie smiled slightly, "Black Velvet."

"Could you tell us about the evening of February 27th last year, where you were?"

"I was performing with my band at the Brit awards."

"What are the Brit awards?"

"The Britannia music awards, it's a ceremony to mark British musical achievements."

"Did you go anywhere afterwards?"

"Yes, I attended a party in Hammersmith, at my record company's office."

"When did you arrive at this party? Were you with anyone?"

"We got to the party around 10.30. I arrived with my husband, my brother-in-law, and Colin Kodjoa, one of my security team. We met my best friend, Lynne Love, outside."

"Mrs Vincent-D'Angelo. "Were you kidnapped and attacked after this party?"

"I was."

"Do you see the person who kidnaped and attacked you in this court?" Vickie looked for the first time at the dock.

"Yes."

"Can you point to the person who attacked you?"

Vickie raised her hand and pointed at Tony. He looked straight at her, and to her amazement, grinned.

"Who is this man?"

"He's Tony Gorman."

"And, what is your relationship to him?"

"He was my band's manager."

"Mrs Vincent-D'Angelo did you ever have any other type of relationship with Anthony Gorman?"

"No, absolutely not." Vickie could feel her eyes welling up.

Anita looked Vickie in the eye. "I'm sorry that you have to be put through this, but it is essential we hear from you."

Vickie nodded. "I understand."

The barrister led Vickie through the events of that evening: the phone call from Catriona, the reason she got in the car, the terror during the journey then what she recalled about the bedroom in Windsor. The court was hushed. There were audible gasps from the public gallery as Vickie's voice, clear and strong, told them of the unwitnessed occurrences during the attack. Several times she paused, trying not to cry in front of the crowded court, as she gave the details of what the man in the dock in front of her had put her through. Her friends and family, watching from the public gallery, knew she was reliving it as she spoke. Anita asked some questions, but mainly she just let Vickie speak.

"Thank you, Mrs Vincent-D'Angelo, I realise this is difficult, but can you tell the court about your mental health since that night?"

Vickie lowered her eyes. "It has been difficult to trust people, even those around me who have been my friends for many years. I found it traumatic to have even my doctors touch me. After the attack, it was three weeks before I could even hug my children or partner. I suffer from flashbacks and night terrors. I find it frightening to be alone. I have panic attacks and problems with intimacy." Vickie blushed and looked at the ground. "When we're intimate, I have to be able to see my husband; I have to know all the time it is him."

The barrister lifted some papers. "Mrs Vincent-D'Angelo, at the time of the attack were you in a sexual relationship?"

Vickie nodded. "Yes, I was." She looked over the court to where Andy and Jamie sat, and smiled slightly.

"Who were you in a relationship with?"

"Johnny Vincent-D'Angelo, lead guitarist in my band, who is now my husband."

"When did this relationship become sexual?"

"Just over a year ago."

"Is your husband the only person you have been in a relationship with since the death of your first husband?"

"Yes."

"Did you have any other relationships of a sexual manner, while you were married, or before?"

"No, Billy and I were together from I was thirteen. I married him a week before my seventeenth birthday, we were mutually exclusive."

"So, you have never had sexual intercourse with anyone other than him, and Johnny Vincent-D'Angelo?"

"No, well not willingly. I was raped by Tony Gorman."

"Objection!" the defence counsel shouted, "this is an allegation."

"Denied, allow the witness to continue!" the judge said looking over at Vickie.

"So, you were never in any sort of consensual intimate relationship with the defendant?"

"No, never!"

"Mrs Vincent-D'Angelo, do you use drugs?"

"No, not my thing I'm afraid."

"Have you ever used drugs?"

"I dabbled a little, when I was younger, but I haven't for a long time now."

"Thank you, Mrs Vincent-D'Angelo. I have no more questions for you."

The second defence barrister, a young pretty woman stood up. "Good morning Mrs Vincent-D'Angelo." She began to ask Vickie about her relationship with Tony Gorman. "Mrs Vincent-D'Angelo you have testified under oath that you were not in a relationship with the defendant." "Yet he claims that on the night of the alleged incident you went willingly with him, even offered him the keys to your lover's car. We have seen the CCTV footage, which appears to support this.

"He's lying!"

"The court has heard what you say the sequences of events were. I have no wish to distress you. You say that he offered to take you home then attacked you. Why would he then ask you to call your house? Is it not true that you and Mr Gorman often indulged in a sexual relationship? You were calling to make an excuse for not going home?"

"That's absolute rubbish!" Vickie said quietly. "Yes, I went willingly with him in the car because I thought my daughter was ill. I was desperate to get to her. I'd no reason to believe Tony Gorman would hurt me. I'd known him since I was a teenager, he appeared sober, he had never ever done anything to make me think he would harm me."

"Yet, you claim he attempted to murder you and brutally raped you?"

"He did," Vickie replied.

An hour later the court adjourned to allow Vickie, who was sobbing, a break. Lynne rushed to her side as she was ushered into a private room. Andy and Jamie followed them in, both still clearly disturbed by what they had heard in court. Lynne wrapped her arms around Vickie and held her, telling her how brave she was.

"Oh, dear God, sweetheart," Andy cried. "Hearing it like that, you must have been terrified? You never said he told you he would kill you and bury you? Oh, fuck, I don't know, I knew he raped you, but I never . . . "

"I couldn't tell you, you were already traumatised. No one was dealing with what they saw. How could I tell you stuff like that?" Vickie sobbed into her hands.

"Lynne stood up. "I'm going to go get you a coffee." She looked at her two friends, "stay with Vickie, until I go and see Anita!" She whispered, "we need to get this stopped, get her home."

"Lynne, I'm okay, we need to get this finished, I'll be fine. Andy, don't crack up, what happened, I should have prepared you for it. I didn't know how to say it to you."

"Does Jovi know? How bad it was?"

"Of course, he does. We're okay with it now, Andy, or as okay as we can be. Dealing with it all, I . . . I just get tired, being strong all the time."

Andy wrapped his arms around her and held her, kissing her wet face. "It's nearly over honey. The defence can't possibly think they can do any more to you."

"I want Johnny, I just want to go home; I can't do this I just can't! I'm back in that room," she sobbed.

Andy held her, speaking softly to her. "Babe you need to keep going. After hearing the details of what he did to you, we need to get him jailed. Vickie, I can't believe that you lived through that. I want to fucking torture and disembowel the bastard."

Jamie, who had been sitting in silence listening, thumped his fist on the table in front of him. "I want to get his fucking barrister in a dark alley. How can a woman do that to another woman? They are just grasping at straws, trying to muddy the water, that fucker needs her head examined! Any fool could see you were telling the truth."

"It's just her doing her job Jamie. They've used a woman to do it because it looks better," Vickie said, holding on to Andy, talking into his shoulder without looking at Jamie, as she spoke. "They just want to put enough doubt in the jury's mind that we could be telling lies."

The door opened and Lynne returned holding a tray of paper coffee cups. She shook her head. "Fuck I had forgotten how bad it was Vickie, until those pictures of your injuries flashed up."

"I think we're all going to have trouble sleeping again tonight hun. I think I might need to vodka myself to sleep." Andy sighed, kissing the top of Vickie's head. Jamie nodded.

In a room along the hallway, Anita was sitting with Johnny and Clinton. Chris stood watching, his back to the wall. Johnny listened as Anita and Clinton told them the salient points of Vickie's ordeal in the witness box. "Fuck why didn't I get called first? I could have been in court, if I had given evidence."

"Johnny, you have to be after Vickie. I need you in case they bring anything else up. You were with Lynne, first on the scene. You're articulate; we'll use you to mop up. Chris we'll need you to be ready, in case they get desperate and bring up you beating him up. They alluded to it whilst cross examining Lynne then just left it." She smiled, "I think Jamie put them off calling you, he was brilliant, so natural, the eccentric act."

"That's no act Anita, that's him, he jumps in and out of it, and he manages to forget things he doesn't want to remember," Johnny said, wiping his eyes. "Do you think they'll call, Toph?"

"I'm not going to because there's nothing that he can add other than giving Tony a pasting."

Chris made a face. "Are they likely to take that any further? I'm ready to talk about the shock and horror I felt, and that I just lashed out. I could always say I was out of my face and can't remember. Although unlike Jamie, I always remember everything."

"Lynne saying you and her used drugs, and being as honest about your sexual pursuits, would allow for that Chris." Anita grimaced and looked at him. "We just need to hope the jury see it was her being truthful because it could have the opposite effect."

"Yeah, I suppose, but she was just being honest, most of the hard drug stuff and sex games were a long time ago. We did a lot of stupid stuff back then, Lynne and I especially. We haven't broken any laws by having a varied sex life. As for the drugs, I'm the young people's ambassador for drug desistance. At least she didn't divulge some of us, still have the occasional toke. In terms of my beating him up, if he was trying to say they indulged in weird masochistic games. Wouldn't he have been better claiming that was why he got so badly hurt? Mind you his nuts must have been inside him, after that kick from Colin." Chris swung his leg to demonstrate.

"I want to do that now," Clinton said speaking for the first time. It's hard to sit there looking at the man who hurt her, Johnny! So be glad you haven't been sitting through it." He stood up, "I'm going to go see Vickie now." He put his hand on Johnny's shoulder. "She'll be okay Johnny; our girl is tough! Stronger than any of us."

Anita nodded her head, looked from Johnny then back to Chris. "Now, I need to get back to Vickie too. Hopefully she's calmer now, able to carry on if needed. I've asked that we adjourn for the day, but I'm not sure if they will? They did it with Lynne, then said they didn't need her and we went straight to Vickie." She too, put her hand on Johnny's shoulder as she left the room.

Johnny looked at his brother then put his head into his hands. "Oh, God, Toph, what if this sets her back?"

Chris looked thoughtful. "Bro, from what Anita said about her evidence, I actually think that it might bring the fight she used to have back. Remember what a fiery wee thing she was; she was always the boss? He took that away from her Johnny; maybe this court case will bring her mojo back."

Anita put her head around the door. "Go home boys, look after that poor little soul, she's exhausted. Medical advice is stop for today. Clinton has taken her home. They've left via the back door. Simon has a car coming for you two in about twenty minutes, drink your coffee and stay in here."

Back at the house Vickie was already in bed when Johnny returned. Clinton had sedated Vickie. Johnny lay beside her as the sedative took effect. He held her and soothed her, each time she cried out. Eventually she fell in to an exhausted slumber.

Johnny returned to the kitchen where the others were sitting around the table, he sighed and took a drink from Annie. "How is she, you haven't left her alone? This is unbelievable Johnny! What they are doing to her in the witness box! She's the victim. They're using all their fucking around and stupid behaviour, against her. Johnny, I'm going to go up and sit with her. We couldn't get her to stop crying, that's why Clinton sedated her," Annie sighed.

Lynne sighed and looked around the table. "The press is going mad about it though, saying she's being raped in the court. The result is the public are getting behind her. Although they're not naming her, it's on the internet that it's Vickie. It's all a bit stupid. I mean, what was the point of protecting her identity then hearing it in public court? All the stories just keep doing the rounds."

Annie stood up. "Last night was like it was at first."

Johnny wiped away a tear from his eyes and sat down with the others. Hopefully she'll sleep all night tonight. Clinton's gone to bed too. Must be hard for him to have sat through it all." He looked at his friends, "I'm sorry about her disturbing you all last night, she wakened up about ten times screaming. I know you must have heard her. God what else are they going to throw at her? She's being raped again in the court. So now you know it all, what she went through. She couldn't talk about it afterwards because she worried about making you all feel worse."

Jamie put his hand on Johnny's shoulder and looked around the table. "Our girl is a survivor, one of the bravest people you'll ever meet. I suppose like the rest of us, she just hoped that bastard would plead guilty, and this day wouldn't come. Poor Clinton, he's done in, Maggie had to stay with the kids and Laura. They are strong folks, aren't they? Vickie, her dad?"

CHAPTER
THIRTY-TWO

Vickie looked up as Anita came into the room. Vickie sat with her father and the others, only Chris and Johnny were not there.

"How are you?" she asked studying Vickie's face, "you don't look as tired!"

"Rested as I can be Anita, I am however, ready to fight." Vickie looked around the room. ***"No one gets to do this to me, not Tony Gorman, not that bitch of a defence barrister, no one."***

"Good girl, stay strong Vickie," Anita looked around the room. "The evidence against him is overwhelming folks. The fact he has put everyone through this trial is going to get him a longer sentence." Anita put her hand on Vickie's shoulder. "You're doing great Vickie, very believable."

"That's because she's telling the fucking truth," Andy cried out. He sighed. "How much more are they going to put her through, whilst that fucker sits there grinning? You know she's not lying about what happened!"

"I know Andy, but the jury has to know that too. I think the judge knows, but we need no doubts from the jury."

"Why is she on fucking trial here?" Jamie asked. "It shouldn't matter if we had gang bangs on the fucking front lawn! He raped and nearly killed her, and she has to prove it? We have to sit in there and have our lives paraded for the fucking world to see. Yet that fucking cowardly, perverted, fucking paedophile, bastard, rapist, twat and fucking woman batterer, sits there and fucking smiles."

"You missed out 'Cunt' in that little tirade," Vickie said, smiling for the first time. "Jamie calm down, it's just the way it is honey. I'm actually a lot tougher than I thought I was! I can be a cunt! I earned the right."

Jamie stood up wrapped his arms around her and held her. "You're the fucking bravest cunt I know Vickie. I'm proud to be your friend." He kissed the top of her head and looked down at her, "I love you babe!"

"Are you ready, Vickie? To go back in and let good triumph over evil?" Anita asked.

Vickie nodded. She kissed Jamie on the mouth, then ruffled his red curls. "I love you too Jamie Connolly." She looked around the small room, "I love you all, no matter what happens here, I'll take that with me. That's what's important, us as friends."

"Ready?" Anita said, resting her hand on Vickie's shoulder.

Vickie nodded.

"Good, I'll go and let the usher know."

Vickie returned to court determined to remain composed. The defence barrister restarted her cross examination. "Mrs D'Angelo I hope you're recovered."

"I'll never be recovered," Vickie said. "I'm ready to continue though, and I'm Mrs Vincent-D'Angelo, kindly address me as such."

The judge nodded. "Counsel for the defence, please address the witness by her correct name."

The barrister cleared her throat. "Sorry Mrs Vincent-D'Angelo. Could you please tell the court what were you wearing at the time you claim you were attacked?"

"When I was attacked, I was wearing a black evening dress."

"Underwear?"

"No!"

"Stockings?"

"Yes!"

"So, you wore no underwear? Only a pair of stockings?

"Yes!"

"Why?"

"Because I wanted to, and as far as I'm aware, it's not against the law to wear no underwear!"

"I put it to you Mrs Vincent-D'Angelo that you were trying to entice my client! The no underwear was to do this!"

"Objection!" Anita cried, looking at the judge. "Mrs D'Angelo Vincent's mode of attire has nothing to do with my learned friend. She is merely stereotyping her.

"My Lady, the question is related to whether the witness did as my client says. Attempt to deliberately entice him."

"Denied. Witness please answer the question. You are straying into dangerous territory here Counsel, so please be careful."

"Vickie shook her head. "No, my stage dress was tight and you could see the outline. My stylist told me to take my knickers off and I did. I didn't bother to put them back on when I came off stage."

"Do you often wear no underwear?"

Vickie shrugged. "If I choose to, yes. I find it more comfortable and liberating to not wear it."

"Did Christopher Vincent announce, on stage, that you were wearing no underwear?"

"I believe he did."

"How did he know?"

"Sorry?"

"How did your brother-in-law know you were not wearing underwear?"

"My husband made a remark about it, just as we went on stage."

"What did he say?"

"Can't remember, something about me being commando, I think."

"Is it common practice to share intimate information with your bandmates."

"We're relatively open with each other."

"Does that include sexually?"

Anita leapt to her feet. *"Objection!"* she cried, "this has nothing to do with the case for the defence! This young woman is the victim of a terrifying, violent attack on her." Anita looked at the judge, white with anger. "My Lady, my learned friend is bordering on interrogation now."

"Sustained, please refrain from what other witnesses saw or how they live! Please concern yourself with evidence which is relevant to the offence being tried here. Mrs Vincent-D'Angelo, do you need a break?"

"No thank you Your Honour."

The defence barrister walked out into the middle of the court room. She pointed to the screen and a photograph of Vickie being carried by Andy to the front of the stage, both laughing, came in to view. The angle of the picture meant Vickie's bare bottom could be seen. "Do you think your mode of dress, and lack of underwear, contributed to Mr Gorman perhaps getting the wrong message from you? You claim you were raped, yet you were half naked, weren't you?"

Anita jumped to her feet, calling "Objection!" Vickie however answered quickly. ***"Even if I was on that stage totally naked! It would have been my choice, and not an invitation to kidnap, torture, rape and almost murder me."***

There was a cheer from the public gallery.

"Mrs Vincent-D'Angelo, I put it to you that you and Mr Gorman indulged in a sexual fantasy that evening. I put it to you that you asked him to hit you, to fulfil a sado masochist fantasy game you often played. We have already heard from your friends Mrs Vincent-D'Angelo. This court is aware, in your circle, there were sexualised games and swapping of partners.

Anita jumped to her feet. "Objection! There is no suggestion, from any of the witnesses, that Mrs Vincent-D'Angelo was involved or even aware of their behaviour. You have no evidence for that statement.

"Sustained, please contain your evidence to facts."

"Mrs Vincent-D'Angelo did you indulge in sexualised games and behaviour? Meaning to show you in a sexual light or otherwise?"

Vickie looked at the barrister. "You've seen what he did to me. He kidnapped me, beat me and raped me. Do you think that was for fun? I've never been in anything other than a professional relationship with Tony Gorman."

"Mrs Vincent-D'Angelo, you say that you're in a relationship with Mr Jonathon Vincent. Yet you regularly cavort on stage with his brother, and the other members of your band. What is your relationship with Christopher Vincent?"

"We've been friends since we were young children; he and his partner Lynne Love, are my closest friends."

"Have you ever been intimate with Christopher Vincent?

"No."

"Are you sure?

"Well we used to play doctors and nurses when we were about 4 years old. Does that count?"

"Have you ever seen Christopher Vincent naked?

"A few times, everyone in our circle has seen Chris naked. He's a bit of an exhibitionist when he's drinking." She heard Andy laugh, from behind her.

"Has he seen you naked?"

"Not totally but we often, particularly in the early days, had to share dressing rooms. So, at times, we got changed in the same rooms."

"Did allow your friends, including Anthony Gorman, to see naked pictures of you?"

"They saw paintings by my late husband where I was partially naked. Yes, it was art."

"Why did you show them pictures of your naked body?"

"Because I trusted them."

"Have you slept with Christopher Vincent?"

"No."

"Have you ever slept in the same bed as Christopher Vincent?"

"Yes, but we have never had a sexual relationship."

"Do you regularly sleep in the same bed as your band mates? Mr Gorman will testify, under oath, he and others have seen you share a bed with men in your band."

"No, not especially. Sometimes on tour and travelling, you're so tired that you sleep where you fall. We're on tour buses a lot, it gets cramped and difficult."

"But, you are in a sexual relationship with Jonathon Vincent-D'Angelo?"

"I am."

"When did the relationship begin?"

"We have been in a relationship since December before last."

"Exclusive relationship?"

"Pardon?"

"Is it an exclusive relationship, exclusive, in that you have sexual relations only with him?"

"Yes."

"Mrs Vincent-D'Angelo, you live with the four men in your band?"

"Yes, we live in the same house. It's a big house, we all have self-contained apartments. "We share a kitchen and reception rooms. Other people also live there, my PA, Nanny's and security team, and the partners of Jamie and Chris. Like I said, it's a big house."

"Who is the owner of the house?"

"I am."

"Do you live as a family?"

"Yes, we consider ourselves a family."

"Your band members help you look after your children?"

"Yes, they help out."

"Your children call them uncle?"

"Yes."

"But none of them, your bandmates, I mean, are actually related to your children."

Vickie looked around she realised what was about to happen. "We use familiar terms." Despite knowing there was a strong possibility that she would be asked about this, Vickie began to panic.

"That's not what I asked you Mrs Vincent-D'Angelo. Are any of the band related to your children?"

Anita stood up. She addressed the judge. "Objection! The defence agent is badgering the witness, who is clearly becoming distressed."

"Denied, it appears to me to be a simple question. Although what relevance the answer has to this trial, I hope the defence will make clear shortly."

"I'll ask you another way Mrs Vincent-D'Angelo in case you did not understand the question. What do your children call Jonathon Vincent-D'Angelo?"

"Daddy. What does this have to do with anything?" Vickie asked, looking around the court.

"Mrs Vincent-D'Angelo, is it true that you refer to your present husband as Daddy, to your daughters?"

"Yes."

"Is it not also a fact Mrs Vincent-D'Angelo, that you have lied to this court about your relationship with Jonathon Vincent? You have been mendacious, in your account of when you began this relationship?"

"I'm sorry, I have no idea what 'mendacious' means."

"Fraudulent, lying, untruthful!"

"No, it began in December 2011."

"Then can you tell the court who the father of your twin daughters is, Mrs Vincent-D'Angelo?"

Vickie looked at the barrister, her head spun, she looked around her. She could see the horror on Jamie and Andy's faces.

The barrister held up a piece of paper, she handed it to Vickie. "Can you tell the court what you are holding?"

"My daughter Billie's birth certificate."

"Objection! Objection!" This has no relevance to the case being tried here. Mrs Vincent D'Angelo is a witness, she is also the victim of a serious assault. The defence is trying to badger her."

"Can you establish why this is relevant to this witnesses' evidence Counsel?" the judge asked, looking from Vickie, who she could see was struggling to breathe, to Anita and the defence barrister.

The defence barrister addressed the judge, "this information is very relevant, particularly in respect of the character and lifestyle of this witness and her friends. Your Honour, if you will let me continue please? It will become apparent, very soon, why I am questioning this witness in this manner."

"Objection denied, but kindly get to the point counsel."

The barrister walked over to Vickie and stood in front of her. She lifted the birth certificate and turned it around.

"What date were your daughters born?"

"19th of September 2011!"

"That is six months after the death of your first husband?"

Vickie nodded.

"Can you read out the part where it says father's name?"

Vickie began to hyperventilate, her face turned pale, and she shook. Andy stood up and shouted at the judge, "stop this, this is unfair! That bastard knows what he did to her. This has nothing to do with it."

The judge banged her fist on the ledge in front of her. "Kindly refrain from shouting in court or I will have you removed Mr Cowan. Mrs Vincent-D'Angelo, please answer this question!"

"What does it say, Mrs Vincent-D'Angelo?"

"Jonathon Allan Vincent."

"Was that by immaculate conception?"

Vickie slumped in the witness box, her head spun and she struggled to breathe.

"Mrs Vincent-D'Angelo? Mrs Vincent-D'Angelo will you answer the question?"

CHAPTER
THIRTY-THREE

"Vickie, darling, thank God you are okay! We thought you had had a heart attack! Clinton put his arms around her and she cried into his shoulder."

"I can't believe I fainted." Vickie looked up at her father. "Is it bad? Just what I'm needing isn't it? Another scar!"

"You're going to need stitches. You'll have a black eye; thank God, it's on the other side from the plate. You hit the deck with force to do that." Clinton lifted the pad from her face and grimaced as he looked at it. "Ricky is on his way love, I got him on the phone."

"Where's Johnny?" Vickie whispered, as Simon and Andy came into the room.

"Outside talking to Anita."

"Oh God, that story is going to be the front page tomorrow! Not what Tony did to me."

Andy sat down beside them. He put his arm around Vickie's shoulder. "I don't think it will make any difference sweetheart. I've been watching the jury; they know you're not lying."

* * *

As Rickie finished stitching the small cut above Vickie's eye the door opened and Anita came back into the room. "They've

273

adjourned for the day; Johnny has gone home. He'll see you at the house. Vickie, you knew this might come out dear. We'll include it tomorrow." She put her hand gently on Vickie's shoulder, "I don't think the judge feels it has any relevance to the rape charge. To be honest she might disallow it as evidence. The defence knew that once it's said it can't be unheard. You're being raped again in that witness box, and she knows it."

Andy pulled Vickie to her feet, "come on babe let's get you home." He put his arm around Vickie's shoulder, pushing away the wheelchair the court usher had produced. "Let's walk out of here with our heads held high."

* * *

Vickie melted into Johnny's arms as soon as she saw him, tears began to flow. "I'm so sorry Johnny. I should have just registered them as Billy's, the way we planned to. It was so stupid, what I did."

"Hey! Look on the bright side babe? Now we don't need to make an announcement! Come through to the lounge babe, you need to rest up." He smiled and kissed the top of her head then gently put his lips to her cut forehead, "you are going to look like a fucking racoon in the morning, both your eyes are turning black."

CHAPTER

THIRTY-FOUR

Vickie woke up screaming; Johnny was holding her, trying to placate her, but, in her head, she was back in Tony's room. Knowing sleep was impossible they went downstairs. Lynne and Andy were sitting at the kitchen table, talking quietly.

"You too?" Johnny asked, pulling out a chair for Vickie.

Lynne looked up and sighed. "I'm struggling to get rest anyway because of the size I am, but every time I shut my eyes I saw you. Chris got really drunk; he slept through your screaming babe. It really freaked me out though; it was like it was last spring."

Andy nodded. "I was struggling to sleep then I heard you screaming, it went right through the house. Just as well the kids are with Maggie."

Vickie grimaced, she took the two painkillers Johnny was holding out. "Sorry folks, the nightmare was bad. I don't realise I'm screaming, Johnny had to waken me this time. It's been a while since I was as bad. I was too warm; I opened the windows to let some of the heat out. I would imagine the press at the gates heard it too."

The door opened and Jamie came into the kitchen, followed by Marnie. "Fuck! you too; I kept seeing things every time I dozed off." He pursed his lips, "I was back in that room again; I

275

think it was seeing you getting taken out by the paramedics that triggered it. You lot the same? It's been a long three and a half weeks."

Johnny switched on the kettle and made Vickie and Lynne herbal tea. "I really need alcohol or drugs." he said quietly. "Want a beer Andy, Jamie, Marnie?"

Andy shook his head. "Rather have something stronger mate." He looked at Lynne, "if Chris left anything!"

Johnny went through to the lounge; they heard him open the drinks cabinet. "Vodka, peach schnapps, whisky, he's drunk the dark rum that was there," Johnny said, coming back through with the bottles.

Andy looked at Vickie. "Vickie just this once, can we have a smoke in the house? I would need to put the alarms off if I go outside at this time in the morning. I built a couple in my room earlier."

"I could do with one too, Andy, so just this once," Vickie admitted, as Andy pulled a cannabis joint out of his pocket.

* * *

Vickie, her face bruised and swollen, was met at the court by Anita, who asked Vickie if she was ready to go back in to the witness box.

"I kind of need to, don't I?"

"Okay we're not going to object to the questions about the twins father because we can actually use it. Given that Gorman got the doctor in New York to drug you. We've got a drugs expert, to say what MDMA mixed with that particular over the counter medication does. Thank God Clinton could remember what the cold medication was."

"My dad was livid, he knew the mix was dangerous. It's banned here apparently. Dad reckons we are actually lucky it didn't leave us with permanent damage.

Anita put her hand on Vickie's shoulder. "So, we'll let the defence finish their interrogation. Then they'll ask if there is anything to add and I'll ask you about your relationship. We'll call the expert witness, they'll object of course but we can argue it's relevant to your history with Gorman. I'll then call Johnny; luckily, we left him until last to mop up. He was so preoccupied with you at the time.

* * *

Vickie stepped back into the witness box. "Ah Mrs Vincent-D'Angelo I hope you're feeling better?"

"Yes, thank you."

"Now we established before you became ill, you had lied to the court."

Vickie shook her head. "I didn't lie."

"You said that you began a relationship with Jonathon Vincent in December 2011?"

"Yes."

"But you have admitted under oath in this court that he is the father of your twins. Who, if my maths is right, were born the September before you began a relationship?"

"Yes."

"So, unless there is an immaculate conception, you were in a relationship with this man before December."

"No, you asked when the relationship began, not when I slept with him. Johnny and I slept together once, a one-night thing, I think you could call it, and I got pregnant. We had been drugged. I didn't know until they were born that he was the father, neither did he."

"You expect this court to believe that? Even if it were true, wouldn't that mean your husband had sex with you without your consent? Please excuse my ignorance, but isn't that rape, Mrs D'Angelo Vincent?"

Vickie shook her head; she remained calm speaking slowly and deliberately. "Although we were hallucinating I remember enough to know it was consensual, so I don't believe it is! We were given mind-altering drugs by a doctor."

"So, it's not rape with your husband, but it is with Mr Gorman?"

"You fucking bitch, don't ever put them in the same context!" Jamie, jumping to his feet, cried out.

"Mr Connolly, please remove yourself from this court until you are calm," the judge shouted, "another outburst in that manner, you will find yourself in a cell."

"Put me in the same one as that lying cunt!" Jamie shouted over his shoulder, as he was ushered from the court.

"So, Mrs Vincent-D'Angelo! You say you didn't know you had sex with your dead husband's best friend. This court would find a story like this hard to believe. Isn't that the same as your bandmates behaviour? You claim you were unaware through drugs and slept together? Then didn't realise you were pregnant by him? Sounds like a fantasy to me."

"It's the truth."

"So, you found comfort with your husband's best friend? The night you both lost your partners? You slept with a man, you had known for years, and you expect this court to accept that you did not sleep with other men. Could what happened with Mr Gorman have been a misunderstanding too?"

Vickie however remained calm. "We began having a sexual relationship that December. In fact, if you want to be pedantic I had intercourse with Johnny at 12.29 am on the 1st of January 2012. It was in a hot tub in my suite in the house. But Tony Gorman battered and raped me. Who my children's father is, changes nothing."

There was a loud cheer from the public gallery, as reporters ran from the court.

"Mrs Vincent-D'Angelo, is there anything else you have lied to this court about?"

The judge banged on the ledge in front of her, "will counsel please approach the bench." The two barristers stood in front of the bench; the judge was obviously unhappy. Vickie glanced over at Tony who nodded and grinned at her.

"Rapist!" she mouthed, her eyes sparkling with fury.

Mrs Vincent-D'Angelo I saw that!" the judge said. "A repeat and you will be in serious trouble. Now counsel, have you got everything you want from this witness? She is not on trial. I won't remind you again. Counsel for the prosecution, do you have anything else?

"Yes, we would like to call Dr Cedric McGregor!

* * *

The drugs expert verified the problems that would be experienced by the cocktail of prescribed drugs. He also advised that MDMA being given in the circumstances, particularly with no thought to what other substances were in the system, would constitute medical negligence.

Finally, Johnny was called to give evidence.

CHAPTER
THIRTY-FIVE

The court buzzed with anticipation as the doors opened and Johnny entered the witness box. He wore a dark grey suit and crisp white shirt. He looked over at Vickie, sitting beside Andy, and winked. After asking him his name and age, Anita turned to Johnny. "Mr Vincent-D'Angelo can you tell the court about the night of Feb 27th."

Johnny spoke about his fear, looking for Vickie and the chase across London.

"You were fearful for your wife's safety then?"

Johnny nodded. "Yes."

"Why were you worried Mr Vincent-D'Angelo?"

"Tony Gorman had threatened us when we didn't renew his contract. He was angry about Vickie and I being in a relationship. He had also sent texts to my brother and I, showing Vickie was with him, and him sexually assaulting her."

"Can you describe these texts?" The court hushed, as Johnny replied, and described the photographs.

"Can I draw the jury's attention to the transcript of the texts and photographs exhibit 112." Anita moved on to ask about Johnny's relationship with Vickie. "Were you hiding your relationship?"

"Not especially, we just wanted some privacy. We realised it might seem odd, Vickie and I had got together so quickly after our partners' deaths, it was just under a year. We were ending our association with Tony Gorman, so we didn't want him to know."

"Mr Vincent-D'Angelo, are you the biological father of Billie and Chiara Vincent-D'Angelo?"

Johnny looked around. "I am."

There was an audible gasp from the public gallery. Vickie looked up at Andy, who kissed the top of her head, and pulled her closer. "It's okay babe," he whispered.

The judge banged the ledge. "Order in court please!"

The barrister nodded. "Mr Vincent-D'Angelo can you tell me how your wife came to be pregnant?"

"It was the night of the plane crash or possibly the following day. After we were told the news, Vickie became hysterical. He got a doctor to sedate her."

"Who is he?"

Johnny looked over at the dock. "Tony Gorman. He came in to tell us, with Vickie's PA, he brought the doctor with him. The doctor stuck a needle in her arm, I saw her calm down. I was very upset myself, so I asked them to drug me too. We didn't know, but they gave us a form of MDMA, which apparently combined with other medication we had taken and caused hallucinations. The effect lasted almost three days."

"You asked the doctor to administer this drug?"

Johnny nodded, "I just wanted to sleep and not think. I actually didn't know or care what they were giving me. Neither Vickie or I take drugs, so we don't have tolerance to them. The result was that we were . . . I don't know how to say it other than out of our faces. We both had bad colds at the time and had taken over the counter medication. No one asked, they just gave us the drugs and left us. At some point during that time we had sex! Both of us thought we were dreaming we were with dead partners, because the mix of drugs left us hallucinating."

"So, you were not aware you had had intercourse with Mrs Vincent D'Angelo?"

"No I thought I'd dreamt it!"

"How did you become aware?"

"The babies were born on September 19th, six and a half months after the crash. Vickie had been ill; the babies were not growing properly in the womb. Initially it was just thought this was the reason they were small. Vickie's father, Clinton Malone, who is a paediatrician, was looking after them." Johnny looked over at the jury and sighed, the pain obvious on his face. "Clinton became concerned that they were premature and therefore Billy couldn't be their father. He did the DNA test."

Anita spoke gently to him, "what happened after you discovered the truth about the children's parentage?"

"Vickie and I fell out over it all, we were in shock. We decided very quickly to try to sort things out. We found out in November, when the girls were eight weeks old. We worked through our feelings then got together at New Year."

"Did you disclose the twins' parentage to anyone else?"

"We didn't know what to do about the situation. We told those closest to us about the babies, at the time we found out. We have been trying to come to terms with it. We never intended to deceive anyone. Because we had all assumed they were fathered by Billy, and we are in the public eye, we didn't know what to do. We knew the truth would hurt a lot of people." Johnny wiped away a tear, "we hadn't told my late wife's family, or my parents. We were working up to it then Vickie was attacked. We had so much to deal with, we just didn't do the press statement, or tell the story. We knew that we would have to as they grew up, but we just needed time.

Anita looked at the jury, then back to Johnny. "The very fact that the defence were able to find out, should show Mr and Mrs Vincent-D'Angelo weren't hiding it."

Johnny was clearly fighting tears as he spoke. "My first wife was pregnant when she died, I was going to be a father. Vickie and Billy were trying to get pregnant. They were snatched away from us. *We made a mistake, but it takes nothing away from what that fucking animal, did to her.*"

The judge banged her table again. ***"Mr Vincent-D'Angelo! That type of language is not permitted in this court."***

"I'm sorry My Lady." Johnny composed himself, he took a drink from the water in front of him. "This is not easy for me, but there is no excuse for the lack of respect I've just shown the court."

Anita looked at Johnny. "Thank you for your honesty, Mr Vincent-D'Angelo. Can I ask you now about the events of February 27th, about when you entered the room in the defendant's house?"

Johnny looked up at the ceiling. "I was frantic by that time."

"Can you describe what you saw?"

"He was on top of Vickie; she was chained to the bed."

"He, being Mr Gorman?"

Johnny nodded. "He was having sex with her." Johnny choked, he stopped speaking, the court usher handed him a second glass of water. Johnny composed himself quickly. He closed his eyes as he spoke, obviously reliving the scene. "She was on her back; her hands were above her head with handcuffs, they were attached to a cast iron bed. Vickie was bleeding; her face was covered in blood." Johnny opened his eyes and his face crumbled, he began to cry. "I could see blood on the lower half of her body, the bedding was white, there was a lot of blood." He looked over at Tony, "he was having sex with her, he had only a white shirt on; it was bloodstained. He had his hand on her throat, Vickie's face was blue, her eyes were staring, she wasn't moving or breathing, she was dead." Tears ran down Johnny's face and his voice cracked. "Someone pulled him off her, and I started to try to resuscitate her. I had seen a video on CPR, so thumped on her chest, along with Lynne, who was with me. I didn't know what I was doing, I gave her mouth to mouth. She started to breathe again, but her lips were still blue. I thought. She was so cold . . . I thought?"

"What did you think Mr Vincent-D'Angelo?"

"I thought I was going to lose her," he sobbed. "Then the paramedic came in and took over." Johnny's face showed the pain of the memory. "Can I stop?" he asked, "I need to get some air." He rushed outside the courtroom, into the toilet; he vomited into the urinal, not making it to a cubicle.

When Chris ran in, Johnny was sitting on the floor, his back to the tiled wall, staring at the ceiling. Andy, coming in behind Chris, with Jamie, shut the door and he and Jamie stood against it, preventing anyone from entering. Chris sat down beside his brother, handing him a handful of paper towels. "Fucking waste of a good breakfast Johnny. You're doing good bro," he said, ruffling his hair.

"Toph I'm reliving it all over again! I want to fucking jump into the dock, and fucking kick, the fucking shit out of him."

"I know bro, but he's an animal, we're not."

Johnny's pain was written all over his face. "I thought I had dealt with it all, but fuck sake, it's all back! The fear, the pain, the whole fucking lot."

Chris nodded, "we have to get that perverted fucker jailed. Just hang on in there, bro, you're doing great."

Johnny nodded. He looked at his brother and friends. "It's so fucking hard boys. She could have died, she could have been dead."

"But she's not bro, she's out there in the hallway, waiting."

The two men stood up and embraced. "You're the best friend anyone could have Topher," Johnny whispered, as he moved away.

"Yes, I know; I have one of them too, best brother." Chris laughed, "I'd kiss you, bro, but you stink of spew."

Johnny splashed cold water on his face then turned and embraced Jamie and Andy. "You two; you're as much my brothers as he is. Thanks boys, for everything."

Vickie stood outside the gents toilet. Johnny came out and wrapped his arms around her. Together, they walked back into the court, he kissed her, then returned to the witness box. Jamie put his arm around Vickie, gently leading her back to her seat.

* * *

"Mr Vincent-D'Angelo you have now been in a sexual relationship with your wife for some time. Is your wife someone who indulges in unusual sexual behaviour?" Anita looked at Johnny, as she spoke.

"Absolutely not, Vickie is a gentle person." Johnny smiled slightly and looked over at his wife, "yes, she can be feisty, but this is a girl who's afraid of thunder. I'm not greatly experienced in these things. Neither is Vickie; I was with my first wife since we were 17. Vickie and Billy were a lot younger; she had only been with him and me, until that animal violated her. We have a fulfilling sexual life, but it's consensual and not violent."

"Mr Vincent-D'Angelo you have a plaster cast on your wrist, I believe you fractured it on honeymoon, how did it happen?"

Johnny smiled and looked over at the public gallery, "I fell out of a hammock, trying to have sex with my wife."

"Mr Vincent-D'Angelo how has your life been since this all happened?"

"It can be difficult. Like my wife, I suffer from night terrors and flashbacks. Everyone who was there that night does, we've all needed counselling and psychotherapy to cope with it. It's difficult to describe the guilt and the pain this has left." Johnny's eyes filled up, "it's also difficult to describe how I feel. I look at Vickie, and I see the daily suffering she has to go through." He looked over at the others in the court. "We all feel pride about how she has dealt with it, but we are all left changed and damaged by it. I feel extremely guilty I did not protect the woman I love."

"Thank you, Mr Vincent-D'Angelo." She turned to the defence lawyer. "Your witness."

The defence barrister stood up. "Good morning Mr Vincent."

"My name is Vincent-D'Angelo."

"Sorry, good morning Mr Vincent-D'Angelo, you are married to Victoria Vincent-D'Angelo, we understand?"

"I am!"

"Why did you marry her?"

"Because I'm in love with her; she's the mother of my children, and an exceptional person."

"Not so you could win your case against Anthony Gorman?"

"No, he raped and almost killed my wife' I didn't need to marry her to prove that." He looked over at Tony. "I caught him attacking her."

"Oh, not this case, but it was fortuitous for you and your brother, wasn't it?"

"What? Fortunate? My wife almost died at his hands!"

"No Mr Vincent-D'Angelo, the embezzlement accusation, you have made. How much is it for?"

"20 million with interest, we think."

"Is it true, that you wanted to end your association with Mr Gorman?"

"It is, I wanted to end our management by him over a year ago. That's not a secret."

"You and the whole band? Or just the males in the band?"

"We do not make decisions unless we all agree."

"Did all the band agree to end your association with Mr Gorman?"

"We all agreed, there was missing money and rumours about him with women."

"Did your wife agree about him? Or did you persuade her to go along with the arrangement?"

"No, he was verbally abusive and threatening towards Vickie, in a telephone call just after last New Year. She decided herself, it was time; we had been waiting for his contract with us to end, so there was no bad feeling."

"Was that what you all wanted? To wait?"

"No only Vickie."

"Do you think that was because she was in a relationship with Mr Gorman?"

"No I think it was because she felt loyalty towards him for things he did when we were starting out."

"You stand to gain around £5 million with interest, don't you?"

"I have no idea; I don't want the money. I intend to give it away, so does Vickie." He looked over at his wife and smiled slightly. "We're all going to donate it to charity."

"You're going to give away £5 million each? That's a lot of money!"

"We don't need it, nor do we want his money, but as you say it's a lot of money. We want it to go to help other rape victims."

"That's very noble of you Mr Vincent-D'Angelo. Did you influence your wife against Mr Gorman?"

"No! One of the reasons this all came about, was because she wouldn't listen to our concerns about Tony Gorman." Johnny stared hard at Tony then looked at the defence barrister. "Vickie trusted him! Vickie is her own person, but she's very loyal. He misused that loyalty, and took advantage of it.

"Mr Vincent-D'Angelo, did you ever sleep with your wife when she was married to your best friend."

"No!"

"Did you ever want to sleep with her?"

"No! She was my friend's wife."

"You tell us you are in an exclusive relationship with your wife. Yet your brother and she are close friends, so close that they have even shared a bed."

Johnny smiled and nodded. "We're all close; traumas in life have left us that way. But Vickie and Chris have always been friends, they just are. Chris, my brother, well his behaviour has always been a bit I don't know, wild. Vickie helps him regulate it, they're good for each other." Johnny looked over at Vickie, sitting between Andy and Lynne, her head resting on Lynne's shoulder. "It makes me happy that they're so close but it is, and always has been, platonic. Before Billy died, he had some sort of premonition of his death. He asked Chris to look after Vickie and the children if anything happened to him."

"Not you, his best friend?"

"No, he knew Chris and Vickie were mates, and it was a safe platonic relationship."

"Does it bother you that your wife goes on stage, half naked and dances seductively with your brother and your friends?"

"No, why should it? It's part of our act. She goes home to bed with me! Men want to possess her, but she is exclusively mine, my wife, lover, best friend." He looked directly at the dock as he spoke.

Tony stood up, his face contorted with anger. *"You bastard; you think you are so fucking cool Vincent, but I had her, I fucking had her!"*

"Mr Gorman sit down please," the judge said.

"Yeah you did, but you had to take it from her, nearly kill her to do it. She's with me willingly, you fucking, perverted, bastard," Johnny shouted back.

Tony tried to climb over the witness box and was immediately restrained by two policemen. *"Clear this court please,"* the judge shouted.

CHAPTER
THIRTY-SIX

In the witness room, Vickie straddled Johnny on the chair, her arms wrapped around him. He was sobbing into her shoulder, she said nothing, just let him cry. When the sobs became quieter, she took his face in her hands and kissed his lips gently.

"Johnny it's alright if it all ends now, the band the success, it doesn't matter. You and I we have something special, you know we do, and we have the kids to bring up. I think Simon's right, we should pick a journalist or ghost writer and tell all."

"Write a book?" Johnny asked.

"Whatever? I bet that if we approached a publisher tomorrow, we could have a book deal pretty quick."

He lifted his head and looked her in the eye, "you think?" he said, smiling through tears. "Our story is so fucking mad; people would think it was fiction! I don't know Vickie; it could make everything worse. I mean, we've got to consider everyone if we do, it's not just our story babe."

"Johnny we've probably got to do it. People are interested in us; we've been dragged through court and everyone knows now. The blackout on identifying me in the UK will only add to it all. You saw the American news headlines this morning? The victim admitted that her twin daughters are not her dead husband's children. Doesn't exactly take Einstein, does it? Tony has had his pound of flesh Johnny; we know he's guilty, but I'm sure the court knows too. His little outburst probably helped convince anyone who was in doubt."

"I'm sorry babe," Johnny whispered, "I wanted to get in that box and smash his smug face in! I promised myself I wouldn't react to him but when he started shouting, it just came out. I suppose we do need to tell the whole story now. How will you feel if all our intimate stuff is made public?"

"I think it already has been made public babe, but we need the truth to come out." Vickie kissed Johnny's face. "Let's get someone to do a sensitive story about the band. We can donate the proceeds to charity. The real Black Velvet, us as people, how we live, how it started. They'll make it up if we don't."

The door was tapped lightly. Simon Forsyth came in. "Are you alright Johnny?"

Vickie nodded. "We'll all be fine once we get this over with."

Simon looked at them and smiled. "Anita just called Tony to give evidence. His defence team refused, but the arrogant fucker, he said he wanted to do it! He's sacked his defence team, this is turning into a circus."

Tony Gorman sat in the dock, he was immaculately dressed and calm, after his earlier outburst. Vickie sat with Johnny, her father and the others, in the front row. Johnny's arm was protectively around Vickie and she leaned into him feeling safe. Anita Robinson stood up. She was a tough woman. She had spent a lot of time with Vickie and the others over the last few weeks. There was no doubt in her mind whatsoever; Vickie was a sweet young woman who had suffered a terrifying and tragic ordeal. Vickie's strength and resilience had amazed Anita. There was no way that this man was going to be found not guilty, not if she had anything to do with it. Within minutes Anita had discredited him and pointed out the police and witness evidence was overwhelming. She stated what the medical evidence was; that the injuries Vickie had suffered, were consistent with being violently beaten and raped. She spoke to him about his management of the group and the financial irregularities that had been uncovered and the fact that the band had sacked him. He slumped in the witness box as Anita finally said. "No more questions."

CHAPTER
THIRTY-SEVEN

"The jury is back guys!"

"That was quick, less than an hour, must be a record." Vickie gasped putting down her coffee cup. "They said it could be days!" The court had found them a private room, away from fans, and press, who were milling around in the public areas.

Their barrister raised an eyebrow. She crossed her fingers.

"Johnny, what if . . . ?" Vickie gasped, looking around at her husband and friends.

"Don't say it honey, they know we're telling the truth." Vickie, shielded by her husband's arms, flanked by her friends, made her way back to court. She looked at the judge as she asked the Tony to stand. Vickie held her breath and she felt Johnny's arm tighten around her. He kissed the top of her head as Andy took her other hand and held it.

"Have you reached a verdict on which you all agree?"

"Yes."

"On the charge of rape . . . how do you find the defendant Anthony William Gorman?"

"Guilty."

Andy and Jamie let out a cheer. Vickie glanced over at Chris, he was smiling broadly.

"On the charge of attempted murder . . . how do you find the defendant Anthony William Gorman?"

"Guilty."

"On the charge of kidnap . . . how do you find the defendant Anthony William Gorman?"

"Guilty."

Johnny hugged Vickie, kissed her and kept his arms around her, weeping with her.

Chris leapt over the seat and grabbed Vickie in a hug. "You did it, you brave, brave, girl."

Lynne ran around and joined them.

"Order! Order in the court!" the judge shouted. Vickie looked over at her and as their eyes met the woman nodded her head and smiled slightly. They sat down. Tony was slumped in his seat.

Jamie jumped over the barrier and began to shake hands with the jury. **"God bless you!"** he cried, as a policeman escorted him from courtroom.

"This court is adjourned until the 22nd of February for sentencing; you are remanded in custody Mr Gorman. Take him down officer."

Vickie looked up as Tony was taken away. He mouthed, 'I'm so sorry!' as they led him away.

CHAPTER
THIRTY-EIGHT

22nd of February 2013

"Vickie, you are sure you want to do this?" Simon asked her. They were sitting outside the court, waiting to go in to Tony Gorman's sentencing hearing.

"Yes, I think I need to do it, for women who are raped, and then have the most intimate details of their lives bared in court. No one could mention the other charges Tony had, because he was innocent until proven guilty. Yet my life and Johnny's, those of my kids, our friends, were dragged into open court. I was raped again by the court system. I was the victim in this, yet I feel I have to absolve myself somehow. I don't want to live a lie about the girls. They're 17 months old and growing fast, they look so like Johnny and Chris now. So, for them, I want the world to know the truth. I also want everyone to know what Tony Gorman did to me. The pain, the fear and the effect of what he did had on everyone around me, including you Simon. You all had to go through it too. It affected everyone. I'm not the only one who has flashbacks and nightmares."

Simon put his arm around Vickie, and kissed her cheek. "Vickie I know how I felt that night. I actually vomited, after

I saw the mess you were in. I think what you are doing is brave and fantastic, I really do. I'll support you all the way. In fact, the ghost writer has almost finished the first draft. Firstly, the impact statement will be released to the press, immediately we leave this court."

"Simon I don't want to make money from it. I want all the proceeds to be split between charities and organisations that help people who are sexually assaulted. I also want their loved ones to be able to access the right type of help. It matters, because most people don't have the support I got. They don't have the funds to pay for psychotherapists, and counselling. I want the system to be there, so everyone affected can be helped through the trauma. I'm living proof that with the right help, you can recover. The whole experience has changed us all, and not all of that change is negative."

"No, the press miss the boys though," Simon laughed. "Even now they still try to start rumours. They have all been helped by the shrinks, haven't they?"

Vickie nodded, "I want to make sure people can be properly supported through the court system. Then they can be protected from what we have had to go through. It's only a matter of time anyway, until the press break the story from court. It's doing the rounds of the internet, social media. It has to be done quickly." Vickie smiled, as Johnny and Andy came back, carrying coffee.

Vickie sat in court with her friends and family around her. She watched as they brought Tony Gorman up into the dock. He looked around and her eyes met his. Vickie did not look away, she met his gaze, she felt Johnny's grip on her right hand tighten.

On her left Jamie reached for her hand and held it, his other arm around Marnie's shoulder. They all stared at the dock. Tony looked away from Vickie, and gazed at the floor. Vickie turned around and smiled at her father and Maggie, who sat directly behind her with Lynne. Lynne was looking amazing despite having given birth to 11lb 11oz baby Jake William Vincent, just four days before. She blew Vickie a kiss as she sat holding hands with Chris and Andy; beside Andy, Mhairi smiled and raised her thumb.

They stood for the judge, who nodded to Vickie, as she sat down. "Before sentencing, I believe we have a victim impact statement."

Vickie stood up, kissed Johnny, and walked towards the witness box. She bowed slightly to the judge. "Thank you, your Honour, for giving me the opportunity to say now what the impact of this man's attack on me has been." Vickie began to speak her voice loud and clear.

"The night I was attacked had been one of the best nights of my career. Along with my band, we had walked away from a National Music Awards ceremony on cloud nine. For the first time in a year, it felt good to be alive. Yes, we had parted company with our manager a few weeks earlier, due to us being ready to move on. I did not for one second, think that this man, who I had known and trusted since I was a teenager, would harm me the way he did. During the attack, I could not comprehend what was happening. I was humiliated and violated, again and again. When I fought back, I was beaten. I was left broken, physically and mentally. I also firmly believe if my husband hadn't had his car fitted with a tracker, I would not be standing here telling you this. But luck was on my side that night, in terms of me having the keys to that car."

Vickie stopped talking and composed herself; she continued to speak after a few seconds.

"I've had to re-live that night here in court. I will not go into the finer details. It took months of painful treatment to mend my broken body. It required much longer, and the love of a good decent man, brilliant friends, and months of treatment from a psychotherapist, to begin to mend my broken mind."

Vickie looked down at her feet and blinked back tears. She took a deep breath, composing herself, before she spoke again. "After the attack, when I was lying in hospital, unable to speak, bewildered and afraid, I panicked when my own father tried to hug me. It took three months of therapy before I could let the man I love, hold me and kiss me without fear." She looked around the court before continuing. "That hasn't gone, I've just been taught how to better control the feelings. I have flashbacks, and even now, a year later, people close to me have to tell me they are going to touch me or I can react. I can only be intimate with my husband if I can see it's him. I slept with a light on for three months. I have panic attacks and am physically sick when I see a Range Rover." She shook her head sadly and looked over at Tony Gorman in the dock; he was still looking at the floor. "I don't think I could go inside one now if my life depended on it."

"One of the worst aspects was though, the fact that this attack on me made me doubt people I love, people who love me, which hurt them. For the first month I couldn't let anyone touch me, I kept everyone, including my children, at arm's length. I was conscious for most of the time he was attacking me." Vickie gulped back tears but continued to speak clearly and articulately. "I was lucky, I was saved. There were moments during the attack, before I lost consciousness, where I thought I would never see my loved ones again. In the last few moments of consciousness, I mentally pictured my children's faces, thinking they would be orphans."

Vickie raised her head and looked at the judge as she spoke. "What this court needs to know though, is this attack affected not just me but everyone who loves me and who I love. My stylist, who chose my dress that night, she blames herself for the way I was dressed; more so now, when the defence questioned my character based on what I was wearing. My security team, for leaving me alone at a party where I should have been safe.

My husband, my friends who rescued me, they have flashbacks too; they also feel they let me down, by not staying beside me at the party. They had to live with the mess I was left in. Johnny, Chris and Lynne, caught him raping me. The others arrived minutes later and saw me half naked and bleeding on a bed, being given heart massage. Those awful pictures live with all of them. They've all needed therapy too; they are as much victims as I am. For weeks, I was locked in a place where all I felt was pain and terror. I couldn't have my children visit because of how I looked. I didn't know if I could hold them as I couldn't bear physical contact with anyone."

Tears ran down Vickie's face as she spoke; she paused and put a tissue to her face before continuing. She could see Johnny and others in the court, crying with her. "My older children thought I was dead. When my young son visited, three weeks after I was attacked, he recognised me from my perfume. I had to stop breastfeeding my premature babies because of the drugs he had given me and the ones I had to take. It is almost impossible to put in to words how much my ordeal affected everyone around me, but I will not be a victim." Vickie looked again at the hunched figure of her former manager in the dock; she knew he was hearing her though. "I will not hide behind a cloak of secrecy and anonymity," Vickie stated. "To do that, allows people to believe I have something to hide. I had no choice in what happened to me! I did nothing wrong but trust someone who did not warrant my trust and who used this for his own ends. I was brutally attacked and violated, yet I had to go through mental torture to bring my perpetrator to justice."

Vickie looked at the judge; she could see the woman was struggling with her own emotions. "Now a year after it happened, I have frequent nightmares. At first it was every night. My husband has become used to gathering me up off the furthest away corner in our bedroom in the middle of the night. He has even found me in cupboards and under the bed, such are the night terrors I face. Johnny has nightmares and flashbacks too. This is the same for the other people in our house, all of my friends who were there that night, have nightmares."

Vickie looked over at Tony; he sat in the dock flanked by two prison officers, still looking at the floor. "Then this . . . " Vickie looked at the judge again, "I can't call him a man because that's not how a real man behaves! This pathetic excuse for a human being, who was caught raping me and would have left me for dead, pled not guilty. Meaning my loved ones and I had to go through the indignities of the court case, where our personal lives were laid out for everyone to hear. My closest friends had to justify the nature of their relationship with me and their own relationships and lifestyles. We had to stand here and answer questions about our intimate relationships. We all suffered from nightmares during the trial, due to having to relive it all in our evidence." Vickie looked at the judge and then at the packed court. "I felt violated, raped again in this court room, that's wrong too! I will campaign for a change in the laws around witness's, in cases like mine."

Vickie turned and looked again at Tony who was sitting with his head in his hands now. "But do you know what Tony? You left me physically and emotionally broken, but you will never take away my dignity, no matter what you did to me. I have something you will never have and that is the love and respect of those around me. I don't hate you because to hate you would use up emotional time I will not give to you. You and I know what happened that night and why you put me and the others through the court case. You failed Tony. What you did to all of us made us stronger, made us grow up, brought us closer. Thank you!" she said, looking at the judge.

Vickie stood up, and left the witness box. The hushed courtroom broke in to applause, as she joined Johnny, who was walking towards her. He reached her, hugged her, tears running down his face, mingling with hers. "I am so goddamn proud of you Vickie." he sobbed, as, his arm around her, he led her back to her seat.

The judge waited until the applause died down. "Thank you, Mrs Vincent-D'Angelo. That was very powerful and moving." She looked over at Tony. "Could the defendant please stand?" Tony stood up, his face white and tear stained. "Anthony William Gorman. You have been found guilty of a heinous crime. You kidnapped a vibrant young woman. One whom you knew would do anything to get to her sick child. A woman you had known since she was a teenager and who you had responsibility for. You staged a hoax call to her, through a frightened young woman. Victoria Vincent-D'Angelo is a tiny young woman. This court heard she is five foot tall and weighs just seven stones. Yet you used extreme force to overpower her. Your crime and the way you humiliated and abused her, from the time you left the venue until she was rescued, there are no words to describe. This must have been the most unimaginable, terrifying and painful time for this brave and articulate young woman. Mrs Vincent-D'Angelo, in her impact statement, told how she suffers a year on, from night terrors and flashbacks."

"We heard during your trial, the evidence from her doctors, as to the extent of the physical injuries. The force used to shatter bones in her face, the pelvic and anal trauma injuries. We heard from her surgeons, of the painful surgery, saw the physical scars she will bear for the rest of her life. We heard from the throat specialist, about damage to her vocal chords and the pressure inflicted to cause this. Lastly, from her and her friends psycho-therapist, who told of the long-lasting psychological damage. We heard of the emotional problems she endures. The impact of what you did, Anthony William Gorman, also had a profound effect on her husband, family and friends. The emotional trauma on them; we also heard of the effects of vicarious trauma, which has caused them pain and suffering over the last year."

"Anthony William Gorman, like Mr and Mrs Vincent-D'Angelo and their friends, I believe the evidence shows, if they had not been fortunate enough to reach her, she would have died at your hands. In fact, when Jonathon Vincent-D'Angelo and Lynne Love arrived, Victoria Vincent-D'Angelo most likely was clinically dead. They performed heart massage, resuscitated her, the paramedic revived her. It is only because of their actions, you are not standing here being convicted of murder. However, I do believe, from the evidence I have heard from the witnesses and from the medical professionals, you intended to kill your victim."

"It is for that reason I am going to hand down the highest

sentences I can, which is life imprisonment for rape. On the conviction of kidnap–life imprisonment. On the conviction of attempted murder–life imprisonment. These sentences will run consecutively and carry the recommendation that you are not considered for parole for 32 years. Before you are considered for parole you must have successfully completed a recent sex offender's programme and you will be a registered sex offender for the remainder of your lifetime. Throughout this process Mr Gorman, you showed no remorse, until the point when you knew you had lost, were going to convicted. I believe you are a damaged, depraved and dangerous man." The judge looked at the policemen flanking Tony. "Take him down."

Outside the court Johnny and Jamie shielded Vickie as they ran to the waiting limo. Colin opened the door for them. A reporter stood waiting at the car. "Vickie, Vickie, how do you feel?"

"Safe!" she said into the microphone.

CHAPTER

THIRTY-NINE

Vickie and Johnny sat holding hands; the makeup lady applied powder to Johnny's face. "Okay!" the director shouted. "We're ready to go." The lights of the studio were bright. Vickie looked at Johnny. He winked at her and gripped her hand tighter. "Three, two, one, you are on air."

"Tonight I'm joined by four of my country-people folks and an Anglo-Irish man. Please welcome, in their first public appearance for seven months, Black Velvet," Camellia Kelly said smiling. "Firstly, possibly the bravest couple we will ever know, Johnny and Vickie Vincent-D'Angelo, the most famous newly-weds in the world! How is married life treating you?"

Vickie smiled and held on to Johnny's hand. "It's been ten months now. So, we're past the newlywed stage. We did live as a family for a while before we got hitched."

"So, you're not kissing all the time?"

"Oh, they are . . . loves young dream!" Chris laughed, rolling his eyes. The others nodded.

Camellia smiled and turned to her guests. "Vickie, can I ask you about the book you co-wrote with Johnny? The story is very powerful and is not just about the tragedies in your lives, it's about the good things too."

Vickie nodded. "We wanted to be honest and open about what happened to us but also to tell the whole story, not just the

301

sensational bits. Everyone was involved because, essentially, it's their story too. To be able to understand why things happened, it was important we explained how it started."

"There are two parts to this book though," Johnny added. "The first part is the story of the band, how we came to be, the story of the town where we grew up. It fits in with why we all needed each other so much. It explains why we made the decision to live together. The crash meant we were all suffering, it helped to be together. Vickie was twenty two, I'm a year older than her, and we were widowed just like that. Andy had lost his mum and brother. Jamie lost the only close relative he had left. My brother, well, he had to cope with all of our grief." Johnny glanced over at Chris. "People assumed that because he didn't lose someone like a partner, sibling or mother, he wasn't suffering. In actual fact, it was even more difficult for him."

"Moving into Vickie's house was probably the best thing we could have done. It allowed us to be together and heal away from the limelight. It's a fantastic big house, and we still live there. Everyone has other homes, here in the UK and abroad, so we do move around." He looked along the sofa at the others and smiled. "It's just home now."

"So," Camellia asked, "you are not there constantly?"

"No, we share a few houses but it's kind of the norm for us to be together," Vickie said, smiling. "We actually do get on, but if we need space there's always somewhere you can go. Chris and Lynne, for example, have their base with us but have other homes too."

Chris nodded. "We're there a lot, now we're parents."

Camelia smiled. "There has been a lot of speculation about what kind of parents you are. What are Lynne and Chris like as parents Vickie?"

Vickie smiled then rolled her eyes "alternative . . . they're eccentric, but that wee boy is the most loved child you could ever meet. He's a happy healthy baby. I'm sure his first words will be interesting, but we're working on it."

Camellia smiled, "so they swear a lot, do they?"

"You could say that! "Johnny laughed and nudged Chris. "Topher can't say a sentence without cursing. Actually Lynne isn't much better."

"I love the nicknames you two have, Johnny and Christopher. The book explains it doesn't it?"

Johnny smiled, "I've always called him Topher, or Toph. When he was born I was only a year old. Topher was my first attempt at his name and it stuck. Our kids call him Uncle Topher too. My nickname came from Billy, Vickie's first husband, who was my best friend. He always called me Jovi; it's obviously the first letters of my name. Vickie and Chris, interestingly, are the only ones in our circle, other than my parents and granny, who call me Johnny."

Camellia looked at Vickie, "Vickie can we talk about the rape case?"

Vickie swallowed hard then nodded.

"You are, firstly, a very brave lady; you were brutally honest, and very graphic, about what happened to you at the hands of your former manager. It must have been a terrifying ordeal; the photographs in the book and the vivid description of what occurred are awful. The book does not leave anything out does it?"

Vickie nodded sadly. Johnny put his arm protectively around her. "Nor should it. I was the victim that night and in the months that followed. I couldn't even let my father hug me without having a panic attack. It took three weeks before I could see my kids. Johnny and I had gotten together a couple of months before the attack. I couldn't let him touch me; I used to have palpitations if he put his arm around me." Vicky looked up at Johnny. "We had weeks of therapy before I could even contemplate being touched without panicking. It was months before we could be intimate. Even now it's difficult for me to be intimate with Johnny unless I can see it's him. His face, his tattoos. We were lucky to be able to afford the help of several therapists to help us to deal with it all. I still have good and bad days, but we have developed coping strategies. They all get it and know when I'm struggling," she said, looking along the sofa and then back to Camellia, "I know when they're struggling too."

Camellia looked thoughtful, "what helped you to cope then? You appear to have come through it all."

"We helped each other, we've been there for each other. Johnny had a counsellor from Rape Crisis who helped him to not just understand what I was going through but to deal with his own feelings about it all. We also had a wonderful psychotherapist who helped us learn to be intimate again. For months I was locked in flight or fight mode. Even now, if anyone makes a sudden move I jump. I gave Jamie a black eye about a month ago when he came up behind me when I had earphones on in the studio. He was only trying to tell me lunch was ready."

"She also kneed me in the crotch another time when I came out of a door at her. We all wear jock straps just in case now!" Andy laughed. He put his arm around her shoulder and kissed her head.

Vickie made a face. "Who I am, who we all are now, is because of what happened. It was a terrifying, very painful ordeal. I did think I was going to die at the time. I only remember parts of it; one of the things I do clearly remember is a moment when I was sure I wasn't coming out of it. I was mentally saying goodbye to my children; trying to picture their little faces, so I would die with that in my head, not what he was doing to me." Vickie took a tissue from Camelia who was dabbing her own eyes and gulped. She leaned closer to Johnny who kissed her. "I'm sorry, I struggle with those parts of the rape, the thoughts, how I felt."

"You are a very brave lady Vickie, to go through what you did and come out the other side," Camelia said, looking directly at Vickie. "When I read your book, I suddenly understood what rape does, to not just the victim but to everyone who loves them."

Vickie nodded, "I never understood until it happened; I read the word rape and thought I knew what it was. I was also attacked by my late husband's father when I was 17. Afterwards I changed how I dressed, taking the blame for his actions. We had just started out at the time. I believed that if I hadn't worn certain clothes then it wouldn't have happened. I remember Billy saying to me that I should be able to wear whatever I chose without being targeted, but I still had that in my head. I never realised, how life-changing a sexual assault can be. Now, I refuse to be ashamed of what happened to me." Vickie looked straight into the camera, "I didn't cause myself to be attacked, and Johnny and I decided we were not going to hide."

"I had, to be honest, such a good experience of sex that I couldn't understand just how awful rape is. That's why I wanted to tell, in graphic detail, just what happened to me and to the other sexual assault victims in our circle. There is nothing remotely sexual about rape; it is just a violent act of control. However, we all learned how to move on from it. I refused to be the girl who was raped. I'm the girl who survived and took her life back. I wear what I want, and I say and do what I want, now!"

Camellia looked thoughtful. "Can I ask about the tattoos?" A picture flashed up from the beach on the tour of Australia. The large group photo featured the band, road crew and staff, all sporting Vickie's face on their hips.

Vickie smiled. "It's a funny story, but the roots of it are serious. After Johnny and I managed to resume our relationship, I could only be with him, without panicking, if I knew it was him. Johnny has a beautiful tattoo which stretches as a sleeve up his upper arm, across his back, shoulder and chest which I focused on if I couldn't see his face." She blushed. "That ruled out some things. When we decided to get married, we got our names tattooed on our ring fingers. Then Johnny decided to get my face and name tattooed on his groin for reasons I won't go into, but it's not rocket science. Anyway, when he went to get it done, he took Chris with him . . . big mistake. In our circle, there are only three forms of communication, telephone, television and tell Chris. He can't help himself, unless you say don't say anything, he just goes for it."

"So, you told everyone?" Camellia asked, looking at Chris.

"Oh yes," Chris said, grinning, "I couldn't keep that one to myself."

"To be fair, I didn't ask him to keep it a secret. If I had, he wouldn't have told anyone, I think." Johnny laughed and nudged his brother.

Vickie shook her head and grinned. "Then he organised the others, our road crew and staff, and they all got it tattooed on them too. Johnny and I, we didn't find out until we got to Dubai, before our Australian and New Zealand tour and were on the beach."

"Everyone?" Camellia asked.

"Oh, yes Camellia. I thought it was a joke at first, but they're all real. It features in a programme about tattoos, our friend and tattooist Sid the needle takes part in. He drew the picture originally then tattooed it on his own thigh; that's where Johnny first saw it. It's kind of become a protest against rape, a way of supporting me. Apparently, tattooists all over the world are being asked to do it. Sid has donated the copyright to our campaign."

"You don't mind people knowing what you have gone through then?"

"My attitude is; why should I? I didn't choose to be violated in this manner. I've done nothing wrong. One of the reasons we waived our right to anonymity was people need to see and hear the truth about what a violent, ugly crime rape is. The taboo of it means that the victim feels they should hide what was done to them. Yet you have no control over what this beast is doing to you. I felt people need to know the truth about this heinous crime, it's not a case of someone having sex with you; it's a terrifying and degrading act which is about control and violence."

"So, you decided to say it as it is Vickie?" Camelia asked.

Vickie nodded. "How Johnny and I chose to deal with it is not for everyone, but it was right for us. I don't think there actually is a right or wrong way, it's about having some control over it all." She gripped Johnny's hand. "Hundreds of women and men are raped every month. The small percentages who report it, well ... they then become victims of the criminal justice system. My rapist's line of defence was me having to prove he did it. We reckon he knew he would be convicted, but he was trying to torture us and make us reveal our private lives. I personally think he wanted to destroy us in the public's eyes. There was no doubt about what happened to me." Vickie paused and wiped her eyes again. "I was nearly killed, yet my whole life and all my friends' lives were displayed and judged publicly, during that trial."

The others nodded. "We had to all justify our lifestyles and relationships, yet we had actually done nothing wrong," Johnny said, looking around him. "Some of our life choices have not been great, but who hasn't made mistakes? What can I say, we're young. We were catapulted into the public domain before we were even out of our teens. Thing was, we knew before the trial about the other victims of Vickie's attacker, which he was later convicted of, yet it was not allowed to be mentioned in court. We had been hearing rumours for years about him. Then we suspected, rightly, it turned out, he was involved in the drugging and rape of Dania Phillips. It was one of the reasons we wanted to change management."

Vickie looked up at the camera, "I think I needed to show how badly injured I was and that was just the visible, physical injuries. I make no apologies for putting the pictures or description in the book. It is meant to make you feel sick. Mine was a particularly violent assault. But, rape is a violent crime. It is a violation of your body, but it is mostly the fear and humiliation that remain with you in the longer term, not the physical pain. The humiliation is heightened when you go through the court process. I felt as though I was raped again in that court. I also still feel extremely guilty about the others having to go through it all to get this rapist jailed."

Camelia smiled and nodded, "and you made no profit from the book?"

"None, in fact we paid the publishing cost of the paperback,

Johnny and I, so the proceeds were higher. We also won a settlement from our former management, of £8 million each, which was embezzled from us when we first started. None of us wanted it because we considered it blood money. So, we all just donated to the fund because we wanted someone to benefit. We picked related charities; everything we raise is going to them. The book is a best seller; we passed our forecasts for the sales in the first month, and the sales went viral. It's gone world-wide."

"Well done, it's impressive," Camellia said, nodding along the line-up. "What about the song?"

"Well, Camellia," Jamie said, "that came about because we felt, after what happened to Vickie, we knew an awful lot about sexual violence. This wasn't Fifty Shades of Grey; it was a brutal, cowardly, attack on a tiny, defenceless woman. The court case that followed was about her proving he did it, when all the evidence was he did. He didn't have to justify his lifestyle. Yet Vickie and us, well, we did. He would have killed her if Chris and Johnny had not stopped him. Yet we all had to live through, as Johnny says, our lifestyle being paraded for the world to see. We wanted to get across not just how awful this crime is but also the fact that it doesn't stop when the rape stops; there are very difficult times in the aftermath. For a few weeks it was awful, she was so traumatised, we were too, we all dealt with it differently. We realised Vickie was the centre of our world, the person who held us all together. We were lucky, we got our girl back; the court system made her so angry, she got her old feistiness and fought for a cause."

Andy nodded, "people have committed suicide, not only after being raped but also after their experience in court which exacerbates the pain. So, we stopped getting drunk and taking drugs to deal with our feelings, and we focussed on doing something to highlight it. We didn't intend it to grow the way it did but when other artists wanted to get involved, Chris, Jamie and me, well, we thought, let's make it a Band Aid concert kind of thing."

"There is also an album and DVD being released for people

who can't get tickets," Jamie said smiling. "Many of the songs have been written by us. Well, Johnny and Andy mostly, but Chris and I did so some of the writing too."

Chris smiled. "The best track though, is the one where Vickie and Jamie duet on a love song Johnny wrote for Vickie. No one realised, until the wedding, Jamie could sing because he is such a lazy git." He grinned at his friend. "Both his parents and his sister, were great singers. Evie Green, who was Vickie's voice coach after she started singing again, had worked with Jamie's mum. Evie remembered Jamie singing as a little boy, so she asked him to try. He has an amazing voice, and in a couple of minutes, he and Vickie are going to sing that song live for the first time in public."

"Is this a change in the direction of the band, Jamie?" Camelia asked.

"What? Vickie and me sharing the singing? Fuck, no, I'm a bass player." He grinned, "sorry, you can't bleep that out on live tv can you?"

Camelia shook her head; she smiled. "Jamie, let's just carry on and talk about your singing."

Jamie grinned, "I don't mind doing an odd song. Duetting with Vickie is amazing because she has such a strong voice, but it's too much like hard work to do it a lot," he laughed. "Chris is the same, okay for a holiday but wouldn't want to live there. The vocalist is actually the most difficult and complicated job in a band. It's all about timing."

"Jamie and I are known as the laziest in the band; we never usually do much but turn up, play our instruments and go home," Chris said seriously. "We only rehearse when we are made to and drive everyone else mad. There have been times when we've turned up minutes before we are due on stage, and many, many times we have gone on stage drunk, drugged or with hangovers."

"They know how to party," Vickie laughed. "Honestly, only half what you read about them was the truth."

Chris smiled and shook his head. "We used to party almost

constantly, and there was a great deal of sex and drugs in our circle, particularly from Jamie and me. We used to keep a tally of how many women we slept with and have wagers on it. At 19, I had been with 400 women then I stopped counting. Jamie was much the same, Andy wasn't far behind us. We're mortally ashamed of how we behaved now. When I saw everything Vickie and Dania went through, heard Annie and Mhairi's stories, I felt I wanted to apologise for being a man. What I thought a real man was, before Vickie was attacked, is not what I now know it is."

"After Vickie was attacked, we were all changed emotionally, and it felt right to do something," Jamie said quietly, "I mean if Vickie and Johnny could go out there, and do what they did for a cause then we reckoned we could too. So, we wrote the song. Music is how we cope with things; we had done the tribute song after the plane crash and set up the memorial foundation for young musicians, which we're still involved with!"

Andy nodded. "We started up the 'right to be me!' campaign, against sexual violence. Just about every recording artist in the country got involved, the result was amazing. People in the music business were shocked by what happened and wanted to help. The song 'Taking Back My Life! Well it's a message from, I suppose, influential people in the music industry, to men who forcibly take what is not on offer."

"Just men?" Camellia asked.

Andy shrugged. "Men rape women, men rape other men, so yes. There are female sex offenders but they're a minority, and usually there's a man involved. The statistics show that 98% of violent sexual attacks are carried out by men. Three out of four women and one in six men will experience some type of sexual assault in their lifetime. In our very tight inner circle, there are four women who have been raped. We live every day with the reminder that rape exists, but we also know that there can be a life after sexual assault, if the support is there. We have all had therapy, and it helped us deal with it."

Camellia looked thoughtful, "Vickie, can we move on to talk about you and Johnny? In the book, you bared your souls, discussed the fact that you had found yourselves in a very difficult and strange situation. You gave birth to your daughters, believing they were fathered by your late husband. Then discovered Johnny was their father but did not remember having sex, due to having been drugged after the crash."

Vickie nodded. "I think I knew, on some level, I had slept with him. I think probably it was grief which caused it, but, the same grief stopped my mind admitting it. I thought it was a dream, Johnny realised first it was real.

Camellia looked at Johnny, who nodded, "I remembered quite early on, but at first I also thought I'd dreamt it. When I realised it had happened, I didn't want to admit it. Then when she told me she was pregnant, I didn't know how to. I never realised though, I was responsible for her pregnancy. Like Vickie, I just thought that because she and Billy had been trying for a baby, they had managed it. Luckily, we both remembered enough to know it was what it was."

"How did you feel when you found out you had fathered the twins?"

"Sick to my stomach actually. I know now, there are many men who take advantage of someone when that person is not capable of consent. Because of the twins' conception, we wanted to be very clear about it all. Not muddy the water for someone who wakes up and finds they've been raped."

"Vickie sighed. "That's what happened to Dania Phillips, another of my rapist's victims. She's young and very brave. She allowed us to tell her story in the book too. She lives with us now. Johnny and I know the difference; we saw Dania after it happened, she was in a dreadful state."

Johnny sighed. "It was difficult for me to come to terms with it all. I had just begun to accept it when Dania was attacked. This made the guilt I felt worse. I simply did not remember; which is not an excuse. We also had the added issue of the twins being

311

conceived when we were unaware, through the drugs. As much as we love our daughters, it's not how we would have chosen to conceive them. We both loved our spouses Camellia; there has never been any doubt about that. I loved Ali deeply; Vickie loved Billy, who was my mate. Ali and Vickie had also been friends, before she was in the band."

"The shock of what we'd done to their memories and their family's grief, being compounded by what we had managed to get ourselves into." Johnny wiped away a tear, and Vickie gripped his hand. "My late wife's parents lost both their daughters and unborn granddaughter, that night. They had to hear the man they were flying to see admitting that the night they died, I had sex with Vickie, a girl my wife trusted me to be with. It took a lot of soul searching and explaining."

Camellia nodded. "You say in the book they understood how it happened."

"Yes, that helps us to move on," Johnny said looking up at the camera, "so we are deeply grateful to Liz and Bobby McCallum for their support."

"The doctor who attended you the night of the crash has been convicted, in America, of medical negligence," Camelia said, looking at Johnny. "During his trial, he revealed Tony Gorman asked him to give Vickie a mixture of MDMA and other drugs, which caused hallucinations. The doctor, who has now been jailed and struck off, has said Tony Gorman suggested they could both abuse Vickie. How do you feel about the doctor?"

"I try not to think about it too much, but the conviction helped us to deal with what he did."

"They were both negligible!" Vickie said. "Johnny and I had bad colds. We had taken over-the-counter medication to get us through the gig that night. I was in a hysterical state so couldn't give consent. He should have checked what I had taken, before they got my friends to hold me down and started sticking needles in me. Chris, in particular, feels a lot of guilt about helping. I mean you trust a doctor, don't you? We were all in a state. Johnny was grief stricken, he asked the doctor to knock him out, yet he was never asked if he had taken any other medication. Marnie, my PA, had bought the drugs for our colds from a drug store but they never asked about it. The mix of drugs could have killed us, as it was, we were in la-la land."

"Andy, who had lost his mother and brother, and Jamie, whose sister had died, were also given drugs but well, what can I say? Their exploits are well documented. They did a lot of drugs! They both knew it was MDMA at the time because they'd done it before and knew the effects. It is used to treat trauma occasionally, but only when everything else has failed. The effect on Johnny and I, who never really did drugs, was greater; no one thought of that."

"Did you realise Tony Gorman meant to abuse Vickie that night?" Camelia asked, looking at Johnny.

Johnny nodded. "Yes, I had no doubt. He told her later, that was his intention. I did think that was his aim at the time, despite my confusion. I got it into my head that he meant to harm her. After what he did to her later, I don't want to think about it, because we now know what he was capable of. For a long time though, I felt I had saved her and abused her myself. We never refer to him by name by the way! If we discuss him at all, which is seldom, we talk about the 'rapist' . . . it's how we cope with it."

"How did you feel, when you both remembered what happened?" Camellia asked.

Johnny looked around at the others. "When we found out, we were devastated. Luckily our friends believed us."

"You told them straight away?" Camellia asked, looking along the row.

Johnny nodded. "We told the others in the band and Lynne, the day after we found out, because we needed to be honest with them. We also trusted them not to tell anyone. We weren't trying to hide it; we just needed time to work it all out in our own heads."

"Their reaction was not typical, was it?"

"Well it was typical for them; they actually thought it was funny. Chris and Jamie especially, were like, this is worse than anything we've ever done ha-ha. Chris made a big thing of the fact that Vickie had forgotten having sex with me."

Chris grinned. "He deserved it. He'd always taken the moral high ground on our behaviour."

"We still don't fully remember," Vickie sighed. "But can guess now." She looked at her friends, then back at Camellia. "They all know us; they knew how we felt about our partners, they shared our grief. It helped, they believed us."

"We knew that if they were saying they were not aware, then they were telling the truth," Andy said, smiling. "I mean, as Jamie said at the time, you couldn't make that story up."

Camellia nodded, "then there was your marriage, in front of 81,000 people."

Vickie smiled. "It was pretty amazing and arranged in four days. When we decided to do it, we knew it was right for us to share the moment."

"Was it a publicity stunt?"

"Yeah, kind of," Johnny acknowledged, "we didn't need the publicity, but we wanted the world to know that we were committing to each other. Doing it the way we did meant we got the message across. We also knew that the trial date was set, and that our relationship would need to come out."

"For some reason the press always focused on me being in a relationship with Chris," Vickie laughed. "Even when it was obvious Johnny and I were together."

"You were a very beautiful bride Vickie; the dress was amazing."

"Thank you. Nicky, our stylist, made it from two shop-bought dresses, and she did it in two days."

"Tell us about the honeymoon, 'Musha Cay!' a whole island to yourselves. Must have been amazing, it costs a fortune too."

Vickie laughed and looked at the band members, "they gave us it as a present; I nearly had a heart attack when I found out what they had paid for it. They could have bought a house in our hometown with what it cost. Google it, there's a website. If you have the money, I would recommend it; there's nowhere on earth as beautiful but also as private. We're all going back there for a holiday, to mark our first wedding anniversary, curtesy of the owner actually, thanks David!"

"All of you?"

"Yes, the five of us, partners and the children."

Camellia smiled. "What about your relationship with each other and the partners of the boys? Is there no jealousy there Vickie?"

"No, not really, over the years those three have had quite a few girlfriends," Vickie smiled, "the ones who didn't cope with the way we are didn't last long. Mostly, I've gotten on with their girlfriends, but there were a lot of girls in the early days. We deal with a lot of things through humour. People might not understand the way we live, think it's odd! Thing is, although it's only Chris and Johnny who are related, we're all as close as siblings. Luckily, all the others partners get that. Lynne and Chris, they got married last month, in the Little White Wedding Chapel in Vegas, by the way, are more than just family."

"Congratulations Chris," Camellia said.

"Thanks."

Vickie smiled. "It could be considered a very incestuous group. Lynne and I have been friends since primary school. In fact, the three of us, Lynne, Chris and I, were, and still are, best friends. Andy and Johnny have also been friends since childhood; Billy was their friend too. Jamie became friends at 15, when he moved to our hometown. "Marnie, Jamie's wife, is our P.A and has been with us since the beginning. Mhairi, Andy's fiancée, nursed me after I was attacked, which is how they met. Anyway, they all have my face tattooed on them. I have their names on me." Vickie smiled; "I got Sid to tattoo all of their names on my bum. I would show you, but I'm not going to flash on live television."

"No," Camellia laughed. "But we do have a picture. Thank you, Johnny, for that, and you Vickie, I was wondering how I could bring it up."

A picture flashed up on the screen of Vickie's bottom, with the large heart, made up of the first names of all her friends and crew. It was woven into an intricate design which made it look like lace.

"It's beautiful!" Jamie gasped, leaning in to look at the monitor in front of them....

"You lot didn't know about this, did you?"

Chris smiled. "We knew she had another tattoo actually but not what it was. We've been trying, since we came back from Australia last year, to find out what it was. The day they were getting married . . . "

Vickie blushed scarlet and looked at him. "Not on live TV Chris! Leave us with something private, please?"

Johnny put his arm around her. "She gets embarrassed about stuff. Let's just say that they walked in on her and saw her bum briefly and leave it at that."

"My brother is a very quick, very clean worker."

"Chris!"

"So, you're all close then?"

Johnny nodded. "Our innermost circle consists of the five of us. Then, the other three partners and Dania, who is engaged to Vickie's brother, Patrick. Annie, who looks after us, is my granny. Her story is in the book; her partner is Doug who's Andy's dad. Then there's Laura and Katie our nannies, Nicky our stylist, Arfur, Colin and Zac our main security; they mostly live with us. Our families then Simon our manager and his partner Rodney, and our crew."

"Compared with other artists we don't actually have a huge entourage!" Vickie added, "we have a trusted circle. We're close, the band, the crew, the staff; I have 23 names in my tattoo. So, I suppose you could say we all know each other well. We do have arguments but they're sibling arguments, stupid things. Johnny

316

and Andy are the worst though; they write most of our material and are always squabbling."

"Do you think there is anything left for you to do musically?"

Johnny nodded. "Oh yes, loads, and we do have lots of time to do it. You also must remember we're all still quite young. Vickie and Chris are still only 24, I'm 26 today, Andy is 25 and Jamie is 27. So, we've got plans. We want to be like the stones and still on stage when we are 70. We've had a six month break, and we are going to make sure we have regular breaks now, enjoy life. Although we have no plans to tour for a few years, we're back working; the new single is out tomorrow."

Camelia smiled and nodded, "Vickie can I ask you something? You don't need to answer, but it's a question that a lot of women, would like to ask you?"

Vickie looked at Camelia, nodded and smiled nervously.

"If you walked into a bar and all four of them were standing there. You could speak to them individually for two minutes then you had to pick one. You'd never met them before. Who would you go home with?"

"I just knew someone someday was going to ask that question. Obviously, I'm in love with Johnny and if history, personality and things came into it, I would definitely say him. Johnny, Chris, Andy and I have known each other since we were toddlers."

"Vickie and I, well, we used to play doctors and nurses," Chris said.

Vickie nodded smiling. "Chris was the first male to show me his penis; it was cute when he was four! However; unfortunately, he never stopped showing it off."

"But if I walked into a bar though and had to pick one, just who I would be drawn to? It would be . . . "

"Come on Vickie?" Johnny laughed. "I actually know the answer to this Camellia."

"Okay then go for it, I dare you?" Vickie grinned.

Johnny pursed his lips and looked along the sofa and back. "I would think; it would be . . . Jamie!"

They all looked at Vickie, "is he, right?" Camellia asked.

Vickie smiled and nodded. "Give that man a coconut. They're all extremely good looking men. I just always think Jamie has an edge on the others. I love his hair, those piercing blue eyes, his beautiful skin; he has this cute little boy smile. He's also very perceptive, funny, hysterical sometimes. Jamie's really quick witted and analyses everything instantly, so his chat up line would be better, he's also insane, mad as a box of frogs." She laughed and leaned back against Johnny, "I would probably go home with any of them if I was single, if I'm honest. I mean look at them? Gorgeous or what? Sex on legs, all of them."

Johnny smiled. "Put it in order Vickie? If you just met us you would go for Jamie first, then who?"

"No way!" she squealed, "It would be you of course darling!"

"She's lying," Johnny cuddled his wife and laughed. "I know you so well." He looked at Camelia, "I'd be last on her list if she did it that way."

Jamie stood up and took a bow. "Victory for ginger men everywhere."

"So, Johnny, you've legally adopted Vickie's sons, admitted to being the father of the twins. Tell us about your children?"

Johnny smiled proudly, "I'm just their dad. However, we talk about the boys' natural father all the time. Obviously, Billy was our mate, so I think that makes us well placed to know what he would want. James is seven now, a brilliant, intelligent little boy, he has inherited Billy's talent for art. Not a lot of people know, but Billy was also a talented musician, so that part is there in the boys too. He didn't want to be in the band, but he could have been. James well, he's going to be an artist; we've absolutely no doubt about it. He also has Billy's calm, confident personality. His favourite person is Andy, who's teaching him drums. He's also sporty, loves football."

"Denis is nearly six; he's funny and a real live wire, very outgoing and confident. He's very talented musically. Chris and Jamie have been teaching him to play guitar and he is becoming good. He's always adored Jamie and follows him about most of the time. He is a wee clipe though Camellia, nothing is a secret with Denis around."

"Scottish word for a tell-tale," Camellia said, laughing. "Yes, I read the book, Johnny. I liked the chocolate milk story."

"The school mums!" Vickie smiled. "It's all so innocent with Denis." She nudged Andy. "I still can't believe he asked a four-year-old to lie for him, although the lady involved did tell her story to the press, so it would have got out anyway."

"He's a grass," Andy said, making a face. "He's Chris's Godson; we think that's where he gets it from."

"I can't wait for them to all have kids though, after the things they let my children do and the presents they bought them." Vickie laughed.

Johnny nodded and continued speaking. "The twins are two now. They are absolutely identical looking, but their personalities are amazingly different. Billie's a real girlie, girl, she loves sparkles, pink, frills and dolls."

"She's amazing," Jamie smiled. "She has the entire band and our crew wrapped around her finger."

"Chris can deny them nothing, and they know it," Vickie laughed.

Chris grinned, "the twins are just adorable and yes, I have been known to be taken advantage of, by them."

Johnny laughed. "Chiara is a tomboy. She's brave and fearless and, very much like Denis, into everything. She runs and climbs everywhere and is very independent and determined. She is definitely the boss in our house. She's so like her mother," Johnny said, grinning.

Vickie smiled. "They're what are known as mirror twins. It means that they're mirror images. It happens, the experts think, with twins when the egg splits late; it's quite funny and rare. They have cow licks in their hair, Chiara's is on the right, Billie's is on her left. They have birthmarks that are identical but on opposite sides on their chests, and Chiara is right handed, Billie is left handed. Incidentally the band, we are very unusual in respect of the fact that, apart from Chris, we're all lefties."

Camellia gasped. "I didn't know that, four left handed. It's usually the other way around, isn't it? One left handed person to four right handed people?

The others nodded, Chris smiled, "the house is set up for left handed people; Lynne, me and Chiara are in the minority. Just a little bit of interesting trivia. I can see that being a pub quiz question somewhere, some-day, you know? What's unusual about Black Velvet?"

Camellia smiled. "Now finally; what about your latest venture, the exhibition?"

Vickie smiled and nodded. "Well we wanted to do something to remember everyone who died in the crash. It was easy with Billy and Ali; they left enough art work behind for us to be able to exhibit it. Their work is really good. I've had offers for Billy's. I want our boys to have it and decide what to do with it when they are old enough. Billy was a superbly talented artist; he hated parting with anything though. That means there are only a few pieces of his work in circulation, they're making funny money. We decided to exhibit some of what we had."

"I hear there are very revealing paintings of you Vickie?"

Vickie smiled. "We met when I was 13, he was 14; we had been together for nearly nine years when he died. He painted me quite a few times. Some of them show me in a certain light."

"There are nude paintings of Vickie, don't you mind, Johnny?"

Johnny smiled. "Billy was my best friend and, other than my brother, the person I was closest to growing up. His work was amazing, he loved Vickie, he painted her a lot and very tastefully done they are too. We decided early on in our relationship, you can never compete with a ghost. So, we don't get caught up in what we did with Billy or Ali." Johnny squeezed Vickie's hand, "we loved them. We still love them. In respect of Billy's work though," he smiled, "personally, I love it. Yes, it's my wife who's the subject, but they are amazing. We'll let the public decide, all proceeds are going to the young musician fund anyway."

Vickie smiled sadly. "It wasn't just our tragedy. The others in the crash, the story of it. Their stories. Ali, Ali studied interior design so there is a lot of her work, her designs too, they are brilliant." Then there's the others, Ali's sister, Caroline, Lindsey, Jamie's little sister, her boyfriend Jack, who we'd never met. Andy's mum, Hannah and brother Jake. The pilot and cabin crew, Jerry, Karen and Alana; we knew them because we'd flown with them before. Andy the journalist, we knew well and of course, Billy's mum, Gillian. They all had lives, and stories to tell."

"There were also the people who should have been on the flight. Johnny's parents, Connie and Martin, and Lynne, were all booked on it. Lynne is the most disorganised person you'll ever meet, she missed the flight. Johnny and Chris's paternal Gran was ill, so the three of them lived, thank God; it just wasn't their time. We've been asked to take it to America next year, as there is a lot of interest, particularly in New York where it happened."

Camellia looked thoughtful. "The burning question I need to ask you two is, if the crash had not happened would you have got together?"

They looked at each other and smiled. Johnny shook his head. "We've discussed this a few times. We don't think we would have, we were great friends. If I'm honest, I always fancied her but would never have done anything about it. It was the circumstances; if it had been different then no, we both think we would have remained with our spouses. We have an amazing life now, we love each other, we are devoted to our kids, but neither of us would have cheated on our partners, we're a bit boring like that."

Vickie smiled and took his hand. "I do think that we would have still ended up together if we hadn't been drugged after the crash though! It would just not have been as quick."

"Thank you, folks, and good luck with everything," Camellia said, smiling. "Now you are going to play us out of the show, with your new single. Ladies and gentlemen put your hands together for Black Velvet and their new single! Loving You is Easy."

Afterwards, they came out of the television studio; Arfur leaned against their car. "Well done boss!" he said to Vickie. "You did well."

"What about me?" Johnny laughed.

"You looked like a very lucky man sitting beside her, you ugly git, talk about punching above your weight. Wish my brother had kept that sex DVD of you in the hot tub. So professional is Colin; he never even told me about it."

"How did you know then?" Vickie asked looking around.

"Chris told me, you told Lynne, Vickie."

"Honestly you lot, it's like Chinese whispers," Vickie gasped.

"Yeah but it's a circle of trust Vickie. What is said in the circle never leaves the circle. If you don't want something shared, don't share it," Chris laughed. "Where's my name on that tattoo by the way?"

"True to life, it's right at her arsehole," Johnny laughed, pushing his brother. "Now Arfur, to the gallery, we want to check it's all in place for it opening tomorrow. It was good of the Prince offering to do the honours."

Thirty minutes later they stood looking around at the exhibits. "Wow, it's good. They have Billy and Ali's paintings absolutely right! They have made the best use of every bit of light," Arfur whispered.

"That's why we chose an art gallery Arfur, so we could have them shown properly."

"Why aren't you selling them?"

"Because they're not mine to sell. Billy's belong to James and Denis, and Ali's, well; Johnny gave them all to her mum and dad. Billy's will only go up in price anyway. So if the boys want to they can sell them. Billy sold about twenty over the years and they are fetching funny money now. We have had limited edition prints of some of them made though. The money from them goes to the fund."

CHAPTER

FORTY

On Christmas day, Vickie looked around her living room.
All of those she loved were present: the band, their
partners, all suntanned from their recent holiday, their
family and friends. The patio doors to the children's play area
were open. She could hear her boys out in the garden. Laura
and Nicky were sitting on the patio steps. Annie was busy in
the kitchen. She would not hear of Vickie getting in caterers for
Christmas dinner, nor would she accept help in the kitchen other
than from Laura who normally helped. All their other household
staff had been given Christmas off work. Doug had tried to help,
but she'd chased him off.

Vickie smiled at Mhairi who was sitting on Andy's knee in the
big armchair. "Bet you're wondering what you have let yourself in
for? Welcome to our Christmas madhouse."

Mhairi giggled, "I can't believe grown men had a nerf gun fight
around the house this morning." She looked over at Jamie, "my
presents were quite boring in comparison. Thank you, Jamie, my
life was missing a double grenade launching toy gun before. Yes,
Vickie but is it just a Christmas madhouse?"

"I prefer to think of it as Santa's House of Fun!" Johnny said,
wrapping his arms around his wife's waist, kissing the top of her
head. "You should have been here the time he bought Andy a
helicopter."

"Yeah that was the year he bought Frankie a one-way ticket to Bora Bora!" Lynne laughed.

"It wasn't supposed to be Bora Bora, it was Bermuda on a boat, got a bit tongue tied in the travel agents. I was hoping the Bermuda Triangle would get her. What can I say, I was shit at geography?" Jamie laughed. "You were right Vickie, by the way, spending £100 each on presents was much more fun."

Vickie looked around the room, everyone she loved was present. Paddy was playing cards with Colin, Zac and Simon's partner, Rodney. Connie sat talking to Clinton and Maggie on the big sofa.

Vickie looked at Lynne and rolled her eyes as she heard Connie say to Clinton "Yes, that baby is much too fat; look at him. I just don't know what they are feeding him." Chris lay sleeping on the floor with the very bonny baby, J.W, asleep on his chest.

Billie, dressed in a pink sparkly party dress, was having a dolls tea party with her grandad Martin, Doug and Simon as the special guests. The men were sipping imaginary tea from Billie's china tea set. Vickie looked over to the door as James leaned in. "Dad, dad, will you tell Denis to get off the big swing, it's my turn," James shouted from the door. "Aunt Laura and Auntie Nicky are helping Granny Annie. Dad I can't come in; Granny Annie says my trainers are all muddy and I don't have time to take them off."

"Dad, Chiara is climbing the fence again, she's too little," Denis shouted from the swing.

Vickie grinned up at her husband. "Well, Daddy, it's you they're asking for."

Marnie stood up as Johnny passed her. "No, sit down doll, I'll go," Johnny laughed. "Now you're pregnant, you better rest, and pray the sprog looks like you and not your man! Look at him lying there like Bagpuss. You're a lazy git Jamie."

"Cheers Jovi!" Jamie laughed. "The haircut has sapped my strength I think." He ran his hand through his newly shorn locks, his red hair now closely cropped; still curling at the edges but tidier and shorter than it had ever been.

"You just look like a poofy boy now, not an ugly girl," Andy laughed.

"I think the short hair suits him!" Vickie said, smiling.

"Vickie thinks I'm the most handsome in the band."

Andy laughed and nudged him. "Yeah, well, Vickie has had a few bumps on the head Jamie."

"So, tell us about Molly and Kieran?" Vickie asked, ignoring Andy.

"She's just the way I remember, and well he's my brother isn't he? I suppose it's a bit like you and Paddy. So, I hope we can be as close as you two are. Hope to spend some more time with them. Life is good Vickie." He looked at Marnie, a smile on his face. "It's all about to get better."

Lynne, sitting on the floor with Dania, stood up and smoothed down her leather trousers. "I'll go with you Jovi." She stood at the door and looked out. "Hey Chiara get down before you bloody fall. That kid is half fucking monkey, half human, I swear."

"Lynne!"

"What?"

"Language!" everyone said at once.

24283326R00194

Printed in Great Britain
by Amazon